FINAL PERFORMANCE

To Lorraine
Thank you for your
help.
Support and
I wish you the best

James Brown
Fahrenheit
451
-D9-

ALSO BY JAMES BROWN

GOING FAST

HOT WIRE

JAMES BROWN

Final
Performance

WILLIAM MORROW AND COMPANY, INC.

NEW YORK

Library of Congress Cataloging-in-Publication Data

Brown, James, 1957–
Final performance.
I. Title.
PS3552.R68563F56   1988   813'.54   87-24793
ISBN 0-688-06842-1

Printed in the United States of America

First Edition

1 2 3 4 5 6 7 8 9 10

BOOK DESIGN BY ABE LERNER

To
Heidi and Marilyn

For believing in this story, and for their advice and encouragement, I thank Oakley Hall, MacDonald Harris, Pat Golbitz, Stephanie Mann, Tim O'Brien, and Orlando Ramirez.

PART I:

The Roof Comes Down

I know I can't be completely sure of myself, or
else I might not recognize the enemy and it'll
creep up on me from behind. But don't you
worry. I try to keep the enemy within sight at all
times, and to remember always that in the end
this monster, Defeat, is an imaginary foe.

A LETTER FROM MIKE

AGAIN I imagine the minutes before Mike's
death. He had bought the bullets at the Big
Five in Hollywood two weeks earlier from a
clerk who told him that they were a good
deal. A summer bargain. In his wallet beside
his SAG card was the receipt, nine dollars
marked down from twelve. The left pocket of
his jeans held car keys and a roll of Certs and
one dollar and twenty-five cents in quarters.
On the floor near the bedroom door sat a
wicker basket full of soiled shirts and towels.
He was on his way to the Laundromat when

he set the basket down and opened his dresser drawer and reached for the gun. A Smith & Wesson .38. The bluing was worn silver where it had rubbed against the holster, the sight was chipped, and the cylinder needed oiling. It wouldn't spin easily anymore. This was an older police revolver, a castoff fired once too often on the academy range by a young cadet. Or maybe a veteran officer. He didn't care. All he needed was a gun with a trigger that when pulled would send a pin down against a cap and a bullet through the barrel into his skull.

That would be it.

Mike stood in front of the bedroom window. As he slipped a shell into the chamber, he watched the neighborhood children playing in the street. They were shouting and laughing. One hollered, "Light it, light it and run." There came a fizzle and a pop followed by faster pops, a string of them with a flurry of light and paper, then more laughter and shouting. The sky wasn't yet dark.

He slipped another bullet into the chamber.

It was a wadcutter, like the other, with a flat lead nose and a copper pinhole in the middle. On impact the lead expanded and mushroomed. The bullet went in small, the diameter of the shell itself, but on its way out it would make a hole larger than a big man's fist. There was no need for a second bullet, though he loaded another anyway. In case of a sloppy hit, he must've thought. A botched job. If he had the fury to fire again, he might need it.

Now he slowly closed the cylinder, heard it click into place, snap and lock. For a while Mike paced the room with the .38 at his side.

On the nightstand rested a fifth of Kessler's, nearly empty already, purchased this afternoon. Through the doorway, into the kitchen, he saw the plates and glasses in the sink that needed washing before he could pack them. The lease on his house was up and he should've been out a few days before. He'd already rented a cheap room in Hollywood, telling himself it was only temporary, that another role would happen along soon. Yet his clothes still hung in the open closet of his bedroom. Hundreds and hundreds of books remained on their shelves. He'd been trying, though—moving a little, resting a little, a little at a time. Each day he combed the back alleys of supermarkets, found cardboard boxes, and hauled them home. The day before he had packed five of them. Today he'd packed none.

There was still the laundry to be done. The phone needed disconnecting, another installed in the new room, and the utility companies had yet to be notified. Somehow, just as the empty cardboard boxes would pack themselves, the details of moving would also find a neat finish.

At this point it didn't matter. Did it? *Did it?*

Test run.

Mike turned the cylinder to an empty chamber and put the barrel against his temple. One great flash of pain and that would be all. He closed his eyes. In his mind, as he squeezed the trigger, he saw himself recoiling from the impact, then frozen lifeless. The blast itself would be deep and hollow-sounding and more sudden than the weak and tinny pop of the firecrackers outside. It would be a true explosion, a big one. Like the cherry bomb that shakes the ground.

Pulling the gun away from his head, he took a deep breath and stared out the window. In the reflection he saw his handsome face, once pictured in *Time* as a major new talent, now bloated from alcohol. The skin had a pasty, pale look to it. His eyes were bloodshot. He blinked. Far in the distance he could see the Hollywood sign sitting cockeyed up in the hills, the letters staggered, the big *H* tilted forward. In better times he'd seen the sign from the street outside Paramount Studios. Here he viewed it from the bedroom of his house in Echo Park for a minute, maybe two, before he glanced down the block. Now the sky had grown dark. Independence Day celebrations had begun. Children and parents stood in their driveways watching flames shoot from cones, showering the concrete, and the black snakes curling in ash, scorching the sidewalks. Mike pulled the drapes shut for the children.

Outside another string of firecrackers went pop, pop.

As he sat on the edge of the bed he turned the cylinder to a loaded chamber and listened for it to snap into place. Slowly he stretched out along the mattress, his body fully extended, his lips around the barrel. He didn't think about his brother. He didn't think of his father or mother or anyone or anything except the cool metal in his mouth and his finger steady on the trigger. Then came the big one, the cherry bomb from inside the house. It slammed his head back against the pillow and left powder burns around his mouth.

Pop.

Pop, pop, pop.

1

When I get sentimental and I want to talk about him, which happens a lot, I almost always mention the *Cannon, M.D.* episodes first. Almost always, whoever I'm telling my story to leans back and says yes, they remember, and that I look just like him. And I smile because it makes me proud. He also starred in *A Rough Kind* but it didn't do all that well. That's why I don't mention it right away unless they've never seen the *Cannon, M.D.* show. Even if it's just for a second, I don't like looking into a blank face. It bothers the hell out of me when they don't remember like they're supposed to, like I think they ought to in my brother's case.

His stage name was Michael Casey. Most people haven't heard of him but when I tell them what he did, all the parts and roles, more often than not they wrinkle their foreheads and nod. Slowly the big brown eyes slip into focus, then the thick dark hair, then the long somber face. They smile, and I return it. He was handsome like most young actors, although it wasn't that all-American clean-cut look of your standard leading man. The publicists thought he looked like a young Jimmy Stewart, or at least that's how they pitched him. Maybe I'm bragging but I'm not lying when I say he was one of the best damn actors Hollywood ever saw. He was nominated for an Emmy at eighteen, and he was one of the youngest and last of Universal's contract players. When they ask what he's doing now, I'll either get up for another drink, if I'm at a bar, or else I'll say something to turn the conversation around. I don't want to pour my heart out, I just want them to remember.

Mention a book, almost any book, and there was a good chance that he'd read it. Which makes me wonder even more why someone so smart and talented, who'd come so close to being an important actor, could crack up and break down so hard, so fast. At first I blamed Mike, then myself, then Mom and Dad for not being there when he needed them. Then I found myself blaming Hollywood, cursing Universal and every producer in town, before I thought that maybe blame and where it rested, if it rested at all, didn't much matter anymore. I'm twenty-four years old now, and it took me six years to see that if I wanted to tell this story I had to tell it pretty much like it happened, like I saw it happen, and how I imagined it to happen. If I came up with some decent answers, good, and if not, well, maybe I'd at least be able to sleep a little better come night.

That's the idea, anyway. To be honest about it. To put the pieces together. The only problem is that I don't know how it all started and where I should begin. I do know that as far back as I can recall my brother was performing, and it wasn't always onstage or in front of a camera. I could start by telling where and when he was born, and how when he was just seven he starred in *Good-bye Blackbird* with Clarence Parker at the Sheraton in San Francisco, or the time he won a talent contest for Weber's bread on a local TV show, or all the radio ads he did. But that stuff isn't the heart of it, and that's what I need to get to. And getting to the heart of it started *before* we got to Hollywood, when Mike and I were lying on the floor watching TV one night, when Dad was out working and they came for Mom.

She yanked us to our feet and pulled us down behind the couch.

"Shhh."

"What's going on?"

"Shhh."

"Mom?"

She slapped him. He put his face between his knees and covered his head with his hands. The beam of a flashlight shone through the living-room window and landed on the wall behind us just above our heads. Mom had her arm tight around my shoulders and I could smell her—acrid, bitter, sweating in her nightgown. One strap had slipped off her shoulder. Her breathing came in short gasps, and she was trembling.

The doorbell rang. Footsteps, gravel crunching beneath hard soles, moved along the side of our house. Two more flashlights circled the ceiling and walls, zigzagging over chairs and tables, searching, scanning the entire room. From around the edge of the couch I saw the half-empty bowl of popcorn on the floor in front of the TV where Mike and I had been lying seconds earlier. The sound was off but the gray-white light of the tube continued to flicker. Mom had turned the wrong knob when she spotted the

16

car, headlights off and motor dead, roll silently up the driveway. By then it was too late. She just grabbed us up and yanked us down behind the couch.

The screen door creaked open, a fist pounded on wood. She moved her arm from around my shoulder to my neck and pulled my cheek against the side of her breast. "GINA McKINNEY, THIS IS THE SHERIFF OF SANTA CLARA COUNTY." The voice was a deep monotone. "WE KNOW YOU'RE IN THERE. PLEASE ANSWER THE DOOR." Mike looked at her, frowning, scared, as if to ask what she planned to do. "WE ONLY WANT A WORD WITH YOU." She reached out and tugged Mike's cheek, the one she slapped, against the side of her other breast. For a second she stopped trembling and stiffened. The heat and stink of her fear made my heart pound. I glanced across her chest and met Mike's eyes, wide and frightened. Then the latch on the back door rattled, Mom trembled again, and Mike and I quickly looked away. Even eye contact seemed like it could jeopardize our safety, expose us.

"You lock the back door?" she whispered, pulling his head closer. He nodded into her bosom. The latch rattled again and another beam of light shot along the living-room floor, this time through a window in the kitchen, down the hallway, inches from my leg near the edge of the couch. Mom's body tensed against mine, and I knew she was nearing tears. "Please, baby, please," she said. "Please don't let them take me." I held my breath, heart thumping, eyes concentrated on the TV. The Blob was consuming a man, his mouth open in a silent scream. She squeezed me harder, closer. A second later the beam of light disappeared and the old Folger's commercial with Mrs. Olsen flashed across the screen.

"GINA McKINNEY, THIS IS THE SHERIFF OF SANTA CLARA COUNTY. I REPEAT, THE SHERIFF OF SANTA CLARA COUNTY." The voice was sharp, louder, no longer a monotone but hostile. "MRS. McKINNEY . . . MRS. McKIN-NEY . . ."

The front doorknob rattled.

Mom shuddered.

Footsteps. The men who had crept around the house were on the porch now. There was the murmur of voices.

Then it was quiet.

We stayed huddled behind the couch until a test pattern appeared on the TV. Finally Mom removed her arm from around my neck and it felt cool there, when the air hit my skin, like rubbing alcohol evaporating. Pushing the strap of her nightgown back on her shoulder, she slowly peeked over the couch. Mike and I watched as she scanned the living room, the front door, the windows, waiting for an expression that might tell us what she saw. A minute passed. Nothing. Then, placing both hands on the back of the couch, she lifted herself into the silver light of the TV. "Go to your room." We stared at her but we didn't move. The outline of her panties showed through her nightgown. "Your Dad'll be home soon. I don't want either of you to say a word about tonight. Understand?" She narrowed her eyes at us. "*Understand? Not a word.*" Mike rose then, shaking, about to speak when her hand flew up out of nowhere. He leaned back, wincing. Only she was reaching for the couch, not him. Her body wavered from side to side.

"Mom?"

"Go to your room."

"You all right?" he said.

She began to tremble and cough, deep, not from her chest but her stomach, until the cough became a gag. She hid her face behind the couch. "*Get out, I said,*" she screamed. "*Get out.*" Mike took my arm and pulled me to my feet and we ran through the living room and up the stairs two at a time into our bedroom. There he slammed the door and locked it. Closed his eyes. Exhaled.

We undressed in silence, in the darkness, listening to each other's breathing. I watched Mike turn the covers of his bed, lift one knee to the mattress, heard the squeak of box springs, saw his slender back and bare white ass disappear beneath the sheets. A window was open near where I stood, and a cool breeze pushed against my shoulders, my thighs. Outside was a full moon and, in the distance, the soft rush of cars on the highway. Our dresser was cluttered with underwear and Mike's books, novels, and plays, a King Kong model holding a firecracker in its paw. Posters of James Dean and Montgomery Clift were tacked to the walls. My brother moved to the far side of his bed and patted the mattress. "Sleep here tonight," he said.

I climbed in beside him. He was warm and his hair smelled

faintly of cream rinse. Closing my eyes, I rested my head on his chest, wrapped an arm around his flat warm belly, listened to his heartbeat, tried to forget the night, the cops, my fear. But I couldn't, couldn't sleep, didn't want to sleep. I rolled away from him, suddenly sweating, and lifted my arms from under the covers. Mike lay with his hands crossed behind his head, staring at the ceiling. Below us we heard the door to the liquor cabinet slam shut, followed by footsteps on the kitchen floor.

"What'd Mom do?"

"Go to sleep."

"I can't."

"Try," he said.

We lay in silence for a while when Dad's truck came up the driveway, engine idling. He'd been working fifteen-hour days on a subdivision in East San Jose for the past few weeks. It wasn't unusual for him to come in late and slip into bed in the room across from Mom's. They'd stopped sleeping together the year before.

The truck door opened and closed. Slow, shuffling footsteps, the clink of keys, the snap of padlocks. Toolbox secure. I held my breath as I glanced at Mike. Moonlight filtered through the bedroom window, illuminating his profile, sharpening the lines of his nose and lips. He was just beginning to grow small dark patches of hair on his chest and under his arms. I envied his handsomeness, his developing masculinity. He was sixteen and I was twelve. To be as old as him, to know all the things he knew, is what I wanted.

The roar of voices traveled up the staircase to our room. Something glass hit the wall below and shattered. I winced. Suddenly the phone in the kitchen rang.

"What'd Mom do?"

Mike frowned, annoyed. He was trying to listen to the fight. Me, I'd given up listening. It was always about the same thing—money. But my brother studied the arguments, tried to make sense out of the bits and pieces we heard from our room those long sleepless nights. Sometimes he even slipped out of bed and crept partway down the staircase so he could take it all in. I usually strained to think of something else, whistled or hummed to drown the voices.

Again glass hit the wall below and shattered.

"How come the cops want Mom?"

19

"I don't know."

"But what'd she do?"

"Shut up."

I turned on my side away from him. The damn telephone was still ringing. Mom and Dad kept screaming and running from one part of the house to another. I pushed the sheet off, intending to go to my own bed, when Mike grabbed my arm. "I'm sorry," he said. "Don't be mad." I let him cover me with the sheet. He propped himself up on an elbow and looked me in the eye and tried to smile. "I don't know what's going on. If I did, I wouldn't hold out on you. You know that." The phone stopped in midring; I heard the crack of plastic.

Mike lay back and crossed his arms behind his head. "But I'll tell you this. It's you and I, you and I who have to be strong." Below, the bathroom door slammed so hard it shook our bed. Mom had likely locked herself in, as she sometimes did, and soon Dad would holler at her to open up. I wondered if she'd told him about the cops and I figured she had. "I might as well be honest even if it hurts. You're entitled to know, Jay, you're old enough, anyway. Okay?" I nodded. "Those cops'll be back." Dad pounded on the bathroom door now while Mom sobbed. I pictured her sitting on the toilet with the lid down, crying into her hands. "Whether it's tomorrow, a couple of days from now, they'll be here. If they get a warrant, they'll take her. I know that much." Sonofabitch, I didn't want to cry, but what I'd held back all night finally came to the surface. "Hey, none of that," Mike said, cradling my head to his chest. "It's going to be okay, Jay. Don't worry. We have each other and that's what matters, huh? You and I. We got to be brave." He shook me a little, trying for a smile. "Am I right?" Right or not, the damn tears kept coming.

The next morning we went downstairs and found Dad sprawled on the couch in his work clothes. One forearm, thick and muscular, rested limp over his eyes. The TV was still on. A set of coasters and a bunch of Mom's *Photoplays* were scattered across the floor. The table lamp lay on its side in the middle of the room. Our father snored. His round belly rose and fell in time with his breathing. Mike put a hand on my shoulder and steered me from the living room to the kitchen.

"Careful."

Glass.

All over the floor. I was barefoot, in T-shirt and boxers. We scanned the kitchen from the doorway. This was the worst, definitely the worst. Every cupboard door was thrown open and the plates and glasses, as if someone had run a hand along the shelves, were either broken inside the cupboard itself or shattered on the linoleum. The telephone jack had been yanked out of the wall and the wires, dusted white with plaster, dangled from the hole. And the jar of nickels and pennies Mom saved for us on top on the refrigerator had been knocked over. There were coins on the counter, the table, the floor, everywhere. Mike and I looked at each other in disgust. His eyes were bloodshot, his face drawn, almost gaunt. Too much worry, too little sleep. Already he'd developed the same worn look of sadness that marked our father's face. It was in the brows, the minute lines around and beneath his eyes, the ashen color of his cheeks.

He shook his head.

"Jesus Christ."

I shook my head. "Jesus Christ."

"Goddamn them."

He stepped into the kitchen, reached into the sink, and fished out the phone. A stack of dirty dishes toppled. Most of the plastic casing was gone and the guts of the thing, the wires and metal, were coated with a thin film of tomato sauce. Mike let it dangle by the cord and wrinkled his nose. Water dripped onto the floor. Then, being careful not to let it touch skin, he held the receiver an inch from his ear and listened. A grin slowly spread across his face.

"Guess what?"

"It works?"

The grin vanished. He threw the phone in the trash under the sink and grabbed the broom from behind the refrigerator. I waited until he'd swept up most of the glass before I stepped into the kitchen for the dustpan. When I turned around, Dad was standing in the doorway, tucking in his shirt. His hair was rumpled.

"You boys sleep last night?"

Mike kept sweeping, head down.

"Well?"

"Not much," he mumbled.

"I'm sorry."

"It's all right."

"Your mother was in a bad mood. You know how she can get."
"We know."
Dad glanced at the clock over the stove. It was a quarter to twelve. Saturday. "Want to go to a movie?"
"I don't think so."
"Jay?"
I shook my head.
"I think you boys ought to go to the movies."
"There's nothing playing," he said.
"Go get the paper."
"Why the big rush?"
Mike stopped sweeping, stood up straight, cocked his head to one side, and squinted. A long moment passed. Dad shifted his weight from one leg to another. Slowly he drew a hand down his face. "Don't make me raise my voice," he said. "Just get the damn paper and pick something." He took the broom from Mike, not in anger, but gently. Then he swallowed and looked at me. "Run put on some clothes, Jay. Get ready to go." So I did. It was a lie, though, what Mike had said—about nothing playing. He watched everything. Good or bad, old or recent, he was willing to sit through *any* movie.

That afternoon we saw a terrible old horror film. Dad dropped us off at the Jose theater in downtown San Jose and told us to call when the movie was over, not before. We watched his truck disappear around the corner and then got in line behind a group of kids. I thought of Mom as we waited, wondered what would happen, what it would be like without her. The urge to cry rose deep from my chest but I gritted my teeth, closed my eyes, and held it back. The line moved forward.

We bought our tickets.

The smell of stale popcorn hung in the air inside the theater. Mike and I settled in our seats in the first row, because that's all that was left. Lousy piped music sounded over the howls of a hundred kids. Soon the lights dimmed.

The curtains parted.

THE UNEARTHLY
Harpsichord music played.

JOHN CARRADINE
ALLISON HAYES
MYRON HEALEY

22

The audience screamed. Mike sighed, irritated, and I did the same. Like my brother I felt contempt for those who lost control and distracted us. You didn't talk or holler in a theater. The Fox, the Studio, the old Jose, they were sacred to us. Second homes. Places to get away from the house, the fights and tension, places to relax and drift. We spent hundreds of hot summer days sitting in the cool darkness of theaters, watching movies and eating popcorn, living the lives of the actors and their stories. They were ours, they belonged to us. A matinee audience was something we usually did our best to avoid. Behind us a baby wailed.

I leaned over and whispered one of Mike's lines. "They shouldn't let them in, you know." He didn't respond. His face was pale in the flicker of light, his lips trembled. I nudged him. "You okay?" He blinked. The corners of his mouth quivered. I put my hand on his on the armrest but he pulled it away. A minute passed. I sank into my seat and tried to watch the movie. Onscreen Tor Johnson was about to attack Allison Hayes in her nightgown.

Mike stood up.

"We're going."

"Now?"

"*Now.*"

Someone hollered at him to sit down. A few others hissed. Grabbing my arm, he jerked me out of the seat and pulled me behind him as he headed for the main aisle. We rushed through the lobby, through the doors, onto the sidewalk, and into the sun. Orange-and-black spots floated before my eyes and I couldn't see where I was going. He kept yanking my arm, throwing me off balance. Twice I stumbled and nearly fell. *"Slow down,"* I said. He let loose of me and ran, dodging people on the sidewalk, running faster and faster. I bolted after him but he was stronger and I couldn't keep up. The farther behind I got the more I panicked. *"Wait,"* I hollered. There was a solid hundred feet between us now and my legs were weakening fast. A woman strolled out of a shoe store on the corner just as Mike passed, and his arm caught hers and spun her around. Her mouth dropped open and she clutched her purse tight against her chest. She was about to curse him when she spotted me, chin up, chest out, barreling toward her.

She wobbled to her left.

I lunged right.

Her eyes opened wide and then, a second before we would've collided, she froze in the middle of the sidewalk and I ducked around her. By this time Mike was a block ahead of me. My chest ached from breathing so hard and my legs, no matter how much I strained, were growing heavier with each stride. "Wait." It was a hoarse, frail shout, no strength left in my lungs. I ran through an intersection as the light turned red. A car jammed on its brakes, honked. People stopped and stared. Now all I saw of him was his T-shirt, weaving side to side, far in the distance.

My ankle buckled.

I hit concrete, my eyes blurred, but I picked myself up and ran a few more yards. Stopped. It was futile. The sun beat hot on my shoulders, my temples throbbed, and my mouth was so dry I couldn't swallow. My brother had left me. I sat down at the curb and hung my head. I thought of Mom last night, saw the flashlights, heard the voices.

"Let's go."

I looked up. Mike stood before me, panting.

"C'mon, c'mon."

Again we ran, only together now, until we tired and then we walked at a fast, clipped pace. Soon we'd turned off Santa Clara Street onto Saint John. Our house sat at the corner across from a small walnut orchard. Two patrol cars were parked at the curb near our backyard gate, where no neighbors could see them. Suddenly, as if he'd felt the same urgency fluttering in his chest at the same moment that I had, he took my hand and we ran—hard, like a race, wind breaking across our faces.

A cop stood outside on the service porch, head bowed, silent. He didn't even glance up, let alone try to stop us. Just as Mike flung open the screen door, Dad stepped into the kitchen, and we froze. His cheeks flushed red, and I thought he was angry, that he was going to shout, but he only shook his head. "I wish you'd listened," he muttered. "Goddamn how I wish you boys'd mind."

His undershirt was soaked with sweat; his strong arms hung at his sides. A fly buzzed over the stack of dirty dishes in the sink.

"C'mere."

Mike let the door close quietly.

"Sit down."

24

I spotted another cop in the living room as we moved around the kitchen table for seats.

"Now you boys gotta see."

Down the hall, in the bedroom, I heard what I thought was Mom going through her dresser drawers.

"You listening?" Dad said.

We nodded.

"Listen good." He stood over us, closed his eyes, opened them. "Your mother . . ." He bit his lower lip. "Your mother is going away for a while but we'll get her back."

I looked at the cop on the service porch, clenched my fists, felt the tears coming. Even though I knew he didn't want to be here, that he was saddened and distressed by the scene, I hated the bastard like I'd never hated anyone before. "No," Dad said. He took my chin in his hand and turned my face up to his. "Cry all you want later but don't you be cryin' now." He glanced at Mike. "That goes for you too." Back to me. "Straighten up and say good-bye to your mother. Understand, try and understand, this is harder on her than us." He pulled my chin a little higher. "Please don't be making it any worse, please." Finally he let loose of me and drew a finger lightly under my eyes.

The other cop sat on the couch with his hat in his lap. As we filed through the living room he uncrossed his legs and leaned forward and pointed to his wristwatch. "Just a few more minutes," Dad said. The cop nodded and sat back. Our father led us down the hall to Mom's room. "Wait here." Her door was open a crack. She was bending over her bed, placing a folded blouse into a suitcase. The smell of perfume was in the air. She wore a knee-length black dress, black high heels, and dark stockings, and her thick black hair was piled in a bun on top of her head. Her hips were narrow and her buttocks were small and firm like a boy's. The sharp lines of her jaw, and the angle at which she held her chin up when Dad approached, almost as if in defiance, as if he were one of the cops, gave her face a hollowed and hardened look. I don't know why but at that moment she seemed more beautiful than I ever remembered.

"Honey?"

"Hmmm?"

"The boys are here." He put a hand on her waist. "They come

home by themselves. I'm sorry, I tried." Closing the suitcase, she smiled weakly. Behind me I heard the cop rise from the couch and walk across the living room. My eyes stung. Mom came into the hallway, set the suitcase on the floor, and wrapped her arms around Mike. "I'll bring you a present soon." I saw his face over her shoulder go stone blank and white, his eyes wide but distant-looking, as if he weren't seeing. She leaned back to look at him. "Baby, I love you. Don't be like this." She hugged him again. His body stiffened, and he pushed himself free.

"I love you, too," he mumbled, stuffing his hands into his pockets. Mom cocked her head as if she hadn't heard right, as if she were confused. She reached for him but he backed away. Dad stepped forward.

"Kiss your mother good-bye."

"It's okay, honey. He's just upset."

"Can I go to my room?"

"No."

She threw her hand sideways. "Let him go." They stared at each other for a few seconds, and it was an angry stare with narrowed eyes, before he turned and went upstairs. "Here's my big man. He doesn't run away." She kissed my cheek. "You been crying, haven't you? My big man's been crying. But there's no reason. I'm only going away on a trip for a little while. Isn't that right, honey?" she said, glancing at Dad. "Tell him." He lowered his eyes. "See . . . Jay." She touched the suitcase with a hand. "All packed. And when I come home I'm going to bring you a present, too." But like my brother, I was no child. I knew she was lying, that the suitcase was a prop, and it was pathetic. I looked away. The cop stood at the end of the hallway now.

"It's time," Dad said.

She kissed me again.

"Mom?"

"What, baby?"

"I love you."

I wrapped my arms around her waist. Breathed the perfume of her dress, her skin, felt her heat. "Don't go, Mom."

She stroked my head. "Your mother loves you more than the world," she said. "Don't forget it." I held her tighter, knowing that when I let go I'd lose her. "I'll be back, though," she said. "Promise." A second later Dad's callused hands were on my arms,

26

pulling them apart, pulling me away. Mom stooped and picked up the suitcase and forced herself to smile. "Why's everybody so sad? I'll be home in no time." She winked at the cop. "Watch and see."

Dad silently escorted her from the living room. I stood in the hallway. Outside I heard one patrol car, then the other start up. I went to our mother's bedroom and opened the closet and pulled her blue summer dress from its hanger and held it against my face. Soft cotton. I breathed deep. Chewed the hem until it soured with my saliva. All I could think was that she was gone, that I wouldn't smell her smell anymore, that I might never see her again. The next thing I knew Dad was leading me upstairs, telling me everything was going to work out, not to cry, not to worry. You need rest, sleep.

Later that night I woke up in a sweat. Mike's bed was empty. A strong wind was whipping the leaves of the walnut trees in the small orchard near our house. The sound of the TV rose from the living room below. I went downstairs and found Dad hunched over the kitchen table with his head in his hands. A single light glowed dimly from the ceiling. The wind outside caught the screen door, lifted it open, then let it bang shut. There was a bottle of bourbon and a glass on the table. Mom's suitcase rested beside the washing machine on the service porch. "Dad?" I said, softly.

He raised his head but he didn't turn around. I stood in the doorway behind him. "I don't want to be disturbed," he muttered. I believe he thought I'd left, because a few seconds later, after pouring himself another drink, he looked over his shoulder. His eyes were bloodshot. There were tears, too, but only tears— no moans, no whimpering. "Please, I need to be alone. I need to think." I'd never seen him cry before and it shocked me. I wanted to run and hold him, tell him not to worry, as he'd told me. Instead I lowered my head and went to the living room, where my brother lay on the floor watching the eleven o'clock news.

"What're you doing up?" he said.

"I couldn't sleep."

"How you feeling?"

I shrugged.

"Scared?"

That's how I felt. "Yeah."

"Me too."

"Dad's crying in the kitchen."

"I know," he said. "He's been in there like that for hours. Better leave him alone." Pause. "Go get a blanket and lie down with me."

Over the television came the popping noise of gunfire. A tally of the American and Vietnamese dead rolled down the screen. We were ahead. In the background marines waded through a muddy rice field. Then the scene jumped. There was Mom, climbing out of a black-and-white, huddled between two cops and a plain-clothesman, walking fast with her head bowed. It cut back to the newscaster behind his desk:

"Mrs. Gina McKinney, local real estate agent, and wife of David McKinney, general building contractor, was arrested this afternoon when police linked . . ."

The screen went black. "No more TV," Dad said. "It's time for bed."

2

"Before the roof come down," as Dad used to say, "we were doing fine, boys. Just fine. If your mother wasn't so . . ." And there he'd pause, maybe shake his head, then either he'd fall silent or change the subject. He didn't like talking bad about Mom because he never wanted us to think poorly of her. Deep down he still loved her. Actually it was against his morals to speak poorly of anyone except Republicans and the Internal Revenue Service. "They have no heart," he'd say. "They have no sense of honor, no respect for the working folk." Roosevelt was a good man because he cared about the poor, launched the CCC, and because he pulled our country out of the Depression. MacArthur was a sonofabitch because of Korea and what he did to the Bonus Marchers. Kennedy was a Catholic, and that was hard for our old man to accept, but he voted for him and stood behind him until he screwed up with the Bay of Pigs and Vietnam. "Listening to the pope, he was," Dad would say. "Did you know that, boys? Kennedy's the one who got into those messes." Then he'd quote George Washington on foreign entanglements and how, as a people, we ought to mind our damn business. America had its hands in the pockets of every country on earth. It was no wonder the rest of the world despised us.

The first thing he'd do when he came home dirty and rednecked from pounding nails in the sun, his khaki pants hanging low around his waist, and his tired body smelling faintly of sawdust, was to get himself a beer. Open a can of peanuts. He'd sigh and sit at the kitchen table and that's when he'd sometimes talk about Mom and then grow silent and finally, almost always, shift the subject to the Chetco River "Boys," he'd say, as we sat watching him drink the first beer. "Someday we're gonna build us a home right on the Chetco. We'll make the fireplace outta natural stone from the riverbed. Haul 'em ourselves." Then he'd lean back and pass his hand through the air as if he were seeing the whole house already built there before him, hidden in the trees, the river rolling below. "Nobody around but you boys and me and your mother. Yep. Good huntin' and fishin'." He'd nod at Mike. "I'll build you a den full of books." A wink for me. "You'll have more trees to climb than a monkey in heaven." And the more he drank the more he went on about this place we were going to build where you didn't have a neighbor for miles, and where the trout just jumped out of the water into your frying pan. To hell with poles. That was the big dream, this house built in his mind, and we heard about it as often as we did his lectures on the "evil bastard Joe McCarthy," a traitor to his race and kind, and whose death Dad celebrated by throwing a party for the entire neighborhood. But that was before I was born, before the roof come down and, with it, dreams of the Chetco.

As a carpenter who became a contractor, our father accumulated more than a few pieces of property over the years. He skimped and he saved, remodeling run-down houses and reselling, buying lots and building from the ground up when San Jose was booming. Thousands of people were migrating from all over the country to Santa Clara County, into what Jack London once called one of the most beautiful, fertile valleys of the world. They all needed a place to live. At one time nearly everywhere you looked there were orchards of plums, cherries, apricots, walnuts, and almonds. But the people kept coming and the building continued and the orchards soon disappeared. If Dad still had the property he did then, we'd be millionaires in today's market.

Only that's not the way it worked out. Mom had a real estate license and she handled Dad's paperwork and somehow or another she wound up in trouble. Here's where it gets foggy. For a long time all we could be sure of was that she'd made a series of bad deals, a lot of underhanded stuff, without Dad knowing about it until it was too late. Mail was hidden. Loans were taken out to cover losses. Checks bounced. More loans were made to cover first and second loans until there was nothing left and no one to borrow from. Dad had no choice but to file bankruptcy.

The details of Mom's scams, the particulars that led to the fall, I wouldn't learn for some time. After her arrest the morning paper disappeared from our doorstep. My brother and I weren't allowed to watch TV or answer the phone or the door. What little we knew about Mom came from eavesdropping and guesswork. Terms like *plea bargaining* and *bail* and *false arrest* filled Dad's long phone conversations with a man we came to know as The Attorney. A kind of god, he was, a man with the power to bring her home, to clear up the mess, to put our family back together again. Whenever the phone rang, no matter what time of day or night, Mike and I were there listening in. If it was The Attorney, we studied Dad's face for some sign of hope, but his expression always remained stern, pensive, giving away nothing. He never told us what was said and we knew better than to ask. Like switching off the eleven o'clock news that night, he did his damnedest to keep us in the dark.

Over the next couple of weeks a lot of our belongings were repossessed, while we just stood back and watched, until there wasn't much left. Some of it was beat-up stuff, too, practically worthless to anyone but us. The dining-room table where we'd once shared meals and conversation, the beds Mike and I slept on, Mom's French dresser, Dad's oak desk, the refrigerator and stove, our washer and dryer, even my brother's file cabinet—the creditors took it all, including Mom's new Thunderbird. By the end of the month we had to up and move from our big four-bedroom two-story house into a one-bedroom apartment on the east side of town.

Cardboard boxes stacked four and five high, taller than me, lined the living room. A narrow path from the kitchen to the bedroom wove through the piles of books Mike refused to leave behind. Clothes that wouldn't fit into the bedroom closet were draped over the chairs. Except for a spot to let the sofa bed unfold, there wasn't space enough to spread your arms. And the walls were so thin we could hear our neighbors talking, watching TV, or making love late at night.

Every morning Dad rose early and went to work, sometimes coming home about noon, showering, and changing into a sports coat and tie. When we asked him what he had to do, where he was going, he'd frown.

"Business," he'd say.

"What kind?"

"Never you mind."

Business, we learned, meant he was either going to see The Attorney or else he was off to the courthouse to sit in on the preliminary hearings. There were a lot of them. And if he wasn't working late, using a droplight to cut and nail by, he was visiting Mom.

Every night, while Mike and I lay in bed, waiting for Dad, the scene replayed itself. Every night I worked out another detail, another ending. The cops came, searched the house, found nothing. They found her but Dad ambushed them as they were escorting her to the patrol car and we jumped in the truck and escaped to Mexico. Or they never came. It never happened. There were a million alternatives, a million different endings, and all of them were better than the one I tried to forget. Sometimes, after Dad came back, my brother and I would lie awake listening to him snore in the bedroom. We'd talk about Mom and how when she returned there would be no more fights, how we'd move back into our house, how it would be like before, only better. Other times we lay awake, staring at the patched hole in the ceiling in the dim light of the streetlamp. Sometimes we held each other in silence.

This night the couple in the apartment below ours were fighting about the Penney's bill. We could hear every word. The woman had charged some expensive drapes. "Turn the radio up," Mike said. He sat at the kitchen table filling out change-of-address cards. I reached across the counter and turned up the volume. Jazz. The clock over the stove read 6:45.

"That about right?"

"What?"

"The radio."

"It's fine."

I opened the refrigerator, more out of boredom than hunger. Eggs, powdered milk, a bowl of green Jell-O.

"You almost done?"

"No."

"When we gonna eat?"

He sighed. "Do I look busy?"

"I guess."

"Then don't bother me."

I shrugged and let the refrigerator door close. Mike covered his ear with one hand while he wrote with the other. The couple below were screaming harder now, and I thought I recognized the woman's voice. Somewhere, someplace, I'd heard it before.

"Who does that sound like?"

"Huh?"

"Downstairs."

"Would you leave me alone?"

I leaned forward and looked over his shoulder. The cards were going to places like the Academy of Motion Picture Arts and Sciences Library, *Films in Review*, the German Film Institute, and *Famous Monsters*. On the chair beside him, packed in two big fruit crates, were thousands of colored index cards. Each one had the name of a dead actor with a brief biography written on it, minor and major credits, birth and death dates. "Quit breathing down my neck, damn it," Mike said. "I can't concentrate." I straightened up, though I didn't step away. As far back as I could remember he'd been collecting obscure facts on obscure dead actors, faithfully reading the obituary column, corresponding with film buffs from Des Moines to France, trading facts and trivia.

"When you wanna eat?"

His face grew red, he slapped the pen down, stood up. "You win."

"Good," I said. "What's for dinner?"

"Spaghetti."

"Again?"

A door slammed in the apartment below. Our walls shook, a man cursed, and then it was quiet except for the radio. The song had ended. A newscaster's voice came over the air. "*American troops suffered a setback today . . .*"

Mike grabbed the cord and yanked it out of the socket. For a few seconds he stared at the radio, kind of stunned, as if he'd surprised himself. "What're you looking at?" he barked. "Get the water ready." I filled a pot and put it on the stove and turned on the fire. As I waited for it to boil I stared out the kitchen window to the carports below, where our father parked his truck. The spot was empty.

"Think we oughta hold off for Dad?" But Mike was struggling now with a can of tomato sauce on the electric opener, trying to keep it from skipping, and he didn't answer me. I glanced outside again. A new complex was going up across the way where there once had been an orchard. Now the trees had been uprooted and plowed into piles.

Suddenly the water boiled over. Orange flames, hissing and crackling, foaming and sputtering, rose up around the pot. "Can't you do anything right?" Mike hollered. He spun around to turn off the fire and the can flew out of his hand. Tomato sauce everywhere. Walls. Floor. Stove.

"Oh shit."

"You did it," I said.

"You *made* me do it."

"No way."

"Clean it up."

"I ain't cleaning nothing up."

He narrowed his eyes at me. I bolted for the door, but he lunged and grabbed my T-shirt and dragged me back a few feet before I wriggled free and leaped over a box of books and scrambled for the front door again. This time I made it out to the hallway when he caught me. We stumbled and bumped up against the metal railing.

"*Jay . . . Mike?*"

We froze.

"*Knock it off.*"

In the courtyard beneath us stood Marissa, our housekeeper and sitter from better times. Even from this distance I could see that her eyes were a little puffy, a little red, as if she had been crying. She shook her head.

"Where's your father?"

"Out working," Mike said.

"So what's the problem?"

"Nothing."

"Nothing," I mumbled.

33

"We're just fooling around." Mike leaned over the railing. Frowned. "I didn't know you lived here."

"Right below you."

I nodded to myself. We weren't the only ones who had been going at it.

The rest was small talk not worth mentioning except to say that she more or less invited herself in and ended up cooking and helping us clean up the tomato sauce. When Dad came home about an hour later, dirty and tired, the dinner was ready. I thought he'd be shocked to see her but he just glanced at the neatly set table and grinned. Marissa lowered her eyes. Once, while we were eating, I looked up and found her staring at Dad with a smile on her face. She offered to come by now and then and help out in whatever way she could. All Dad said besides thanking her was that he couldn't pay. And because he couldn't pay he didn't think it would be a good idea. I could understand that. It was a matter of pride. But what I couldn't understand was the coincidence. We just happened to move into the same complex as Marissa and her husband? I didn't believe it then and I don't believe it now.

3

Miss Gloria Millicent Miles of the James Lick High drama department was in charge of the fall production of *Guys and Dolls*. I suspect she'd been there years before my brother came along, years after, and as far as I know she's still there, tormenting students and parents with the same tired show. When we moved we switched schools, my brother signed up for her class, and I registered at Pala Middle School. Our schools were built back to back, separated by a football field and a chain link fence, and when my day was over I'd go to the auditorium to watch him practice. He'd had training with Al Copen in San Francisco when Mom was around, and modern dance with Tessa Child, who studied under Isadora Duncan, but Miss Miles topped them both.

She was a stout woman with a heavy bosom and a hearty laugh. Her hair she wore in a beehive, from her ears hung two golden hoops, and her eyebrows were completely plucked. In their place she painted black oval lines. Her voice carried from one end of the auditorium to the other. "You must reach the back rows," she'd say, seated behind her big white piano. "This is not a nightclub. There is no room for Jimmy Deans and Brandos on my stage. Your models are John Barrymore and the Gielguds, not your mumblers of Hollywood." My brother and all the other guys who had worked hard developing intense mumbles would sit up straight and swallow.

"Mr. McKinney?"

"Yes, ma'am?"

"Come forward, please."

He approached the piano.

"Put your fingers on the side of your throat . . . no, not there." She rose from the bench and took his hand and put it where it belonged. "Ready?" She hit the first key as my brother hummed through the first vowel, prolonging the A sound until his face reddened. "Before you can act, you must learn to communicate and you, Mr. McKinney, *you* are an infant of the stage. No one can hear you," she'd say. "Louder this time." Again she'd hit another key, and Mike would stretch the vowel out as long and as loudly as he could. "Can you hear him? Class? Can you?" The students would shake their heads. I'd nod. Finally, when he'd broken a sweat, she'd order him to take his seat and call up another. As Mike made his way down the aisle, red-faced and frustrated, he never looked up at me seated in the back row, watching him.

Sometimes I thought he didn't like me hanging around, his little pest brother, only he didn't have the heart to tell me to get lost. He knew how it was. At Pala I was known as "the kid whose mom . . ." and then their voices would drop to a whisper. They all knew my name, and they all spoke it in hushed tones as if it were something filthy. A fucking curse. I felt sure they knew more about what had happened than I, that their parents had told them, and though I wanted to know what they knew, I wasn't about to ask. After a while, I didn't know if I even wanted the facts.

So I stuck with Mike. Where he went, I went. When he'd walk me to the gates at Pala in the morning, then turn and head out of sight, I'd take off in the opposite direction about as often as I found myself in the classroom. Once Mrs. Wharton, my teacher, kept me after the last bell. She sat me down and placed her hand on mine.

"I read about your mother, Jay."

"Read what?"

"I just wanted to tell you that I understand what you're going through."

"Read what?"

"About what happened."

"Nothing happened."

She patted my hand. "I know how you feel."

"No, you don't."

"How're you getting along at home?"

"Fine."

"Does your father know you're upset?"

"I ain't upset."

"Am not," she said. "Does he know how much school you've missed? Does he know the kind of problems you're having with reading? With writing? I'd bet he doesn't. Would you like me to tell him?"

I shrugged.

"Your mother wouldn't be happy with that attitude."

"Don't talk about her."

"You need to talk, Jay."

"Go to hell." I rose from my desk. "I don't need to talk about nothin' to nobody."

That day I left I didn't come back to class for a week. On Monday a letter arrived with the return address reading PALA MIDDLE SCHOOL. But I got hold of it first. It was from the counselor notifying Dad of my absences and recommending that I see the staff psychologist once a week. They also wanted to put me in a different class for what I knew were the dumb kids. Down the toilet that letter went. Others came but I was always there to get them. As for the phone, they couldn't call. Dad had taken out an unlisted number because the creditors and collection agencies wouldn't quit hounding him. From here on out, I decided, school was a thing of the past.

Every day for a month, when my brother left me off at the Pala gates, I'd circle the block and head up to Alum Rock Park. There was a beat-up picnic bench where I'd wait out the mornings with Eddie García, a.k.a. The Shrinking Man. Little Eddie G. About

36

my size, five-two, only skinnier. He was a foster child, though actually he wasn't any child, not in age anyway. We lived in the same complex, and each morning his foster mother would dress and feed him, hand him his radio and a pack of Marlboros, then point him in the direction of Alum Rock. Half the time his zipper was undone and the buttons on his shirt were one off. His head was shaved nearly to the skull to save on haircuts, and he always had a little stubble on his chin with a couple of fresh scabs where the lady nicked him shaving.

There wasn't a hell of a lot to talk about, as Eddie knew only his name and two other words, but it didn't much matter. That's not why I came to the park.

We sat on the bench.

I held up two fingers. "How many?"

"Hey."

"Two?"

"Yeah."

"You got it." I patted him on the back. He smiled. I held up two fingers again. "Two?"

"Yeah."

"Two and two makes twenty-two."

He stared up into the trees above our bench. A squirrel was out on a limb, making it bend. I waited until I had his attention again.

"That's how old you are."

"Yeah."

"About twenty-two," I said. "Can I have a smoke?"

I reached for the Marlboros in his shirt pocket and he winced and leaned away from me. "Relax, man," I said, pulling my hand back, holding both up, palms open. "I ain't gonna hurt you." Slowly, when I saw the fear leave his eyes, I reached for the pack and shook two out. Together we smoked, his radio playing. It was a big one the size of a lady's purse but we kept it on low. Occasionally cops patrolled the park, and though we were off the path, hidden by trees and brush, they could've heard the music. What I didn't need was to get nailed for truancy.

Around two in the afternoon I'd have a last smoke, say good-bye to Eddie, and head back to meet Mike at the auditorium. For a long time no one ever knew what I was up to. Not Dad, Mike, or Marissa, who'd taken it on herself lately to do our laundry and sometimes make us dinner when her husband was out. No one even suspected me. I always carried my books wherever I went, and at night after dinner I opened them and made like I was cramming for an exam when really I was off dreaming.

Our father had strong notions of right and wrong. He believed in the virtues of hard work. Always be truthful. Never cheat, lie, or steal. "There's no room for the half-assed," he'd say. "The world's plenty full of 'em already. You got to rise above, boys. Got to work harder than the next guy if you're going to make something of yourself." Every chance he had he gave us this sermon, or one close to it, and he gave them more often as the days passed. I've since wondered if it was these things—his notions of honesty and hard work and success—that kept him from telling the truth about Mom.

All he'd ever say, when we asked about her, was that she was away. "She's okay, though. She's doing fine and sends her love. Don't you worry." But that wasn't the point. We all knew where she was but I wanted to hear it from him. I thought if he'd admit it, say "locked up" or "jailed," that it'd be easier for us all to accept. As it was, not knowing the facts, I figured the worst. Something unmentionable. She'd done a thing so unscrupulous, so evil, that it burned his heart to talk about it.

"You're a McKinney. Remember that, boys. There's not a sonofabitch alive can keep you down because you got this." He'd pat his chest. "Heart. And you got this." He'd nod. "Brains. And this." He'd make a fist. "To fight with. Don't matter how poor we are because we been poor before. We made it once, we'll make it back again. If your mother hadn't been so greedy . . ." And there he'd stop, the passion gone, his face suddenly pale and slack. We were the McKinneys all right, and I believed it was something to be proud of, but not a single relative on either side had phoned, written, or dropped by since the arrest. No one offered a loan, which Dad would've declined anyway on account of his pride, or to help out by looking after Mike and me—that is, everyone except Marissa, who offered both, and who probably had the least to give.

It was hard not to like her, even though I felt that she was trying to take Mom's place. She had a friendly face with warm brown eyes and a warm smile that made a person smile back. Her hair she usually wore short, and her dresses were simple in style but bright in color, pulled in tight at the waist with a sash that swung as she walked. She was a few years younger than Dad, a small-boned woman, a gentle woman with a smooth, white complexion. At least twice a week she brought up a tray of enchiladas or hamburgers or a pot of *menudo* cooked just right so that the tripe was tender, not rubbery. I don't know how her husband, Louie, took to her charity, but I suspect he didn't take to it well. They fought a lot, anyway, and when he drank too much we sometimes heard him slapping her. The next day she wouldn't come out of her apartment. But for the most part she visited so often that it got to where Mike and I were afraid to horse around, for fear she'd think we were fighting. In no time she'd be pounding on the door, asking what was the matter. "Your mother was good to me," she'd say, after scolding us. "She hired me when I needed work. Now I want to be good to you people, and if that means keeping you from killing each other, then that's my job. *Behave.*"

If our apartment happened to be messy at the time, and according to her standards it usually was, she would sigh. "Let's get this place picked up before your father gets back. You think he wants to come home to *this*?" If she got too ambitious, and stayed too long, after a while we'd hear a thump on the floor. Marissa would look at us and then stomp her foot a couple of times to let him know he'd been heard. "*Pendejo,*" she'd mutter. Then she would finish whatever it was she was doing—washing dishes, dusting, making Dad's bed—and return to her apartment.

The night *Guys and Dolls* opened she made it her job to iron my best white shirt and gray slacks, had me shower, and helped me slip into a sports coat she'd picked out. Dad wasn't home. Mike had already left. Marissa stood before me, a black tie in her hand, biting her lower lip as if she were threading a needle.

"Is my dad coming?"

"I don't think so."

"Why not?"

"He has business."

"With Mom?"

"Uh-huh," she said. "Look up at the ceiling." I did, and she knotted the tie. "Tonight he finds out when she's coming home." She adjusted the tie, tugged on it. "Too tight?" I said it wasn't.

Marissa stepped back and looked me up and down and then smiled. "Better hurry if you're going to make it on time."

As I headed downstairs onto the street I thought about Mom. She had been gone now for three months and two weeks, yet it seemed a lot longer. For a while I even considered skipping the play and heading back to wait for Dad. I wanted it to be good news so badly that I expected it had to be, and I wanted to hear it now. At the same time I couldn't let my brother down. He'd feel awfully low if no one, not even me, was there to watch him. So I kept walking. As I crossed the street I heard Eddie's radio turned up loud. I thought to myself, If that was my brother wandering around when it was going to be dark soon, I'd do something about it. I wouldn't let him stay out at night, not in this neighborhood.

At the auditorium I paid for my ticket and took a seat a few rows from the stage so that I could watch Mike up close. Soon the houselights went out. A spot shined on. Miss Gloria Millicent Miles came out smiling from behind the curtain, clasped her hands together, and welcomed everyone to a fine night of theater. She had her hair done up for the occasion, and instead of the gold hoops she wore pearls in her ears. In that powerful voice she carried on for nearly ten minutes about how she enjoyed coaching all the fine young actors and actresses of James Lick High School until I found myself yawning. Finally, when even the most polite parents began shifting in their seats, she stepped down.

The curtains parted.

What the play was about, I do not know. I couldn't concentrate. A few seconds after Mike stepped out onstage, a kid in the seat ahead of mine turned to his mother.

"That's the guy I was telling you about," he said.

"Which one?"

"On the right."

"The skinny boy?"

"Yeah," he said. "His mom's the murderer."

A buzzing, humming noise sounded in my head. My ears burned. Not once during the entire first act did I look away from that sonofabitch for more than a minute. At intermission, when the houselights came on, he rose from his seat. I saw he was taller than me, older, too, but at this point it didn't make a damn bit of difference. And I was sure, as I followed them both to the back of the auditorium, that I'd seen him before, on my way home from

Alum Rock. He had been working on a dirt bike in his garage, listening to rock and roll.

His mother bought him a Coke at the concession stand. "Dean" I heard her call him, and I've since never been able to hear the name without recalling the scene, his face. They talked. Smiled. Laughed. They were having a good time without ever noticing that I was standing beside them, waiting. He finished his Coke when the houselights flashed on and off. The mother returned to her seat. Dean headed for the lavatory. I took a deep breath and followed.

There he stood at the urinal. Another kid was combing his hair in the mirror. I waited until he'd left and we were alone before I cocked my head.

"Hey."

Dean glanced over his shoulder.

"What'd you call my mother?"

"You talking to me?"

"I'm talking to you."

He zipped up and walked past me to the washbasin without a word.

"I said what'd you call my mother?"

He looked at me in the mirror. "I didn't call her anything," he said. "I don't even know who you are."

"Liar."

The guy frowned like he didn't understand what I was talking about, and I knew he did. There's no mistaking Mike and me for brothers. But this bastard just looked away and reached for a paper towel as if I weren't there, like I was nothing, because I was younger and smaller. "Fuck you," I said, while he was drying his hands. He tossed the paper towel into the wastebasket and opened the door. "You're a fucking liar." I reared back and hit him as he was stepping back into the auditorium, only I had to jump to do it. I missed slightly. He tried to grab me and I threw another. This one landed good, square on his cheek. Solid. Then the door closed, the auditorium was dark, and the stage curtains parted. I couldn't see much but I kept throwing them, faster now, from all different angles. I had him moving back, he had his arms up, and that's what I kept hitting—the damn arms, trying to break through to his face.

Suddenly the houselights flashed on. Out of nowhere a man

came from behind and locked his arms around me. Lifted me off the ground. "Calm down," he said. "Calm down."

"Lemme alone."

"Soon as you relax."

About that time I noticed that everyone in the place had turned around in their seats. The stage curtains swung closed. Dean stood rubbing his cheek with one hand, patting his hair down with the other. His mother was there now, too, asking what had happened. Was he hurt?

"The kid's crazy."

"You started it, man," I said.

"I didn't do anything to you."

"Fucking liar."

"Watch your language," the man said. He carried me outside with everyone watching. When he figured I was calm enough he let me down. The night air was cool on my face. My heart pounded. I saw the lights of the auditorium go out. The second act was beginning. "Where's your parents?" he said. "They here?"

"No."

"You came by yourself?"

"Yeah."

That surprised him. He was quiet for a few seconds. "What happened in there?"

"Nothing."

"Something happened."

"It's none of your business."

He looked at me long and hard. "I'm the principal," he said. "It's my business. Are you going to behave if I let you back in?"

But by that time I was already walking away, and I didn't turn around to answer him. Seconds later I heard the doors to the auditorium shut and lock.

I went and sat in the quad and waited.

Close to an hour must've passed before I heard the applause go up. Soon parents were strolling out of the auditorium, talking and laughing, headed for the parking lot. When I figured just about everyone had left, and I began to get edgy, my brother walked past me. He carried a gym bag and had changed into his jeans and a T-shirt.

"Mike?"

He stopped, glared at me, then walked on. Go, I thought. If

that's the way you want to act, go, walk it alone. But as I watched
his figure grow small across the quad, fainter down the open corridor, I cursed and ran after him.

"Hey, I'm sorry."

He kept walking like I wasn't there.

"C'mon, Mike."

"You almost ruined the play."

"I said I'm sorry."

A long silence passed.

"You know something?" he said. "You're turning into a real
punk." He stopped in the corridor and hit one of the lockers with
the butt of his hand. It made a hell of a noise through the empty
school. I winced. "What're you doing fighting some guy twice
your size? Huh? You could've gotten killed."

"He started it."

"That isn't what I heard."

"What'd you hear?"

"*You* started it."

"Bullshit."

"Quit cussing. You're cussing too much lately."

"You know what he said?"

"I don't care what he said."

"The fucker called Mom . . ." I looked down the corridor. A
light burned at the end of it. "Forget it."

"Say it."

"I don't wanna."

"A murderer?"

I bit my lower lip.

"That what he said? So what? I've heard it before around here.
Is that any reason to fight?"

Mike walked on. I watched him head down the corridor, the
gym bag slung over his shoulder now, until he passed under the
light onto the street. Then I ran after him.

"The bastard's a liar," I hollered.

"Maybe."

"Whatta you mean *maybe*?"

"Maybe he's telling the truth, Jay. We don't know." He threw
his hand in the air. "It could be true."

"You know something I don't?"

He shrugged.

"Don't hold out on me," I said. We crossed to the next block. I waited for an answer, a response, anything. "C'mon, Mike. I can fuckin' take it."

"I don't know anything for sure yet."

"It's a lie, though."

"That's what I want to believe."

"She wouldn't do nothing like that," I said. "You know she wouldn't, she just wouldn't." Ahead down the street I saw the light on in the kitchen window of our apartment. My heart rose. I thought of telling him what Marissa had said, if only to prove him wrong, but I kept quiet.

Soon we climbed the stairs home. "You okay?" Mike said, stopping me in the hallway. "Let me see." He held my head up to the light for a second. "You look fine."

"Of course."

"You're lucky he didn't hurt you."

"He's fucking lucky I didn't hurt him."

"Watch yourself next time," he said. "Don't be fighting anymore. Don't be cussing, either. And quit smoking, okay?"

"I don't smoke."

"Jay?"

"Yeah?"

"I can smell it on your breath every day after school."

At least he didn't know I'd been cutting. That could change, though, and I knew I had to be more careful now because of the fight. He'd be watching me closely.

We let ourselves into the apartment.

"Dad?"

No answer.

"We're home," I said.

I went to the bedroom. A reading lamp glowed on the nightstand. The bed was disheveled, a pillow at the foot of it, another on the floor. In the kitchen I found my brother squatting before the oven, peering inside. The air was hot and still and something cooking smelled good. On the table rested a bottle of whiskey and two glasses. I went to open the window over the sink and that's when I saw them, as I parted the curtains—what I thought was them, though I couldn't tell for sure at first, because it was dark. Just two figures. They were down in the carport, standing beside the tailgate of Dad's truck. A load of four-by-fours was on the

44

lumber rack, roped and flagged with a red rag. I thought at first it was her husband because they were leaning to one side under the lip of the roof in a shadow. Only Marissa was visible. Then I saw it was our father. He had his arms around her waist. She rested her head on his chest. I watched them for what seemed like a long time before I realized I'd been holding my breath and that my brother stood behind me. His forehead was sweating.

I let the curtains fall back in place. Mike stared at me.

"Don't say a word."

"I won't."

"You didn't see a thing."

"Nothing," I said. "Nothing."

At that he poured himself a shot of whiskey and downed it and winced. "We better get out of the kitchen," he said, turning. "Try to look natural, like nothing happened, because nothing did. Right?" I nodded. But before we could get to the living room, we heard Dad coming up the stairs, singing, and we knew then he was drunk.

"Hey, boys."

"Hey," I said.

"How was the play?"

"Good," Mike said.

"You bowl 'em over?"

"I think so."

"How about a drink, Mike? You feel like you're old enough to handle it? C'mon." He motioned us to sit at the table and then went and got another glass and a can of Dr Pepper for me. "I have some news," he said, his voice suddenly serious. "It may not sound all that good but believe me it is. It could've been a whole lot worse." As he poured the whiskey, slopping a little on the table, he laughed. Only it was a strange laugh, one I'd never heard before, as if his voice were going to crack. "You'll need some water to cut that, son. It's too strong." Mike tossed it back and swallowed without wincing and then set the glass down hard on the table. "Who taught you to drink like that?" Dad said. "Not your old man. Sip it." He turned the bottle around so that the label was facing us. "Chivas Regal, some of the best. This is an occasion, boys, and that's why your old man bought the good stuff. I have news . . . about your mother." He nodded to Mike. "Another shot?"

"Yeah."

He poured him two fingers' worth.

"What's the news?"

"I'm getting there," Dad said. "Put a little water in your glass."

But Mike tossed it back like before. "You're gonna get sick drinkin' like that," Dad said, shaking his head. Already Mike's eyes were glassy, and he was sweating more, too, around the neck and face. Dad took an even, deliberate sip of his drink. "*That's* how you're supposed to do it," he said. Mike reached for the bottle slowly, as if he had to concentrate on it, and poured his glass half full. This time, though, he couldn't down it without gagging. "What I tell you?" Dad slapped the edge of the table and left his hand there, hanging, his heavy forearm bending the fingers back. A long silence passed as they stared at each other. "You mad about something?" Dad said. "Something I did?"

"No."

"You're acting like it."

"I think he's just drunk," I said.

Mike glared at me.

I looked away for a moment.

"The news. What is it?"

Dad bowed his head. Slowly he traced a finger through the spilled whiskey on the table. "If it wasn't for liquor," he said, as if to himself, "if you couldn't come home to a drink now and then, you know what we'd have in this country?" He looked up now. "Do you?"

"A revolution."

"You're damn right."

"C'mon, Dad."

"You know why?"

"We've heard it a hundred times," Mike shouted.

But he went on, anyway, about how liquor tranquilized the masses into civil obedience, and how it was another reason why Prohibition was repealed—to avoid an uprising—until finally he sat back, sighed, and began to sing in a deep and drunken voice.

> *Eight more months and ten*
> *more days, they're gonna*
> *set her loose . . .*
> *Eight more months and ten*

46

more days, they're gonna
cut the noose . . .

As he ended the last verse he reached across the table and patted Mike on the arm. "C'mon, you know it now. It ain't hard to
sing." And again he sang it, and another time after that, too, before Mike interrupted him.

"Finished?"

"Let's sing it together once."

"I don't want to," Mike said. "It's sick."

"I'm just trying to make things a little easier."

"Come off it."

"*You* come off it," Dad said. "*You* relax."

Mike's face was red from the heat and the liquor and his eyes
were bloodshot. His words were slurred. "It doesn't make anything easier," he shouted. "I want to know what happened, damn
it. That'll make it easier."

"It doesn't matter what happened."

"The hell it doesn't."

"Not anymore," Dad said, slamming his hand down on the
table. "It's over and done with. There's nothing to talk about."

"A woman *died.*"

"Be quiet."

"That matters, doesn't it?"

"Let's have another drink."

"What was the evidence? The proof?"

"They didn't find nothing, son."

"Oh great," Mike said. "Great help. Let's just have another
drink and pretend it never happened." He reached for the bottle
and poured himself some more. Sat back. "Everything's fine,
huh?"

"Knock it off."

"So why they holding her?"

"I said knock it off."

"Did she do it?"

"Your little brother's here. Please." He closed his eyes for a
second and then opened them. "Please, Mike, please be quiet."
His voice cracked, he fell silent, and that's when I told them I
needed to get some air, that I'd be right back, not to worry.

Outside I jammed my hands into my pockets, hunched my

47

shoulders, and walked, just walked, not caring where I was headed. Halfway up the block I spotted Eddie at the corner with his radio blasting. "Whatta you doing out?" I said, when I got to him. "Ain't you supposed to be home?" He just smiled, and I knew he was glad to see me. I turned the radio off for him, took hold of his arm, and was planning on bringing him back to his foster mother when I thought to hell with it. He wasn't dumb. There was a reason why he wasn't home, and it was probably that he didn't want to be there. And I sure as hell didn't want to go back myself.

I spun him around. We walked on.

"You're a good friend, you know that?"

————

"Sometimes I think you know what's going on but you just don't say nothing. Am I right?"

————

"Bet you hate that lady."

————

"Bet she treats you like shit."

————

"If she cared, man, then where the fuck is she? Huh?" I said. "Gimme a smoke, Eddie. I need a smoke."

We walked and smoked Marlboros until we were a good mile from the apartment. I told him about what had happened tonight with my fight at Lick, the argument at home, about Mom and everything else on my mind. He listened, he even understood a lot of it, except he just couldn't speak. Instead he'd cock his head, frown at the right places, smile when I smiled. He knew what I was saying, maybe not the words but the feelings behind them, and that's all that mattered.

On Alum Rock Avenue I spotted a bus. We crossed against the light and caught it and got off downtown. Most of the stores were closed and the streets, except for a couple of raggedy-dressed men and a few passing cars, were empty. Some of the stores had boards over the doors. Another had an old sun-bleached GOING OUT OF BUSINESS sign in the window. There was nothing inside except the fixtures. It was kind of depressing, as I could re-member when downtown was *downtown*—the place to go—but for Eddie it was still a big deal, even though there wasn't much to see here anymore. His eyes wandered from one building to an-other and he liked to stop a lot and look into the windows. I

48

thought maybe he'd never been downtown before, or else it had been a long time ago.

I looked up at the marquee of the Fox. The lights flashed, throwing shadows on the sidewalk. I checked my wallet to see if I had enough money and found that I did. "C'mon." I took him by the arm and tugged. He didn't budge. "How long's it been since you saw a movie?" I tugged harder, smiled, and he relaxed.

We stepped up to the box office.

"When's the last show?"

The lady furrowed her eyebrows at Eddie. "It started a couple of minutes ago."

"Two, please."

I gave her the money.

"Is he going to behave?"

"We come here all the time."

"Just so you know."

Know what, I thought. What did she think he was going to do? We got our tickets, finally, and I handed them to the teenager working the snack bar. Eddie gripped my arm tight on our way down the aisle. "It's just a movie, man," I whispered. "Nothing to be afraid of."

The title ran as we settled into our seats.

THE INCREDIBLE SHRINKING MAN

There was hardly anyone in the place, the way my brother and I liked it—no screaming kids, no shouting—but when I sat back into my chair I felt my eyes grow heavy. I yawned. It was an older movie I'd seen once before with Mike. A young couple are on a boat in what looks like the middle of nowhere. A warning crackles over the shortwave radio. Military bombs at sea. The woman runs below. The man remains on deck. Soon the screen is covered with radioactive fog. Seconds later, even though I wanted to watch the man shrink, I let my eyes close. That's all it took. I don't know how long I slept, but it was for the length of the movie, anyway.

I woke up to a finger jabbing me in the arm.

"Show's over, buddy."

The teenager who had taken our tickets stood now with a broom in his hand. "It's over," he said. "We're closed." I sat up and turned to Eddie, only he wasn't there. I scanned the theater. The screen was white; the houselights were on.

"Did you see my friend?"

"When you came in."

"You didn't see him go?"

"Nope." He stooped to pick up a paper cup. "Maybe he's in the head."

I ran up the aisle into the lobby and checked the men's room. No one. I ran back into the lobby. The lights around the snack bar were out. A clock over the popcorn machine read a quarter to twelve. The lady who sold us the tickets was searching through her purse as she pushed open the front door with her hip. I ducked past her outside onto the street and hurried down the block. "Eddie?" I called. *"Eddie?"* But there was nobody around. I circled the block once and looked into every alcove of every store with no luck. The cops, I had to call the cops. I started back to the theater to use the phone, and that's when I heard him, in the parking lot behind the old Fox, behind the trash bin near the exit doors. A whimper, it was.

"Eddie?" I said. "Say hey."

"Say yeah."

His radio was busted on the asphalt. A plastic knob lay cracked beside it, and the antenna was all bent. When I stepped closer I saw that he was curled into a ball on his side. He was hugging himself and shivering. I kneeled beside him and he jerked away and whimpered again. "It's okay. It's me, man. Jay. It's okay." Bits of gravel clung to his forearm, and when I pulled his hands from his face I saw that the bastard or bastards had hit him hard. There was a purple bruise down the center of his forehead and a cut over one eye. "I'm sorry, man, I'm sorry." He'd lost a shoe, too, which I found next to the exit door. I put it back on for him. The radio I left behind. I just wanted to get out of this damn parking lot and find someplace to clean him up and then get him home. I kept thinking, Why, what reason, what kind of mother-fucker would do this? For the hell of it? Twice I tried looking Eddie in the eyes, and twice I ended up staring down at the ground.

On the way back we stopped at an all-night gas station. There in the men's room I washed the blood from his forehead. Then I brushed off his shirt as best I could, straightened the collar, spot-cleaned his pants with a paper towel, and walked him the rest of the way home in silence. The buses had stopped running for the night.

At his apartment I knocked on the door and ran to the end of the hallway and watched from the edge of the stairs. His foster mother opened the door in her bathrobe.

"Where's your radio?"

———

"You let somebody steal your radio?"

———

"You know how much that radio *cost*?"

———

She stepped into the hallway and grabbed his arm. Looked at his face. "What happen? You get in a fight? How many times I tell you not to go to that park at night? There's no hope for you." After she pulled him inside, when I heard her slap him, I left for my place.

The light was still on in Marissa's apartment, and I thought about going there as I passed, talking maybe, but then I thought better. It was too late. She'd want to know what I was doing out. So I climbed the stairs home that night, one of the worst of my life, and cursed myself for ever having gone out in the first place. They had left the door unlocked for me, and as I entered I found Mike asleep on the couch in his clothes. Dad snored, slumped in a chair. The kitchen light still burned, and the bottle of whiskey on the table was empty. A tray of Marissa's fine enchiladas rested on top of the stove untouched, burned black, completely wasted. As I closed the door, moments before they woke to give me hell, I thought of Eddie. The radio. I should've taken it. Could be the insides still worked. A plastic knob, an antenna can be replaced. I might've been able to fix it.

4

Four months in the neighborhood and I had a scar over my eye, my nose was set to one side, and I got a couple of knots on the back of my head that are still there today. The kid who gave me the knots busted a hand in the process because, as Dad used to say, I had a hard head. So I changed my ways, how I dressed and how I walked. I wore what the *cholos* wore, pleated slacks or creased Levi's, and always with a perfectly ironed T-shirt from Penney's or a flannel Pendelton, untucked. I walked with a swagger, my shoulders thrown back, and my hair slicked straight. I cussed about every other word. And I slouched in my chair in class, as I was back in school now, which I'll go into in a minute.

Dad wasn't happy with the changes, but he understood the reasons and never said much about them except not to cuss. Mike, though, was angry with me. If I was leaning toward the hard side, he was leaning the opposite direction. Miss Gloria Millicent Miles and another teacher eventually saw how smart he was and stuck him in a special accelerated program for gifted students.

Every day he met me after school, rather than the other way around like before, and made sure I went straight home. Made sure I did my work. He'd be waiting at the front gates after the last bell, always with a pile of books under one arm—some for his classes, others that he checked out from the library for himself. At sixteen he'd read all of Dostoyevsky and most of Tolstoy. He read everything on Stanislavsky, and everything the man wrote about acting. The Method became my brother's method, and the main technique, memory recall, though it helped make for some fine performances, eventually came to haunt him.

Together we'd sit at the kitchen table and pore over boring textbooks. I could stand it only for about an hour.

"My eyes burn."

I rose from my chair.

"Sit down. You're not finished."

"I wanna walk."

"Where you going?"

"To the park," I said. "To see Eddie."

"That crazy guy?"

"He's not crazy."

"You know what I mean," he said. "What d'you and him do there, anyway?"

"Nothing."

"You can do that here."

"Ain't the same," I said.

"Can't you make other friends?" He put his pencil down, as he always read with a pencil so he could take notes, and stared at me with those big brown eyes of his. "You realize what's happening to you? If you keep hanging out at the park with those hoods, you're going to become like them."

"I don't hang with any hoods."

"They're going nowhere, man, and I don't care why, only I don't want you following them." He wagged his head. "I can't believe you sometimes. Cutting school and smoking and cussing. Better change your ways, Jay."

"Don't worry."

"I'm worried."

Then I'd take off. And I made a point now of passing Dean's house on my way to and from Alum Rock. Usually he was out in the garage with his dirt bike, revving it up or wiping it down, and he never noticed me. On a workbench above a shelf full of paint cans was a radio like Eddie's. The problem was that either the garage was locked or Dean was there. Not that I was afraid to fight him again. Nine out of ten fights, I won. I had developed, like my brother developed, a solid reputation. His was as a good ambitious student; mine was as a badass. He had to study and work to maintain his image. I had to hang out and work to maintain mine. It was all equal as far as I could see.

They found me out two weeks after the night Eddie and I went to the movies. As usual I'd been cutting school and fooling around at the park, but without music the mornings passed slowly. We were still buddies, although I felt like I'd betrayed him by falling asleep and letting him wander. Now and then the guilt rose up inside of me, I'd get teary-eyed, and I'd curse the bastards who could do such a thing. I told Eddie I'd get them someday. Slice them from the belly up and dump them in the Alum Rock creek for dead. I also had a new nickname for him, as the movie had taught him two words. Shrinking Man. He said them constantly, bobbing his shaved head, grinning. I vowed to get him another radio if for no other reason than to quiet him down. Those words reminded me of that night and my failure.

In the meantime, while I was bumming around Alum Rock, Dad completed the tracts off Story Road. He spent most of his waking hours now coming and going, looking for work, and I could never tell when he might show up at the apartment. Previous years whenever he finished a big job, and the places sold—usually before the drywall was even hung—there was a lot of cash floating around our house. The family went on vacations. Mom sometimes bought a new car. But this time the money went to the bank that financed the construction loan, and what was left the creditors devoured. Dad was still on his own, still a contractor, but no loan officer would back a bankrupt man. He was like other carpenters now, hunting for work, for jobs that didn't require more material than he could afford to put out for, small jobs, labor jobs for old neighbors who needed something done around the house, who knew our father needed work. It was also a lot tougher to check the mail now before Dad. His hours, like I said, were unpredictable.

Our mailbox was one of those standard cheap apartment kinds that anybody can open with a knife. The postman came at one sharp, and I was there as usual, across the street watching, waiting until he left to make my move. Today there were no letters but in the rack beneath the mailboxes I found a small package addressed to Mike and me. The return address read HEDDING CORRECTIONAL CENTER, MILPITAS, CALIFORNIA. My heart skipped a beat. It was wrapped in brown paper and tied with a string and it felt soft when I squeezed it. I wondered, because it was for both of us, if I ought to open it. At first I thought, No, it was his, too, and I'd have to tell him. Then he and Dad would ask how I got to the mail before them and that would be it. There was every reason to put the package back in the rack, pretend I never saw it, and act surprised later when I saw it again. Yet it was in my hands. I couldn't just walk away. Suddenly an idea hit me.

Around back near the carports was the laundry room. On weekends it was packed but this was Friday, most everyone was at work, and as I hurried down the driveway I found the place deserted. Setting the package on a washing machine, I carefully peeled off the tape, untied the string, and unfolded the brown wrapping without tearing it. Inside were two handkerchiefs. One had my name embroidered in the corner beneath a finely sewn picture of a pirate's ship. The other had Mike's name in capital letters on the picture of a theater marquee. I raised mine to my mouth and inhaled, but it smelled only of the paper it came wrapped in. I stared at it for a long time, and I thought of Mom. Imagined her face. For a moment it felt as if she were there beside me. I neatly folded the handkerchief and replaced it along with my brother's in the package.

A letter was enclosed. I leaned against the washing machine and read it slowly twice.

Dear Boys,

I hope you both like your presents. I made them myself, you know. How are you doing in school, Mike? Jay? How do you like your new place? Is it nice? Does it have a pool? Mike, you watch out for your brother, and please give my love to your dad. I love and miss you both dearly and think of you all the time.

Mom

My plan was to return the package to the rack, but as I slipped the letter inside, and began to rewrap and tape the paper, I heard the laundry door creak. In came Marissa carrying a basket full of dirty clothes. My mouth fell open. There was nowhere to hide. She furrowed her eyebrows.

"Why aren't you in school?"

"It's a holiday."

"Try again."

"The teachers had a meeting," I said. "They let us out early."

"One more time."

"Got a cold?"

"Now the truth."

"I cut."

"That's more like it." She sighed and turned the basket upside down, dumping the laundry onto the folding table. "Put the whites with the whites," she said. "I'll do the colors."

We sorted laundry in silence for a while.

"You're not going to tell my dad, are you?"

"Have to."

"Please."

"Don't *please* me," she said. "You knew what you were getting into."

She dug through her pocket for change. I wondered for a second, as she slipped quarters into the slots of two machines, if I should use what I had against her. It was my only chance. I held up a dirty T-shirt. "This Louie's?" I asked.

Marissa glanced over my shoulder. "Yeah," she said. "Most of the whites are his."

I dropped the shirt into the white pile. Took a deep breath.

55

Gathered my courage. "Got a letter from my mom today," I said, casual.

"How is she?"

"Fine. She thinks everything's fine with us, too."

"It is, isn't it?"

"Not really."

"What d'you mean?"

I gathered up my load of laundry, as I couldn't look her in the eyes. "You know what I mean."

"No, I don't."

"I mean you and my dad."

Marissa was pouring detergent from the box into the machine, only she didn't realize how much she was using. "That's a lotta soap," I said. She glared at me and stopped pouring. I glanced down at the clothes in my arms. "Where do you want these?"

"In there," she said. "Who you been talking to?"

I dumped the whites into the machine.

"Nobody."

She pushed the slot with the quarters hard into the box. The machine hissed, hot water steaming. "But I won't say anything," I said. "If you don't say anything about me." Here she turned, dropped the lid on the laundry with a loud clang, and stared hard at me. I bowed my head. Now that I'd said it I felt ashamed.

"I like you," she said.

"I like you, too."

"I like Mike and I like your father."

"You like him a lot, though."

"You don't understand."

That word irritated me. My shame passed for a second. "I understand," I said. "I know. I got eyes."

Both of the machines were churning now, slopping water back and forth, vibrating. The room had grown hot fast, and I felt myself sweating. Marissa moved closer and put her hand on my shoulder. I bit my lower lip, ashamed again of myself or her, I'm not sure, and I looked away to the dryers, the folding table, anywhere but into her eyes.

"You love your father?"

"Yeah."

"You love your mother?"

"Yeah."

56

"And your brother?"

"Yeah."

"Then whatever you saw, whatever you think you saw, or whatever you think you know, you'll keep to yourself." She squeezed my arm once. "But I'm not making any deals with you. It would be wrong, Jay, if I didn't tell your father."

So she brought me to her apartment and made us lunch. That's where I stayed, feeling rotten for what I'd done, until Dad and Mike came home about the same time, around three. Marissa delivered me to my door and, in the hallway as I stood staring down at my feet, told them she'd found me skipping school. Mike shook his head in disgust. Dad frowned and asked me why, why would I do something like that? And I shrugged, not knowing what to say.

He sat me down at the kitchen table and lectured about how as a family we had to pull together, how he was working and couldn't look after me like he ought to, like he wanted to, how times were tough but we would weather them, and how important school was. "Like a house," he said. "You gotta have a good foundation to build on. You gotta get an education to get along later in life or you're gonna fall on your ass. You'll dig ditch for a livin'." He put his hand on mine on top of the table and I noticed, as he carried on, how his fingers were thick and strong, how his palm was calloused and rough. "I dropped out in the tenth grade because my family needed me to work. You don't gotta work, not yet. My father, *your* grandfather, signed his name with an *X* till I taught him how to write. You got an opportunity a lot of folks don't, and you'd be a fool to waste it. Look at your brother now. He studies hard. He doesn't skip school. He knows what's important and he's gonna amount to something because he's smart, sometimes a little too smart. . . ." Dad chuckled. "But he'll amount to something, and so will you, damn it." He nodded firmly. "I was an A student all through school, I wanted to be a doctor, and I woulda been a good one if my family didn't have to work to eat. Now you tell me why you're playing hookey, son . . . you go ahead and tell me." I felt terrible, guilty, and I said nothing. "That's what I figured, no reason, no good one, anyway."

I'd hoped that if I just heard him out, and promised him I'd never do it again, that he'd let it go at that. But he called the school. Dad wagged his head at me as he dialed the last number.

"What's your teacher's name?"

"Mrs. Wharton."

A second passed. "This is Mr. McKinney," he said. "I'm calling about my boy. Can I speak with Mrs. Wharton?" I sank into my seat. Dad curled the cord around his hand and squeezed it while he waited until she came on the line. "Mrs. Wharton? I'm Jay McKinney's father . . ." I tried to sneak off but Dad caught me out of the corner of his eye and waved at me to sit back down. "Uh-huh, I see. . . . No . . . no, I didn't know that. . . . *How* long? Are you sure?" Now a grave expression came over his face. "Hmmm, yes. . . . I didn't get anything in the mail. That might explain some of it. . . . Uh-huh, uh-huh." His eyes grew wide. "You sure about that?" A long pause. "I'll talk to him. . . . I appreciate it. . . . You bet. . . . You too now. . . . Thank you, Mrs. Wharton. . . ." I hung my head between my knees.

Click.

The roof had come down.

I expected an explosion. Instead he said, "Don't you move, don't you go anywhere, you understand?" He felt in his pocket for his truck keys, motioned to Mike—who'd been sitting on the couch all this time pretending to read—and together they left the apartment. About a half hour later they returned with a bag from Woolworth's. In it was a small blackboard and a box of chalk. Dad set the board on a chair in front of me, opened the box of chalk, took out a stick, and printed the word FORWARD on the board. Mike crossed his arms over his chest and leaned against the refrigerator.

"What's that mean?" Dad said.

"To walk straight," I said. "Something in front of you."

"Good." He covered the word with his hand. "Now spell it."

I spelled it.

"Good."

Next he erased the board, handed me the chalk, and told me to write it. I did. He shook his head and looked at Mike. "The teacher was right," he said sadly.

"About what?" I asked.

"It's nothing to worry about, son. You'll learn."

I stared at the word. It was spelled right.

"What's wrong with it?"

"It's backward."

"No it ain't."

"Look at the *r*'s and the *d*."

"So?"

"He can't see it," Mike said.

"They're backward, son."

"Reversed."

I squinted, stared, and they grew quiet watching me. "No," I said.

"Yep."

"You're dyslexic," Mike said.

"What's that?"

"It means you see things a little different than some people," Dad said. "Lots of folks have it."

After dinner that evening they worked out a strict schedule for me. They would both tutor me but the major responsibility for making sure I made it to school and back would be my brother's. Dad speculated that maybe I'd gotten a good knock on the head and had a certain loss of memory. He'd heard of it before. It was possible, he said. Anything was possible. My brother thought it might be caused by something emotional that Dad felt we ought not to talk about. Later, as I lay in bed with Mike, listening to him breathing in his sleep, I wondered what he had meant. I saw clearly, I thought—objects, people, things around me—and even if I got words reversed now and then, they still made sense. I decided not to think about it, as the worst was over for the day, being found out and all, when I remembered the handkerchiefs. The letter. I got up and dressed and hurried outside.

The package was still there, resting on the washing machine where I'd left it. I saw it through the laundry-room window. The light was on but the door was locked. A dryer, empty, went round and round.

At Pala they put me in a special class. The pamphlet I brought home to my father called it a "Program for the Learning Disabled." A couple of the kids stuttered so bad you couldn't hardly understand them. A few couldn't understand the teacher and the teacher couldn't understand them because they spoke Spanish. Some were just slow. Two were truly dumb. One was like Eddie, and three others had what I had. We could handle mathematics well enough, especially verbal exercises, although we sometimes blew it in the end—not in the process—by reversing the sum numbers. And we could read all right except that it took us a little longer than the average student. If a word in a sentence appeared out of order to us, we had to stop and figure out where it belonged, had to rearrange.

Why Mike and Dad never knew about my "word blindness" up until now was partly because I'd been passing my classes, though barely. And partly, too, because although I couldn't write well, I knew the meanings of words. If, for instance, I saw the word *house* I might read it as *home*, or *see* as *look*. And, say, if I had to spell *baseball*, I didn't so much see the word as the leather ball and the red thread flying through the air. I saw images instead of letters.

Once in the third grade my teacher sent a note home to Mom with my English paper attached to it in an envelope. "Sloppy, illegible writing, gross mechanical errors," she wrote. "Needs to concentrate on penmanship and spelling." What Mom did was sit me down right then and there, as Dad had done, only she had me read aloud my own work. I had no problem deciphering it, as my teacher had, and when I'd finished reading Mom saw that I understood what I'd written and she thought I'd done sloppy work on purpose. "Be more careful," she said. "Use a dictionary if you don't know how to spell a word." She didn't know, like I didn't know, that there was something wrong with me. Somebody who knows what they're talking about has to tell you those kinds of things.

Still, to be safe, she took me to an eye doctor to be sure that wasn't my problem. It wasn't. Then she took me to an ear doctor, but I checked out fine there, too. In the fourth and fifth grades I survived by reading my English assignments over and over until I'd memorized every word in every passage. No one was the wiser for it. I could stand in front of the class and read aloud without stuttering, stammering, or getting the words mixed up. In the sixth grade I took a battery of so-called intelligence tests and came out on them with the same good scores as the others in class. Yet I still sometimes wrote *Jonh* for *John*, *an* for *am*, and occasionally I read the STOP sign as SOTP, knowing exactly what it meant, but not always able to spell it correctly. In any case, I got by in school for quite a while before anyone caught on to me.

60

It was here in this class for the learning disabled that I wrote my first short story. Not a full-blown one, more of a sketch really, about an old man who used to live up the block from us. I'd seen him one morning slumped in a chair on his porch as Mike and I walked by on the sidewalk. A glass of wine was clamped between his thighs. My brother figured he'd drunk too much and passed out. To me, he looked asleep. But he was still there later that evening, slumped in the same position, and an ambulance came for him.

I titled my story "The Battle of the Cuff." Death, I wrote, had been hiding in the cuff of his pants leg, ready to attack when his guard was down. I didn't know if the man had actually served in the military, but in my story he was a decorated army sergeant in his youth. My teacher, Mr. Walter Lewis, thought it beyond my years despite all the grammatical errors. He read it to the class, and I sank into my seat with embarrassment.

Later that afternoon I showed it to my brother. He smiled when he finished.

"You know something, Jay?"

"What?"

"This is pretty damn good."

"Really?"

"I'm not lying. You have a feel for the character. I mean I can *see* him, and it's not just me, not because I was there. It's the same old man, right?" I nodded. He grinned and patted me on the back. "Didn't know you had it in you, man. Seriously, you ought to keep writing."

After I'd soaked up the praise, we sat down at the kitchen table and went over the grammatical errors and misspellings together. When we finished, my story was marked up all to hell. Mike saw the disgust, the disillusionment in my eyes. "Don't worry," he said. "The point is you've kept in character with this old guy, you're trying to tell the truth here, and you've got hold of some of it. The heart, anyway," he said, tapping his pencil on my chest. "That's the most important thing. Now you have to go back and make what's good about it clear, sharp. What is it Mrs. Miles said about me being an infant of the stage? Remember? You were there." I said I did. "So you're an infant of writing. It doesn't mean you're dumb, though. Don't let anybody ever let you think that. Because you're not, Jay. Thomas Edison, man, Albert Einstein, General Patton—they all had the same problem. You're smart, got it?" He patted me on the back again. His voice rose. "We'll be dynamite, we'll explode. *Boom*." He waved a hand through the air. "There it is . . . in lights . . . The McKinney Brothers. Actor. Writer."

"Yeah."

"Famous."

"Yeah."

"Can't you just see it?"

"*M*," I said, rising to my feet. "Small *c* . . . capital *k* . . . *i* . . . two *n*'s . . . and an *e* . . . and a *y*."

Mike grinned. There was no other way to spell it.

One morning, not long after I'd written the short story, Dad gave us a sealed envelope. "There'll be a young man coming by this afternoon," he said. "His name is Derek. Don't invite him in, understand? All I want you to do is give him the envelope and tell him I'll see him again in three months. Got it?"

"Got it."

"What's the man's name?"

"Derek," Mike said.

"What're you going to tell him?"

"That you'll see him again in three months."

"Right." Dad handed him the envelope. "See you tonight."

"About what time?"

"You just be ready to go."

"See you."

"See you."

"Derek, right?"

"Don't give it to anybody else, and don't open it yourself. I'm trusting you. This is important."

As soon as we heard the truck leave the carport, and saw it disappear down the block, Mike told me to put the kettle on. Soon the water began to boil. He drew the envelope back and forth through the steam until the seal came unglued. I turned the fire off and followed him into the living room, where he peeled the envelope open. Hundred-dollar bills were enclosed. We glanced at each other wide-eyed, never having seen that much cash before. I grabbed it out of his hand.

"Give it back."

"In a second."

I counted ten. Fresh and crisp. "A thousand bucks," I muttered, amazed. "A thousand goddamn bucks." Where Dad came up with that kind of cash, when we'd been eating spaghetti and beans, I still don't know.

I handed him the money.

"What's the letter say?"

Mike showed me a piece of paper with nothing on it. Clipped to the top, though, was an old snapshot. Mom was holding me in her arms and smiling. Mike sat on a two-by-six stuck into the dirt. He couldn't have been more than four years old, and he wasn't smiling. Dad stood to one side behind us with his arm around Mom, grinning. In the background was the skeleton of a building, just the frame and foundation. I'd never seen the photo before.

"Where's that?"

"That's our house."

He flipped it over. On the back it read MANY THANKS FROM THE MCKINNEY FAMILY. "That all?" I said, shrugging. No letter. No name mentioned but our own.

Mike folded the paper around the bills and slipped it back into the envelope. "That's it," he said. "Where's the glue?"

Late that afternoon an overgrown teenager wearing a varsity jacket knocked on the door and introduced himself as Derek. My brother gave him the envelope and told him what Dad had said. The teenager nodded, thanked him, slipped the envelope into a book he was carrying, and walked off.

Mike closed the door.

"I hope I didn't screw up."

"He said the right name."

"Maybe he overheard us talking."

"Dad said he was young."

"But that young?"

"They're training him. You know like they do. They get 'em young."

"You're crazy."

"He looked Italian, too."

"This isn't a movie, man." He glared at me. "This shit is for real."

The rest of the afternoon we spent getting ready to visit Mom. Showering. Dressing. Rehearsing what we would say, Mike telling me not to get too sentimental, to just relax. It had been nearly five months since we last saw her. I was anxious. Once I slipped outside and had a quick smoke while Mike was in the bathroom. By the time Dad came home and cleaned up we'd been ready to go for over an hour.

Soon we were climbing into the truck, driving across town. A Skilsaw with its black cord wrapped around the blade guard rested on the floorboard. The smell of fresh sawdust and the Old Spice our father wore filled the cab. We drove and drove. In the parking lot Dad eased the truck into a stall and switched off the engine. We stared at the building ahead. L-shaped, concrete, three levels tall, with small windows in neat rows on each level except the first. Some of the windows were lighted, others were not. The sky was clear and growing dark. In the distance was an apricot orchard. A slight breeze moved the branches. The Chevy's engine ticked itself cool. I watched a drop of sweat slip down the side of Dad's jaw and hang there for a moment, slowly stretching itself longer until it beaded and fell. He blinked. "Well?" I felt for my brother's hand but it wasn't there. He stood outside, holding the door open for me, waiting so he could lock it.

Seconds later we walked together across the lot.

"What're you going to tell her?"

"Me?" I said.

"You," Dad said. "You're going to tell her how much you miss her, aren't you?"

"Yeah."

"Mike?"

"Sure."

"What else you boys going to say?"

Silence.

"What'd she send you awhile back?"

"Handkerchiefs."

"So what do you say?"

"Thank you," I said.

"Don't forget it," Dad said. "I shouldn't have to remind you."

Just before we entered the building he stopped and nodded at us. He ran a fist gently across my chin, then Mike's. "I want to tell you boys something else, too." His voice became deep, very serious. "If your mother cries when she sees you it's because she hasn't seen you in so long and she loves you. She might not cry now, but if she does, don't you guys go getting upset and start howling. We don't need a scene in there. For her sake, mainly." He grinned and straightened the collar of my shirt. "All right? I'm counting on you now."

Mike had to wait in a room outside the one where the visitors met the prisoners. Only one person at a time was allowed in, and I would've had to wait, too—while our father visited—if I wasn't younger. The guard felt it might be better if I went in with Dad. He opened a heavy wooden door. Somehow, as we stepped into the room, I had the notion that Mom would be standing right on the other side to greet us. But she was behind a sheet of wired glass, thinner than I remembered her, wearing a shapeless green smock. Her faced looked aged; her eyes seemed set deep into her skull. Her hair was pulled back and her skin seemed drawn back with it, tight across her forehead, taut and bony. She was without makeup, dark eyeliner or rouge, and her complexion was sallow. Mom smiled faintly at me and took a seat on her side behind the glass.

A woman in uniform stood in the corner of the room with her hands behind her back. There was a phone receiver on the counter on Mom's side and one on the counter on our side. In the doorway behind her stood another guard. Three chairs down from the one where I sat was a black woman speaking to an old black man who might've been her father.

Dad handed me the receiver. I placed it to my ear and smiled.

"How's my Jay?"

"Fine," I said.

"You behaving?"

Dad squatted on his haunches beside me.

"Uh-huh."

"You look so handsome all dressed up. I miss you."

"Mom?"

"What, baby?"

"You be outta here soon?"

Dad squeezed my hand, as Mom had winced at my question. I tried to cover my mistake. "Thanks for the handkerchief."

"You're welcome."

"Mike's here, too."

"Lemme talk to your father."

"Bye."

65

"Bye."

"I love you."

"Love you too."

I gave the phone to Dad. He placed the receiver to his ear and smiled. From a pocket in her smock Mom produced a letter, unfolded it, and pressed it flat against the wired glass. Dad's face went blank, pale. It was signed by Louie.

Her voice on the phone was amplified. I could hear them fine.

"Honey?"

"You bastard."

"Louie's a drunk. He's mixed up."

"You bastard."

"He doesn't know what he's talking about, honey. Listen to me . . ."

But that's all they said. Mike didn't get to see her. Mom began crying, then dropped the receiver and rushed through the door where the guard stood watching. Dad lowered his head for a long time before he raised it. For a longer time he stared at the empty seat behind the glass, blinking every few seconds. I wondered if he was waiting for her to come back, to talk, but I knew it wasn't going to happen. After a while I put my hand on his shoulder. "Let's go," I whispered. "Dad, c'mon." He rose and I walked him to the door.

Outside the building I told Mike about the letter. Dad didn't try to stop me. All I said was that it came from Louie and that Mom knew. It was enough. As we were getting into the truck I looked up at the building once more. In one of the lighted windows on the second floor I saw a hand waving to me. I wondered if it was Mom's.

For a few miles, on the way home, nothing was said. Light from the passing streetlamps shone through the cab. We listened to the hum of the engine. Finally Dad glanced at Mike.

"Did you give Derek the envelope?"

"Yeah."

"No problems?"

"None."

"You open it?"

"No."

"I expected you would the second I left," he said. "A boy with a sealed envelope, a secret envelope. You and Jay always peeked at

66

your Christmas presents. Everything under the tree, yep. Tape got so worn pulling it off and on you couldn't stick it back." He chuckled, smiled. "Nothing was ever a surprise for you boys. You remember?"

"I remember."

"There was money in the envelope."

"Oh?"

"For your mother. They dropped the murder charge," Dad said, "as I suppose you know by now. It was a gift. For the attorney to give to the judge." A long pause. "Because I love your mother and I want her back. No matter what happens, you need to know I'm sorry and I want her back, son. You need to know that. There's nothing between me and Marissa." He furrowed his eyebrows. "Maybe there was at one time but not anymore." Another long moment of silence passed. The road passed. My brother turned and stared out the window. I stared down at the Skilsaw on the floorboard.

"I don't believe you," Mike said. "I think you're going to have to choose between them now." Dad stepped down hard on the accelerator. The road came fast. Lights on the street came fast and blurred. Something rattled in the door frame. I concentrated on the noise, tried to pinpoint it, if it came from the crank or if something was broken inside the panel. It was hard to tell unless you undid all the screws and looked inside. Hard to tell about anything, I thought that night. I couldn't know what would happen when they let her out. Mike couldn't. Dad couldn't. Years later I learned two things about the day of our visit. One had to do with the snapshot in the envelope. He had enclosed it, he said, to maybe make the bastard feel bad, maybe good, but to show him who we were. To show him this was a family.

The other thing had to do with Mom.

She returned to her cell for just a short while. The details on this aren't clear but there were no more letters, no more handkerchiefs sent to us after our visit. And I wrote, too. Nothing went in, nothing came out. All I know for sure is that she returned to her cell. She got in a fight. She bit off half of a woman's ear and they locked her in solitary for the remainder of her sentence.

5

In our family album there's a metal plate photo of our great grandfather wearing a bearskin coat without a shirt underneath. He's posing on horseback. His chest is thick and muscular and his hair is long and scraggly. There's a Bowie knife in a sheath on his belt. In his hand, held over his head, is a Winchester .30-30. Tied to the barrel with strips of leather, and tied to his belt with more strips of leather, are what in the photo look like black balls about the size of your fist. I've held the picture under a bright light before and counted seventeen of them. In the background is a flat open Kansas plain. My father once told me that in our great grandfather's room in a shack of a house he had another twenty-six Indian scalps dangling from his ceiling.

There's a reprint of that same photo on page 328 of Roger Darby's *Outlaws and Settlers of the Old West*. The caption below it reads: JOSEPH ZACHARIAH MCKINNEY, AN IRISH IMMIGRANT, WAS KNOWN THROUGHOUT KANSAS AND MISSOURI AS ONE OF THE MOST FIERCE INDIAN HUNTERS OF HIS TIME. ABOVE, HE IS PICTURED WITH SIXTEEN OF HIS "TROPHIES."

Darby miscounted.

Joseph was barely five feet five, but he's said to have had shoulders thirty some inches across, and he was not only feared by the Cheyenne and Sioux but by his wife and child as well. He was a mean, dense sonofabitch who at any other time in our nation's history might've been tried and hung for murder or who, if he hadn't sailed over from Ireland, might've become a peaceful potato farmer like his father. At age fourteen his son Harold married and ran away west with his first child already in the belly of my grandmother. Nine more would follow, the seventh being my father.

Harold was a gentle man, though a demanding, often stubborn one, but by no means was he an Indian killer. The only problem he had coming west was with Mormons, not Indians, as he passed through Utah in a covered wagon. Two bearded men directed him down a path he soon found led nowhere, he suspected they were

68

trying to steal his wife, they had pistols, they pointed them at him, and he shot them dead with a double-barreled shotgun. I still have that gun. The bluing has long since worn off, the stock is cracked, and one of the triggers is jammed. My grandfather, by the way—by his own account—was the last man to cross the Oregon Trail by wagon. It was pulled by horses he stole from his father, although he didn't consider it theft. They were *owed* him. Joseph had worked him since the age of six for a wage he held only long enough to hand to his father.

Harold and Majorie McKinney settled in Klamath Falls, Oregon, for ten years, where they raised six children. At times Harold left town to pick hops, other times he felled timber, but mostly he shoveled sawdust and pulp in the local lumber mill. Someday, he hoped, they would train him as a saw filer. That was a good job—it paid well and it wasn't back breaking—yet there were others in line ahead of him. And Harold, like my father and brother, was an anxious man. Another ten years might pass before they made him a saw filer, and then there was no guarantee. So one day Harold packed up the wagon again, loaded his children and wife, and headed a little farther south. It was here, from out of the mountains, the great redwood and pine and the damp green fern along the California coast in the town of Eureka, that my father, David Michael McKinney was born.

They rented a ranch, raised chickens and cows, planted a tiny farm, and sold what produce they couldn't eat themselves. They fished, hunted deer and rabbit and pheasant and quail, panned for gold in the Mad River, and cut and sold cordword to the folks wealthy enough not to have to cut their own. This was the good life, my father used to say. Clean air. Fishing. Hunting. But his father made the same mistake as Joseph McKinney had. He worked his children with the same fierce determination with which my great-grandfather had worked his boy. At the age of fifteen my father dropped out of school, as had his older brothers and sisters before him, found a job, and every week faithfully gave his wages to Harold.

One by one each McKinney would fall in love and grow fed up living at home and would leave to start his or her own family. Dad was no different, although it took him much longer than the others to break free. He worked for the Southern Pacific Railroad, and by seventeen he was making more money than his father or

69

any of his brothers ever had. Old Georgie Bottenhatter, the line boss, was a master plumber, carpenter, welder, and electrician. He taught Dad the trades inside out. When Georgie died, my father took his job, and for fifteen years he worked a crew of red-necked, hard-nosed young men before the SP again promoted him. Now he traveled from one town to another along the California coast, supervising the servicing of rail equipment and the construction of storage houses and new stations. Meanwhile he fell in love with and married a fisherman's daughter. He was happy. Content. His life had direction. But the long nights of his absences soon proved too much for the fisherman's daughter, she grew lonesome and frustrated, and two years later she ran off with a young marine.

David was now thirty-five. Still young but bitter. He still handed over a large chunk of his checks to his father, and he still considered the ranch in Eureka his home base, though he'd moved out long before. It was his mother who, sensing his disillusionment, told him that a man of his caliber and ambition had no business working for the Southern Pacific Railroad. "You have to get out on your own. You have to work for yourself. Do you want to rot in this town like the others? Like me and your father? Look around, Dave. What do you see? Is there opportunity here for you? No. You're a young man." She made a shooing gesture with her hand. "Go. Leave. Get out from under your father, much as I love him . . . and you, my son. This isn't easy for me. But your debt is paid. Start your life over again. Your blood, and I tell you the God's honest truth, will sour and go bad if you stay."

But he didn't take her advice. Not at the time, anyway. Instead, for another year, he resigned himself to a life with the Southern Pacific.

Then one day he met Gina Maria Corallini.

Cor-ah-lee-nee.

The name rolled simply and smoothly across his tongue the first time he spoke it.

They met at a dance hall in Hunter's Point in San Francisco. The SP had sent my father south to oversee the nearly finished construction of an annex to the station downtown. They put him up in a decent hotel. He had a wallet full of money. He was lonely, he hadn't slept with a woman in so long he couldn't remember, and on his last night in San Francisco he went out looking and hoping for a woman only to bed.

She was twenty-two.

A beauty. Hair black and shiny as her eyes. She wore a tight dress that showed off her fine figure, silk stockings, and a diamond ring on her finger given to her by a young sailor off in battle. When David mustered the courage, and asked her to dance, she smiled and accepted. Her friends looked the other way. Later that night they went out to dinner. The next morning David quit the SP. That same day Gina slipped the ring inside a letter, sealed the envelope, and mailed it off to Korea.

Antonio Dominic Corallini was best known for a device called the Bouncing Pencil. At sixteen he had sailed from his native Sicily to the promised land on a freighter bound for New York's Little Italy. He was a cook's helper, a skinny boy with blackened teeth, who had great dreams of becoming rich. All it took was one good idea, he thought. Just one. Something that everybody needed without knowing they needed it. But when they saw it, ah, their eyes would light up. "Of course," they'd mutter. "Why didn't I think of that?" But for Antonio the idea that would someday make him wealthy never happened. Royalties for the Bouncing Pencil were small and arrived infrequently.

At one end of the device was a spring with a base the size of a dime. An inch up from the bottom was a wooden ball for balance and weight. The sticks were dyed green while the balls varied in color. Reds. Purples. Blues. They were in every five-and-dime in town. The idea was to hold the pencil a few feet from the ground, drop it, watch it spring back, and then catch it. The problem was that though the colors caught the eyes of nearly a million children, and though it was priced cheap enough at a nickel a shot, the device itself didn't work well. It rarely bounced straight, it was too light, the spring too weak. Antonio also invented a potato peeler with a revolving blade, but found when he went to patent it that someone had beat him to it years before. He invented other things, too, mostly improvements to household appliances, and he even sold a few of the patents. None of them, however, was ever made. Manufacturers bought the rights only to protect their own already-marketed gadgets.

71

He married Angelina Maria when he was twenty-six, shortly after his first and only halfway successful invention was produced. A few rough years followed. Angelina convinced him to move to San Francisco after she received a letter from her cousin, who was opening a shoe store. Would she like to work for him? He'd train her. Because she was *familia*, he wrote, and because he trusted her. It was a job where he promised to move her up into the business end of it if she proved herself a good employee. Her husband, after all, could do his line of work anywhere. So it was in North Beach, working as a cobbler's apprentice and later as a partner in Robert's Italian Shoes & Repair, that Angelina gave birth to her first child, my mother, Gina Maria.

Another, my mom's sister, came along the year after.

Angelina doubled up on her work hours. Antonio cared for the girls while he struggled with his inventions, until eventually one sold well enough to send his daughters to a Catholic high school. This device had an attachment that clipped onto the top of the front seat of a car. A length of elastic ran from the attachment to an oak bar about a foot long. As the car moved down the road, a child could hang on to the bar and pretend he or she was water skiing or surfing.

In her junior year at St. Mary's, Gina dropped out to attend business school. Here she learned shorthand, filing, minor accounting, and how to type at a speed few in her trade could match. She went to work for a shipping firm on the Bay, and moved out into a studio apartment with her first month's wages. My mother often said that one of the reasons she left home early was that her father favored her sister. He would go, say, to the corner market and return with a bag of groceries and one ice cream bar. The treat went to her sister, as did other things as the girls grew up. Mom didn't like to talk about her past much, though, especially the teenage years. But I do know that her mother was crushed when she left the house and that her dad was glad to see her go. She was a nuisance. Always coming and going, slamming doors, cupboards, always jabbering and playing the radio too loud, always breaking his concentration. His other daughter was quiet by nature.

The day Mom came home with David on one arm, a bottle of champagne in the other, Antonio was hard at work in his room. She pushed open the door. Inside, tools and scrap metal hung from nails in the wall. There were steel rods here and there. Hinges and ball joints. Glue and tacks, leather and cloth. In small boxes were some rusty springs.

"Dad," she said. "I'm married."

Antonio glanced up from where he sat behind a table cluttered with hardware. His hair, she thought, had more gray in it since she'd last seen him. "I see," he said, squinting. He looked my father over. "Just like that?"

"Just like that."

"I see."

"Don't you wanna know his name?"

David stepped forward with an open hand. Antonio wiped his on his pants leg first.

"Dave," she said, "this is my father, Antonio."

They shook.

"What d'you do for a living?"

"He's not working right now."

"I see." He pursed his lips. "Come back when you have a job."

"He had a job, Dad. He's making a better one for himself. We're moving."

"Where?"

"To a better place."

My father tried to be friendly and change the subject. He smiled. "What're you building there, sir?" Antonio took off his glasses and rubbed his eyes with a fist.

"This here," he said, holding up a piece of angle iron, "will attach to a connecting rod. There'll be a switch at the end of it, a button. It will run underneath the bathroom floor and when you step on it, this switch, this button flush with the floor, if you're a *man*," he said with spite in his voice, squeezing the iron, "the toilet seat will rise for your purpose. When you take your foot away, it will descend." He stomped his foot on the floor. "Just like that."

"Aha."

"Aha?"

David nodded politely.

"Dad, I'm *married*." She raised the bottle of champagne. "Let's celebrate."

"Have you told your mother?"

"Not yet."

"You'll break her heart."

"Don't say that."

"You will. You'll break her heart in two." Antonio turned back to his table and put on his glasses. "You can't live here," he muttered. "You know that, don't you? There's no room anymore."

But she didn't answer him.

David had already taken her arm. They were on their way, headed down the stairs, outside into the fog that had spilled into the city like water rising over coaming.

Out of the woods and into the city is where you got to go if you want the money. The trees may be pretty, and the country may settle your soul, but if you're going whale hunting you got to dip your pole in the sea. This was my dad's way of saying he had to leave not only Eureka and his parents but San Francisco as well. Except for an occasional new skyscraper, employing mainly iron-workers, and except for remodel jobs on Victorian houses built after the big quake, San Francisco was as still as its fog for the tradesman. But fifty miles south in the Santa Clara Valley was the rapidly growing town of San Jose. Here my mother and father settled. In the newly erected city hall he made application for his B-1, passed the exam, got his contractor's license, a loan from the B of A, and bought his first lot.

On the lot he built a house and sold it. He repaid the loan, bought two lots, built on them, sold them. He bought older, run-down homes, fixed them up, and sold them. Meanwhile Mike was born. A few years later I came along. With the help of a dozen sitters and housekeepers, including Marissa, our mom found time to take her real estate license. "That's about when the trouble started," Dad later said. "The damn license gave her the opportunity. Up till then your mother and me had ten beautiful years together, son."

During this period Mom also found time to drive Mike to his different lessons and pick him up afterward. Dance. Swim. French. Acting. "All the things," she said, "that my parents couldn't afford for me." I was about ready to start the same regime when the roof came down. In a way I was glad, not for the collapse, but for the lessons. I saw the pressure my brother was under taking this and that, trying out for the swim team, auditioning for plays and radio commercials, and I didn't envy him.

74

Now I'm nearly back to where I started, and yet even after tracing the family bloodline I still don't know much more about what happened to us, and why, than when I began. Something changed, though. Mom and Dad drifted apart after eighteen years of marriage. They took to sleeping in separate beds in separate rooms. She became involved with a crooked lawyer, not intimately, but in business. My father, on the other hand, became involved with Marissa—if not intimately, something damn close to it. Maybe they weren't making love back then but they were moving toward it. Dad gave her some long rides home when she'd finished cleaning our house and baby-sitting us for the day. As for the crooked lawyer, he went underground after Mom's arrest. Today he's a prominent district attorney for a city I best not name. He found the clients from out of state, Mom pushed the paperwork through escrow, one of them forged a bogus owner's name, and that was it. People were sold properties that didn't exist. How long they thought they could get away with it, I don't know. One of the victims who lived in Arizona, a retired man named Glass, lost his life savings. It ruined him as much financially as it did emotionally and later physically. Mrs. Glass was bitter and angry, but where her husband's spirit was broken, her own was fired up.

Why Mom felt she needed scams to get ahead is beyond me. "We were making money hand over fist," Dad used to say. "I never knew what was happening until it was too late. A man come to our door. You boys weren't home. He was in a suit. He says to me, he says . . .

"Mr. McKinney?"

"Yes?"

"I'm Mr. Jackson from the B of A."

"Yes?"

"You're six months overdue on your payments."

"Payments? What payments?"

"Your second mortgage, sir. On the house."

"This house?"

"Yes, sir." ˙

"You got the wrong McKinney, buddy. I *own* this place. I built the sonofabitch."

Dad would wag his head, finished. The man was right, yes, the man was right. "Your mother forged my name," he said, at another point in time. "On checks and contracts. Everything, son, and she hid my mail, too. The creditors were after me as much as they were your mother. Don't think I didn't have my reasons for what I did, or for what I didn't do, that I ought to have done— mistake that it ended up being. I did you boys wrong in the worst way a father could," he'd say, lowering his eyes. "I realize that now."

I wonder sometimes if Mom didn't bring the roof down on purpose. Other times I wonder if it had to do with a life so much better, so much wealthier than the one she left behind, that she just wanted more of it faster. Maybe she only wanted to secure it. Maybe she was plain greedy. Maybe just one ambitious venture slipped, and to keep it afloat she had to take a risk and that risk failed. Then another risk, one after the other, all failures. Could be it fell like an avalanche, suddenly, and there was nothing she could do to stop it. We didn't know, she never said, and yet Mike and I loved this woman who sold, as Dad put it, "her own home from under her children's heads."

I imagine the love had at least a little to do with how she held us in her arms as babes, how she cared for us, how a kind of closeness that can't ever be erased moves through your blood and lodges in your heart. There are some things I just can't explain. Once I knew a woman who locked her three-year-old in the car while she went into a bar for a drink. A couple of hours later she returned and found the kid passed out in the backseat from the heat. It wasn't the first time she'd done him wrong. What I'm *trying* to say here is that that kid loved his mother even though she hurt him. And he kept on loving her because there had to be some good times and kind moments in between the bad—ones to remember, just as there had been with our mom. Times, say, when I fell and she was there to paste the Band-Aid on my knee, times, too, when she baked bread and our house filled with the sweet smell of it. I remember her at the kitchen sink with her hands up to the wrists in dishwater, how her stockingless legs were pale in the winter, and I remember the corn on her small left toe. I remember how Mike would help her dry the pans, and how when Dad came home from work she used to kiss him, and I remember smiling watching them, and thinking that this was the way it was supposed to be. A good family. Now, when I remember, I only get angry. Mom must've known her world was coming down. She could've backed off on the scams before they broke. She could

76

have talked with Dad. They might've been able to work it out. Mom didn't have to hide night after night in another room. She didn't have to start the fire that led to her arrest. That my brother told me about.

He was with her the day it happened.

6

In July our mother was released from prison. The final days of waiting passed slowly. Each morning an old flatbed Ford with wooden pallets for railings rolled through our neighborhood at the break of dawn. My brother and I would hop in back with the Mexicans at the corner where the truck idled and honked its horn. Apartment doors opened. More men, women, and children climbed up and in. We rocked back and forth against each other and the pallets as the Ford rattled down the street. Some sipped coffee from thermoses, others shut their eyes and tried for a little more sleep. The season was plums, later cots.

Soon the truck stopped on a dirt road. A cloud of dust rose and dissipated. Mike and I jumped out with the others. Another day, it was. Another long one. "I think I was with her," my brother said. "With Mom the day . . . you know what I'm talking about?" We crossed the road into the orchard. When the others were out of hearing distance, and we'd gotten our crates, he continued as we walked. "I'm almost sure I was there—no, I am sure. She took me to my dance lesson, right? She picked me up. We were on our way home but she said she needed to get a prescription filled. So we stopped at Bain's and I waited in the car. Nothing to it, right?" We dropped our crates on the ground under a tree. The branches were heavy with plums. Fat. Purple. "She was in there for a long time, though, and I mean a *long* time. First I thought she had to wait for the prescription, maybe there was a line, or she was shopping. You know how she is in stores. Takes forever sometimes. I was just about to get out of the car and see what the hell was keeping her when here she comes down the street, except it was from a different direction, Jay, and she didn't have the prescription. That's the day of the fire."

"So what?"

"Don't you see?"

I yanked down a plum and threw it. "Big deal," I said. It hit the ground and split. "There was a fire. Big fucking deal."

"Dad owned the building."

"Not around Bain's."

"A half-mile."

"That's a long way."

"I said she was gone a long time."

"Don't mean shit."

"What's the matter with you?" he said. "An old lady burned to death, man."

I ignored it. "You know how those guys are," I said. "Her prescription wasn't ready. She hadda wait but she got tired of waiting."

"Believe what you want."

"Fuck you."

"Fuck you, too."

I picked another plum and shot it hard at a tree. Watched it split. "I'm just trying to put the pieces together," he said. "Because I thought you might want to know. Marissa said it made the front page." A humming noise sounded in my head, and my cheeks suddenly felt hot. "Whatta you listening to her for?" I said. "You know what she's after, you can't believe her."

"Just made it up, huh?"

"That's right."

"She saved it. I saw it."

"Shut up."

"Now do you believe me?" he shouted. "Headlines, man. Capital *m* . . . small *c* . . ."

I grabbed my crate and headed for another tree. For the rest of the day we worked different parts of the orchard. I kept thinking about the night they came for her, the night we heard the newscaster, the visit, and I told myself to forget it all. Mom would be home soon. It was the past. I worked alone again the next day, and the day after that, too. But by the end of the week we were picking side by side. Soon the trees were naked of fruit and we moved on to another orchard.

At that time of the year the trees smelled of the fruit they bore, and the smell was sweet. A good smell, it was, but one I could only stomach first thing in the morning. After a while it became sickening. After a few hours of stripping branches, retrieving fruit from the ground shaken loose by the shaker man with a long pole, filling crates, and carrying them to the trucks, you forgot about the smell. You thought about your back, your arms, and the sun.

With the winter had come the rain, and with the rain had come unemployment for our father. Derek in his varsity jacket had made two more pickups during the eleven, nearly twelve, months that Mom was gone. I'm not sure how Dad found the money. Borrowed it, I suppose. On the weekends in the summer he came out to the orchards with us, but on the weekdays he searched for better work. Sometimes he found small jobs. He didn't talk about Marissa anymore. None of us did. I think he stopped seeing her, too, or at least we didn't know about it. She didn't visit like before. If we spotted her or Louie in the courtyard or down around the carport, we maybe said hello, or we maybe looked the other way. It depended on the distance, whether we were close, approaching them, or if we were far enough away to turn our heads and pretend we hadn't seen them. They did the same.

Now it was toward the end of July. We were finished with plums and on to cots and some of the fruit had already begun to rot on the branches. Dad had told us the night before that Mom was coming home tomorrow. He didn't know what to expect and neither did we. We were told to be careful with what we said and to give her a warm hug without any tears.

The time was noon.

My crate was full of cots. The fuzz from them was in the air and in our nostrils. Our hands were sticky from the juices of the rotten fruit and the sap from the branches and leaves we pulled off with the cots. Nothing except turpentine could cut it. We carried a can of it with us. Mike used the stuff, then passed it to me along with a rag so I could clean up. We sat under a tree and opened our bag lunches. The sandwiches smelled and tasted like turpentine.

"What're you going to say to her?"

"I don't know."

"Me either."

"It'll be good to have her back, though."

"Really good," I said. "I miss her so fucking much."

"Don't let her hear you cuss."

"I won't."

Across the orchard I saw some of the younger Mexican men still working. Using tickets, the management paid by the crate, not by the hour. More tickets, more money. At the end of the day or the week you cashed them in. The Mexican men worked the fastest.

"You see Marissa lately?"

"Yesterday," Mike said.

"Did you tell her about Mom?"

"She already knew."

"Dad must've told her."

"Had to."

I wrapped my sandwich back up. No appetite. "Shit's gonna hit the fan tonight," I said.

"Definitely."

At the end of the day we used up the last of the turpentine and hopped in back of the flatbed Ford. My brother put his arm around me on the ride home. The smell of sweat filled the air each time the truck stopped for a light and then faded when we got going again. "How many tickets you get?" I said. But Mike didn't hear me, or else he didn't want to answer. He was staring over the side of the truck, watching the road pass beneath us.

An open fifth of Beefeater rested on the kitchen table. Under her eyes were black streaks where her mascara had run. Mike nudged me. I smiled as she rose from her chair. The dress, it was the same one she'd worn the day she left. "Here they are," she said. "My boys."

"Go on."

"Huh?"

"Get out of here," Dad shouted, waving his hand. "Go on, go. Anywhere."

"Hey."

"Hey like hell."

"Mom," I said.

"Baby."

She held her arms open. Dad pointed to the door. "Get," he shouted. "Come back in a couple hours."

"Let them stay."

She hugged me, then Mike.

"You look good, Mom."

80

"So do you."

Her hair was styled short, curled in the front, and she smelled of hair spray. She'd had to have been to a beauty shop before coming home. Mom held Mike's face in her hands. "So tan," she said, leaning back, staring at him. "Where'd you get such a tan?"

"Working."

"Your dad got you learning the trade?"

"It's plum season," I said.

"Cots now."

"They're picking," Dad said. "You boys go unload the truck. There's scrap gotta be stacked under the locker."

Mom looked at him and laughed. "Just like the Mexicans. You got them in the fields like the Mexicans." She reached for her drink and took a long swallow. "Like the one your daddy's screwing. They know, don't they?" She shrugged. "Of course they know. You been screwing her right here. In the apartment." She looked at Mike. "Hasn't he? Your daddy been screwing our little housekeeper?"

Mike bowed his head.

"Go on, son. Take Jay and get out of here."

"Was she good?"

"Shut your mouth."

Mom narrowed her eyes. "She come, David? You make the little slut come good? You do it in our bed?" Suddenly she turned to us. "Get your things packed. We're gonna move and let your daddy have the place all to himself. Just him and Marissa so they can screw in peace." She threw her hands up. "All yours, David. All yours, just like you want it."

"Don't listen to her."

"They better listen."

"She'll calm down," he said, as if she weren't there.

"Calm down?"

"You're drunk is all. You don't know what you're saying."

"I know exactly what I'm saying."

He started to lead us out of the apartment but Mom stepped in front of him. She took Mike by the arms. Her eyes suddenly became soft, her voice changed. "Who do you wanna live with, honey? Huh?" She stroked his head once. "You wanna live with me? Jay? What about you? You wanna stay with your father and

Marissa or do you wanna be with your mother who loves you? I can't live here, honey. You know that. What's it gonna be?"

"Leave them alone," Dad hollered.

Mom glanced at him, then turned to Mike again. "C'mon, honey. Tell him. You don't wanna stay in this little town. It's no place for someone like you." She shook Mike. "Tell him."

I reached for my brother's arm and pulled and we stepped around her. Out the door, we ran downstairs to the carport. There we worked in silence, unloading odd lengths of lumber, stacking them neatly under the locker on the cement floor behind the parking bumper. Next we restacked the drywall. Three-eighths with three-eighths. Half-inch with half-inch. Scrap rock, it was, the edges frayed, spilling the white chalk inside. When we finished with the drywall we rearranged the different cuts of plywood by dimension and width. Then we set to work ordering the two-by-fours.

I paused to wipe sweat from my brow.

"Who should we go with?"

"Who do you want?"

I thought for a while. "Dad," I said. "I wanna stay with Dad."

"So do I."

At that moment I spotted Louie cross the lot to his car and get inside. We watched him drive off. I had a short cut of two-by-four in my hand and I thought, for just a second, how good it would've felt to have sunk it deep into his skull.

Late that night I awoke to whispering. Dad was snoring in the bedroom. Mom had passed out on the couch. Mike and I had spread blankets on the floor and fallen asleep, but when I woke up now he wasn't beside me. A light in the hallway shone through the kitchen curtains into the living room. I closed my eyes again and listened.

"You coming with me?"

"I don't know."

"I don't wanna leave you, baby."

"You don't have to go."

"My name's no good here anymore," she whispered. "I have to find work and nobody'll hire me. You know I can't live with your dad after what he did. You know that."

"Can't you both just make up?"

There was a long silence.

"Honey?"

"Yeah?"

"It isn't possible."

"Can't you try?"

"Come with me, baby."

"Where?"

"Wherever you want," she said. "You name it. Tell me."

"I don't know."

"Los Angeles?"

His voice became strained. "I have to think, Mom."

"Shhh."

"I love Dad."

"I know you do."

"I do."

"That's where you belong. Los Angeles. You can't do anything with your talent here. You'll end up a carpenter just like him. Wanna do that kind of hard work the rest of your life?"

"No."

"Then come with me."

"Jay, too?"

"If he wants."

"Mom?"

"Hmmm?"

"I don't want you to be alone anymore."

"Tell your father that tomorrow."

"Okay."

"Try and get some sleep now."

I heard my brother cross the room, felt him slip under the blankets, his back pressing warm against mine. Soon he was breathing smoothly, asleep, while I lay awake. The hall light went out a few minutes later. It was already edging dawn. Mom was crying into her pillow.

Whatever my brother did, I did. Wherever he went, I went. When he told me the next day, while we were picking cots, that he had changed his mind and planned to leave with Mom, I told him I'd go along. "You're sure now?" he said, looking me square in the eyes. A lump lodged in the back of my throat.

"I'm sure."

"You don't have to go."

"I know."

"I'd understand."

"We're brothers, man. You and me." I slugged him in the arm. "Where you go, I go."

"It'll work out." Mike put his arm around me. "Remember when you were, what, maybe three or four, and Mom gave you some watermelon seeds? You planted them in the garden?" He smiled, and I shrugged. "Remember you kept checking on them but they never grew and then one morning you came out and there were two big watermelons sitting in the dirt? I wish you could've seen your face." He squeezed me around the shoulders. "Remember that?"

"I remember you telling me."

"It was Mom's idea."

"She bought 'em."

"Because she was thinking about you, man. She'd been watching you, she cared. It'll be all right with her again," he said. "We can always visit Dad."

"Yeah, visit."

"And phone."

"Every day."

"If you want," he said. "We can write, too."

I stooped and picked some cots up off the ground. "Sure," I mumbled. "Let's get back to work." My hands were gripped so tight I crushed two trying to hang on to them. The other cot I dropped.

He took it well. Inside, though, I knew he was hurting bad. As Mike explained himself, stuttering, pausing to find the right words, Dad only nodded. He'd been sweeping out the truck bed but had stopped to listen. "I understand," he said, when Mike had finished. "I understand. Someone's gotta look out for her, and this could be for the better. But I doubt it." He shook his head. "The creditors are gonna be coming around here, soon as they learn she's out, and it's best they don't know where she is. I'll try and keep the bastards off her tail and maybe, after a while, when this shit blows over, your mom and I can get back together again." He squeezed Mike's shoulder. "But lemme tell you something, son. It's gonna be seven long years before your mother's a truly free woman unless we can settle up early. There's things you boys don't know. I think you ought to reconsider." Dad turned to me. "Jay?"

"Yeah?"

"This what you want, too?"

I stared down at the asphalt.

"He told me it was," Mike said. "Today in the orchards."

"C'mere."

Dad rested the broom against the truck and then wrapped his arms around Mike's neck and mine and pulled us close. Hugged us. "Gonna miss you. Gonna miss you boys something terrible." He roughed up Mike's hair. "You take care of your little brother now. Understand? Any problems down there, no matter what, you're coming back." He winked at me. "We'll make a go of it again, huh? I think so."

Then he turned us loose.

Early that evening Dad phoned a friend who he knew had a car for sale. He let him have it for twenty-five down and fifty a month. It was an old Chevy Nova but the engine had been rebuilt, the transmission supposedly only had ten thousand on it, and it ran beautifully. We loaded it up that night with boxes of books and Mike's obituary collection, Mom's clothes, and our own. The plan was to leave the next day at dawn, although it didn't work out that way. In any case, I had unfinished business to take care of before we left.

While Dad was off picking up the Nova, I slipped out of the apartment and headed for Dean's house. His garage was wide open. At the end of the driveway was a fence behind which I crouched, watching Dean tinker with his dirt bike. He wore dirty coveralls. A good five minutes must've passed when the screen door along the side of the house swung open. His mother leaned over the threshold.

"Dinner," she shouted.

"Comin'."

Dean dipped his hands into a can of grease remover on the workbench beside the radio. He wiped them clean with a rag, then stripped out of his coveralls. The radio he left on, and his tools he left scattered across the garage floor. "Eight Miles High" was playing. Soon as he'd gone into the house I exhaled once, took in a deep breath, and crept up the driveway until I reached the screen door. There I stopped, my arm pressed against the side of the house, listening to the clink of silverware and plates from inside. Do it, I told myself. Do it fast and get the hell out of here. Stepping past the door, I glimpsed his mother sitting at the dinner table, head down and eyes closed. Dean sat with his back to me. A few seconds later I had the antenna pushed down, the volume off, and the radio tucked under my arm. They never noticed me. That's how quickly and quietly it went. Halfway to Alum Rock, when I turned it back on, "Eight Miles High" was just ending.

I found Eddie at our regular bench, grinning as I approached, as if he'd been expecting me all along.

Mike and I were camped out on the floor again when Dad slipped into the living room on the night that we left. Mom slept on the sofa bed. He sat on the edge of the mattress, a slumped, sorry-looking figure in his bathrobe. His hands were folded in his lap. "I want you all to stay," he whispered. "Forgive me, please." Mom was silent until he touched her shoulder. She jumped to her feet. She tramped around in her nightgown, flipping on lights, waving her arms.

"Get dressed. We can't sleep here," she shouted, entering the bathroom and slamming the door behind her. Dad bit his lower lip. Mike and I crawled up off the floor, folded the blankets, and hustled into our clothes.

A minute later Mom came out dressed. Our father followed us downstairs to the Nova. I gave him a hug, tried not to cry, and then squeezed into the front seat. Mike did the same. Inside, the door shut, he rolled down the window. Dad rested his elbows on the frame as Mom started the engine.

"Call me when you get there."

She stared over the wheel, refusing to look at him.

"You make sure you call."

Silence.

"I'll do it," Mike said.

He reached into his bathrobe pocket and handed him a fifty-dollar bill, a five, and two singles. "Give this to your Mom for gas. I'll have more at the end of the week. I'll wire it. I need an address, though. Let me know where you're staying."

"I will."

"Bye."

86

"Bye," I said.

"Love you."

"Love you, too," Dad said. "Gina?"

No answer.

"You take care of them. You watch out now."

More silence.

"Ain't forgetting anything?"

"Nothing," she said.

"You can still change your mind."

"Good-bye."

"Bye," Dad said.

She slipped it into reverse. Dad stepped away from the car. We were moving. We waved to him as he stood there alone in his bathrobe in the glare of our headlights. He waved and waved. He was still waving, smiling weakly now, as we dipped down the driveway onto the street, en route to U.S. 101.

All night we drove through small sleepy towns, past wide-open fields barely visible in the night, past farm communities that smelled of manure and diesel fumes, past towns along the coast that smelled of the sea, and past a dead cat on the side of the road near Pismo Beach. Only once did we stop for gas. Mike stared out the window, and I moved closer, my thigh against his. Often, as I felt my throat tighten, I'd take his hand in mine and squeeze, he'd squeeze back, and the tightness would pass. I tried to sleep but each time I nodded off, my head on Mike's shoulder, I thought of Dad. I wondered what he was doing right now, if he too was unable to sleep, if he'd poured himself a drink, why he had let us go, and when I pictured him alone in the kitchen my eyes sprang open.

Come dawn we were past Santa Barbara. Gradually the highway filled with more and more cars. A semi shot past on the left, rocking us, blowing exhaust. Mom tightened her grip on the wheel. A Harley roared by on the shoulder. Others drove fast, close, switching lanes, trying to get ahead. In the distance, as the highway fed into a freeway, a thousand city buildings spread before us. Mom flipped on the radio. *"Two months after the May fourth antiwar protest at Kent State University in Ohio, in which National Guardsmen shot and killed four students, President Nixon . . ."* Mike

87

winced, leaning forward to listen more closely, when Mom spun the dial.

A disc jockey came on the air:

"Ninety-two-point-two in Hollywood, giving you the best in easy listening around the clock. It's seven-oh-three in what's going to be another sunny, sunny day . . ."

For the first time since her release she turned to us and smiled. "Hollywood," she said. "Hollywood, honey." At the Sunset ramp we pulled off the freeway. Soon we were cruising a wide three-lane street, stopping for a light, the Nova bouncing under the weight of boxes and books as we braked. Mike rolled down his window and stuck his head out into the sun. A big smile crossed his face. Mom reached over me and patted his knee. "We made it, baby. That wasn't so bad of a drive now, was it?" The light dropped to green. "Keep your eyes peeled for a decent motel," she said, driving on. A few blocks later Mike pointed to a sign shaped like a cowboy hat. THE STARLIGHT MOTOR INN. FREE COLOR TV. REASONABLE RATES. Below it another smaller sign of pink neon flashed VACANCY . . . VACANCY . . .

In the parking lot she shut off the engine and we climbed out of the car. Behind a clear plastic fence was a pool that had been drained. The white bottom had a crack in it. Already the air was warm, hazy, a dull yellow glare that made us squint. Again my brother smiled, spreading his arms, stretching. We followed Mom into the office, where a short shaggy palm tree grew in a planter in the corner. The clerk had a dark tan. He sipped coffee from a foam-plastic cup.

"We'd like a room for three."

"Single beds?"

"Fine."

"It's thirty-two fifty a night," he said. "How many you staying?"

"Only one."

"The maid comes in at eleven A.M."

"We'll be gone by then."

"Just leave the key in the room when you go."

Mom reached into her purse. "You take checks?"

"Sorry."

"It's good."

"Sorry."

88

She turned to us. "C'mon, boys, we'll find another place."

As we started for the door the man called to her and we stopped. He looked us up and down once, sighed, then clicked his tongue.

"You sure it's good, lady?"

"Of course."

"I just manage the place, you know. I get stuck for it if it bounces."

"I promise it won't."

"One night?"

"That's it."

Mom made out a check while the man filled out a form. He asked for her name as she wrote. She answered calmly, naturally. Mike and I glanced at each other but we didn't say a word. In a sharp, elegant hand she signed the check and tore it from the book and gave it to him with a smile. Then she put her license on the counter. The picture was hers all right, but, like the check, it was signed Sheila Taylor.

PART II:

Hollywood

"Hollywood . . . I'd go there if I only could . . .
Hollywoooddd . . ."
     —"Hooray for Hollywood" by
     Johnny Mercer and Richard
     Whiting, from the movie
     Hollywood Hotel.

AMONG my brother's personal effects, aside
from the quarters and his SAG card, the
Certs and the receipt for the .38 shells, was
Dad's recipe for turkey. On stationery from
the Chateau Marmonte, inside the billfold of
his wallet, were the basting ingredients. The
list was written in his own quick small
scribbling, which only he could decipher
easily. His plan was to have a moving party.
Friends would help him pack and load his
belongings. Afterward he'd serve them
turkey, and cranberry sauce, potatoes and

gravy, green beans, beer, wine, and whiskey.

He called late one night to talk with Dad in San Jose. This was a few weeks before Independence Day. They hadn't seen each other since May.

"Hello?"

"Dad?"

"Son, how are you?"

"Good. Did I wake you?"

"It's okay."

A Bob Dylan ballad played on the stereo in Mike's living room. "I want your recipe for turkey, the one you always made for us," he said. "Just had it on my mind, you know. The other day. I don't think I can wait until Thanksgiving rolls around to have it again."

"You been drinking much, son?"

"A little whiskey."

"You watch it now."

"I can handle myself."

"You worry me, your drinkin'," he said, serious. "You there in Hollywood with those people."

"What people?"

"You know what I mean."

"Hey," Mike said. "You going to watch me next week?"

"Get yourself another part?"

"It's just a *Cannon* repeat."

"I'll be watching for you," he said. "Got a pen?"

Dad gave him the recipe, oven temperature, and basting schedule. Later, after they hung up, Mike took a ride down to the twenty-four-hour Safeway on Alvarado near his house. He bought all he needed, but the moving party never came off. Unopened jars of garlic powder, Old Hickory Smoked Salt, and a box of Bell's poultry seasoning stood lined along the windowsill in the kitchen. He even bought a new roaster and set it on the counter, price tags and stickers still on it, never to be used—like the twenty-pound turkey, frozen solid in the freezer.

7

Theodore Marrin was known throughout Hollywood as a sonofabitch. He ran a powerful actors' studio just off Melrose near Paramount in a remodeled warehouse. Competition for enrollment in his workshop was fierce. Marrin had trained some of the best of his time, knowns, and unknowns, big names and small character actors. Studios still sent him their brightest talents for a quick polish while agents and casting directors continued to scout his players for another young up-and-coming star. Although a slot in his class didn't guarantee any breaks, his name on your résumé meant interviews, maybe a reading. Marrin was the Stanislavsky of Hollywood. The Strasberg of the West Coast. The man was respected and revered and despised. He was fifty-seven years old when my brother first met him, but he looked more like seventy. Gray-haired. Gaunt. Bitter. Marrin had contracted multiple sclerosis five years before and now he walked with a cane. The disease had worked first on his legs, so that one was bowed and the other paralyzed from the knee down. Inevitably it would do more damage. In the meantime he dragged his lame leg behind him.

We'd been in L.A. two months before Mike signed up for Marrin's yearly orientation, or recruitment lecture, if you could call it that. He did his damnedest to discourage newcomers. My brother knew of the man from his autobiography, *An Actor's Schedule*, about a life dedicated to theater, the rejection that came with it, and finally success as a drama coach. Twice Mike read the book, both times inspired and impressed by Marrin's triumph over the odds. This man was a veteran. A master. No small-town Gloria Millicent Miles. No washed-up Al Copen.

On the morning of the recruitment my brother tucked the autobiography under his arm and left our apartment. We had settled into a one-bedroom place in Westlake, and he had to catch the bus into Hollywood. Melrose and Vine. The rear doors hissed open. His palms were sweating, maybe his throat was dry. He had to be a little nervous, because he knew of Marrin's reputation, and yet at the same time he couldn't know exactly what to expect of him.

Somehow he had to impress the man. Show him he was good. Better than the others.

At the theater he took a seat in the back row beside a young guy wearing a tight T-shirt. His biceps were round and strong. He had dark hair and green eyes and a cleft in his chin. But his lower lip twitched every few seconds and, when it did, the handsome face looked somehow confused and awry.

Mike put his feet up on the chair ahead.

"Get 'em down."

"What do you care?"

"You wanna get into the class?" the guy said. "I'm telling you, man, put 'em down."

My brother did.

"I'm Saul," he said. "Saul Leiberman."

"You new here?"

"Shit, no."

"Sorry."

"The man is fucking great. That's why I'm around." His lip twitched, and he laughed. "I like to watch him work."

Ahead Mike stared at a spotlight shining on a wooden chair in the middle of the stage. Soon Theodore Marrin hobbled into the theater with a woman on either side. He wore baggy pants held up with bright-red suspenders, and there was a couple of days' growth of gray beard on his face. The two women took seats in the front row. The older one turned and glanced behind her and caught Mike's eye. He matched her glance for a few seconds, then looked away. The class had grown dead quiet. Suddenly there came the clatter of wood on wood. Marrin had dropped his cane.

A teenager sprang from his seat.

"Leave it."

The teenager nodded, embarrassed, and sat again. Marrin pointed a finger as he counted the heads in the audience. "Twenty-four. Too many. Does anyone," he said, clearing his throat, "want to leave now and save us time?" No one moved. He sighed, paused, then launched into them with a shout. "You're garbage. *Trash*. You waiters, you students and dishwashers, you dull bored housewives, you vain dense beauties." His voice grew suddenly soft. "All of you come to me for help? Hmmm?" Then it went up again—loud. "No, you come to be told that you're good, that you're special." Marrin waved his hand in disgust.

"From Wisconsin or Indiana or the San Fernando Valley, you come to Hollywood with big dreams and little money and you think you're daring. This is what it takes, eh? Commitment?" He tossed his hair back, long and gray, his forehead large. "Who told you you could act? Some high school teacher?" He laughed. "Someone else who doesn't know shit? Still you believe it because you have nothing else to believe in. Because your friends and parents saw you in a little play in a little town and they applauded and the applause made you feel good." He undid the top button of his shirt, as he'd already begun to sweat under the spot, leaning forward and backward in the chair, shouting. "Laugh. That's what you ought to do. At yourself. You ought to get back in your cars or the bus you came on and return to your little towns and your little lives and do what you were made to do. Fuck. Fuck, reproduce, and die."

A bar of sunlight shone into the theater. The teenager in the front row had opened the door and let it slam behind him. "Follow the kid," Marrin said, glaring at each student one by one. Another rose and left. "That's two . . . who's next?" A dozen seconds passed. "A little town, a little job, a little wife or husband. C'mon now, be honest. You'd be much happier." He pointed to the back row. "You, you think you have talent?" Mike swallowed, shifting in his seat. "And you . . . and you . . . all of you will fail and give up. Maybe, just maybe, a couple here might get a small role in a cheap film sometime in their life. You'll think bigger and better parts are on the way just as soon as the world recognizes your brilliance. And when the world doesn't, and the roles never materialize, and the years keep passing, you'll become bitter. You'll wise up and realize that you were never much good, anyway."

Again a bar of sunlight fell into the theater. Two young women had left this time, heads held high—indignant—one quickly following the other, as if leaving together made it easier. "Anybody can take off when they want," Marrin shouted. "To hell with politeness. There's no time for that here." He undid another button on his shirt and continued. "Now the years are gone, it's too late to do anything of value with your life. You're caught in a stinking job that you hate. You're drinking more and feeling sorry for yourself." He held up one finger. "So tell yourself the world often fails to acknowledge genius in its time. Your case is no different.

97

Now look in the mirror and say it." Marrin drew a hand in front of his face as if he were peering at his own reflection. "Say it to the wrinkles around her eyes and your thinning hair and then pour yourself another drink. Call one of your failed friends. Console each other. Lie some more. It's all you'll have left."

Another student slipped out the door.

When it had closed, and it was dark again, he nodded to the two women in the front row.

"How many is that?"

"Three," one said.

"Five, honey," the other said.

"Good enough. I'm bored." Marrin leaned over and grunted and reached for his cane. From that position he looked out into the audience. Again his voice was barely audible. "Auditions tomorrow," he said. "Sunday morning at eleven. Study *Major Barbara*." Slowly he lifted himself from the chair and held out his hand to the younger woman.

She rose and took it.

Saul Leiberman clapped. One student joined him, then another and another, until everyone was applauding except for my brother. Saul nudged him.

"What's with you?"

Mike didn't answer.

"He was brilliant."

"I don't know."

"The man is a fucking genius."

"Maybe."

"Maybe, shit," Saul said, still clapping. "Take my word."

Maybe. Maybe he was just a pompous asshole, Mike thought, though he didn't say it. Instead, as he followed Saul down the aisle, he glanced at the two women helping Marrin toward the door.

"Who are they?"

"Cynthia and Leitha."

"Students?"

Saul laughed. "Wife and daughter, man," he said. "Nice stuff, eh? Leitha."

"Which one?"

"The daughter."

"Yeah."

"Don't even look. You'll never make it here if you do."

As Mike stood behind them, sunlight shining through the opened door, his eyes traveled up her lean, almost frail body to her blond hair. A thin blue vein showed at her temple. One arm was wrapped around her father's waist. She looked beautiful, he thought, about his age, too. But it was Cynthia—not her daughter—who was peering over her husband's shoulder, giving my brother the eye, smiling as she helped Marrin out the door.

I figured Mike must've stopped off at Larry Edmund's Book Shop on the boulevard on his way home. First of all, it wasn't far from the theater, and Edmund's was the best bookstore in town for my brother's tastes; and second, he had to pick up a copy of Shaw's *Major Barbara* for the next day's audition. I imagine he felt put off by what the old man had said, yet he also must've felt—as Marrin likely did—that the lecture had accomplished what it was designed to do. It emptied the theater of dabblers. Or maybe it only got rid of the ones who didn't much like Marrin's approach and personality. Maybe that was more like it.

On the bus home that afternoon he studied every character in the first act. Mainly, though, he concentrated on Stephen and Lady Britomart's lines. For all he knew the tyrant would have him read for the mother character, not Stephen, the son. It didn't matter. Mike had the kind of mind that could absorb information just by following his hand down the page a few times, as if he were sucking up the words through his fingertips. Now and then, as the bus rolled along the street, he scribbled notes to himself in the margins of the play. They had to do with character traits and quirks, gestures, movements, how he imagined them to look at one another, and how he imagined them to respond after a certain exchange of words. Anyway, he probably had the first pages of dialogue memorized, and a solid sense of the first act, by the time the bus stopped for his exit. When he stepped off, a copy of *Major Barbara* in hand, I was there waiting for him with bad news.

But I'm getting ahead of myself here. First I need to mention that Mom was at work. I was alone. The month before she'd landed a job as a secretary for a storage company, and though it didn't pay much, it was enough to rent a cheap apartment in Westlake across from MacArthur Park. The neighborhood was on its way down. Our new name, she had told us, was Benson. "Don't answer to anything else," she'd said.

Benson. I didn't like it.

Taylor sounded better because it reminded me of Elizabeth Taylor, only it was hot now. Worn out. If Mom had another phony driver's license for the new name, or the others that came after it, I never saw it.

Our new apartment was a nine-story brick tenement house with low water pressure, so you couldn't take much of a shower, and it had faulty wiring that shorted out every so often. The first night there we spent in the dark. It also wasn't in what some folks considered a good part of L.A. Mom wanted out fast as possible. She put in ten hours a day at her job, seven days a week, trying to save up enough to move us to another, safer side of town. In the meantime she decided not to enroll us in the local p.s. "Not in this area," she said. "You'll just get in fights." So Mike and I stayed home not only on the weekends but every day. If I'd gone, the teachers would've flunked me anyway, as I'd quit caring about school, or else they would've stuck me in another class for the learning disabled. Which was almost the same thing, and I didn't need it—the shame, I mean—the embarrassment.

I'd been making decent progress with my brother tutoring and drilling me for hours every damn morning. And as far as Mike falling behind, he could've skipped two years and still wound up at the head of his class.

Before he'd left this particular morning, after Mom had gone to work, he'd sat me down in the kitchen, and slapped a pencil and a notebook on the table. "Write a story," he said.

"About what?"

"Whatever."

"Gimme an idea."

"Make one up. Invent. Imagine," he said. "Just *do* it."

So I did it, mistakes and all, while he was off at Marrin's studio. This one was about a kid who joins a street gang and becomes its leader. He falls in love with a beautiful girl who wants to reform him, and then he gets killed in a motorcycle wreck. The inspiration came from "Leader of the Pack" by the Shangri-las, a song Eddie and I liked listening to at Alum Rock Park. It was a rotten story, and I lost interest in it about halfway through, but I kept writing because I felt that I had to finish it. I had to have something to show Mike, if only to prove I wasn't fooling around all day while he was off making a break for himself. I titled it "The Motorcycle King." Just as I was tying up the seventh and final page with a funeral scene, there came a knock on the door. I rose from the kitchen table and answered it. A man in a suit stood in the hallway.

"Is Mrs. McKinney in?"

"No."

"This is the McKinney residence?"

"Uh-uh," I said, glancing at the floor. "Wrong place."

"Don't lie to me."

"I'm not."

"You tell your mother. . . ."

"This is the Benson residence."

I slammed the door. My heart beat fast. When I heard his footsteps trail off down the hallway, and figured he'd had enough time to ride the elevator to the lobby, I went to the window and opened it. Peered over the ledge. Below on the street I watched him climb inside a car parked at the curb, only he didn't drive away. I didn't know who this guy was but I knew he was bad news and that I had to find Mike. Quick. He might know what to do, because I sure as hell didn't.

That's when I left the apartment. Through the back way, not the front. I hurried to the bus stop and waited, wishing I had a smoke, something to do with my hands. Something to calm my nerves.

An hour later his bus came rolling up the street, blowing exhaust behind it, brakes squealing as it pulled to the curb.

First he wanted to see it for himself. So we walked past the car on the other side of the street and I pointed it out to him with a quick nod. "That's it," I said. A blue Plymouth. Government plates.

"You sure now?" he said, almost whispering, though there was no need for it.

"I'm sure."

"How long has he been there?"

"A couple hours, I guess."

"Damn."

"Whatta you think he wants?"

"Who knows?" he said, disgusted. "Really. Who knows what Mom's done."

The man rolled down his window and flipped a cigarette butt out. Mike nudged me. "Don't look," he whispered.

"Did he see us?"

"Just come on." He walked faster, and now I had to double-time it to keep up with him. At the end of the block, I looked over my shoulder to see if we were being followed. We weren't. "What're you doing?" Mike barked, grabbing my arm, tugging. "C'mon, we have to tell Mom."

We ran half the way, walked the other.

At the storage company he talked to the receptionist. "It's important," he said, shifting his weight from one leg to the other. "We really can't wait." The woman led us through the lobby into an office area built inside the back of a cool, dark warehouse. As we entered Mom glanced up from behind her typewriter, looped a strand of fallen hair around her ear, then quickly reached under the desk for her purse. Right away, not saying a word, she hurried us out of the office to the employee lounge, where nobody would hear.

She placed her hands on her hips. "Okay," she said, "what is it?" Mom sighed as he told her, as if she'd been expecting it, as if it were no news at all. When he finished she looked me in the eyes. "You tell the man we were the Bensons, Jay?"

I nodded.

"You did good," she said. "The first rule is never admit different. Never, baby. You understand? Because they don't really know. They're just testing you. But you know what you did wrong?" I shook my head. "You shouldn't have ever opened the damn door. Don't," she said, waving a finger, "don't *ever* answer it again unless I tell you. That goes for you, too, Mike. We gotta work together."

On the wall nearby hung a pay phone. Mom went to it, fumbled through her purse for change, dropped a coin into the slot, and dialed the operator. A collect call to San Jose. As she listened to it ring, she rested her shoulder against a coffee machine and shook her head at us. "He better be home," she said. "I don't know how else they could've found us." It probably rang three or four times before it was picked up.

She turned her back to us.

"David? . . . You told them, didn't you? . . . The IRS—who the hell do you think? . . . Then how'd they know where we were? . . . Settle with the government? Ha. Keep dreaming, honey. . . . Too late now. The boys are staying with me."

She hung up.

We were told to wait outside while she went for her last check. If the government knew where we lived, they likely knew where she worked, or they would soon enough. Then they'd attach her wages and we were just scraping by as it was. I didn't believe our father told them a thing, and I don't believe it now. Still, they had found us. We learned from Mom later that afternoon as we drove around town, waiting for the blue Plymouth to leave, that you can't file bankruptcy against the federal government. "We owe them," she said. Mike asked her how much, and Mom smiled, almost as if she were proud of it. "About a hundred thousand." She said it again, only this time she drew the words out. A beautiful-sounding figure. "A hundred thousand dollars." How in the hell she ever drove up a debt that large, I do not know. The amount had to be based on scam money, or at least a good part of it. It's strange, I thought then as we continued to drive, how the government demands its share of even dirty money.

Finally, when the sky grew dark, the IRS agent called it a day and left. Upstairs in our apartment, Mom kicked off her shoes and collapsed on the bed in her room with an arm draped over her eyes. She was exhausted, burned. Mike and I packed boxes while she slept. Tomorrow we had to find another place to live, another name. My brother picked out Clift, after Montgomery Clift. Did I think Mom would like it? I told him she would, though I thought to myself, What does it matter? After we finished packing I pulled down the Murphy bed, undressed, and climbed under the covers. Mike stayed up to study *Major Barbara*.

I woke as he turned off the lamp and slipped into bed beside me. "I read 'The Motorcycle King,'" he whispered. "You left it on the table."

"What'd you think?"

"I liked it."

"Honest?"

"Would I lie?" he said. "It's moving too fast, though. You need to slow it down and expand and *feel* like the King. Like you did in the other story with the old man." He reached over and mussed my hair. "We'll talk about it tomorrow," he said, turning on his side. "Right now I'm too tired."

For a while I stared up at the ceiling. A pipe knocked inside the wall behind us.

"You miss Dad?" I said.

"Huh?"

"Dad. You miss him?"

"You know it."

"So do I," I said. "You think maybe they'll get back together?"

"Quiet, Jay."

"Sorry."

"I really have to get some sleep."

But it was time to load up the car. The alarm clock in Mom's room had gone off.

8

Usually our father called every Thursday night when the rates went down, but this time he phoned on a Tuesday around two in the afternoon. I answered it. We were living in an apartment in Hollywood now and no one else was home. "Watch out for your mother," he said. "Tell her I called. Have her call me back soon as she gets in. Right away, son. I'll be waiting by the phone. Tell her old Mrs. Glass just left here with the sheriff and she's on the warpath." As usual Dad wanted to protect me from the truth, as if it would damage how I felt about Mom, or my image of her. But the question I had, and still have, is a bigger one, which has to do with why—now that Dad knew the IRS and Mrs. Glass were on to Mom—just why he didn't come for Mike and me. If he'd thought he was doing us a favor, keeping the creditors off Mom's back as a kind of decoy, he had thought wrong. I don't have the answer unless I want to think he didn't give a damn about us, and that I can't believe. Maybe, like Mom once said, he wanted to be alone with Marissa.

In any case, Dad didn't mention the details about Mr. Glass dying and why the old lady was on the "warpath." Those, along with the fraud charges she brought against our mother, were things I wouldn't learn about until much later. The Glasses were a retired couple from Arizona who had invested their life savings in one of Mom's scams. They bought a beach house in Santa Cruz that didn't exist. The old man had a heart attack and died a few months after he found out he'd been conned. His wife, knowing she'd never see their money, decided instead to subpoena Mom on fraud charges. If nothing else, she wanted her locked up again. That was the woman's real goal, anyway, according to what my father eventually told me, and even then he couched it in soft terms. For now, though, it's enough to say that we had to up and move a lot, just as we did that Sunday, the day we left the apartment in Westlake. We dropped Mike off at Marrin's studio in the morning, after we'd loaded the Nova with boxes of clothes and books.

Across the street a 'family, all dressed up, headed down the block toward a church. Mom glanced at her watch as Mike got out of the car and stepped to the curb.

"We'll pick you up about two or three."

"Thanks."

"Good luck."

"See you," I said.

He waved to me with his copy of *Major Barbara*.

While Mom and I scouted around town for a new apartment, the one I mentioned earlier, Mike auditioned for a spot in the workshop. Only ten of the sixteen who showed up were accepted. His heart must've beaten fast after his performance, as the old man read the cut list aloud. Mike shifted in his seat. Swallowed. Second to last his name was called, and he let out a sigh.

Saul Leiberman turned in the seat beside him.

"You made it," he said.

"Barely."

"You don't sound too excited."

"I'm excited," Mike said. "That isn't it."

In the seat ahead another student was writing a check. Mike glanced to his side. A young woman searched through her purse. For a pen, he thought, or maybe cash. Another reached for his wallet. Mike leaned toward Saul.

"When do we have to pay?"

"Today." Saul smiled, proud. "I'm what you call a working scholar. It's free for me."

"How'd you do that?"

"He's got to like you."

"Think he liked me?"

"Ask, man." Saul shrugged. "I mean what else can you fucking do if you don't have it?" He winked. "Go on, get him before he takes off."

A mumble. "I hate asking."

"You got two thousand bucks?"

"No."

"Your parents?"

"No."

"Can you make payments?"

"I don't have a job."

"Give it a shot then, man," Saul said. "Whatta you waiting for?"

He took a deep breath and headed down the aisle. Marrin sat in the front row, hands crossed and balanced on top of his cane, talking with his daughter. A minute passed. Mike stood a few feet away, silent. He wished they'd acknowledge him so he could get it over with before he lost his nerve. A quick Yes or No. But they kept talking as if he weren't there. As he waited he concentrated on Leitha's cheekbone, her ear, and the way her hair rested on the back of her neck. She wore tight Levi's and a loose blouse and he wondered what she looked like without them. Good, he imagined. Great. Then suddenly he realized he was staring and he looked away. Finally Leitha laughed and kissed her father on the cheek. He smiled. "I'll be right back," she said, turning, nodding at Mike. "I think someone wants to talk to you."

Marrin glanced up at him with a bored look on his face. "Go ahead," he said. "What do you want?"

"I was wondering . . ."

"Out with it."

"Sir?"

"You're wasting time."

"About the tuition?"

"You pay Cynthia, not me."

Mike blinked. "I don't . . ." He paused. "I don't have it right now."

"This is a fucking business, not a charity," Marrin said, voice rising. "You think I do this crap for fun?" Slowly, carefully, the old man lifted himself to his feet. "Stand back, damn it." As he hobbled past Mike, toward the door, he glanced over his shoulder. "If we need you, you can work it off. Ask my wife. She handles that shit." Then he made his way out the door into the parking lot, looking this way and that, calling for his daughter.

Saul came up behind him.

"What'd he say?"

"To ask his wife."

"No problem." Saul patted him on the back. "I mean I love Marrin, man, don't get me wrong. We're tight. I respect him like a father. It's just that Cindy's a whole lot friendlier."

"I hope so."

"Hey."

"What?"

"You know what I'm saying, man? Watch out. I mean I been with the workshop five years. Since I got out of the service. Twelve months in 'Nam, man." Saul gave him a hard look. "I know what the fuck I'm talking about. Just don't blow it, okay? The man don't need any more problems." He nodded toward the door, and together they walked outside into the parking lot. Marrin was gone. Saul pointed to a house in back of the theater. "That's where they live during the week. Marrin don't like driving much now. Traffic, you know? He's not so patient. His legs, too, they ain't getting any better." He nudged Mike. "Let's do it."

In the den on the wall behind Cynthia's desk hung a Picasso lithograph of Don Quixote. Saul told her what Mike needed as they stood before her.

"When can you work?" she said.

"Any time you need me."

"Nights and weekends?"

"Sure," he said.

"Do you need a helper, Saul?"

"I'm way behind."

"What about today?"

"I got work for him."

"Can it wait until tomorrow?" she said.

"That's up to you and him."

"Michael?"

"I'll start whenever you want."

She looked to Saul. "I could use him at our place today." Then she leaned to one side of the desk toward the doorway. In the living room Marrin and Leitha were playing dominoes on the coffee table. "Honey," she called.

"What?"

"I'm taking Michael here up to the house."

"What for?"

"The guard rail," she said. "It needs fixing."

"I can do it," he hollered.

"Don't be silly. Do you need anything while I'm gone?" Marrin didn't answer. Cynthia reached for her car keys on the desk and handed them to Saul. "Would you warm up the car?" she said. "We'll be out in a few minutes." When Saul had left she flashed Mike a smile. "You had lunch yet?"

"No, Mrs. Marrin."

"Cindy."

"Cindy," he said.

"I'm starved." She stepped out from behind the desk. "When do you have to be home?"

Mike shrugged.

The Marrin family spent weekends and holidays at their home in Malibu. Years before their other house behind the theater had been used only as an office. A place for opening- and closing-night parties. Now they stayed there most of the time. As Marrin's disease worsened, so did his nerves, and the daily trips from Hollywood to Malibu became too much for him. Traffic was a bitch. And he refused to let Cindy or Leitha slip behind the wheel when he was in the car. But he wasn't in the car now, Cindy and Mike were, and it was a Mercedes 280 SL.

My brother must've known, as they drove up the Coast Highway, that he was getting off to a bad start with the old man. Being alone with his wife was bound to have nasty complications. Yet he was only seventeen, so maybe he realized what was involved, but just not how much was involved. Maybe he was just enjoying riding in a Mercedes with the top down, speeding along watching the waves and the brown bodies sprawled on the beach on a sunny California day. It had to be a good moment. He'd just passed his audition, the anxiety of failing was behind him, and there beside him was a beautiful woman. He figured her to be about forty, maybe a little older, and she looked a lot like her daughter. Blond. Tanned. A good tight figure in jeans and a loose blouse, though not quite as thin as Leitha. She was a bit huskier, a heavier bust, more of a woman than a little princess. Only her skin wasn't as soft and smooth as her daughter's, and when Mike looked at her from across the seat, it didn't do the same thing for him. With Leitha he wanted to lightly kiss her neck. With her mother he wanted to lightly bite it.

When they turned off the highway up into the Malibu Canyon, as Mike sensed they were getting closer to the house, he began to sweat. If she wanted him, if that's what this was about, and he couldn't know for sure, it would be his first time. A young man's fantasy come true. Only she'd have to initiate it because he couldn't take the chance. Because he couldn't risk being wrong about what she wanted, or didn't want, and because he didn't think he'd have the courage, anyway. Yet he felt sure that she wanted him. There were too many smiles, too many long stares, to believe otherwise. Twice he'd had to look away before he blushed; twice she had reached over and squeezed his leg and laughed. Both times he felt like a little boy, flustered, awkward, not knowing how to react.

The road continued to rise up and up. Every once in a while when they rounded a bend he saw the ocean below in the distance. In those moments, when he glimpsed the blue water, he forgot about Cindy. He relaxed. "That's where Bob Dylan lives," she said, pointing. "Down that road."

"Really?"

"Really."

"Down that road?"

Again he felt like the little boy. Repeating what she'd said with too much enthusiasm. Like a little groupie. He looked at her legs, her hand on the stick. Cindy downshifted at the top of the mountain and pulled into the driveway and shut off the engine. They went inside.

The house was built on the edge of the cliff with half of it hanging in the air, supported underneath with steel beams, and the other half solid on granite. In the living room, white shag carpet covered the floor. The back wall was all window, overlooking the ocean, and nearby, next to a wet bar, was a sliding glass door that opened onto a redwood deck. "We can lunch out there.

That's where the railing is," she said. "Now you see why I didn't want my husband to try to fix it." She put a hand on his shoulder and he felt his neck tense. "Once I drove Saul over to do it. He couldn't. He's afraid of heights . . . what's the word? It doesn't matter. Poor Saul." She laughed. "He's been with the workshop for I don't know how long, and I don't think he's ever gotten a part. Nothing. But you . . ." She took his face in her hands as if to study him. "You're going to do just fine." She smiled. "I was there today, you know. I watched your audition. You have the looks and the talent, too, which is rare."

When she kissed him one kind of tension faded—the one where he'd wondered if this was what she had wanted, and it was. So that tension was gone, but the other that replaced it was worse. He didn't know what to *do*. She led him to the bedroom, not her own but Leitha's, where they undressed. There she had to help him with the buttons on her blouse, had to place his hands on her breasts, had to teach him how to use his mouth and his tongue the way she liked, and how to pace himself. Cindy licked his ear. "We have three or four hours," she whispered. "There's no hurry. No one's home, no one's going to come home, and no one's going to find out unless you tell."

"I won't."

"Just deny it. Always."

"I will."

She placed her hand on his chest and pushed. "Lie back," she said. "Relax."

The first time he came after a few strokes. But he was young, and in a couple of minutes he was hard again. They worked up a sweat, both of them playing gently, sometimes roughly, until the muscles in his thighs felt good and sore and strong. She hung on tight the second time in a way that showed her hunger. He knew then that Marrin couldn't do what he was doing, going fast and hard, if only because of his condition. And he wondered how long she'd gone without making love, if she had had Saul or anyone else in the class, and if there were still ways she could enjoy her husband as she was enjoying him now.

The room was growing dark when they finally turned away from each other. On the wall, as Mike crossed his arms behind his head, he noticed a picture. In it stood a young woman dressed in an English riding outfit.

"Who's that?"

"Where?"

He nodded at the picture.

"Just Leitha."

A high school pennant hung on the closet door, and on the dresser were riding trophies. "Stinking horses. It's all the little bitch cares about." Cindy kissed him again, then rose from the bed. "Better hurry," she said, slipping into her pants. "There's a hammer and some nails in the kitchen in the bottom left drawer." With one hand she held her hair off the back of her neck, turning this way and that in front of the dresser mirror, checking for marks. She glanced at Mike in the reflection. He was still staring at the picture. "Get *dressed*," she said. "We can't go until you fix the rail."

While my brother and Cindy rolled along the Coast Highway, headed toward Hollywood, Mom and I sat waiting in the Nova outside Marrin's studio. Light from a streetlamp shone through our windshield. Mom rested her head against the steering wheel for a moment. She needed sleep. Her eyelids were heavy, her nerves shot. She looked down at her watch. Ahead I saw a figure walking toward us up the block.

"Where the hell is he?"

"Is that him?"

"It better be," she said.

But when the figure passed under the streetlamp we saw that it wasn't Mike. Mom sighed. We'd been waiting off and on now for hours. Earlier, in the afternoon, she'd chosen a two-bedroom place not far from the workshop. Later we'd had dinner at McDonald's and saved Mike a hamburger and fries and a Coke. At that point Mom was already angry and worried. We'd unloaded the Nova ourselves, rather than wait any longer for him, and the extra work had only put her that much closer to the edge. She was under pressure.

About a half hour later Mike slipped into the backseat. Mom started the car without saying a word. Halfway down the block he leaned over the top of the seat. "I'm sorry I'm late," he said. "Really, Mom. They needed me up at their house. I got a working scholarship for my tuition."

"That's nice."

"You're not mad?"

"I understand."

We turned off Melrose onto Highland. The street was busy with people and traffic.

"Did you find a new place?"

"Yeah," I said. "It's got a pool, too."

"Great."

"We already unloaded everything," Mom said.

"I wanted to help," he said. "You know I would've."

"How'd it go today, honey? Tell me."

He smiled, leaning forward more. "You wouldn't believe this instructor. You either, Jay." As he was telling us about his audition, and how hard it was to get into the class, Mom turned in her seat and slapped him with the back of her hand. The Nova swerved over the line. Another car approached, honking.

"*Watch it,*" I hollered.

Mom jerked the wheel straight and then reached around and swung and connected again. He took it in silence. Maybe that's what did it. Maybe that and the honking of the cars around us and all the other worries on her mind combined in one instant that set her off. Because she lost herself then. Snapped. Her eyes opened wide. She clenched her teeth and pulled the wheel left then right, left then right, throwing us across the seats.

"What're you doing? *Please,*" Mike shouted. The car beside ours pulled off the road, and another ahead slowed down to get behind us.

"*I'll kill us all,*" she screamed, stepping hard on the accelerator. The engine roared, the Nova shot forward. I clutched the dash.

Ahead the light dropped to green. A truck started across the intersection. "*Stop, Mom, please,*" Mike shouted. Just after I'd braced myself, saw us slamming into that truck and the glass flying, the metal crunching, she hit the brakes. The tires squealed. Mike sighed as he fell back into the seat. I sighed. On the corner a group of people stared at us. Mom wiped sweat from her brow with the back of her arm and turned off Highland onto a quieter street. The inside of our car smelled of burned rubber.

At the apartment she walked ahead of us, her purse swinging at her side, hurrying. I stayed a few steps behind Mike as we climbed the stairs after her, his dinner in a bag in my hand, watching him drag his feet. He stopped in the hallway outside our new home. Mom had left the door wide open, and all of our boxes were piled in the middle of the living room. Some of them hadn't been unpacked since we moved from San Jose. I didn't know what to tell him. He looked at the boxes and the cheap furniture that came with the place and then he turned and rested his elbows on the railing. For a while he stared down at the soft blue light underneath the water in the swimming pool. I did the same.

A minute later Mom came out with a wet washcloth. She took his chin in her hand and turned his face around. There was a small bruise under his left eye. Gently, she placed the cloth against the skin. Mike winced. She held it there for a few seconds before she reached for his hand, brought it up to the cloth, and let him hold it himself. "I'm sorry, baby. Please don't stay mad at me," she said. "I didn't mean to hurt you." He turned away and stared back down into the water. Into his other hand she pressed a ten-dollar bill. "Buy yourself something," she said softly. "Take your brother to a movie. Have a good time, baby."

When she'd left I opened the bag.

"You eat yet?"

"Leave me alone."

"Hey, you gotta eat."

"Go away," he mumbled. "Just get out of here."

For two, maybe three minutes I didn't say anything. A pump in the pool hummed. Overhead, a plane flew by, one light blinking red. "Forget about it, okay? C'mon inside." But he was frozen there, distant. I shook the bag for him to hear. "It's cold but it's still good. I'll warm it up if you want." No answer. Somewhere in the complex music played. I took the Coke out of the bag and offered it to him. "Thirsty?" Then just like that his hand flew out from his side and the bag split and the Coke spilled. He threw the washcloth down.

"Get the fuck away from me," he shouted. "I don't need your sympathy."

I stooped and picked up the hamburger and then threw it back down. "Fuck it," I said. "If that's the way you wanna be, just fuck it, man." So I left the food there, left my brother, left the complex, too. He made the mess—let him clean it.

That night I went to the movies by myself. *The Dirty Dozen* was playing at the World in Hollywood with Lee Marvin, Donald Sutherland, and Charles Bronson. Only when I got to the box office, and reached around for my wallet, I remembered that I was broke. I'd been broke for weeks now. I thought, To hell with that. I was going to see the movie, and I would, because I was determined. First I checked the side exits, but they were locked. Think, I told myself. Then I spotted a man leaving the phone booth in the parking lot of the Regal car wash. From the bed of a truck I found an old tire iron, cuffed it under my arm, and ducked across the street. No one was looking. The car wash was closed. It took about three minutes, and maybe seven or eight tries. Finally, with the flat end of the bar, I got a good bite under the lip of the coin box and pulled hard.

Jackpot.

Nickels and dimes and quarters spilled out, ricocheting off the glass walls, landing right at my feet.

9

I'd guess they made love about a dozen different times before her husband caught on. Too many things needed fixing too often up at the house in Malibu. Other times, after the workshop, if Mike was mopping the stage or sweeping the aisles with Saul, she'd send Saul home early. They'd make quick love in the dressing room with his pants down around his ankles, her skirt pulled up around her hips, and her blouse spread open. But it wasn't as good as it could've been, good like it was up in Malibu, because he was too nervous. His eyes kept flashing toward the theater door, expecting it to open, Marrin or his daughter happening onto them. He imagined noises. Once they made love on the edge of the makeup dresser with her legs wrapped around his waist, her ankles locked, so he couldn't pull away. Cindy almost screamed when she came, as if she wanted her husband, who was in the house nearby, to look up from the television he might've been watching, or the book he may have been reading, or the game of dominoes he and Leitha could've been playing in the living room. It was as if she wanted him to raise his head and wonder at the noise and then lower his eyes and pretend he had heard nothing.

Maybe the old man accepted it, wasting away like he was,

knowing his wife needed a lover, or, if she didn't, how she was bound to take one anyway. There were a lot of young men around the workshop. She was still young herself, still pretty enough to turn heads, and still very much used to getting what she wanted. As the affair continued Mike learned that it was her father who set Marrin up with the studio. A wedding gift, it was, although you'd never know it from his autobiography. There he read as a self-made man, working himself up from nothing. He left New York for L.A. because he thought he could make it easier here, and he did, but he had more help than he cared to admit publicly. Cindy had just dropped out of UCLA for a role in an off-Broadway production of *Golden Boy* when they first met and fell in love. He was the male lead. She played the scamp.

For a while Marrin encouraged her talent, advised and rehearsed with her. But shortly after their marriage she became pregnant with Leitha and she gave up performing. Temporarily, she had told herself, only until her daughter was ready for school. "I was like you, Michael," she said one day, lying in bed. "Dedicated. Acting was all I cared about." In the meantime she devoted herself to her husband and child while the studio continued to grow. Yet when Leitha finally entered the first grade, and Cindy had free hours, she never got around to acting again. Something had been lost.

It was years before she felt as if she'd been cheated, short-changed on life, having settled down too quickly with a man who turned out to love himself, the workshop, and his daughter more than he did his wife. Once she left him for a month. Life alone, though, was even more miserable. Out of habit, love, or maybe loyalty she returned to her family on her own. Marrin had never asked her back. Neither had Leitha. And it was strange, too, because she had raised the girl while Marrin built his reputation. Cindy didn't know anymore, but when she said she'd quit caring, and rolled over in that bed in Malibu, Mike knew different. She cared. A lot. After her husband contracted his disease any thought of leaving him dissolved. She would stand by him, yes, but no more than that.

So maybe she figured she had a right to the young men. That wasn't what she told Mike, though. He only suspected it. Instead she'd stroke his chest and tell him how good it was to be with him, and how she felt Marrin might never have married her if not for her money. She told him other things about herself, too, but exactly how much of it was true, he couldn't be sure. There was Marrin and Leitha's side of the story, which he hadn't heard. Yet he didn't interrupt her, he let her carry on, because he knew she needed to talk to someone and he was that person. Only the more he heard, the more he realized that their affair had to end. Theodore Marrin had been coming down harder on him in the workshop over the past three months, and he knew damn well that it involved something other than just acting. He longed now for the daughter, a woman his own age. One he could laugh and joke and cuddle with like he imagined it ought to be—not an affair with an older married woman and all the complications and secrecies and lies that went with it.

At night he'd dream of Leitha, recalling the color of the blouse she wore that day in workshop, or how her jeans gripped her thighs, the way her ass swung as she walked, and the sound of her voice. Soft but deep, not high-pitched like other girls her age, but a little raspy, as if she were a heavy smoker, only she wasn't. Often, as he tossed in bed, or he was walking home alone, he rehearsed entire conversations with her. Somehow it would get mentioned that he was a serious actor going places, big places— like her father—except he would never say it directly. No bragging. Always she ended up admiring him for his determination, his modesty and talent, and she'd accept when he found the nerve to ask her out.

But damned if she wasn't always by her father's side, his right-hand girl, his assistant tagging along like a puppy. Once, up at the house in Malibu, after he'd just made love to her mother, he passed by Leitha's room on the way to the bathroom. Her door was open. He stepped inside. On her dresser were a dozen wallet-size photos, cut and separated along the white borders, ready to be sealed into envelopes stacked beside them. Graduation invitations. He picked up one of the pictures. In it she wore a black gown that ran low across her shoulders, her hair was done up, and a thin gold necklace encircled her throat. She wasn't smiling.

From the living room came Cindy's voice.

"Michael?"

"Be there in a second."

"We have to get back."

Leitha wouldn't know the difference, he thought, cupping the

116

photo in his hand, later slipping it into his wallet when he dressed.

On the night before *Major Barbara* opened, the old man ran my brother through a scene. The rest of the class watched, and after a while a few bowed their heads, because they must've known the reason, too. Because it became obvious fast. It started off as a dress rehearsal, but Marrin had dismissed them one by one until only Mike remained onstage. He was playing Stephen. The old man watched from a chair upstage corner, his bad leg crossed over the other, hanging limp with the ankle turned inward.

"*Stop.*"

Mike dropped the line in midsentence.

"I don't believe you," Marrin shouted, glancing around the theater. "Does anyone?" He hadn't shaved in a couple of days, his gray hair was uncombed, and his eyes had a fevered look about them. He nodded at his daughter sitting beside Cindy in the front row. "Do you?" he said. "Do you believe him?"

"No."

"And my wife?"

She glared at him.

"Cindy? Darling? Was he any good?"

Silence.

"Was he?"

"Go to hell."

Leitha shifted in her seat. Marrin thumped his cane on the floor. "Do it again, boy," he shouted. Again Mike went to the spot downstage where he would deliver his line, take two steps, then deliver another. Only he never got past the first.

"*Stop.*"

"What'd I do wrong now?"

"You don't know yet?" he said, eyes wide, feigning disbelief. "You really don't know?"

"No."

"Tell him, Cindy."

She didn't answer.

"You used to act, darling. A long time ago. Tell the boy what he's doing wrong. Why always leave it up to me?" He put his fingertips to his chest. "I'm not the only teacher here," he said. "Answer him." But she just folded her hands in her lap and stared

117

at Marrin. Again he thumped his cane on the floor, except this time he grinned. "You act without thinking," he said. "You're young, you don't know what the fuck you're doing—the emotional journey, the implications of your character. He's cardboard. He's stiff. You're young and pretty but there's nothing here." The old man tapped his temple with a finger. "Nothing. What you're doing isn't acting, boy. It's shit." He waved his hand. "Try it again."

His face felt hot and flushed and he wanted to tell the sonofabitch to stick it. Give him the finger and walk out. But he wouldn't, and he knew it, because the play was an important one. Because he needed the exposure. So Mike returned to his spot onstage, swallowed and collected himself, and ran through his lines again. Be calm, he thought, when the old man raised his hand, silencing him. Be calm. Mike rubbed his forehead. "What do you want, Mr. Marrin?" he said. "I'm doing my best."

"I want honesty."

"How?"

"Emotional honesty, boy. Do you know what that means?"

"I think so."

"I don't think you even think."

Somewhere in the back of the theater a student chuckled. Mike gritted his teeth. In the front row he noticed Cindy shaking her head. "Imagine," the old man said. "Lady Britomart is your mother. She's just told you that your father doesn't give a damn about you. Can you understand that? Is the emotion too complex?" Another student laughed. "Now do it with honesty and conviction. Open up, boy. Quit lying to us and yourself, because we see through it. We're not all fools."

Again and again he ran him through the scene, stopping him every time, hollering, correcting, scolding, until his voice was hoarse. Until he was sweating. Until Cindy rose to her feet and left. Finally, with a wave of his hand, he dismissed him from the stage. Rehearsals ended early that night. Mike took a seat in the back row and stayed there, watching the others leave, listening to his ears ring for how long he didn't know. Soon the theater was empty except for Saul. His job was to shut off the lights and lock up.

The stage was dark as he stood beside the open door, his hand

118

on the last light switch. Outside, traffic passed on the boulevard.
An engine roared in the parking lot.

"What I tell you?"

"Shut up."

"Let's go."

Mike climbed to his feet. Kicked the chair ahead.

"I told you, didn't I?"

"Shut up."

"Hey," Saul said, throwing the switch. Darkness. "You ain't
the first, man."

The Mercedes pulled up beside him as he headed home down a
quiet side street. Slowly the passenger's window hummed open.
Mike stopped. Leitha leaned over the seat and shouted to him.

"Get in."

"No thanks."

"C'mon, get in."

"I'll walk."

"This wasn't my idea, you know," she said. "My mother sent
me. She's worried."

"Tell her I'm fine."

A car passed, headlights blinding them for a second, then disappearing.

"I could just say I brought you home."

"Do whatever you want."

"Like you do? Lie?"

Mike jammed his hands into his pockets and glanced down at
the sidewalk. "You think you're so goddamned great," she said.
"So pretty. So talented. But you're not." She shook her head.
"There's thousands like you in this town. Why don't you just quit
the workshop and leave us alone?"

"Maybe I will."

"Not maybe. Do it."

"Don't push me, okay?"

"Then quit."

"Go on," he said, raising his chin. "Go back to your daddy."

"Screw you."

"He's all you care about. You don't know me. You don't even
know your own mother."

For a moment she sat stunned. Mike walked on. At the end of the block she veered around the corner and cut him off as he stepped down from the curb. He lurched backward. Leitha glared at him through the open window, one hand on the wheel, the other on the stick. Slowly a smile appeared on her face.

"Would you do me a favor?" she said.

"Maybe."

"If you don't quit the workshop?"

"Yeah?"

"And my father doesn't kick you out?"

"What do you want?"

"Quit fucking my mother."

Then she hit the gas, leaving him there in the street, wagging his head, wondering what the hell he'd gotten himself into. What the hell he could do about it. Forget the workshop? The play? Mike watched the Mercedes disappear down the block. No, he couldn't quit. Not yet.

Ten P.M. He flipped on the TV and poured himself a drink of Mom's gin. Downed it. Poured another and drank it down. "Jay," he called. "You home?" No answer. He checked the bedroom but found it empty. Where was the kid? Screwing around, probably, when he should've been sleeping or studying. Mike sighed. His brother was blowing it more every day since they left San Jose.

Suddenly the phone rang in the kitchen. He dashed for it.

"Hello?"

"Michael?"

"Yeah."

"It's me," Cindy said. "I'm just calling to see if you made it home all right."

"Thanks."

"Are you okay?"

"Uh-huh."

"You know he doesn't have any proof," she said, her voice dropping low. "He's bluffing. Just remember to always deny it."

"I will."

"Good."

"He's asleep now. I'm going out for a ride." Pause. "Is your mother awake?"

"She got a night job."

"So you're free."

"Not tonight."

"You don't want to come up to the house with me?"

"I better not." Mike wrapped the cord around his finger. "Do you think he's going to kick me out of the play?"

"He knows how far he can go and he's gone too far already. I'd never let him do that to you. Never." Pause. "Sure you don't want to go up to the house with me?"

"I'm sure."

"See you."

"Bye."

"Bye."

"Oh, Cindy?"

"Yes?"

"Tell Leitha thanks for the ride."

After he hung up he poured himself a nightcap and sat down in the living room. The eleven o'clock news was on. American soldiers marched along a dirt road. In the background rose the smoke from a burning village. The scene cut to Richard Nixon standing dressed in a suit and tie behind a podium marked with the presidential seal. "Asshole," Mike muttered, flipping the TV off, heading for the hall closet. There he rummaged through a box of clothes, found his swimming trunks, and stripped naked. As he slipped into the trunks he thought of Marrin and cursed. He thought of Cindy and Leitha and the play. He thought of Dad and wondered if he ought to call him. For advice. Mike smiled to himself. Dad knew about affairs.

Outside, as he headed down the open hallway, a towel draped over his shoulder, he stopped and looked over the railing. The deep end of the pool shimmered in the light. Fifteen feet down and maybe five or six feet out, he estimated, figuring he could make it. It wasn't that far. Mike climbed over the railing and tossed the towel and watched it flutter to the concrete. For a while my brother stared into the soft blue water as he exhaled once, inhaled, and then the sonofabitch just did it. I know because I was there for this one, watching from a window in the laundry room, holding my breath.

And it was a beautiful dive, because I saw it, and because he'd been trained in it. To leap. To rise. Up and up. At the highest point he spread his arms, arcing as he hung frozen in the air for just a second, then falling fast now with his legs stiff and straight and his palms together. There was barely a ripple in the water where he broke its surface, only it wasn't in the middle of the pool. He'd gone up, up too far—not out quite far enough. My heart dropped. Shy another couple of goddamned feet and he would have done himself in a hell of a lot sooner than he ended up doing.

I wasn't washing clothes in the laundry room. And the reason I happened to be at the window when he dove off the railing wasn't any coincidence. I was looking to see if anyone was around, if it was safe. In one hand I had a tire iron, in the other a heavy-duty screwdriver, and on my belt a canvas sack hung by its drawstring. I'd taken to busting into machines whenever I needed a little money, and sometimes even when I didn't. Sometimes I did it for the hell of it, which I knew was even worse than stealing for a reason, though that didn't stop me. Any machine was game except for the bill changer. They had reinforced steel-plated faces with double recessed locks and direct bell alarms. I found that out the hard way one night at the Wash-and-Drive across from Sears. The alarm must've woken the entire neighborhood.

But I did get into fourteen washers and twenty-seven dryers on three different occasions down at the all-night Speedymat on Cahuenga. There also wasn't a phone booth within a mile of our apartment that I hadn't hit on at least once. This was before the phone company put in silent alarms, although that wouldn't have made much difference. Those cases were built flimsily compared to the bill changer, and I had learned to work quickly but calmly. In and out. Fast. Now I used a screwdriver to jimmy a hold on the box, then the bar, and I carried a canvas sack for the change so I wouldn't be scrambling around picking up coins and stuffing them into my pockets. They weighed you down.

One time I got into the cigarette machine at the Sunset bowling alley in the morning before it opened. The janitor had left the door ajar while he was sweeping out around front in the parking lot. Ten minutes later I had a sackful of coins tucked under my jacket.

The cigarettes, all I could carry, lasted me a month. With the money from that job and others I bought a diamond glass cutter, a pair of tight-fitting rubber gloves and a roll of duct tape, some bolt cutters, and a corduroy jacket for Mike when he went out on his interviews. So he could look sharp. I told him I found it at the World. "Almost brand new," I said, holding it up for him. "Hardly worn. Try it on." He slipped his arms into the sleeves and shrugged, hands out, checking the length. It fit perfect. Mike cocked his head.

"You sure you found this?"

I frowned, giving him a hurt look. "Why?" I said. "You think I stole it?"

"I mean the man could've returned for it."

"Finders keepers."

"That's no way to think, Jay."

"So bring it back. Give it to the manager," I said. "Maybe he'll like it."

But he was already headed for our bedroom to look at himself in the dresser mirror. In the four months of his affair with Marrin's wife, while I was busting locks, Mom had found another job as a secretary on the night shift at a plastics company. My brother and I were also back in school, as Mom felt that our new neighborhood was a good one. Our new last name on the registration forms was Bain, and I didn't much like the sound of it, but by this time I didn't care one way or the other if it wasn't our own.

Mike was completing his senior year now, studying hard, working evenings and weekends at Marrin's studio. Mom slept days. I was pretty much on my own, with no one telling me what to do or when to be in. I went to school when I felt like it, and I didn't feel like it a hell of a lot. This new place didn't send out truancy letters, either, or none I knew about, and as far as writing was concerned, I'd quit for a while. There didn't seem much point in sitting around staring at a boring piece of paper when I could be out making money.

Tonight I had to forget about my job in the laundry room. My tools I hid in their usual place, up in an empty locker in the carport. Before I entered the courtyard, I stopped and peeked around the corridor. Mike was still swimming. When he dove under, I hurried for the apartment, hoping I could slip inside unnoticed. Climb into bed. Sleep, or fake it. He surfaced and spotted me just as I reached the stairs.

"Jay?"

I stopped, sighed.

"Where've you been?"

"Around."

"What kind of answer is that?" he said. "C'mere."

"Later."

"*C'mere.*"

Mike swam to the edge of the pool and rested his arms over the side. I shrugged and went to him and squatted on my haunches. "You staying out of trouble?" he said. Water dripped from his arms down the concrete into a crack. "You watching out for yourself?"

"Yeah."

"How's school?"

"Okay."

"You're not cutting?"

I stared at the diving board at the other end. "No."

"Look at me."

Here it comes, I thought. The third degree. Instead he smiled and reached out and patted the top of my tennis shoe. "That night with Mom?" he said. "You know what I'm talking about?" He looked up at the hallway outside our apartment. "I don't think I ever apologized for it. It was me, I was in the wrong, man. You were just trying to help and I exploded." His hair was slicked back wet, and his shoulders were covered with goosebumps. I listened to the water lap against the drain flaps along the sides of the pool. "Sometimes I wonder if we did the right thing leaving with Mom. For you mostly, I mean." He shivered. "I have to be here if I'm going to make it but you . . . hey, you know you can go back anytime you want, Jay." He looked me in the eyes, and I shook my head. Again he patted my tennis shoe. "You positive?"

I nodded.

"You know I wonder too . . ." This time when he paused I smelled alcohol on his breath. "Man, I wonder sometimes if I can really act."

"Whatta you talking about?"

"I have my doubts."

"You're great."

"Think so?"

"I know it, I've seen it. Something'll break for you," I said. "To the top, right?"

"Right," he mumbled.

"It's the truth."

"And you're being objective, huh?" He smiled weakly. "My play opens tomorrow.

"Aha."

"What?"

"You're nervous is all." I slapped my thigh. "About the play."

"That's only part of it. I'll turn eighteen this year." He closed his eyes for a moment, then opened them. "The draft, man. The fucking war," he said, clenching his teeth. "I don't want to fight." He gripped the edge of the pool. "Somehow, some way I've got to get out of it." I went to fetch his towel.

"We'll split to Canada or something," I said, my back to him. "Me and you. Let's talk inside." But he'd dived under by the time I turned around, and I don't know if he heard me. The light beneath the water made the surface, as it rippled, shine the color silver. I watched him swim the length of the pool, and when he rose at the other end, and called out to me that he'd be in after a couple of more laps, I sighed and headed upstairs.

Later in bed, while I waited for Mike, I decided to give it up—the machines, anyway. Little nickels and dimes and quarters. Pocket change, I thought, not worth getting caught over. For I believed, as my brother believed about himself regardless of what he'd said earlier, that I was destined for bigger and better things.

Up until his seventeenth birthday I don't believe he worried a whole lot about the war, or if he did, he sure didn't talk about it with me except by the pool that once. Of course that doesn't mean he didn't think about it, because he had to. Mike was next in line as he approached eighteen, and a perfect specimen, being the strong, healthy young man that he was. My brother would've made a fine soldier.

But he had better things to do with his life than to waste it on a fucked-up war that never needed to be fought. *Major Barbara* soon set his career in motion. *Variety* called his performance "outstanding." *The Reporter* said it was an "impressive and powerful debut," and the *L.A. Times* wrote, ". . . the handsome male lead played by Michael Casey demonstrates a fresh talent deserving of recognition." And on and on they went, all praise, which only made Theodore Marrin angrier, because the reviews contradicted what he'd said about Mike in class. Because they showed that others thought differently about my brother than he did. It could also be that he believed Mike had what it took to make it in Hollywood, only he didn't want to admit it to the workshop or himself. In any case, Marrin was in another bad mood the night the play opened. Instead of taking it out again on Mike, though, he used Saul Leiberman.

And it was too bad, it wasn't right, because he'd rehearsed damn hard for *Major Barbara*. Everyone in the cast had. Saul played Rummy in Act II, not a large role, but a good one, and he was proud of it. He and Mike arrived at the theater early to open the doors and air the place out. Iron the period costumes. Starch shirt collars. Sweep the auditorium. This was two hours before the opening performance. Now Mike was stapling programs in the dressing room, trying to keep his mind clear and hoping Cindy wouldn't wander in. She'd want to talk. He didn't. Saul had a bottle of Windex in one hand, a rag in the other. He was wiping down the makeup-dresser mirror.

"You up for it?" he said.

"As up as I'm ever going to be."

"We're gonna shine."

"I hope."

"Shine," Saul said, shooting the mirror with Windex, wiping it down. "I'm talking *shine*. This production is tight." He grinned at himself in the reflection. "A full house, too. You want to see acting?" He laughed. "Just watch me from the wings, man."

Marrin hobbled into the dressing room then. Mike bowed his head and pressed another staple into another program. The old man tapped his cane on the floor. His face was clean-shaven for the first time in days, and he was dressed for the occasion in slacks and a turtleneck sweater and a houndstooth jacket. "Turn around," he said. "Sit down and relax, Saul. There's been a change." He hung his cane on the back of the chair beside the dresser, placed his hands on Saul's shoulders, and pushed until he sat. "I want your understudy on tonight." He massaged the muscles. They looked at each other in the mirror.

"What'd I do wrong, Mr. Marrin?"

The old man sighed and dug his fingers deeper into the shoulders, the flesh, kneading it. "It's nothing personal, boy. You have to understand that," Marrin said. "You do, don't you? I know you do." He worked the neck now, his own head thrown back and his eyes at half-mast. "You're getting tense . . . I can feel the muscles tightening. Let those negative feelings pass . . . close your eyes." And Marrin let his own eyes close for a moment, kneading the muscles still harder.

"Please, sir," Saul said. "I'm always here for rehearsal, I'm never late. I've been working hard on this."

Marrin ran a hand farther up the back of his neck, beneath the hair, so that Saul had to bend his head toward his lap. "Don't beg, don't whine, boy. You'll get your chance. Relax and lift your head now . . . No, very slowly, keep your eyes closed and let the tension leave your body, your mind, and when you open your eyes and look into the mirror you'll know there's a purpose for what I do and that it's a good purpose and you ought never to question it."

The old man narrowed his eyes at Mike and then, reaching for his cane, hobbled out of the room. Slowly Saul raised his head. For a few seconds he stared at himself in the mirror.

Mike pounded a staple hard into a program.

"He can't do that."

"You heard him."

"Tell him to stick it."

"You don't understand." Saul rose to his feet. "We have to trust him. I know. I do. He has a purpose." As he started for the door Mike grabbed his arm. "What's the big deal?" Saul said, shrugging. "This little play? Shit, I landed another job on *All My Days*." His lower lip twitched once. "I work a lot, you know. Always lines to memorize. Sits. Soaps. They're always rushing me. Lemme go." He jerked his arm free and stepped outside into the parking lot. "New scripts, work to do. Out of the blue, they call my agent. Out of the blue." Like a song, he said it, wagging his head. "Out of the fucking blue."

Midway through the third and final act Mike knew he had performed better this night than he'd ever before in his life. No simple pretending, acting the stock, the expected. When he showed anger it came first within his chest, vibrating there as it grew and grew, then rising to expression in his face, and finally into his voice. It was a kind of fluttering, wavering note that made the audience freeze, concentrate, and follow him as he moved about the stage with confidence and power. And then came the applause when the spots went down, and the curtains closed, opening a second later on the rebound. Mike rushed out onto the stage with the cast, his shirt wet with sweat, his brow damp, and his heart pounding from exhilaration and exhaustion and relief. It was over. He'd done a fine job. Bowing, he looked into the audience. All ninety-nine seats were full. The applause grew still louder. He smiled, bowing once more before hurrying offstage again, thinking, *Yes, I shined like Saul said.* He shined, all right, but why and for what reason and for who other than himself, he wasn't sure.

Marrin hobbled into the dressing room a few minutes later. Three actors who were congratulating each other fell silent. The others had already left for the cast party at the house in back of the theater. Marrin scanned the room. Mike was inside a dressing booth, changing into his street clothes.
"Where's the Casey boy?"
"Over here."
Mike heard the thump of his cane, the drag of his bad leg. On the floor beneath the drape he saw the tips of Marrin's shoes.
"You need to sweep up."
"Tonight?"
"Tonight."
Jackass, he thought, as he heard Marrin leave. He didn't want to celebrate with them, anyway. Not Cindy and Leitha and Marrin. Not all in the same space.

He swept the stage and the aisles. He picked up the spare programs and pushed the seats back into place and shut down the houselights and finally he locked up. As he crossed the parking lot, a gym bag slung over his shoulder, he glanced through the living-room window of the house. Inside, people were drinking and smoking. Music flowed through the open door. For a second he wondered if he ought to go in and have a couple of drinks after all. Then he thought better and continued on his way when he heard a screen door slam.
"Leaving already?"
He stopped. Looked.
Leitha stood on the porch, smiling. In her hand was a glass of wine. "Pretty good job," she said. "For an amateur. I really don't

give a shit but I think you'd better come in for a while." A pause. "Betsy Grotz wants to meet you."

"Who?"

She laughed. "You really are a hick, aren't you?" she said. "Better start reading the trades." Leitha dug into her pants pocket and came up with a ring of keys that she twirled on one finger. "Don't forget to thank my mother. She's the one who called her," she said, holding up her drink as if to toast him. "Any ideas why?" A grin spread across her face. Mike kicked at the ground for a second and, when he looked up at her, his eyes were narrowed. "Be a good boy and do me another favor, huh?" Leitha laughed again, finished her wine, and handed him the glass as she stepped down from the porch. "Take this in for me. I have to get out of here." She crossed the parking lot and hopped into the Mercedes, started it up. Mike watched her drive off as he had the night before, except this time he wondered where she was going. To see a lover? Somebody older? He looked down at the glass. There was still a sip left, which he drank, holding it in his mouth, stepping inside the house before he swallowed.

A minute later he found Cindy, who filled his glass and took his arm and led him through the crowd to Betsy Grotz. She gave him two business cards. One was her own from the William Morris Agency in Beverly Hills. The other had the name of a photographer on it. "Call him," she said. "Tomorrow. Call me, too." He slipped the cards into his wallet in the compartment beside Leitha's picture. As he looked up he noticed Marrin glaring at him from across the room. *You . . .* But he stifled the thought, sliding the wallet into his back pocket, giving him his best smile.

10

Success came quickly for my brother. Sometimes I wonder if it didn't come too quickly. Not long ago I was sorting through some old letters that he sent our father, and in one of them he wrote ". . . it's amazing, Dad, how much my life has changed in the last seven months." At the bottom, beneath his signature, was the P.S.—"We all miss you, especially Jay. I'm enclosing a money order for a plane ticket. Please use it." The word *please* was under-lined twice. There was no date on the letter, no return address, and the postmark had been torn off when the envelope was first opened years before. Yet I remember those months that he wrote about, and the changes they brought. He had professional eight-by-ten, black-and-white glossies taken. He went on three audi-tions, getting callbacks on the first two but losing out in the end, finally landing the third. As for the return address on the letter, its absence, my brother had left it off for fear that the IRS or some other creditor might intercept our mail and find us. Up until now no one had bothered Mom, not since we had last moved, and we wanted to keep it that way.

The third audition he got was for *Vice Squad*. He played a re-tarded kid whose father, an army sergeant, frames him for the murder of his mother. The day before the shoot I found him in the bedroom with a portable radio pressed to his ear, his shirt off one button, staring at himself in the dresser mirror with a vacant look on his face. He had cut his hair almost to the scalp and dyed it black. Mike grinned dumbly and rolled his eyes.

"Who am I?" he said.

"Eddie García."

He winked. "How'd you guess?"

"Luck," I said. "But you sure you wanna look like that on TV?"

When Mom saw him later that day she was furious. "It'll grow out," he told her, drawing a hand across his temple, ruffling what little hair remained. "This is important, Mom." She shook her head in disappointment. It wasn't the role she liked to imagine her son playing.

But Mike didn't care what he looked like offscreen, so long as he looked the part onscreen. And he did. He played Eddie down to every detail, every gesture, including the way he used to flinch when I'd reach into his shirt pocket for a Marlboro at Alum Rock. The difference was that Mike spoke in a slow, stumbling manner where Eddie couldn't speak much at all, and the flinching he used for when the father character raised his hand, even if it was only to scratch his head. This guy was a sonofabitch. In one scene Mike takes off his shirt, and on his back are welts. He even talked the director into letting him carry the radio around in a couple of scenes. How my brother understood Eddie well enough to play

him so well, without ever actually having spent time with him—
just by having watched him around the apartment complex—impressed me. Yet I knew then, as I know now, that there was a lot
more that went into the making of this character than just Eddie
García.

Shortly after the *Vice Squad*, before it even aired, he beat out
two dozen other actors for a lead in a TV movie-of-the-week
called *Where Are the Children?* This one had to do with a group of
teenagers who fall prey to marijuana. The show was a commercial
success, being the seventies as it was, with lots of worried parents
of children who smoked the stuff. One by one the teenagers suc-
cumb to heroin and ruin their lives—all except Mike's character
who loses his high-school sweetheart to an overdose in the first
half hour. The emotional impact of it spins him straight, and in
the end he goes off to college. It was a ridiculous show. Naïve and
dated. But my brother played his part well again, and his agent,
Betsy Grotz, for she'd signed him the day after *Major Barbara*
opened, couldn't have been more pleased. She took a big interest
in him even though he wasn't yet one of her top clients.

Vice Squad happened to be my favorite show, a cops-and-robbers
program, and every day for a Week when he returned home from
the set I'd ask him who he saw. Who he talked with. I was infatu-
ated with one of the young cops played by Lynn Slade, and I
needed to know everything about him. Was he tough like in the
show? How did he look in person? What was he *really* like? I
wanted the true-to-life inside scoop, but my brother wouldn't give
it to me. He'd just shrug and say, "He's a nice guy."

"And what else?"

"I don't have many scenes with him."

"So?"

"So I don't see him much, Jay."

"Can you take me on the set?"

"Not now," Mike said. "It's not the right time for me to ask
favors."

If it wasn't the right time for a favor, at least the timing was
good for the money he made. We needed it as much as we ever
had before. Mike was still a minor when the breaks came his way,
though, and the checks went to Mom. She doled out fifty or sixty
dollars here and there and told him that she was keeping the rest
for him in an account until he turned eighteen. Which wasn't far

off. With his share he bought a file cabinet to replace the one that had been repossessed in San Jose. In it he stored the three-by-five index cards of his obituary collection. Once he brought home a beautiful canned ham. Another time he bought Mom some roses and a bottle of perfume and me a hunting knife for the day when he said he'd make enough money to buy some land up on the Chetco for Dad. We'd build that house yet, one with a natural stone fireplace, and a den for Mike's books. A real home. No goddamn dream. No lousy apartments anymore. "You'll need a good knife to clean all the trout we're going to catch," he said, smiling as he handed me the present, then laughing. "That'll be your job."

I'd have thought that since his career was going well he would've quit Marrin's studio. Why stay now that he was working? I suppose he did on account of Leitha, or because he was the star of the workshop and the feeling was a good one, or it could be that he actually thought Marrin was teaching him to be a better actor. Whatever the case, now that he was coming up in the industry, Leitha wasn't so cold to him. One time she let him carry a box of old business files to the Mercedes, and once she gave him a lift home. Her father still despised him, yet Mike had landed a couple of roles with the prospect of more to come, and if one day he hit it big Marrin could add him to the list of famous alumni. The studio's reputation and his name as an acting coach must've meant one hell of a lot to the old man. I can't think of any other reason why he'd let someone who had had an affair with his wife stick around. What's even stranger, though, was that he gave Mike a full ride, no tuition or work required for it. Maybe he knew the affair had ended, and he'd forgiven my brother. But I doubt it, the forgiving part, anyway. I don't see how anyone could forget something like that so easily.

This all happened about the time Mike sent off the letter to Dad. His reply came quickly, a few weeks before Easter on a lazy Saturday afternoon. I was lying on the floor watching *The Three Stooges* on the portable. Mom had just gotten out of bed and sat now drinking coffee in her bathrobe at the kitchen table. She was flipping through a copy of *Movieland*. "It says here that Lynn Slade you worked with married a Negro." Mom held the picture up for us to see. "She is pretty, though, isn't she?"

My brother didn't say anything. He sat beside me on the floor with the morning paper. I turned the TV up.

A couple of minutes passed.

"Damn."

"What?" I said.

"Bebe Daniels died."

"Who's that?"

"*Rio Rita?*" he said, as if I could've possibly known. "*Forty-second Street?*" A sigh. "She had a cerebral hemorrhage."

Mike shook his head and went downstairs for the mail. He came back with an envelope in one hand, a letter in the other, reading it. Mom glanced up from her cup of coffee and nodded at him. "Whatcha got there, honey?" she asked.

"A letter from Dad."

I jumped to my feet and looked over his shoulder and read as he read. The writing was impressed deep into the paper by a hand more comfortable holding a hammer than a pen.

Dear Mike, Jay, and Gina:

You got yourself a deal, Mike. I feel strange taking money from my own boy, but I'm proud you're making it and I sure need to see you all again. It's been a long time. I'll be down on Easter on PSA Flight 306, arriving into Burbank at 9:50 in the morning. When is your *Vice Squad* going to play? I've been looking for it in the *TV Guide*. You don't know how proud I am of you and Jay, son. Tell your mother hello for me, and I'll see you on Easter.

Love,
Dad

Mike handed her the letter.

"What's he want now?" she said.

"Dad's gonna visit," I said.

"Just for a couple of days," he said, swallowing. "I sent him the plane fare."

"You what?"

"I sent . . ."

"With the money I gave you?"

"It was mine."

"Not to throw away. What the hell's the matter with you?" She tossed the letter aside. "Where's he going to sleep? You wanna tell me that? Huh?"

"He can have our bed," I said.

"The hell he can."

"Me and Mike'll sleep on the floor."

She slapped the table. I looked away into the living room. "He isn't staying in this apartment," she shouted. On TV Curly made whooping noises while he struggled to free his hand from the vise. Moe clubbed him with a broomstick. Larry ran in circles, shrieking. "That goddamn idiot box," Mom screamed, clutching her head, rising. "It's driving me crazy." I went to turn it off when there came a knock on the door.

Mike answered it without a pause. He just wasn't thinking. A fucking sheriff stood in the hallway.

"Is Mrs. McKinney in?"

"Who?"

"McKinney," the sheriff said.

"No one here by that name."

"Oh?"

"Might want to check down the hall." Mike paused to rub the back of his neck, to lower his eyes. "We're the Bains."

"Then let me talk with Mrs. Bain."

"She's not in."

The sheriff half smiled and stepped past Mike into the living room. Now he could see her as I could, huddled beside the kitchen table with her mouth open, holding her breath. He pulled a sheet of paper from his back pocket and pushed it into her hand. "Mrs. Virginia Glass wants to see you in court, ma'am," he said, just before he left, quickly as he'd come. He slipped past Mike without another word.

I turned off the TV.

For a full minute Mom stood barefoot in the kitchen, her bathrobe hanging slack on her body, staring down at the paper in her hand. Finally she moved to the couch and sat and hung her head between her knees and took long, deep breaths. Mike went to her side. "I'm sorry," he mumbled. "Really, I am, really." Without raising her head she held the subpoena in both hands, between both thumbs, and she tore it in half.

My brother grabbed the newspaper off the floor and I followed him into our bedroom. Closed the door. He tossed the paper on top of his new file cabinet. Later he'd record the obituary onto an index card and file it away under D for Daniels. For now, though, he just stared at me.

Stacked in the corner beside the cabinet were the empty crates that once held his collection. Mike pointed to them.

I sighed.

"Better start packing again," he said. "We have to get out of here fast."

11

Debra Swanson had starred in dozens of films. Mostly she played one character. A streetwise blonde with a quick wit. What set her apart from the others of her time wasn't so much her beauty as her gruff voice and the sexual innuendos she became famous for. Her last home was built on a quiet street in the Fairfax district, only a few miles from our old apartment in Hollywood. Birds-of-paradise grew along the path that led to the front door. Roses bloomed beside the porch. It was a beautiful two-story Spanish-style house made of white stucco with a terra-cotta tile roof. Sycamores shaded the lawn. This was the second time Mom had seen the place inside and out. It was our first. We pulled up into the driveway in a brand-new rented Cadillac.

Mom shut off the engine. "The realtor's name is Mr. Conroy," she said, looking at me, then Mike. "And your father is what?"

"An executive," I said.

"For who?"

"Lockheed."

"And where is he?"

"On a business trip."

"Good, but where?"

"Texas."

"When's he coming back?"

"In two weeks."

If Mike was listening, Mom couldn't tell. He was staring at the house. "Did you hear me?" she said. "What's your name?"

"I don't think we can afford this place."

"That's not what I said."

Mike exhaled. "Miller," he said. "The Millers. We've gone over it a hundred times."

She glared at him. "Don't get smart with me, damn it. If you hadn't screwed up we wouldn't have to move. C'mon now and smile," she said, opening her door, climbing out. We did the same. "Mr. Conroy wants to meet you. Remember, we've just come back from church."

Mike and I wore slacks and white shirts. Our shoes were shined. Mom wore a pants suit with a low neckline. Her lips were painted red, and her hair was piled on top of her head in a neat bun. Together we walked up the path lined with birds-of-paradise.

"Call him *sir*."

"I will."

"Mike?"

"I know," he said.

"And don't slouch," she told me. "And tuck in your shirt."

Suddenly she smiled and waved her hand. Mr. Conroy stood in front of the living-room window, waving back. A few seconds later Mike and I were standing in a tiled entrance hall, shaking hands and introducing ourselves to the man. Behind him was a staircase with a solid oak banister. A spacious living room looked off to our right.

Mr. Conroy nodded at Mike. "I heard you're an actor," he said. "Do you know who used to live here?"

But Mom pulled Mike to her and hugged him before he could answer. "I already told him," she said. "You should've seen his face light up. He couldn't wait to get here. Isn't that right, honey?" She pulled me under her other arm. "So was my youngest. Weren't you?" She paused to smile at us. "You wouldn't believe how long we've been looking for a house in this neighborhood. My husband says, 'Honey, find our family a decent home in the Fairfax area. Rent one if you have to.'" Mom turned me loose so she could pat her own chest. "Of course that's easy for him to say, he's always off flying from one state to another. That man," she said, shaking her head. "He just doesn't know how hard it is to find a decent home in a good neighborhood nowadays." A big pout crossed her lips. "I'm sorry my husband couldn't make it again." She pulled Mike closer.

136

"He's in Texas, sir."

"Only for a couple of weeks," Mom said.

"Our dad's an executive for Lockheed," I said.

She laughed. "Mr. Conroy knows that already. Why don't you boys go look around?" Her voice dropped suddenly. She frowned. "If it's okay, I mean. There isn't any problem, is there?"

Mr. Conroy winked at Mike and me. He said he thought we seemed like fine young men and that the owners, who were in Europe for the holidays, would be pleased to have us. "So long," he said, raising a finger, "as you behave yourselves." He reminded us that the furniture was worth thousands of dollars. It couldn't be played on. Mr. Conroy pointed into the living room. "That couch," he said, "was owned by none other than Miss Swanson herself."

Mom touched his arm and assured him that we'd take excellent care of the place. "You and the owners are welcome to visit any-time," she said. "My boys are very well mannered." Mr. Conroy nodded. Finally there was the matter of a year's lease and other papers to sign. "Go on and pick out your rooms," Mom said over her shoulder as she followed him into another room.

Mike and I glanced at each other and rolled our eyes. The living room was furnished with a French couch, two love seats, and four armchairs, all covered with clear plastic. The carpet was bright white and a thicker, heavier plastic runner stretched from the fire-place into a den. Even the lampshades were wrapped in plastic. We wandered up the oak staircase and down a long hallway. "This is no place for us," Mike mumbled, looking into one of the bed-rooms. "Two damn months here and our money's gone." He snapped his fingers. "Like that. What if I don't find more work? How are we going to pay the rent? Ridiculous," he said. "Ridicu-lous."

Down the hall were three more bedrooms, each furnished with oak headboards and dressers. One had a fireplace and a window that overlooked the front yard. "At least Dad'll have a room to sleep in," I said, more to myself than Mike. At the end of the hall was a sun parlor, where we waited until Mr. Conroy had left. Below was the backyard and a three-car garage. Soon we heard the front door close, then an engine start up. Seconds later Mom let out a whoop that sounded through the house. She called up to us.

"Honey?"

I punched Mike in the arm. "C'mon," I said. "Cheer up. There's nothing we can do about it now." So we shuffled back downstairs to the living room.

Mom threw her arms around Mike and hugged him. "If you want to make money," she said, "you gotta look like you have it. And you're gonna make it, baby, lots of it." He smiled, though it wasn't much of one. She stepped back and held a ring of keys over her head and shook them and turned in a circle. "Can you believe it? Us here?" She kicked off her pumps and fell back on the French couch. The plastic made a crinkling noise. "It's just the beginning, too . . . just the beginning of a lot more to come." Mom ran her hand over one of the cushions. "Miss Debra Swanson sat here, right here, right in this room." She tossed her head back and laughed. "Didn't think he'd rent to us, did you?" Batted her eyes. Laughed again. "Help the butler unload the Cadillac," she said dramatically, tossing Mike the keys. He caught them. "I'll be upstairs freshening up."

Outside, in the driveway, Mike unlocked the trunk.

"Do you think he was bullshittin'?" I said. "That Mr. Conroy?"

"About Debra Swanson?"

"Uh-huh."

"I could find out," he said. "Know how she died?"

"No."

"A car wreck. Decapitated."

From inside the trunk he pulled out a pile of Mom's dresses on wire hangers and draped them across my arms. "I believe she was even riding in a Cadillac when it happened. What do you think of that?" he said, reaching into the trunk again. He rested a box of books on the rear fender and removed a paperback from it. "Ever read *The Man with the Golden Arm*?" I shook my head. "You'll like it," he said. "It's your kind of book. You have to read if you're going to write, you know." Mike stuffed it into my back pocket. "You're still writing, aren't you?"

"A little," I said, lying. "Off and on."

"Anything you want to show me?"

"Not yet."

He reached over and roughed up my hair. "To the top, right?"

"Right."

138

"Then you'll have to do better than off and on. Let's get this boat unloaded." As we started along the path to the front door he stopped for a second and looked up at the house and sighed. "Damn it, Jay, that was *my* money." He smacked his lips. "What a waste."

I finished *The Man with the Golden Arm* in six days. They were nearly full days, though, because I was a slow reader. Words within sentences sometimes jumped ahead of themselves. I'd have to reread lines over and over until they made sense, and in doing so I memorized whole passages. By the time I reached the end I knew as much about the story as I did about how it was put together sentence by sentence, paragraph by paragraph, page by page. Details of character and plot stuck in my mind. Nelson Algren wrote about the people I thought I wanted to write about. When I finished *The Man with the Golden Arm* my brother gave me another by Algren called *A Walk on the Wild Side*. I read it in five days, mostly at night, lying in bed waiting for Mike to get home.

We had our own rooms now, which I didn't like much, as it was awfully lonely. I missed the talks we used to have while we lay in bed and grew drowsy. In those moments before sleep it seemed we could speak more openly and freely than we could during the day. Knowing he was near helped me rest easier, though I don't suppose our sharing a room would've made any difference now. He'd taken to staying out late and stumbling home drunk. Twice in two weeks I'd woken up in the early-morning hours and found him passed out with his clothes on. The room would reek of alcohol. I'd open the window to let in some fresh air, and with it would come the moonlight. A poster of Montgomery Clift in *Judgment at Nuremburg* hung on the wall over the bed where my brother lay, his chest rising and falling. For a while I'd stand there, shaking my head and looking down at that handsome face, the thick dark hair and long eyelashes. I'd take off his shoes and cover him with a blanket and then return to my room. Come dawn I'd hear him closing the window—shivering, I thought—because it was cold out.

When Mom went to work in the evening, and Mike was out, I'd take a walk around the neighborhood. The houses were like our place in that they were all spacious and expensive, but it didn't seem as if anyone lived in them. Even during the day or on weekends, when I thought most people would be out mowing the lawn or working on the car, our neighborhood was empty. Quiet. There were no kids around, and only occasionally did I see another person. Usually it was a maid in one of the living-room windows, or maybe a gardener hosing down the driveway. Now and then I noticed the same couple walking a Pekingese. And once, on a night before Easter weekend, I spotted a paper boy.

His bike was parked on the sidewalk outside a big brick house. Ivy covered the walls. He was on the porch, talking to an older man. "We'll be gone for a few days," the man said. "I want you to stop delivery until the first." The paper boy made a note of it on a small pad he carried and the man opened his wallet and gave him a dollar. At the time I just walked on, not thinking anything of it until later. It was like our mother used to tell Mike about opportunity, and how sometimes it can be staring you straight in the face and you won't recognize it. I didn't then, but I would soon enough. That next day Dad flew into town.

Mom kept the Cadillac for the occasion. Our Nova, which Mike had picked up two weeks earlier, was parked out of sight in the garage. We arrived at the PSA gate in Burbank just as Dad was stepping off the plane. In one hand he held a small suitcase, and under his other arm he cradled a brown grocery bag that was leaking at the bottom. On his face was a smile. His cheeks were pink, flushed from working in the sun. He had on a bright-blue Hawaiian shirt open at the throat and he smelled of Old Spice. We hugged him. I took the suitcase, Mike the bag.

"Where's your mom?" he said.

"Out front."

"Circling around," Mike said. "She couldn't find a parking place."

The sliding glass doors of the terminal hummed open. Dad put his arms around us as we headed to the sidewalk. Cars passed on the street. "Good to see you boys," he said, grinning. "Goddamn how I missed you all." He squeezed us. "How's your mother?" Just then she maneuvered the Cadillac into the loading zone. His grip on my shoulder grew slack. I glanced up at him a second before Mom tapped the horn. Those red cheeks of his had suddenly gone pale.

"Relax now, Dad," Mike said, stepping off the curb. "Please try not to lose your temper. I want us all to get along for a change."

*   *   *

In the bag was a twenty-pound Butterball turkey. With it he brought a jar of Old Hickory Smoked Salt, garlic powder, a box of Bell's poultry seasoning, and a bottle of Andre sparkling wine. "Cheap stuff," Mom called it, as he was unpacking the bag. She was leaning against the stove. Her hair was fixed with a curl at each temple, and from her ears hung chrome hoops that shook when she let out a shrill laugh. "The least you could've gotten was Korbel." Mike and I exchanged looks. "You still haven't said what you think." she said.

"About what?"

"The house."

"I'd rather not say in front of the boys."

"Why's that?" Mom said, raising her eyebrows. "You ashamed of something?" Dad didn't answer. We'd already shown him around and he'd done exactly what Mike had done when he first saw the house, which was to wag his head in disgust, or disbelief—maybe both, I'm not sure—but Dad's silence certainly irritated her. "I'd say we were doing pretty good for ourselves without your help, wouldn't you?" Dad shrugged and carried the turkey to the kitchen sink. He was stripping it out of its plastic wrapper as she came up from behind and slipped her arms around his waist. Her voice was sweet in his ear. "Better here," she said, "than that slum you had the boys living in. I mean I think I deserve a little credit. You haven't even given me a kiss yet." Dad set the turkey in the sink, turned, and leaned over to kiss her, when she pivoted on her toe and stepped away. "So tell me," she said, matter-of-factly. "How's Marissa?" He inhaled deep through his nostrils. A long moment of silence passed. "Is she still cleaning houses?"

"Let's not start, honey."

"Start what?"

"You know," he said. "Not now, not in front of the boys."

"What's to hide?"

"Nothing."

"It's over, isn't it?"

"Yes."

"It's in the past."

"Yes."

"Forgive and forget. The kids understand that." She flipped her head back and laughed. "I don't know why you're afraid to talk about her." Again, when Dad returned to the sink, she slipped up from behind and put her arms around him. "Marissa was such a good little housekeeper. The best we ever had, wasn't she, David? It'd be a shame to lose her."

Dad winced and jammed his hand inside the turkey and pulled out the gizzards and threw them into a saucepan. "They've moved," he muttered. "Her and Louie are getting a divorce. Now don't push it anymore, Gina. I've about had it." He turned the water on over the turkey, rinsing it. "I didn't come four hundred miles to fight."

At that my brother rose from the kitchen table where we'd been sitting listening to all of this. "Can I help with the turkey?" he asked. "I want to learn how to do it."

But Mom spoke before Dad could respond. "Makes it awfully convenient, doesn't it?" she said. "I mean now with Louie out of the way."

That snapped him. His face turned bright red. Down came his fist on the counter. "Stealing the boy's money, damn you," he shouted. "How else could you get in this house? You think I don't know? You think the IRS is gonna settle up with us when you're living here?" He pointed a finger toward the front door. "They see this place and they're gonna say what? Huh?" He made a dumb face. "Square it with the poor McKinneys? Nooo. Why they got all *kinds* of money."

"You been talking with the IRS?"

"Our attorney has."

"Is that how they found us?"

"Bullshit."

"You told. Did you give them our new address too?" She looked at Mike. "Hear that, honey? That's your daddy for you."

"It's a lie, son."

"Now do you boys understand?"

"I'm trying to settle up."

"For what?"

Again Dad slammed his fist on the counter. "For what we can afford," he shouted. "*Payments*. Just to get them off our backs, Gina, just so we don't gotta hide anymore. You got no business," he said, shaking his head. "No business driving a Cadillac and living here with Mrs. Glass and the goddamn IRS and who else I don't know on our tail."

Mom began pacing the kitchen. Slowly a grin spread across her lips. "I'll drive that Cadillac to Arizona," she said, laughing. "I'll ride right past that old bitch's house."

"Like hell you will."

"And then I'll drive it by the IRS."

"Shut up."

"And I'll honk the horn. I'll wave." She threw her hands into the air. "Fuck the IRS. Fuck Mrs. Glass," she screamed. "I hope the bitch rots in hell with her husband." Suddenly Mom pushed past Mike and grabbed the bottle off the table. "Let's celebrate, David. C'mon, honey, it's Easter." She glanced at the clock on top of the refrigerator. "It's almost noon. I'm sure you could use a drink about now. Open your cheap wine." She shoved the bottle into his chest and he took it. "You know," she said, turning, staring at Mike and me, "your daddy isn't perfect like you boys think."

Finally she stormed off upstairs.

For a long time none of us said a word. Dad put the bottle down and patted the turkey dry with a towel while my brother rummaged through the cupboards for the roaster. He wanted to learn, as he'd said, how to cook a turkey. And Mike watched, all right, while our father seasoned the bird and stuffed it, but there was a blank, vacant look in his eyes. I knew then that he wasn't paying a damn bit of attention and that later, if I asked him what spice was what, he wouldn't have been able to tell me. After they'd gotten it into the oven Dad washed his hands, took two glasses from the cupboard, and went upstairs with the bottle of wine. He was gone for quite a while.

Clear from the kitchen I heard the cork pop and hit the ceiling. A few minutes later I wandered into the entrance hall for Dad's suitcase, which was sitting beside the front door, and I heard the headboard rattle against the wall. Her bedroom was right above me. I'd intended to haul the suitcase to the guest room—out of sight, out of mind, I thought. I hoped that if they drank enough and it got late enough that any question of Dad sleeping in a motel tonight would be forgotten or dismissed. Instead I left the suitcase where it rested and listened to the sounds coming through the ceiling. I imagined it was powerful and good love and that they were sweating. I felt sure that if Dad hadn't been seeing Marissa, if he hadn't lied, then it had to be a long time for him and even longer for Mom and that this was what they needed. Then I heard her scream. At first I actually smiled to myself, because I thought it was from pleasure and that they were enjoying themselves and it would help them to make up. But what I thought at that moment was blind. The screams continued. I took a step up the stairs, then stopped, as did Mike, who was standing beside me now, holding my arm. Once she called out our names. Not until I was years older did I realize that my brother hadn't been trying to stop me and that it wasn't simple cowardice that kept us standing there quietly, listening, until I felt dizzy. We returned to the kitchen and basted the turkey. Mom didn't come down for Easter dinner that night and later, when our silence proved too much for Dad, he phoned the airport.

Mike rose from the table in the middle of the meal. He just set the napkin on his plateful of food and left the house without his jacket. And it was cold outside. When I walked Dad out to his taxi soon afterward, down the path past the birds-of-paradise, I could see my breath in the night air. A checkered cab idled in our driveway behind the Cadillac. Dad kissed the top of my head.

"You comin' back?" I said.

"Sure."

"When?"

"Hard to say, son." He stared down at the ground. From inside the cab a radio dispatch squawked, crackled. "It won't be for a while."

"But you just got here."

"I'll be back."

"You can't just go."

"Tell your mother I'm sorry," he said. "For what good it'll do, I don't know. Tell Mike the same. I'm sorry." He opened the door and set his suitcase inside and then hugged me. "Soon as I get on my feet, I'll send for you. We'll take a trip, huh? Maybe up to the Chetco. Do a little fishin'." He slipped into the taxi and shut the door. I stepped back. The cab rolled down the driveway onto the street. I watched until the red taillights faded and disappeared up the block.

A light burned in Mom's room above the porch. Her hand was just pulling the drapes shut, and for a moment it seemed to me as if she could've been waving. I thought I ought to go up and find out how she was getting along, if there was something, anything, I could do for her, but I didn't want to see her. Not now. My throat swelled. I feared seeing her just as I'd feared seeing that side of our dad, the ugly side, the one that kept me from the bedroom then as it did now. It was the side of the man who had gotten into a taxi, not my father, but an imperfect stranger.

I drew an *X* on the back-door window with a diamond glass cutter. In my rear pocket was a flashlight and a roll of duct tape. Rubber gloves covered my hands. The idea was that when you tapped along the lines, after you'd taped them, that the pane would snap into four neat triangles. Then you reached inside and unlocked the door and that's that. A clean, quiet entry. I'd seen it done a dozen times on *'Thief for Hire,* but I soon discovered from this experience, and one other, that cutting glass in the frame was plain, simple bullshit. It just didn't work. After tapping my lines with the butt of the cutter for what seemed like forever, glancing over my shoulder all the while, sweating and growing more nervous, I ended up busting it out. The crack sounded through the neighborhood. Glass shattered and fell to the floor inside. For a minute I crouched close to the ground, listening for noises or footsteps, but it was quiet except for the crickets in the garden. I rose and reached through the broken window and felt for the doorknob. Seconds later I was inside the kitchen of the brick house around the block from my own.

I wasn't one of those messy, inconsiderate burglars—the kind who tears a home apart. I believed I could go about my business quickly and well without disturbing the order of things. As I moved from one room to another I kept the beam of my flashlight below the level of the windows, so that anyone who might've passed outside wouldn't spot it skirting along the walls. My heart beat fast, but it was more from excitement than fear. There wasn't much in particular that I wanted, except money, and I went through every closet and every drawer without finding a cent. But in the dining room, inside a walnut china cabinet, I did find a box of real silverware, which I thought I could pawn for a decent price. That I put on the floor near the back door, where I could pick it up on my way out. Then, in the living room, next to an expensive stereo, I flipped through a shelf of records and came across a Byrds album I'd wanted. The stereo itself was too big to carry.

And upstairs in the master bedroom I spotted a nice portable tape recorder. It was on the nightstand, where, in the drawer, I found a Smith & Wesson .38 police special. Seeing it gave me a jolt, as I knew that the man who lived here—if he'd been home— just might've used it on me. Only when I aimed the flashlight on it, I noticed the chambers in the cylinder were empty. What protection was an unloaded gun? I thought, holding it in my hand, feeling its weight. The bluing was worn silver in places, and the sight was chipped. For a moment I considered leaving it, because I had no use for a gun, let alone a beat-up one, yet I figured it was too good of a find to pass on. So I emptied a pillowcase and dropped it inside, along with the tape recorder.

That's right.

That's what I did. Then I left through the back door. It couldn't have been more than fifteen minutes after I'd entered. My entire shirt was damp with sweat. The pillowcase bounced against the side of my leg as I walked quickly, but not too quickly, down the driveway of the brick house. In it was the box of silverware, the tape recorder, the *Fifth Dimension* Byrd album, and that fucking .38 I never should've taken.

12

Saul Leiberman was scared. He'd spent a year on active duty in Vietnam and four in therapy after he was discharged. Once, on his way back from a motel, having already dropped Cindy off at home, a crop duster buzzed his car on the Ventura Freeway outside Encino. His breathing became short. Soon his hands began to shake, his jaws locked, and Saul swerved across traffic into the emergency lane. The driver behind him hit the brakes, fishtailed, and cursed out the window in passing. Two others honked. Saul cut the engine and stared over the wheel, resisting the urge to drop to the floorboard and cover his head. The radio faded in and out between stations. Static. Then the weather report. A constant rush of cars continued to zip by his own.

An hour later night fell and the streetlamps along the freeway came on. He reached for his wallet and flipped it open. There in the weak light he studied the picture on his license, silently repeating to himself, *Saul Leiberman . . . three-four-seven-oh-eight Sherman Way, Apartment two-oh-nine . . . Saul Leiberman . . .* until he found the courage to start the engine, put the transmission into gear, and maneuver his Mustang back onto the road. He vowed then and there that if he made it home he'd never again take his life or that of another into his own hands. Not with two tons of metal. Not in his state of mind.

At his studio apartment he swallowed two Miltowns, washing them down with vodka. His doctor had prescribed the pills for times like these, when memories kept him from sleep and his nerves on edge. But Saul had gone through three bottles of them in as many months and the doctor had cut him off. It had to stop. The next day he woke up groggy and entered therapy at the VA in Santa Monica, only he rode the bus to his appointment. His red Mustang with yellow flame painted on the fenders sat now, gathering dust in the carport. Mechanically it was still in fine condition, except for the battery, which had gone dead a long time ago.

Saul's affair with Cindy, like my brother's, began as a working scholar. At his audition he'd shown not exactly talent but a kind of raw anger—one, Cindy thought, that if harnessed might someday make him a fine actor. Range would come with control. He was also handsome, with brown hair and a square jaw and long powerful arms. A week after Saul was given the scholarship, though, Marrin checked into the hospital for extensive tests. What first began as a numbing of his right foot, and later the leg, before the paralysis set in, was thought to be the result of a stroke. The tests soon proved otherwise, and the next day the bad news circulated through the class. Saul bought a card and had the others sign it and then gave it to Cindy that evening as she was climbing into the Mercedes on her way to the hospital. She thanked him and then, suddenly turning away, began to cry. He put his arms around her to console her. She wrapped her arms around him, too, feeling the muscles in his shoulders that before she'd only been able to admire from a distance, the tanned, hard biceps, breathing in the scent of his hair. Soon her lips were on his neck, but he didn't pull away out of fear or loyalty to Marrin, because he wanted her, too. He had from the first audition. The card didn't make it to Marrin that night.

It started off as a tender, quiet, gentle kind of love. They were in need of comfort, they told themselves, of warmth, because they had their problems—yes, they had them and this eased them— and the sex was only a way of consoling each other. But the sex soon got better, stronger, more urgent, sometimes almost violent in its power. They made love at Saul's studio apartment, occasionally in a motel, and once they shared a weekend in Palm Springs. For months, while Marrin was checking in and out of the hospital, they carried on in what they thought was secrecy. Only it wasn't secrecy. Leitha suspected from the beginning, after the second late-night phone call from her mother telling her she was visiting a friend. "I'm on my way home," she said. "Don't wait up for me." Then when Marrin finished the tests, the phone calls changed. "Don't wake your dad," she'd say instead. "He needs all the rest he can get. I'm on my way home now." And Leitha never did wake her father, not because he didn't already suspect, and not because she didn't want to disturb him, but because she didn't want to hurt him with the knowledge that she herself knew what her mother was doing. Those nights she would lie awake listening for the jingle of her mother's house keys, the front door opening and closing, then footsteps down the hall into the bedroom, followed by her father's voice rising out of the quiet. Leitha turned twelve that summer, and for not waking her father, for remaining silent, Cindy bought her a championship Arabian mare.

The affair ended like it did with Mike—Marrin grilling Saul in front of the entire workshop, embarrassing the hell out of everyone. The difference was that by this time Saul had fallen in love with Cindy. He wanted to marry her, and he told her so, but she had never taken him all that seriously. He was a handsome young man, a nice man, and that's where it stopped. That's also about the time when they last made love in the motel, after she turned down his proposal, when he dropped her off home, the day he vowed to quit driving.

It was Saul who told my brother that if he let himself be drafted, and he made it back alive with all of his limbs, that he might be wiser for the experience but that no one would give a damn. He resented those who split for Canada or who went off to college on a deferment while he, Saul Leiberman, was watching his buddies die. Because he hadn't hid. Because he hadn't run. Because he had fought and fought hard. Yet there were many times since his return, as the war dragged on and the protests mounted, that he felt like a fool for ever having supported it. Now he no longer wished 'Nam even on the supposed enemy. But what hadn't changed, and what really bothered Saul, were those in the class who asked him if he'd ever killed anyone and what it was like. How did it *feel*? They needed to know for a scene, a character. And they'd say it so innocently, like children—stupid fucking children—as if he had no conscience, no memory, no heart. That question Saul always answered with a cold, indignant stare.

My brother had sense enough not to ask him about his experiences, but rather how the hell to escape them. Two years in the service were two dangerously spent years away from Hollywood. Work had just begun to come his way, and if he left now and he returned intact when his stint was up, who in the business would remember him? Who, like Saul had said, would care? Leaving the country or going underground was out of the question.

It was failure, though, not the war, that became Mike's greatest fear. He once told me that he'd be either a bum or a star and that nothing, no one, not the draft or anything else, could get in his way. If he even thought of falling short of his goal then he might one day compromise it, and that in itself was a disgrace. Minor success was a tease one step shy of failure. Acting had been his dream since he was five years old, when he'd see a movie and then come home and do skits and impersonations while Mom and Dad watched. They'd applaud, laugh. To them at his age it may have been cute, but to my brother it was serious even then. Now he had a career to protect. He'd wanted to discuss it with Dad on Easter, if only to hear his own voice, except the timing had been rotten. Mom had no advice. So it was in Saul Leiberman, minutes before the workshop began, that my brother confided.

They were loosening up onstage. Stretching their muscles. A dozen other actors had also paired up, one leaning over the other, patting along the spine in short quick chopping motions. Saul rolled his neck and spread his feet. "I'm not exactly the best guy to ask, if you know what I mean. I pulled my weight." He bent over and touched the floor. Mike did the same but he couldn't quite make it, as he wasn't as limber, and the strain showed on his face. "Did you ever fuck up when you were a kid?" Saul said.

"Like how?"

"A felony, man. You got a record?"

"No."

"Ever see a psychiatrist?"

"No."

"Got flat feet?"

"No."

"A bad back? Ulcers?" he said. "A bad heart? Anything like that?" They were looking at each other from upside down. "You could cut off your hand."

"Be serious."

"Split to Canada."

"I told you I can't."

"What can I say then? There's no more college-boy shit, and you're prime material." He laughed. "You'll look sharp in uniform."

"It's not funny."

"Try for a C.O."

"I'd still have to serve."

They straightened up together. "At least you wouldn't see action. They'd give you some office job. Easy time, man, easy time." He ran a hand through his hair, which had gotten messed from bending over. "That's what I'd do if I had it to do again. The board call your number?"

"Not yet."

"So relax."

"How? I'm eighteen. My ass is on the line."

Saul grinned. "You got, say, a year left. I'm talking between the time they call your number, the physical, and boot camp." He laughed again. "Better have a good time now, man, because you ain't gonna get many in the 'Nam."

Mike clasped his hands behind his back and stretched as far forward as he could so that the muscles in his legs and arms ached. Somehow, some way, he had to get out of it. He held the position while he counted from ten backward, staring hard at the floor, until he saw silver specks floating around his head.

"Please just *sign* them," she said. "I know, I know, but it's too late for that. . . . We've gone over this before, haven't we? . . . No, you can't come by for a drink. . . . You know how it always turns out. . . . There's nothing more to talk about. . . . Yes, yes,

I'm listening. . . . Baby, I wish you wouldn't say that. . . . Do we have to go through all this again? . . . Of course I still love you. . . . No, it doesn't involve Mark. . . . Please don't call him that. . . . He didn't know. . . . Yes, I'm alone now but we're going out later. . . ."

Marrin thumped his cane on the floor.

A young actress sat Indian-style centerstage under the spots, cradling an imaginary phone receiver on her shoulder. She uncrossed her legs and pulled her knees to her chest and hugged them.

"Intense," he shouted. "You must be intense."

Silence.

"What is it you want?"

She blinked, confused.

"What? Tell me."

"For him to sign the papers."

"Don't be simple-minded."

"I want a divorce."

"You want to hurt him."

In the back row Mike shifted in his seat next to Saul's, watching like the others, only he kept his head partly lowered. A hand covered his brow. They were doing sense-memory improvs today, emotional warm-ups. The girl onstage had picked her own subject. "I still love him, though," she said. "We just couldn't make it work and we tried, we tried."

"Clichés."

"That's really the way it happened."

"Bullshit," he growled. "You had another man."

"But I still loved my husband."

"Before you met this Mark?"

"I know what you're thinking," she said. "But you're wrong. That's not the reason."

Marrin pointed his cane at her. "I still loved him, I still loved him," he said in a high-pitched voice, mimicking her. "Such a sweet line of shit. If you loved him then why the hell did you fuck around? Why the divorce? The point that brought you there was painful and frustrating and it haunts you and it ought to. And because it haunts you, it hurts you, and because it hurts you, you need to absolve yourself by hurting him. The least you can do is be honest to your art." He turned in his seat and smiled at the

151

class. "Is that simple enough for her? Am I being clear?" When no one answered he faced the stage again. "Don't ever, and I mean ever, waste our time with a scene involving memories and emotions either you don't want to understand or which you're incapable of understanding. How it happened in your life," he said, slowly now, as if speaking to a child, "and how you reenact it onstage are two fucking completely different matters. I'd hoped you were beyond the lies, but I was wrong."

"But I am."

"You're what?"

"Beyond the lies." She got to her feet. Glared at him. "I thought, of everyone here, that you'd know the feeling too . . . but I was wrong."

The class was dead quiet.

"You're out."

"I quit."

"*Out.*"

Marrin slammed his cane against the armrest. The young woman stepped down from the stage and grabbed her purse and sweater from her seat and left. The old man remained quiet for a full minute. Finally he glanced over his shoulder to the back row. Mike sat up straight. He put his fingertips to his chest.

"Me?"

"No."

"Me?" Saul said.

Marrin nodded.

He hustled down the aisle up to the stage. Mike sat back and sighed.

"Close your eyes."

Saul did.

"Let your arms hang free, listen to your heartbeat. Now think of an image, a scene, a memory you don't want to remember, that hurts to remember, and I want to see you cry like you're never going to stop." He paused for a few seconds. "You have the memory?"

"Yeah."

"Is it fixed?"

"Yeah."

"Open your eyes."

He did.

"Move around, use the space. *See*."

Saul paced the stage wagging his head, sobbing loudly, but it was forced, faked, and there were no tears. Marrin shouted for him to stop. "Don't play with us," he said. "We can see through the shit. What's the memory, Saul? How old are you?"

"I'm five."

"And?"

"My parents are fighting."

"About what?"

"I don't remember."

"Oh, Christ."

Frowning, glancing at the floor, Saul slipped his hands into his pockets. Marrin took a deep breath. "Be serious, damn it. This is no game. Think again, think of a bagging party." A grin. "You took part in those, didn't you?"

He swallowed. "Once."

"Try that."

"No."

Marrin pointed to the door. "Anytime, Saul, anytime like the little bitch. It's your choice." For a while he paced the stage again, exhaling hard through his nostrils so that they flared. "Be specific," Marrin shouted. "Sights. Sounds. Objects. Smells. Recall the *moment*." Saul closed his eyes, his hands began to shake, he whimpered. "You're there now," Marrin said. "Open your eyes and *believe*." As he did the tears came quickly and the whimper became a sob and it was real.

"What'd you see?"

"Blood."

"Just blood?"

"Bodies."

"How many?"

"I don't know."

"Count."

"I can't, man."

"Try."

"Legs. Arms, man. Fucking *pieces*."

"Who do they belong to?"

"I don't know."

"Vietnamese?"

"Our own, my buddies." He grabbed his head in both hands.

"But I don't know who, man, *who*." Saul kneeled, grimacing as he reached for an invisible arm or leg, holding it out in his hands from underneath. A cry came from deep in his throat, he swallowed, and you could see the sickness rising from his stomach. Suddenly he dropped the arm, or the leg, and jumped to his feet. He reached over his shoulder for his rifle. Aimed it. Slowly he backed up to the edge of the stage and stopped, crying still, but without the tears now. Just the heaving of his chest. His face was sweating and his eyes were fixed.

"What'd you hear?"

"Moaning."

"Someone's still alive then?"

"Yes."

"Who?"

"Sergeant Davis."

"You see him?"

"Yes."

"All of him?"

"His leg's blown."

"Can you save him?"

"Yes."

Saul snapped the bolt back, then forward, throwing a shell into the chamber. He crept toward the spot onstage where his eyes were fixed, where the sergeant lay dying, and put the barrel to his head. He clenched his teeth. "Motherfucker," he screamed. "Motherfucker." Saul pulled the trigger and the gun recoiled. Again he pulled the trigger, again the gun recoiled.

"Beautiful," Marrin said. "Beautiful."

Again.

"That's enough."

Again and again.

In the back row Mike closed his eyes for a moment, trying to imagine what Saul was imagining, seeing if he could understand it, and he believed he could. The fury, the anger, the power. Blood for blood. No fucking around. That they would understand. He smiled and opened his eyes. Onstage Saul continued to fire over Marrin's protests, the rifle jerking in his arms with each blast until the clip was finally spent.

The next morning Mike phoned his agent. A secretary answered.

"Is Betsy in?"

"Who's calling?"

"Michael Casey."

"One moment."

A few seconds later Betsy came on the line. "I was just about to call you," she said. "Your *Vice Squad* airs next Wednesday."

"Great," he mumbled.

"Are you scared?"

"Very scared."

"I'm sure you did terrific."

"That's not what I'm nervous about."

"What is it then?"

"The draft."

"I see," she said.

"Do you know any psychiatrists?"

"Plenty."

"A sympathetic one?"

"Let me call and make an appointment," she said. "It'll be expensive, though."

"Thanks, Betsy."

"Don't tell your friends."

"I promise."

"And it doesn't always work."

"I know."

"They have to believe you're telling the truth."

"I'll make it true."

"You have to convince them, too."

"No problem," he said. "Thanks, Betsy, thanks."

"And one more thing."

"Yeah?"

"Can you ride a horse?"

A minute after their conversation he gathered his courage and phoned Marrins' house behind the theater. No one there. He dialed the Malibu number. It rang four, five, six times and he was just about to hang up when he got an answer.

"Hello?"

"Cindy?"

"Hang on."

"Leitha?"

"Who is this?"

"It's me, Mike," he said. "I need your help."

"Forget it."

"Could you just listen for a second?"

"I'm busy," she said.

"Please?"

Silence.

"I heard you're an expert with horses."

"I'm good," she said.

"You ride all the time, right?"

"So?"

"I mean you know horses."

"Get to the point already."

"I'm up for a role, a really good one, but I have to know how to ride. I need a coach," he said. "Will you?"

"Let me think about it."

"Maybe we could go out to dinner after?"

"Don't push your luck."

"Sorry."

He was about to tell her that his *Vice Squad* was airing the next week when the line went dead. Mike stared at the receiver for a good five seconds before he shrugged and returned it to its cradle.

Cindy came in from the redwood deck, where she'd been sunning herself. She wore her daughter's one-piece. A towel was draped over her shoulder.

"Who was that?"

"Mike."

"Why didn't you call me?"

"It wasn't for you."

"Oh?" she said, frowning. "Then what exactly did he want?"

"He wants me to teach him how to ride. For some part."

"You told him no, I hope."

They glared at each other from across the living room. Leitha, who had been wading her way through *Anna Karenina* before the phone rang, looked away and stretched out on the couch. "Why?"

she said, opening the book. "He's one of our best actors. Aren't we supposed to help them?"

The role was a two-part TV movie based on the life and times of Jesse James. The casting directors needed a half-dozen young men to play opposite Peter Fox and Iris Pane in what then was the biggest budget for a TV production in Universal's history. But they didn't want to use stuntmen any more than they had to, as a lot of it was to be shot on horseback, and so Mike had to at least learn how to rock in the saddle. He'd told his agent that he used to play polo, when actually he'd never been on a horse in his life. Water polo was what he meant. The audition was on Thursday. His lesson came on the Wednesday that his *Vice Squad* aired. He rose early that morning and shaved and showered and dabbed his cheeks with cologne. Gargled twice. He almost put on a good pair of slacks before he realized what he was doing and slipped into his Levi's.

They met at the workshop. From there they drove across town toward the coast and followed a winding road up through dry mountains opposite the ocean, down into the Malibu Canyon, and then along a dusty, poorly paved section more gravel than asphalt. At the end was the stables where Leitha boarded her Arabian mare.

Mike had to rent a horse. It was Leitha's pick. She'd phoned it in the night before so that when they arrived, parked, and climbed out of the Mercedes, the horses were already saddled and hitched outside the corral. "This is the one my father always rode," she said, drawing a hand along its neck. "We came here almost every weekend when I was a little girl. My dad used to be very athletic, you know." Leitha smiled at the horse. "Ebony's just an old gelding, though, not the liveliest anymore, but then you don't want a lively one to learn on." Mike stared at the horse, watching it flick its tail and shiver, the skin along its haunches shuddering. It was a huge smelly damn thing with a runny snout and flies buzzing around its eyes.

"Isn't he still beautiful?"

"Definitely."

"Look at his croup," she said. "Look at the way he holds his head."

"Nice."

"And those eyes."

They were large and brown and bloodshot around the rims. Foam hung from its lower lip. "It must weigh a ton," he said. The animal snorted then, its flanks quivering, its hoof pawing the ground. Mike stepped backward.

"Don't be scared," Leitha said. "They can sense it, you know, and they'll take advantage of it. Now grab the horn." She took hold of her own horse's saddle. "Slide your left foot into the stirrup like me, bounce once . . ." In one quick movement she straddled her horse. "And you're in."

Easy enough.

Only when Mike tried the maneuver he didn't give it enough bounce and he had to grasp the far end of the saddle so as not to fall. He pulled himself up with both hands, grunting, his face gone red from the struggle before he made it. He smiled sheepishly. "You'll have to work on your mount," Leitha said. "That won't cut it on film. Now take the reins . . . yeah . . . but like this." She held them in her right hand, her left planted on her hip. "When you want to turn right, lean right with the reins. Opposite for the left. Got it?"

"Yeah."

"Keep your back straight."

"Like this?"

"Perfect."

He expanded his chest, proud.

"It's not so hard."

"Not once you get the feel of him," she said. "How he moves, and the rhythm of his steps."

Mike had the reins in hand now and his back straight and his ass firm in the saddle when he turned and looked at Leitha there on her horse in Malibu Canyon. She was his own age, and maybe because of Cindy, or maybe in spite of her, he felt a sense of confidence rise inside of him. Not the little boy here, not the nervous kid, not like he would've been with her now if he hadn't first known her mother. So he thought, anyway. Leitha had her hair tied back in a ponytail and her legs looked lean and strong in blue jeans down to her cowboy boots, her thighs slightly flattened against the horse's ribs. A bit of sweat shone beneath her upper lip. She glanced away. The sun was hot in the canyon.

"How do you make him go?"

"Press your heels in gently."

He tried it and the horse clopped forward. A big smile spread across his face as he turned to look over his shoulder. She returned it, following him past the gates and up along a trail into the mountains. When it widened she came up beside him. "Don't hang on to the horn. Do like I'm doing and move with your horse," she said. "What's this part for, anyway?"

"A TV movie."

"A western?"

"Right," he said.

"Is it a lead?"

"No, but it's a good role."

"You'll get it."

"Think so?"

Leitha winked. "Easy," she said. "My mom says you're going to go far."

"What does your dad say?"

"He despises you."

"Do you?"

"Do I what?"

"Despise me."

"Oh please," she said. "I don't need this again."

They rode without talking for a few minutes. The canyon was barren except for the dry brown shrubs and some sickly trees. Farther up Mike could see the top of the mountain black from a fire.

"Does he know you're helping me?"

"You kidding? He'd kill me," she said. "I told him I was going out with a girlfriend. Mom knows, though, but I've got so much on her it's pathetic." She reached out and stroked her horse's mane. "When I think about how they've fucked up their lives, I don't see what right they have to tell me how to run mine. They don't take me seriously. I'm sick of pretending that everything's fine."

Leitha pressed her heels into the horse and trotted past him. He watched her in the saddle, her back arched, her hair swinging from side to side against her shoulders. Soon she'd reached the top of the mountain and waved down to him. He waved back and then jabbed the horse's sides. A few minutes later Mike drew the

animal up alongside hers, his knuckles white around the saddle
horn, both feet out of the stirrups. He was sweating. A cool
breeze blew. The view was of the blue Pacific as far as they could
see. He took a deep breath.

"You still haven't answered me."

Mike waited for her reply, staring at the burned ground, a
scorched rock. Ahead a charred tree lay in ashes.

"Do you?"

"Not too much," she said.

"It wasn't all my fault."

"There's nothing to explain."

"Just listen for a second."

"*You* listen." The horse shifted, startled, because she'd raised
her voice. Leitha yanked the reins. "I can't blame you completely,
okay, or I sure as hell wouldn't be here, would I?"

"Spite maybe?"

"Drop it."

"That's what I need to know," he said, "if that's the reason."

She jerked the reins again and headed back down the mountain.
For a minute he watched her, not knowing what to do, if he
should follow her or not, and wondering why the hell he'd ever
opened his mouth, or why he had pushed her. Damn it. He
pressed his heels hard into the horse, except he did it in the flanks.
The animal bucked and shot along the trail with Mike half in the
saddle, half out, hanging first on to the horn and then falling flat
to the side of it and wrapping his arms around the horse's neck.
The ground moved fast beneath him, and that's all he could see—
dust and black ash—because that's where his head was aimed.
Down. The hooves pounded the earth. He sped past Leitha.

"Pull up on the reins," she shouted, taking after him. "The
reins."

But he couldn't find them, although they were in his hand.

They drove back to Hollywood in silence. In the studio parking
lot Leitha let the engine idle while she stared over the wheel. A
dozen seconds passed. He didn't know what to say, or if he
should say anything. She looked bored and impatient. Finally he
felt for the handle, opened the door, and stepped to the ground.
The damn horse had bounced him around in the saddle all the

way to the stables before he discovered the reins and stopped it. Now he was stiff and sore from the waist down.

"My *Vice Squad* plays tonight," he mumbled. "You plan to watch it?"

No answer.

"Can I see you again?"

No answer.

"I apologize, okay?"

"Close the door," she said.

"Can I call you?"

"You have the number."

She put the car into gear. Mike shut the door and walked as she drove off. The first couple of steps made him wince. What he needed was a drink. Something cold, something strong to numb the pain. Something powerful enough to wash away the dust and ashes caught in the back of his throat.

Later that night Leitha polished off *Anna Karenina*. Her father was sitting on the couch in the den watching TV when she finished the book, closed it, and slipped out of her room. *Vice Squad* was playing. She came up behind him.

"You and Sharon have a good time today?"

"Huh?"

"At the stables."

"Yeah," she said. "It was fun."

On the TV two plainclothesmen grilled Mike. He was mumbling his lines, stuttering, trying to get the words out. Leitha put her hands on her father's shoulders and massaged the muscles around his neck while she stared at the screen. The plainclothesmen smiled at one another. Mike bowed his head, caught in a lie, but one not his own, not for himself. He was protecting the murderer.

"What d'you think of him?"

She shrugged.

Marrin looked up and put a hand on top of hers. "Is everything okay, honey?"

"Fine," she said. "He's good, isn't he?"

"Yes."

"But not really good."

"Not yet."

"Think he will be?"

"It depends on his agent," he said.

Onscreen Mike placed his fingertips to his temples as if he were trying to think, to remember. There was a confused look in his eyes. One plainclothesman rose from the interrogation table and ordered the other to book him.

"Same old shit," Marrin said.

"Seen enough?"

"Too much."

"Want to play a game of dominoes?"

"You set 'em up."

She went to the TV and reached for the knob as Mike was being escorted down a hall to a holding cell. Suddenly a close-up of his face filled the screen. His expression was fear and worry. She smiled faintly, eyes fixed on his until the cut. A Listerine commercial. The volume rose. Several seconds passed before she looked away, sighed, and remembered to turn off the set.

Mike wagged his head and blinked. Haze outlined the TV above the pool table where the same Listerine commercial was playing. It was his first time in a bar, and he'd been prepared to be carded and kicked out, but the bartender had served him without a glance. That was hours earlier. The place was practically dead, dark, and empty except for himself, the bartender, and a couple in a booth in the corner. He took a sip of his drink and set it down. After the commercial break, he watched himself onscreen sitting alone in a concrete cell. He held his head in his hands. Mike blinked again, trying to clear his vision, and smiled. They had had to retake the shot three times to get it right.

He caught the bartender's eye.

"Know who that is up there?"

"On the TV?"

"Yep."

But the scene had changed by the time the bartender turned and looked. "The little blonde, you mean?"

"Not her."

"Sweet, eh?"

"Just keep looking."

Mike nodded to himself, smiled. A minute passed. The bartender glanced at the clock next to the cash register. "The Dodgers are playing the Pirates tonight," he said. "I'm gonna have to switch the channel on you, buddy."

When the Dodgers came on Mike finished his drink and left. He didn't know or even care whether he'd given a fine performance or not. For now he was thinking of his stomach, his head, his vision. As he walked he took deep breaths and concentrated on his steps so as not to stagger or weave. He thought of Leitha and he held his chest up and out and he was able to walk straight for a couple of blocks. He wondered, too, if she had watched him tonight and if she'd been impressed, if he should phone and find out. But no, he thought, no. Tomorrow maybe, when he was sober and when she'd had time to cool off, maybe then he'd call.

Cars moved along the boulevard, headlights glancing off the buildings, making shadows of his body against the walls, then the sidewalk, stretching, then disappearing. As he continued along the street a faintness overcame him and he had to take hold of a lamppost to keep his balance. He closed his eyes. His head reeling, he saw himself, as if from a distance. A long shot viewed through a long dark tunnel full of traffic noise, echoing, looking in on himself there on that street in Hollywood. Happy, he should've been happy; anyone else in his situation would've been. Another actor, yes. Only he wasn't happy, not at all, but instead he was depressed and much much too drunk to wander home stinking of whiskey. He winced, feeling the dull pain move through his thighs, his buttocks. If not home, where? He couldn't just stand there. Walk. Open your eyes, he thought, doing it. Take long deep breaths, exhale and inhale, and let the scene dissolve now, fade.

Fade to black.

13

My brother was nominated for an Emmy as outstanding guest performer in a drama series for his role in *Vice Squad*. The night it aired I watched it alone, as Mom was working and Mike was out, but the next day I asked him about the part he'd done. How did he play my friend Eddie García so realistically? He gave me the dopey grin and rolled his eyes. "You have to become," he said. "Through detail, you place yourself into the mind and body of the imagined. The specific," he said, bobbing his head, "is what makes a performance convincing." But that was the workshop talking more than my brother. I don't believe Marrin taught him so much how to act as how to articulate what Mike already knew intuitively.

The point of it all is that being nominated for an Emmy before his nineteenth birthday made him a hot property around town. From here on out he was called in for interviews by name, not a composite, not just another actor thrown in with a dozen others who happened to fit the character description. Overall, things seemed to be looking up for the family, in that Mrs. Glass and the IRS hadn't shown themselves and there was enough money around the house not to worry about the rent. Mike also landed a different role in the TV movie based on Jesse James. *The Great Last Raid* is what it was called, and he was filming it on location in Montana the night of the Emmy ceremonies in Hollywood. The director told him he could fly into town for the night at studio expense. They'd shoot around him for the day. I imagine my brother thought a hell of a lot about hopping on a plane, but in the end he decided that the professional thing to do was stay on the set. Work came first. The director was impressed, not just with his commitment but his acting, too, and he used him again a few months later in another TV movie-of-the-week called *Bull Fire*.

Mom and I watched the Emmys together in the living room. She was in her bathrobe on the couch with her feet curled beneath her. I was stretched out on the floor. During the commercial break she nodded toward the mantle over the fireplace and grinned. "We'll put the Emmy there, huh? How about it?" She laughed and tossed her head back. "We'll have us a new El Dorado before the year's out. Watch and see," she said, "and it isn't going to be a rented one, either. I tell you your brother is going places, baby, big places."

Finally the moment came.

The host stood behind a podium and read aloud the names of the nominees. When he announced Mike, I took a deep breath and held it. Mom let out a small yelp.

The envelope was opened.

"And the winner is . . ."

Not Mike.

I slapped the floor and climbed to my feet. Mom smacked her lips.

"Turn it off," she said.

"Sonofabitch."

"Watch your mouth."

"They cheated him. The god . . ." But I caught myself as I flipped off the TV. "They cheated him."

Mom paced the living room, brooding, quiet. At the mantle she stopped, passed her hand along the top of it, and sighed. Then the phone rang. As she went to the den to answer it, I hurried to the kitchen and picked up the other line. I suspect we both thought it was Mike calling from Montana, only it wasn't.

Her tone was curt.

"He's not here."

"Could you tell him Leitha called?"

"Leitha who?"

"He knows me."

"I bet he does."

"From the workshop," she said. "I just wanted to congratulate him."

"For losing?"

"It's still an honor."

"Thank you," Mom said. "I'll be sure to give him your message."

Less than a minute after she'd hung up Dad phoned, but Mom wasn't speaking to him anymore, and she cut him short before I could even say hello. "I need to keep the line open," she said, in an uppity voice. "My son is trying to get a hold of me. Goodbye."

And she was right, as it turned out, because Mike did call seconds later, drunk in Montana, slurring his words. The connection was faint, fuzzy. "What the hell," he said, laughing. "It's a popularity contest." But despite the laugh he sounded depressed, and for good reason, I thought. He'd come so close.

A few days later, when Mike returned from Montana, he and Leitha began seeing each other for dinner, a movie, and occasionally they rode together at the Malibu stables. I don't know if she truly liked my brother or if she was dating him to anger her parents or if it was his career that made her warm up to him, as Mom might've suspected. Maybe she liked him for reasons I don't know a damn thing about. Whatever the case, my brother certainly liked her enough, loved her, even, and he was proud of his successes, too, although he wasn't what I'd call happy. Driven, yes, but not happy. Twice in the next six months his picture made the pages of *Tiger Beat*, and after *Where Are the Children?* aired he began getting fan mail from all over the country, not lots of it, yet enough to show that he was on the rise. All the things he'd dreamed about and worked for were finally taking shape and still there was something wrong, very wrong, which I'll go into soon enough. For now, at least, life was looking up for him.

As for myself, nothing much eventful happened in the coming months. I went to school off and on, made a couple of casual friends, though none worth mentioning, and I read two more novels in my slow plodding way. With *The Catcher in the Rye* I realized that Holden and I didn't have much in common. But when I read *Studs Lonigan* I felt here was a story I could connect with. It was a long one and I read the bulk of it while waiting, like I did a lot, for my brother to get home from wherever he happened to be. Other nights I read to calm myself after I'd been up to no good, so I could drift and sleep, as I had to rise early now before the sun rose. I'd gotten a job.

The ad in our neighborhood weekly read:

> YOU TOO CAN BE A WINNER
> BIG PRIZES/GOOD PAY
> DELIVER THE
> HERALD EXAMINER
> FOR YOUR NEIGHBORHOOD

The pay was bad but the contacts were good. Mike thought it was a great way for me to keep busy, to make a little money, to learn, as Dad often said, "the value of hard work," and he bought me a bike for my deliveries. I was doing fine, I figured, so long as I didn't get caught. I did another house when the husband of the place asked me to hold off delivering for a week, and I was on the lookout for still another opportunity. Summer would be the season, as that's when most people went on vacation.

What I took from the first house, which was actually my second, counting the house before I became a paper boy, was a Rolex watch, a pair of diamond earrings, a half-dozen records, a 1954 class ring from Dartmouth College, and a brand-new portable typewriter still in its box. I stole only what I could carry in my pockets or in the sack that hung on the handlebars of my bike.

Most of the stuff I stashed in a cardboard box overhead in our garage until I could decide what to do with it all. If I was going to pawn it, I wanted to do it all at once and be done with it. In the box, along with the .38 Smith & Wesson and the silverware I'd stolen earlier, were old textbooks that Mike no longer had a use for but couldn't bring himself to throw away. It turned out not to be a very safe spot, or a very bright idea, but then again I wasn't a very bright kid to be robbing houses in the first place. I do regret what I did. I don't feel any pride.

The typewriter I put in my room. "It was a prize," I told my brother, when he asked me about it. "For getting the most new subscribers."

"Do you know how to use it?"

"I'm trying."

"Want me to show you?"

He'd had typing in high school back in San Jose, and he taught me where to place my fingers, how to let them do the thinking, how not to look at the keys. "It takes practice before it becomes like second nature," he said. "Don't get discouraged. I have a typing manual around here for you someplace, only I don't remember where I put it." He furrowed his eyebrows. "It'll come to me."

Anyone with a lick of sense might've realized right then that I'd set myself up for one hell of a lot of trouble. But not me. My mind was on *"The Motorcycle King,"* and seeing it changed from longhand into type, which was about the only respectable thing I accomplished during those months. I stretched it from four pages to seventeen and felt that I could've gone on even longer with it. Above all, though, were the letters and how they came out when I hit the keys—no upside down *e*'s, no reversed *d*'s—and it was me doing it, doing it right, and I gained confidence. Seeing them appear on the page without having to think about them was like imprinting the letters in my mind over and over until, finally, it almost became like my brother had said—second nature. I had begun to see things in their proper perspective.

167

I decided, too, that after I finished the story and showed it to Mike, if he liked it and thought it was good, and if he'd correct my grammar for me, I just might send it off to a magazine. What magazine, I wasn't yet sure. I was hoping he'd have a few suggestions. The story had a whole new angle to it, as I'd made my main character a cat burglar and the new scenes were real with detail—the kind of detail I thought my brother would like.

And then I had another idea.

The more I read, the more I realized I couldn't tell the story I wanted to tell, the one that was growing now inside my head—not another "Motorcycle King," but something different, about a family like my own—without making it a long one. I had the characters, I thought. I had some of the scenes imagined, too. What I didn't have was the discipline to just sit down and figure out what was going to happen to this family, where I ought to begin, where the story would go, and how exactly it would end.

PART III:

To the Top

I imagine him back: his beauty
of feature wastreled down
to chin and wattles, his eyes
ratty, liver-lighted, he stands
at the door, and we face each other, each of us
suddenly knowing the lost brother.

—"The Sadness of Brothers"
by Galway Kinnell

I IMAGINED a late-night call. It came at the
end of a dream. An operator's voice crackled
over the line. Long distance. "Will you accept
the charges from Michael McKinney?"

"Is this some kind of joke?"

"No joke, Jay. It's me."

"Will you accept?" the operator said.

"I accept."

There came a click. Our line was private
now.

"Hey, little brother. How you doing?"

"Pissed off."

"Speak up," he said. "I can barely hear you." The line crackled again. Mike laughed. "It's a bad connection."

I raised my voice.

"Why'd you call?"

"You think Mom could handle it? Dad?" He laughed again. "How's my Frankenstein? I just wanted to see how you were getting along."

"How come you did it?"

"Because I had to."

"It was cowardly."

"I was depressed and tired," he said. "I needed rest, man. I humiliated myself and I wanted out."

"Coward."

"Let's not fight, okay? I can't do anything about it now."

I switched the receiver to my other ear.

"Mike, I want to know when you did it. What was the date?"

"Who gives a damn?"

"I do."

"It was last month."

"I know that."

"So forget it."

Scratchy, static noises sounded over the line. "You still there?"

"Yeah."

"Tell me."

"Really, I wasn't much concerned about the date." A long pause. "But I think it was the Fourth of July, or maybe the night before. Anyway, lots of firecrackers were going off."

"Good."

"Good what?"

"I guessed closer."

"Than who?"

"The coroner," I said. "I told him I

thought you'd been dead for a couple of days. He figured three or four. From the time you were found, I mean."

"Glad to hear you won the bet," he said sarcastically. "Still writing?"

"No."

"What's the matter?"

"Nothing to say. Nothing worth telling."

"Here's some material for you, little brother. Listen to this, man . . . *listen*, little brother."

The .38 went off in the background. The receiver bounced against the floor or a table or a countertop with a sharp bang. The line crackled, faded, then came the dial tone. Disconnected. Again.

14

My brother began spending long hours locked in his room reading, adding to his obituary collection, and reciting aloud lines from the different characters he'd played. Sometimes late at night I'd hear him creep past my bedroom on his way downstairs. A minute later he'd pass again with a glass, ice clinking against the sides, and I knew damn well he wasn't drinking water. Once I woke up to the roar of voices. Both were his, but one was that of an older man. Deep and authoritative. I sat up and listened. My brother shouted.

"Draft me."

"We just might."

"Go ahead. See what happens."

"Don't threaten me."

"No threat, man," Mike said.

"Sit down, boy."

"Up yours."

The other voice was silent for a few seconds, and when I heard it again it was calm. "Tell me, son. Be frank. Why . . ."

"I'm not your son."

"Mr. Casey."

"You got it, man."

"Why aren't you fit to serve?"

"Give me a gun," he said. "I'll serve."

"Cut the sarcasm."

"Give me the bullets, too," Mike shouted. "Fuck with me, I'll burn you. Don't mess with my life."

I rolled out of bed then and went to his door and tapped on it. Suddenly it was quiet in the room. "You all right in there?" I tried the knob; it was locked. "Open the door."

But instead of letting me in, after another long silence, he muttered that he was fine. "Go back to bed," he said. So that's what I did, except I couldn't sleep, because he kept pacing most of the night.

The next morning at breakfast, after I'd finished my paper

route, he acted like nothing had happened. And maybe nothing had, maybe he was just getting into character. Up until this time, although he drank a little too much, he seemed like he had matters under control. Nobody could've suspected him of being anything other than a healthy, ambitious young actor.

I first noticed a change when Mike stepped off the plane from Montana with a Stetson pushed back on his head. He spoke with a country drawl. At the time I figured he was just clowning around, making fun of himself and the character he'd played, and I enjoyed watching him in the way I might any decent performance. Mom, I suppose, thought the same in that he was behaving a little strangely, but what could she say now that he was working a lot? Now that the money was about to flow? Acting, after all, was the business of eccentrics. Only it was a good two days before he stopped wearing the cowboy hat, speaking with a drawl, and strutting around the house bowlegged as if he'd been riding horses most of his life.

Then there was the psychiatrist. Mike saw the man once a week for a few months before his draft-board interview, never missing a session except for when he was off filming in Montana. The particulars of what they discussed, I'm not clear on, yet I suspect that what started off as a ruse to dodge the draft turned up a lot more inside of him than he, or at least I, ever imagined there. Shortly after the suicide, as I was going through his belongings, I came across a copy of the psychiatric report that was given to the Selective Service. In it I read of a brother whom I did not know.

> The Selective Service System for him represents a critical situation. He expects to kill himself or to kill those who would come to take him away in self-defense, fully expecting in this instance to either be put in jail or again to terminate his own life . . .

The report said that Mike described Mom as a domineering, pushing, hysterical woman with a criminal background. As for Dad, he thought of him as being weak, at times distant, someone with whom he "yearned to have a better relationship," and also hoped to help financially. The doctor then went on to say that Mike had first come to him with the "chief complaints" of "symptomatic alcoholic abuse" and "recurrent feelings of failure." The report ended with a recommendation:

> An induction of this young man would result in a personal catastrophe of either suicide or homicidal violence. In either condition he would be of no service or use in the Armed Forces.

So it was, just a few months shy of his nineteenth birthday, that my brother received his notice to appear at the Armed Forces Entrance and Examining Station in Hollywood. The day before the appointment he stayed locked in his room, pacing back and forth, stopping to stare out the window, then sighing and throwing up his arms and pacing again. He skipped breakfast. He skipped lunch and he would skip dinner, too. Late that afternoon he wandered downstairs into the den and picked up the phone. Dialed. No one answered. He muttered a curse and headed back to his room. An hour later he tried calling again but without any luck.

That night he lay in bed sweating, scared, unable to sleep. His heart beat fast, and the hair along the back of his neck was wet, heavy. Finally he rolled out from under the sheets and headed to the den in his boxers and picked up the phone. Moonlight shone down the hall into the living room. He squinted at the numbers as he dialed, the receiver pressed to his ear, listening to it ring. One finger he kept poised over the hang-up button. A groggy voice answered.

"Hello?"

"Leitha?"

"Do you know what time it is?"

"Eleven?"

"More like one," she said.

"I've been trying to get a hold of you all day," he said. "Where've you been?"

"Out."

"Where?"

"That's my business."

Mike cupped the mouthpiece with his hand. "I need to talk," he said.

"I'm listening."

"I might be drafted tomorrow."

Suddenly her voice fell to a whisper. "My dad's up," she said quickly. "I have to go."

"Wait."

"Bye."

"Can you give me a ride in the morning?"

"I'll call you back in a minute."

"Seven-thirty, okay?"

"I gotta go."

They hung up. The minute passed, then two, then three. Mike stared down the hall into the living room. The plastic cover on the couch glistened in the moonlight that shone through the window. Debra Swanson sat there, he thought, starting for the kitchen to make himself a drink. Only it must've been without the damn plastic.

She picked him up in the Mercedes wearing a terry-cloth bathrobe over her pajamas. An empty cup of coffee rested on the floorboard. Her hair was tousled, held in place with pink barrettes. Loose strands curled around her ears. They drove into Hollywood, and on the way he told her about his plan. In the loading zone outside the station she turned in her seat and faced him. He looked like he felt. Hung over and scared. Red-eyed. Mike hadn't slept all night.

"Think it'll work?"

"It has to."

"But what if they don't believe you?"

Mike shrugged.

"You can't mean it."

"What?"

"This dumb plan of yours."

"It's not dumb."

"Part of it is, and you know it. All that killing stuff." She slapped the dashboard, and he turned away. "If it gets you out, fine. Good. But it's stupid if you really mean it." Mike reached for the door handle because he couldn't listen to her right now. Because he had to mean it if it was going to work. Still, he didn't want to scare her.

"Hey, you going to write to me if I'm drafted?" he said, as he climbed out of the car. She smiled.

176

"Need a ride home after?"

"If you can."

"Call me," she said. "Ring twice and hang up."

"See you."

"Mike?"

"Yeah?"

"I'm worried for you." Pause. "It's just an act, though, right?"

"An act."

He gave her a kiss, then shut the door. Turned toward the building. Sixty, maybe seventy or so others stood in a line that stretched halfway down the block. Marked men. No, marked boys hardly ready to shave, let alone die. Some were talking, joking around, trying not to act scared when he knew damn well that they were. Others stood silent, brooding. Mike swallowed. Be cool, be calculated, he thought. Tell the bastards the truth. Another teenager stared at him as he made his way to the end of the line. Mike stopped and glared back. The kid was chewing gum fast as his jaws could work.

"What're you looking at?"

The kid dropped his eyes.

"You think I don't mean it?"

He walked on as the Mercedes passed him on the street. Leitha honked and waved but he didn't see her. I do, he told himself. I do.

The psychiatric report had been sent to the medical board the week before. Mike figured, or at least he hoped, that they'd take one look at it and he'd get to skip the physical exam and go straight to the real matter at hand—the psychiatric evaluation. Except that's not the way it worked out. The clock on the wall showed ten forty-five. Nearly three hours had passed and all he'd done so far was fill out forms, strip down to his boxers, and wait in a crowded room. Three times he tried to explain his situation to the man at the desk who took his name when he first came in, and three times he was told to take a seat. "You'll get your chance, pal. Relax," the guy said. "You're not the only one here."

At eleven a man in a dingy white coat strolled into the room and cleared his throat. "Fall out when I call your name." He wore thick horn-rimmed glasses, which kept slipping down the bridge of his nose as he read off a list, and which he kept pushing back into place with his thumb.

"Barnes?"

"Here."

"Brooker?"

"Here."

"Casey?"

"Here."

He called out nine other names and then turned to the group, removed his glasses, rubbed his eyes with the back of his sleeve, and pointed to the floor. "Follow the yellow line," he said. But the group called before them hadn't yet budged, and there was nowhere for the new group to go. Mike glanced up at the clock. Another five minutes had slipped by. Why stand? He headed for his seat when the man behind the desk barked at him.

A half hour later the line moved forward.

The yellow one led down a hall to two lab technicians. There they took a blood sample and pointed him to another line. This one was blue. It led to the proctologist, who ordered Mike and the others to put their toes up to a red line.

"Pull down your shorts."

They did.

"Bend over."

They did.

After the inspection Mike and the group returned to the yellow line where they had first started, waited another half hour, and then advanced along a green line to another lab technician. Here Mike was given a plastic cup and directed to a stall with a toilet, a washbasin, but no door. Finally, after he'd returned the little cup, another man in a white coat approached him. This one had a pen and a pile of forms attached to a clipboard. He wrote and made check marks as he spoke.

"Full name?"

"Michael Casey."

"Ever spent the night in jail, Casey?"

"No."

"Are you a homosexual?"

"No."

"Ever been treated for drug abuse?"

178

"No."

"Alcohol abuse?"

"I'm seeing a psychiatrist," he said. "For that and other things."

"Come with me."

The man led him down another hall into a large room divided into offices with movable partitions. At one he stopped and nodded for Mike to have a seat and then left. The chairs, like the walls, were painted gun-metal gray. On the desk was a name plaque: DR. JASON HOWELL. Again Mike sat and waited, hands folded in his lap. All around he heard voices, bits of conversations in the other cubicles, but none that he could make out clearly.

The doctor entered with an unlit cigarette hanging between his lips. In his hand he carried a file. He squeezed past Mike to his desk and opened the file, removed the report, and read it silently. Another minute passed. Slowly a drop of sweat slipped down Mike's side, paused on a rib, then rolled to the waistband of his boxers.

The doctor looked up.

"Tell me," he said, shaking the report. "Is this true?"

"Word for word."

"It says here you're an actor."

"You got it, man."

"Aren't you acting now?" He tossed the file onto the desk and pulled the cigarette from his mouth. Sighed. "You'd actually kill yourself or someone else over the draft?" A smirk. "C'mon, kid. You expect me to believe that shit?" He leaned forward on his elbows and stared him square in the eyes. "What," he said, "just what if I decide you're bluffing?"

"I'm not."

"But what if I think you are?"

"Draft me and see."

The doctor sat back, sighed again. "There's a lot of other boys out there," he said, pointing to the doorway. "Some with legitimate *physical* problems. We don't have time to play around."

Mike nodded as if he understood, as if he respected what the man had said. "Seriously, sir . . ." Now it was his turn to lean forward and stare him straight in the eyes. And he spoke clearly, calmly, convincingly, without a threatening tone. "If you draft me . . . when I'm issued a rifle . . ."

Pause.

"And I'm issued the bullets . . ."

Pause.

"One night I'm going to blow my commanding officer away."

The doctor slipped the unlit cigarette between his lips and then suddenly jerked it out and crushed it into the ashtray. "Get your clothes on and get the hell out of here." He slapped the file shut and rose to his feet. "You'll be hearing from us."

Outside on the street Mike jammed his hands into his pockets and walked without looking back. His heart beat rapidly. He walked faster and faster until soon he pulled his hands free and broke into a run. People on the sidewalk stepped aside. Up the block, at the corner, he spotted a phone booth and he slowed to a trot. Crossed the street. He steadied his breathing, wiped sweat from his forehead. Then, reaching into his pocket, fumbling for loose change, he stepped into the phone booth and shut the door.

The Marrin family was having what her father called a round-table discussion. Leitha called it a fight. "I don't even *want* to go to college," she said, stamping her foot.

"You have to."

"I don't have to do anything."

"Don't talk like that."

"Why Barnard, then?" Leitha shouted. "Why not UCLA?" She glanced at her mother sitting in a chair, flipping through *Cosmopolitan*. "Mom, you went there. How come I can't?"

"Can't what, honey?"

"Aren't you listening?"

"Of course," she said, turning a page. "But you're missing your daddy's point, honey."

"Don't call me *honey*."

"Barnard's better for you," Marrin said. "It's smaller, more intimate."

"It's for snotty girls."

"You don't mean that."

"I won't have any friends."

"C'mere."

She sighed and went to her father on the couch. He looked up at her and smiled, reached for her wrist, and pulled gently until she was sitting on his lap. "My legs aren't that far gone yet," he said. "Not for my little girl, anyway." He stroked her hair. "Your mother and I'll miss you but we've talked it over, baby, and we both think going away to college is the healthiest thing for you."

Just then the phone rang.

Twice.

Leitha made a dash for it in the other room. There she stalled for a half-minute, talking into a dead receiver, feigning a concerned voice. She came back into the living room with a worried look on her face.

"Who was that?" Marrin asked.

"Sharon again," she said. "She's still having problems. I have to go."

"Can't she talk with her parents?"

"They don't listen."

"Has she even tried?"

"Like I have," she said. "They're the problem."

"Baby . . ."

"Can I borrow the car again?"

"Ask your mother?"

"Mom?"

"It's fine with me," Cindy said. "The keys are in my purse."

Marrin took hold of his cane and lifted himself from the couch, hobbled down the hall, and locked himself in his study. Leitha dug through her mother's purse on the coffee table. Cindy glanced up from the magazine. "It's one thing for me to fool around," she said, "and another for you. Don't forget your father's an acting coach. He knows a good performance from a bad one." Leitha found the keys and started out of the house. Her mother looked back to the magazine and flipped the page. "And one thing you're not, *honey*, and that's an actress."

She slammed the door behind her.

I'd like to think it was on Debra Swanson's old couch in our living room that my brother and Leitha made love for the first time. She'd picked him up again and given him a ride home, and he invited her in before he climbed out of the Mercedes. A long silence passed. In it was the clumsy moment where they both knew what would happen if she accepted, or at least what might happen, which made it just as tense. "Really, I shouldn't," she said, reaching for the door handle. "I can't stay long, you know."

The house was empty, as he'd expected, and as he thought she must've expected, too, because there was no car other than her own in the driveway. Still, she asked, when they stepped inside, "Is your family home?" And he told her no, and then, to reassure her, he called out for Mom and me. There was no answer. The place was theirs, and they could've made use of the bed, but getting there from the living room when they were both so damn unsure of each other seemed impossible. That's why it likely happened first on the couch.

For a second, when she lay back along the cushions, her bra unfastened and her blouse unbuttoned and her breasts soft white against the darkness of cloth, just for a second Mike must've thought about how lucky he was to have her. And Leitha, maybe she didn't think about luck—maybe, instead, she wondered what she was doing with one of the young men who had slept with her mother. Maybe what had happened earlier, the fight about college, and the resentment she felt toward her mother was what drove her straight into my brother's arms. Then again maybe that had nothing to do with it at all. If it made any difference, he was as handsome as she was beautiful, and she likely wanted him as badly as he wanted her. But still that damn couch was awfully small and cramped and a couple of times, as they made love, my brother must've considered moving upstairs to a bed, where they'd be more comfortable. Yet getting up now, giving pause to the heat, would've been awkward, senseless, even dangerous to suggest. A delay, a pause, and she might suddenly fasten her bra and button her blouse, zip up her pants, apologize, and rush out to the car. If Mike got up at all, it was to close the drapes, and he probably did that before they started.

So as they held each other he tried to forget about the damn plastic covering that stuck to his arms and her shoulders when she arched her back. He tried to ignore the crinkling sounds it made when he moved against her and how, every so often, they had to stop and rearrange themselves because the couch was too narrow. Finally they both must've thought to hell with it and pushed the coffee table aside and moved to the floor. There whatever awkwardness and nervousness they might've felt was lost.

It wasn't yet dark outside, and I'm hoping that when he closed the drapes there was a space left between them and that a ray of sunlight fell into the room. It fell across Leitha while she lay on the floor, and Mike stared at her, and she watched his eyes. She lifted her arms over her head and spread her long hair and let him look awhile longer before she reached for him. I'd like to think it was now, not in the car after she picked him up, but now, when they'd finished making love and they lay naked side by side, that she asked him about the draft. And it was now that she held him as he told her and all the fear and anger and humiliation he'd felt passed. I'd like to think that's how it was best for them.

Then she must've told him about the old man and how he wanted her to go off to Barnard in the fall. For a long while Mike said nothing. He slipped his hands under, around her waist, smiled.

"Is that what you want?"

"I don't know," she said. "Maybe I should. I mean why stay?"

"For a lot of reasons."

He could've said then he loved her and that he didn't want her going anywhere, and maybe he almost did, but he stopped himself. Because he didn't want to barter. Because it wasn't up to him or her folks and because even if he loved her, and he believed he did, they would never last together if she didn't come right out and tell the old man herself. Face to face. So he just stared at her, and after a while she got a little mad, seeing that he wasn't going to say what she maybe wanted to hear. She put her hands flat on his chest and pushed.

"I gotta go. Let loose."

But Mike had his arms wrapped around her, locked at the wrists. "Call home. Make something up," he said. "Tell them you're going out to dinner with Sharon again."

"Would you let go?"

"In a second."

"I'm probably already in big trouble," she said. "I don't even know why I came here."

"You do, too."

"I thought I did."

"Why don't you just tell your father the truth?"

"Oh sure."

"It's not like we're doing anything wrong."

"He'd strangle me."

"I'll tell him if you want."

"Let go."

Leitha pushed on his chest once more, and this time she meant it. Mike let her free and climbed to his feet and slipped into his boxers. He pulled on his shirt. "Hey," he said, shrugging. "If he doesn't know already, he's going to find out soon." She slid one leg, then the other into her panties, her pants, and then scanned the room. Her arms were crossed over her chest.

"He's my father," she said, "and I don't want to hurt him again, like you and my mother." Leitha dropped to one knee and peered under the couch. Her voice rose in anger. "Don't just stand there," she barked. "Help me find my bra."

Alone later that evening, my brother sat in the dining room with a drink. He didn't know what to think about Leitha. About the draft. About failing. Where that last worry came from, I don't know, as it seemed to me he was doing damn well for his age. Likely he was reading the paper spread out on the table, because he always read the paper, and he hadn't had a chance at it this morning. He drew his finger down the obituary column and stopped at Rochelle Hudson. *Dr. Jekyll and Mr. Hyde.* Found dead in her Palm Desert home. He sighed and tore the clipping out when the phone rang, only he didn't answer it. He didn't want to talk. Later, upstairs in his room, he heard the doorbell. Again he didn't answer it. For now he was exhausted, not having slept the night before, and all he wanted was rest. This was about the time I came wandering home, with Mike upstairs and Mom at work. I'd been shooting baskets at Hollywood High, my newest school—though I didn't attend it much—until it got too dark to see the hoop. I was a freshman now, at least on paper. That's the year Mom registered me for when we had moved to Fairfax.

On our doorstep was a manila envelope with Mike's name written on it in black felt pen. The return address was the William Morris Agency. There was no postage on it. I brought it upstairs and knocked on his door.

"Mike?"

"I'm sleeping."

"I got something important for you."

From inside the room I heard the boxsprings jangle. The door opened. I handed him the envelope and he broke the seal. Out came a script with a note attached to it. His eyes widened as he read, and he smiled. "We might get that place on the Chetco sooner than you think," Mike said. He locked my neck in the crook of his arm, hugged me, and then turned me loose. "Could you make me a pot of coffee? Strong, too. I have a lot of work to do."

At the time, as I headed down to the kitchen, I figured he was just up for another TV part, except a really good-paying one. But I was wrong. The script was called *A Rough Kind*, it was to be a major feature, and the role my brother was up for gave star billing. There were some complications, however—ones that don't quite fit in the telling just now. Meanwhile I'd like to mention that *A Rough Kind* still plays the revival theaters and occasionally the edited version airs on TV. And the New York Film Festival recently ran it as one of the best ten films of the last ten years. So it's still around, though I don't make a point to catch it anymore.

As for there not being any postage on the envelope, I suspect it was delivered by special messenger. The audition was the following day. All that night my brother stayed up studying his character and, in the morning, when he emerged from his room as I was rolling out of bed for my paper route, he wasn't Michael David McKinney. No, he was Evan Easton from Greenville, Ohio. The year was 1865. The Union army was recruiting for its ranks by hauling every able-bodied young man into its service. Evan was a nineteen-year-old draft dodger headed west.

15

The warrant for Mom's arrest must've gone out around the same time Mike went up for the starring role in *A Rough Kind*. That's the way I have it figured according to the way things fell into place. What happened was that our mother missed her court date with Mrs. Glass. I suppose the old bitch, as Mom liked to call her, was happy with the warrant but disappointed that she didn't get her just day at city hall. I suspect, too, that had Mom shown up she would've met with a couple of IRS agents interested in her whereabouts. The fact was she knew better than to plead her case, because she was guilty—which is why, I imagine, that she tore up the subpoena a minute after the sheriff served it. If she appeared in court, they'd likely jail her; if she didn't appear, they'd still do their damnedest to lock her up. Either way she was a loser. But our mother was free now, and I suppose anyone in her situation who had already spent time, rightly or wrongly would've done whatever was humanly possible not to spend more.

Mom was still working the night shift at a plastics company about a month or two after the missed court date. If there's one thing she excelled at it was work—hard, long hours "to better ourselves," she often said, "because money is power, and baby, that's what it's all about." How they found her out this time, I'm not sure. I've come up with a few ideas, although they're mostly elaborate, ridiculous ones that have more to do with fantasy than fact. The simplest explanation was that someone informed on her. Someone who knew of her past, someone close to the family, or maybe a co-worker who she'd gotten too friendly with had tipped off the authorities. Whatever the method, it occurred while my brother was probably least able to handle yet another complication. *A Rough Kind* was no small movie. No TV special.

Mike got an interview because the producer had seen him on *Vice Squad* and thought the performance outstanding. He and the director both wanted talented but fairly unknown actors not just because they could work them cheaper, but also because new faces would give the film an edge of authenticity. It was a big break for my brother. Even though Paramount wasn't exactly hot on the project, they'd agreed to a nationwide distribution contract, which meant exposure and reviews for Mike from all over the country in what was likely to be a high-quality picture. The director, who was also the writer, had landed an Academy Award nomination for best original screenplay the year before.

The day of the interview Mike went in wearing cowboy boots and a black three-piece with a western bow tie. His hair was slicked back. He spoke with a slight country drawl, confident yet humble in tone, like a young Jimmy Stewart. That's also the comparison a movie reviewer for *The Washington Post* later made. Now Mike stood before the producer, Kent Morton, and the director in a small office on the back lot of Paramount. A copy of *A Rough Kind* was tucked under his arm. They looked him up and down. Morton did the talking.

"Have you read the script?"

"Yes, sir."

"Any scene you'd like to try for us?"

"It's your choice."

"We have one in mind." Morton opened the script in his lap. "The Union army is at your parents' door," he said. "You're hiding under a table in the parlor. It's covered with a black velvet cloth, and on top of it is your dead brother's shrine—a photo, a Union Medal of Honor, a gold pocket watch, some other things." He held his hands out, framing the table. "He served but he didn't make it back. Your parents don't want to lose you, too, so they're on your side. Got it so far?" Mike said he did. Morton sat forward and continued. "The army searches the house, they don't find you, and now they've left. It's safe to come out. You're still scared as hell but you can't let your parents know it. For them you act brave. All right?" He looked to the director in the chair beside his own. "He'll read the father, I'll read the mother. Remember, your parents are sending you west until the war's over. You might not see them again for a long time, if ever." Pause. "Any questions?"

Mike shook his head.

"You understand the situation?"

"Very well."

"The emotions?"

"I know them," he said, "like I know the situation. It's not a problem. I'm ready when you are."

Morton folded the script back. "We're on pages three going through to seven." But Mike didn't open his copy; he set it on the desk and then sat on the floor, hunched his shoulders, and made like he was hiding under a table.

They must've thought he was a little strange when he first came in dressed as the script pretty much described the character. And when he put down his copy they probably thought he was taking an awfully big risk, though that changed. Because he didn't miss a line. His dialogue came smoothly and honestly, as if it were being spoken for the first time. And it was as if the actor Michael Casey, not Evan Easton, had himself experienced a similar situation because he had, and his understanding of the feelings involved showed. Shone. They ran him through another scene, and with a couple of cues he knew those lines, too, the emotions and motives behind them. Again he delivered with power, but it was a power that drained him, one that could've only come from reliving the memories he'd tried to forget.

They were impressed.

An hour later Mike left the interview exhausted but exhilarated. On the way out, passing through the lobby, he spotted three other young men waiting on the couch with scripts in hand. One wrinkled his forehead at him. Another rolled his eyes. The third stared blankly. Mike walked right by them. Kent Morton and the director had to know, as he knew, that if they wanted a better Evan Easton than himself they weren't likely to find him in the lobby. Not here, he thought, stepping outside into the sun. No, if not him, they'd have to drag one back from the Midwest of the 1800s.

Waiting was the hardest part. Morton and the director didn't let him know if he'd gotten the role for nearly two months after the interview. The days slipped by slowly for him, almost painfully. He did get a callback for a reading with another young actor up for the other lead, and again he did well, yet they still wouldn't confirm the deal. My brother took to drinking in the mornings now and then, maybe just a beer, later another, and whenever the phone rang he ran for it.

Toward the end of the second month a letter arrived from the Selective Service. His heart skipped a beat as he split the envelope.

> The Medical Examining Board of the United States Armed Forces has determined Michael Casey unfit for military service for reasons noted in the classification marked below.

In the box labeled 4-F was a check mark. Beneath it was the scribbled signature of Jason Howell, Doctor of Psychiatry.

He reread the letter, then let it drop from his hand and flutter to the living-room floor. Made it. He closed his eyes in relief. The next thing he did was get on the phone and call his agent. The secretary put him through.

"Guess what?"

"Sounds like good news."

"Great news," he said. "I'm unfit for the army."

"Fantastic."

"I'm *free*."

"That's what Universal's been waiting to hear," Betsy said. "They want to sign you."

He pulled the receiver from his ear. Looked at it for a couple of seconds. Replaced it.

"Did I hear right?"

"I hope so."

"Universal?"

"Don't get too excited," she said. "It's for seven years. You better think before you sign it, if you sign it. I can't advise you on something like this." Pause. "I'll send it out today for you to look over. I'm on another line right now. Let me call you back."

"When do I have to decide?"

"Soon."

"How soon?"

"Very soon. Bye."

"Bye."

When Mike hung up he wasn't sure exactly how he should feel. Happy? Maybe he would've been if he'd known what to do, only he didn't. For all he could tell they might want him for bit parts in sit-coms, voice-over work, or maybe they planned on using him in good movies. But seven years? And what about *A Rough Kind*? Mike picked up the phone to call Betsy back, dialed the first three numbers, then hung up. She'd be irritated with him. A drink, he needed a drink to help him relax, to figure it out. He headed to the kitchen. Too much, too fast; he could hardly think straight.

Mom bought two bottles of Dom Perignon when Mike told her about his 4-F and the contract. A special messenger had delivered it in the afternoon. She herded us into the dining room and opened one of the bottles. "Baby," she said, as she poured him a glass, "this is the big time. I always knew you were gonna make it except I didn't think it'd be so soon." She poured herself a glassful, then me. "You're going places, honey, big places. No damn war in your way, no nothing now. Thank God I got us out of that little dead town." She put her arm around him. "Aren't you glad you listened to your momma now? Huh? Aren't you?"

"Sure," he mumbled.

"Didn't I say we'd go places?"

"Yeah."

"I was right, wasn't I?"

"Uh-huh."

He took a long drink, finished it. Mom poured him another and set the bottle down and reached for the contract lying on the table. "Big time," she muttered, as if to herself. "Big time." There were a lot of pages to it, and for a couple of minutes she sat silent, flipping through them until she found what she wanted. Her eyebrows went up, her voice rose. She put a finger on the page. "They're gonna pay us five hundred a week for the first year. That's two thousand a month, baby, whether you work or not. And it goes up from there." Mom jumped to her feet and wrapped her arms around him again. Gave him a kiss. "Stay right where you are, honey, I'll be right back."

I looked across the table at Mike when she left the room, expecting him to be looking at me, either grinning or frowning, maybe rolling his eyes because of Mom, but he had his head down. Slowly, by its stem, he turned the champagne glass round and round. "What's wrong?" I said. Mom returned then, smiling, a pen in her hand. She put the contract in front of Mike and folded it over to the last page. She tapped the pen on the bottom line.

"Sign here, baby."

Silence.

"Go on, sign it."

He just kept turning the glass, which was already empty. Mom poured it full, then placed her hand on his shoulder. Her voice was soft. "Whatta you waiting for?" she said.

"I'm thinking."

"What's to think about?"

"If I want to do it."

Her lips grew taut. "You crazy?" she shouted.

"It's for seven years."

"For a lotta money."

"But I'm up for a movie."

"That can fall through, *this* can't." She slapped a hand flat on the contract. "Sign it." When he didn't move she threw her arms over her head and shouted, "Who got you started? Huh? Huh? I did." She pointed a thumb at her chest. "Me. If it wasn't for me you'd be back in San Jose pounding nails like your father. Picking plums like the Mexicans. I've worked too hard, too long for you."

Mom jammed the pen into his hand and pushed his fingers down around it. "Don't you dare pull this crap on me now, baby."

I rose to leave.

"Where the hell you going?"

"Upstairs," I mumbled.

"Sit your ass down."

So I sat. She turned back to Mike. "Think of your little brother," she hollered. "Think of what that money means to him. New clothes, maybe a special school. He never had what you got."

Mike slid the contract and the pen across the table to me. "Here," he said, though he was looking at Mom. "Let him sign it then."

"You selfish bastard."

I didn't move, didn't say a word.

My brother raised himself to his feet. "Maybe he can take the job. We look enough alike." He grinned here, which was a mistake. Up came the hand, fast, sharp across his face. Mike gripped the back of the chair and clenched his teeth. "That's the last time," he said. "No more, ever. Don't ever hit me again."

Mom made a face, pretending to be scared. "Whatcha gonna do? Huh?" she said. "Gonna hit your momma? Wanna be a big tough guy like your daddy? Huh, baby? Put Momma in her place?" She stuck her chin out. "C'mon, baby . . . c'mon, hit your momma. See what happens." He glared at her and then, swallowing, lowered his head. "Show your little brother what a man you are," she said, jabbing him in the shoulder. Mike gripped the chair still tighter. "Looks, baby, is about as far as you and your brother go and that ain't saying much." Suddenly she laughed. "Sign the contract? He don't even have brains enough to spell his own goddamn name right." I got up from my chair to leave because I understood it was partly her anger talking, partly truth, and I didn't want to hear any more of it. Mike grabbed the bottle of Dom Perignon, nodded to me, and I followed him upstairs to his room.

There he locked my head in the crook of his arm. "Hey, don't listen to her. She doesn't know what she's talking about." He mussed up my hair and let me go. "You know better. Am I right?"

"I guess."

"No guess," he said. "Well?"

"Well what?"

"Where's that story you've been writing?"

As I went to fetch it from my room, I heard Mom storming around the kitchen below, slamming cupboard doors and busting what sounded like plates. Soon I returned to Mike with seventeen typewritten pages of "The Motorcycle King." We sat Indian-style in the middle of the bed with his poster of Montgomery Clift staring down at us. While my brother read I studied his face, trying to guess what he was thinking, if he liked it, or if he thought it was garbage. My palms began to sweat. A couple of times Mom shouted a curse up the staircase, but he kept on reading as if he hadn't heard her, one page after another until he reached the end.

I'd hoped he would think it was good enough to publish. If not that, I at least could've used some approval, some praise. Instead he asked me point blank if I wanted him to be honest, and of course I said yes, though I didn't expect him to be as honest as he was. "Jay," he said, passing me the bottle. I took a drink and passed it back. "This needs a lot of work." Then he went on to say I had too many characters that didn't really belong in this story, maybe another one, that there were too many loose ends and coincidences. As a short story it "simply doesn't hold together . . . and your typing," he said. "It's not so much your spelling, because I know you know how to spell most of these words, as it is you hitting the wrong keys half the time." He held up the first page. "Look at the errors."

About the only thing he liked was the burglary scene. In it I had lines about how a glass cutter made a crackling noise as it passed along the windowpane and, when the window finally gave way, how the pieces sounded falling to the linoleum floor inside the kitchen. There were other lines, too—ones that he liked— about the tension and exhilaration my main character felt while he made his way through the different rooms with a flashlight. "How can you know this?" he asked, frowning. "How could you make it so real if you haven't done it?"

"You," I said, shrugging. "How do you play your scenes so real?"

At that we each had another drink and laughed. But mine was a strained laugh, for my brother suspected me now, and I knew damn well if he found out the truth I'd be in a deep trouble. **Deep disgrace.** So I began to feel pretty low sitting there on the bed with the manuscript and my lies, and a little later, when his criticism sank in, I felt downright miserable. Mike clapped me on the arm. "Don't be so depressed," he said, jumping off the bed, squatting before his bookcase. He pulled a paperback off the shelf. "Read this next. Maybe it'll help." He tossed it to me. "This guy's great." Then he sat back down beside me and we had a last drink of champagne. "You have to do one of two things, I think. Either cut your story down, or," he said, smacking his lips, "expand, expand. That's what I'd do." He spread his arms wide, the bottle empty now, cradled between his legs. "Take in everything you can. Be quiet, like you are, and *listen*, man." He cupped a hand to his ear. "Listen to the voices in your head, all the different ones. See if you can't make out what they're saying. Watch and imagine. Remember and become." He grinned. "Put all the pieces together and see if they don't somehow connect in the end."

A knock came on the door then.

"Baby?"

"Yeah?"

"I've calmed down," Mom said. "You?"

"Pretty much."

"I'm sorry I lost my temper, honey. You know I didn't mean to." She rattled the doorknob. Locked. "Is Jay there?"

Mike glanced at me. I shook my head.

"No," he said. "You check his room?"

"It's empty."

"I don't know where he is."

"Tell him I'm sorry, okay?"

"Sure."

"I gotta go to work now."

"See you."

"There's still a bottle of champagne in the refrigerator." She drummed her fingers on the door. "If you really love me, honey . . ." Her voice faltered. My brother stared down at the bedspread. "Just think about it, baby," she said. "Please?"

Mike moped around home waiting for Betsy's call. It didn't come, though, and by the time he decided to phone her himself she'd left the office. I'd gone to my room to read the novel he'd given me, except I fell asleep, not from boredom but because I was a little drunk from the champagne. The last time I saw Mike that night he was sitting in the den with the phone in his lap, fingertips pressed to his temples, willing the thing to ring. Seven years, he must've thought. Seven long years. But the money was good. Think of all the things he could buy. Books. A car. Fine dinners and theater tickets to the best shows in town for Leitha and himself. Yet he couldn't get his mind off Evan Easton, what the role could do for his career, and how if he got the job, but he signed the contract, Universal might not let him take it. What were Morton and the director waiting for? Not knowing was a bitch. Considering how the script arrived special messenger, and how little time he'd had to prepare for it, you'd think there was a great urgency to get the film going. To cast it. To set up a shooting schedule. Mike put the phone back on the desk and looked through the doorway into the living room. The clock on the mantle read nine o'clock. The house was quiet. There was no sense staying home, as Betsy wasn't going to call this late, so he went out for a drink to the same bar that served minors. Meanwhile, our mother put in her last night on the job.

A tape inside a transcribing machine flapped around and around. The reel was empty. Mom pressed the "off" button, then pulled the set of earphones from her head and placed them beside her typewriter. Glanced at her watch. Nine-thirty. At another desk sat a young trainee, her second night on the job. They were the only ones working the swing shift tonight, as the other regular had called in sick. The new girl already looked beat—red-rimmed eyes, a sallow complexion under the glare of the florescent lights. She'd get used to it, Mom thought. Sure, sure she would, just as soon as she slept through a full afternoon. The first week was always the toughest.

"Want a cup of coffee?"

"I don't drink it."

"You will soon, honey."

Mom headed to the reception room at the front of the building where the coffeepot was kept. Venetian blinds covered the window but the slats were open a bit, and outside she saw the streets empty and deserted like the buildings across the way—factories and warehouses, wholesale distributors. Off in the distance, as she measured a spoonful of coffee, she heard the steady rush of cars on the freeway. A moment later came the faint sound of a train whistle followed by the rumble of its great wheels. One went by at nine-thirty every night. Another rolled through in the early-morning hours as she locked up, headed to the parking lot out back, wide awake but exhausted, wishing the drive was already over and that she was warm in bed. Home with her sons. Soon maybe she could get a regular job with regular hours like other people. Or maybe just part-time, maybe no job at all, if things kept up for Mike. It looked the case. The boy was going to be famous. As for Jay . . . She sighed, turning the spoon, watching the coffee tumble into the strainer. She wished she could spend more time with him.

The train passed.

Now it was quiet except for the distant rush of cars on the freeway and the ticking of the young girl's typewriter. Mom went to the water cooler near the window and filled the pot, watching the bubbles rising inside the bottle, hitting the top, bursting, when she spotted the headlights of a car glance across the wall. For a second she didn't think anything of it, because cars did pass by occasionally even if it was a deserted street, only this one stopped. She heard the motor die. She put the coffeepot on the counter and went to the window and lifted a slat. Her heart dropped. Parked at the curb was a black-and-white.

Turning, letting the slat fall, she hurried out of the reception room into the office, passing the girl on the way. "The pot's on the blink," she said. "You need anything while I'm out?"

"Where you going?"

"Winchell's."

"Get me a couple of twists."

"See you in a bit."

"Need some money?"

"I got it."

Mom grabbed her purse from under her desk, her coat from the coatrack, and let herself out through the rear door leading into the warehouse. There she switched on the light and broke into a run down a path lined with clear plastic tubes tall as herself, past shelves of plastic sheets of all different colors and widths and lengths. At the back was a steel door with a pulley attached to the handle and she pressed on it. The door slid open with a clang. Her heart pounded.

The Nova stood parked in the darkness behind the loading dock. She fumbled through her purse for her keys and opened the driver's side, threw her coat in back, and slid behind the wheel. Her hands shook, her ears felt hot. She jabbed the key into the ingition. Turned it. The motor growled, died, and she looked into the rearview mirror, but saw no one, nothing. Again she tried it. This time the engine roared—loud, much too loud. In that instant she saw in her mind the beam of their flashlights through the windshield, imagined the footsteps and voices, and finally the door opening and a strong hand latching on to her arm, pulling. It wasn't going to happen again. She slipped the transmission into gear and drove with the headlights off. In her mouth was the metallic taste of pennies.

Seconds later she maneuvered the Nova down the driveway onto the street. The black-and-white was there. She saw it as she passed. Two cops stood in the doorway talking with the new girl. Mom glimpsed her hand go up, point, and she knew then that they had turned to look, although she didn't see them do it. She pressed the pedal to the floor. The Nova vibrated, picking up speed.

Ahead was the freeway entrance.

My brother stumbled home around midnight. The house was completely dark. As he felt his way to the staircase he heard a voice and stopped.

"Baby?"

He stiffened. Stared into the darkness.

"C'mere."

"Mom?"

"Over here."

"What're you doing home?"

The click of a switch. A lamp cast a circle of yellow light across the *Photoplay* and *Movieland* magazines on the coffee table. "Honey," she said, "we have to talk." As he went to her he saw that her eyes were dark, streaked with mascara, almost racoonlike in the glow of the lamp. She patted the cushion beside her. "Sit down, I won't bite." Mike sat on the edge of the couch, elbows resting on his knees, fingers laced together.

"Why you crying?" he said, looking down at the floor.

Mom put her hand on top of his. Her voice was strained. "You

196

know your momma's a hard worker. You know I only want the best for you and Jay. I never mean to lose my temper. Honest," she said. "Sometimes I don't know what gets into me." She closed her eyes and shook her head. A lump rose in Mike's throat, and he felt a fluttering in his chest, a softening of the heart. "You have to make the right choice—not for me, for yourself. But you need to know something." She squeezed his hand and opened her eyes. "There's been trouble, baby."

"Like how?"

A long silence.

"I can't go back to my job."

"They fire you?"

"I wish it was that simple."

Suddenly she began to cry. "Why can't the bastards leave me alone? I've *paid*." The sobs grew louder. Mike put an arm around her and rested his chin on top of her head. Maybe for a minute, maybe two, he held her there on the couch in the yellow glare of the lamp that shone across the cheap movie magazines, hoping to calm her but failing. Finally he rose to his feet and left her, bent over with her hands pressed to her temples, her hair reaching toward the floor.

In the den he switched on the desk lamp. As he picked up the phone he heard Mom sob again and he winced, wishing she'd stop. Just stop. He dialed slowly, leaving his finger in the hole, letting it circle back, click into place. Seven times plus three for long distance. He listened to it ring and ring. Seven years, he thought. Seven fucking years.

Groggy. "Hello?"

He opened his mouth but said nothing.

"Hello?"

Nothing.

"Who is this?"

The voice was Marissa's. Over the static he heard what sounded like boxsprings creaking, then fumbling noises followed by another, more urgent voice. "Hello . . . hello?" Gently, quietly, he returned the receiver to its cradle and turned off the desk lamp. For a few seconds longer he stood in the dark staring at the phone, wondering what to do, what to think, or why he'd even bothered calling in the first place. Advice? He didn't need it anymore. The old man had a life of his own now. Mike went to the kitchen for the other bottle of Dom Pérignon, unraveled the foil, and popped it open. The cork hit the cabinet and skittered across the linoleum. Taking two glasses from the drainboard, sighing, he walked back to the living room.

Mom was still bent over, crying. She looked up when he handed her a glass of champagne. Mike smiled weakly.

"Where is it?"

"The contract?"

"I'll sign it."

She drew a hand across her eyes. "I knew you'd change your mind. I knew it all along." Mom nodded toward the mantel over the fireplace. "It's right there, baby," she said. "So's the pen." Then she held up her glass to toast.

16

The Adventures of Augie March was the book Mike gave me after he'd dissected and criticized what I once believed was a perfectly good short story. But I was wrong. I hid *"The Motorcycle King"* in a drawer in my desk and vowed never to look at it again. The thought that I'd ever written it made me wince. Instead of re-working it, I decided that just as soon as I got my confidence back I'd start another, longer one from scratch, and in the meantime I'd read Saul Bellow. I carried his novel around with me most every-where I went, even after I'd finished it, because I liked rereading certain paragraphs and chapters when the notion struck me. A lot of what I saw in Augie I saw in myself in the way I imagined my brother saw himself when he watched James Dean or Montgom-ery Clift perform. Acting was only the tool. It's what you made with it that counted. As our dad used to say, "If you haven't got good tools, son, you can't do a good job." When he made that remark, or one like it, he was usually sharpening his wood chisel, just before he put it to use. "A dull blade," he'd say, passing the tip across a whetstone damp with oil, "is a hell of a lot more dan-gerous than a sharp one. Take the time to put an edge on it." The logic was that with a dull blade you were either bound to gouge the wood or else slip by forcing it and cut your hand. I've thought about this analogy, and I believe it applies to my brother even though he had the good and sharp tools to do his job properly. Still, he slipped and screwed up, like myself and Augie March, only the outcome wasn't quite the same.

Up to this point I haven't much discussed my schooling because there's not a hell of a lot to say about it that isn't boring. I hadn't completed my last year, though I went on to the next grade when we moved into Debra Swanson's old place. The school didn't ask for transcripts, and Mom certainly didn't volunteer the information. The less they knew about us, the better—for her and myself. I probably could've passed my freshman year if I'd just shown up for class, did at least half the assignments, and treated the teacher politely. The problem was that I couldn't manage to sit at a desk all morning into the afternoon for more than two or three days a week. Flunking was inevitable, and the idea of it did bother me if I let myself think about how far behind I was falling, but usually I pushed those thoughts out of my head as fast as they entered it. What worried me more was how I could keep the news from getting back to Mom and Mike come report-card time.

After my paper route I'd ride home, eat breakfast, grab my books, and then make like I was headed for school. Lately I'd been spending a lot of my days at Poinsettia Park across from what used to be the Samuel Goldwyn studios. Old Russian men shot shuffleboard there in the morning. Later, when the sun grew too hot, they'd play chess on the benches under the shade of the trees. I'd watch them for a while, then read *The Adventures of Augie March* for a while, watch again, read some more. Sometimes I wrote in my notebook. Sketches of dialogue in broken dialect. Pictures of the old men and how they dressed and how they moved. I tried to imagine their lives, the houses or rented rooms they lived in, and how the insides might've been decorated. In the late afternoon I'd slap the notebook shut, the novel if I was reading, and hop back onto my bike.

Where before our house was quiet, maybe empty, when I came home, now I'd find Mom humming in the kitchen. She'd be wearing an apron, chopping tomatoes or onions, and there'd be a pot of sauce bubbling on the stove, maybe a casserole in the oven. Dinner was on the table at six every night.

"How was school?" she'd ask.

"Fine."

"Lots of homework?"

"I did it in study hall."

"Good for you," she'd say, wiping her hands on the apron, smiling. "Kind of nice having your momma home for a change, isn't it?"

And in a way that I'd forgotten, I thought, Yes. Calmness had replaced most of her anger, she wasn't as edgy now, and there was a certain order about things in the house that before had been lacking. Our laundry was always done. The refrigerator was always full of fresh foods, no TV dinners. It was good to come home to the smells of her cooking and the soft sounds of her humming, like I imagined it was good for other families, but I had a feeling the situation couldn't last.

She and Mike had had another big fight about whether or not we ought to move again. He lost it. "If they found you at work," he said, "what's going to keep them from finding you here?" Yet Mom held to the idea that either Dad had somehow slipped up and let our whereabouts be known the first couple of times, which I didn't believe, as he was smarter than that, or else the authorities had traced her through the name Bain. It'd been her alias on the job, though she told us she'd given her boss a different address. The police would've had to trail her home to find out where we lived. In that way she'd been careful.

"Believe me, baby," she said. "I don't just drive straight home without looking behind me." No one except Dad, Mike's agent, and Leitha knew our actual address, or at least they were the few who were supposed to know it. Another slipup I could see was with Mike and the Selective Service. They could've checked and found out that the name he'd given them wasn't his real one, although that sounds like a hell of a long shot, considering the bureaucracy involved and how the military works. Or maybe the IRS, if they'd known his stage name, could've traced us through Mike on account of the exposure and publicity he was getting.

"We're as safe here as anywhere else. Besides," Mom said, "it wouldn't be right to break our lease." This was the first time I'd heard her concerned about right from wrong, and I didn't believe her any more than I thought my brother did, which couldn't have been much. The truth, I figured, was that she liked this place not only because it was a nice house but because Debra Swanson had once lived here. Somehow that made it special. And who was to

200

argue? There'd been so damn many fights lately that none of us wanted another. So the subject was dropped the same morning my brother had brought it up, the night after Mom lost her job, the night she forged his name to the contract.

About a week later Paramount made its choice. Earlier in the day Mike had had a meeting with Betsy and some executives at Universal. Mom and I were just sitting down to dinner when he got home. He leaned against the doorway in the dining room, one hand on the jamb, drumming his fingers. "You know the movie I was up for?" he said. "*A Rough Kind?*"

"Yeah?" I said.

Only he wasn't looking at me when he spoke, and he wasn't smiling, either. His eyes were on Mom. She set a bowl of fresh-cooked peas on the table and wiped her mouth with a napkin. "Come sit down," she said. "We're having your favorite, honey. Veal." She nodded to me. "Your brother needs a plate."

I started to get out of my chair when he raised his hand. He glared at Mom. "They want me," he said. Now a smile appeared on his face but it was a spiteful one. "We'll get a steady paycheck just fine, just fine. Don't worry, Mom." The smile vanished. "But they're going to make plenty more."

"Who?"

"Universal."

"How much?"

"What's the difference? I got the role and they're letting me do it," Mike said. "For a lot of money we'll never see." He headed past us into the kitchen, opened a cupboard, slammed it shut. Shouted. "Where's the vodka?" At about that point, when I knew the fight was only going to get louder and more vicious, I left the table and hurried outside. No way did I want to deal with another argument so soon after the last.

In the garage I hopped on my bike and rode it out and down the driveway onto the street. It was the second week of the month, and there was this one lady named Mrs. Turner who still owed me for the paper. I hadn't been able to catch her at home this month or the last. So I thought I'd give her another shot, as the money came out of my pocket if I couldn't collect. Either she paid up tonight or I had to cancel her subscription and take the loss. No more second chances. Her car was parked in the drive-way when I arrived, which might normally have been a good sign, but it'd been there before without anyone being home, or at least no one who wanted to answer the door. As far as I knew she lived alone. I parked my bike on the front lawn and walked up to the porch and rang the bell. Waited. The first thing I noticed when she opened the door was the strand of pearls around her neck.

"Collecting for the *Examiner*," I said.

"Come in."

She gave me a smile and then disappeared down a hallway. I stood in the foyer, scanning her living room. On the coffee table stood two silver candlesticks. A pair of French doors opened up onto a sun porch that faced the backyard. Soon Mrs. Turner strolled into the foyer with her head down, looking into her purse, searching through it.

"What do I owe you?"

"Eight-fifty," I said. "We missed each other last month." From her billfold she took out a ten-dollar bill and handed it to me. "Keep the change," she said. I thanked her twice, because it was an excellent tip, then wrote her a receipt. Before I left she asked me for my name.

"Jay."

"Jay what?"

"Miller."

"Tell me, Jay. If I want to stop delivery, what do I do? Call the *Examiner*?"

"You can."

"It'll only be for a week."

"Taking a vacation?"

"I wish," she said. "No, it's a business trip. I don't want the papers stacking up while I'm gone. There's been some burglaries in the neighborhood."

"Really?"

"Right down the block."

"They catch him?"

"No, and I doubt if they will. What can you do but hope that you're not the next? All the cops do is file a report." Mrs. Turner wagged her head, and I did the same. I told her then that it was no problem about the paper, either call the circulation desk or tell me personally. All I needed was a day's notice. She snapped her purse shut and thanked me. I thanked her again and headed back to my bike.

When I heard her close the door, I glanced up at the house. It was like ours in that it was large, grand, and built Spanish-style. But here cinder-block walls separated it from the houses on both sides, and the trees, which lined the curb, masked the light from the streetlamps. I rode then, not wanting to go home even though it was getting late, getting dark. Mom and Mike were probably still fighting. When I thought that I pushed harder on the pedals. My legs got to working so fast that finally I just threw them out to my sides and coasted, flying, the wind at my face as I shot straight down the middle of the street. The feeling was a good one and yet, there in the pit of my stomach, burned a touch of guilt for reasons that ought to have been clear. At the time, though, I blamed it on Mrs. Turner's tip. More generous than deserving, I thought. I really shouldn't have accepted it.

17

In his first month under contract Mike made sixteen hundred dollars. Universal made twenty thousand. The money he lost working in *A Rough Kind* certainly bothered him, though not as much as it did Mom. What concerned my brother more was the movie's fate. If it happened to do well at the box office, and he was later offered other starring roles from other studios, he'd be in a bad predicament. For the next seven years his talents and services would likely go to the highest bidder, not necessarily the best filmmaker. And Mike, who took pride in his performances and the characters he played, wouldn't have much, if any, say as to whether or not he wanted to accept the job. His career depended on good roles in high-quality features, not trash—not just for the big money—and he knew it. Knew it well. As many actors made stars by a studio contract had also been ruined by one.

It happened that Mike's particular contract was one of the last of its kind that Universal or any major studio ever made with a player. The days when an actor would be groomed and trained in a stable of talent, nursed along from one fine role to a better one, the days of this type of star-making machinery had all but come to an end. Guarantees once offered no longer existed. Priorities were changing, shifting from long-term goals to short ones, and my brother was caught in the middle. I suppose the contract could've been broken if he'd told his agent that he'd signed it under duress, only that might've gotten our mother in more trouble than she already was. The business end of it, too—the director, the producer, the executives—they might have hired someone else instead of waiting on Mike to untangle any legal complications. Actually, there was no breaking the contract short of risking his role in *A Rough Kind* and that, like involving Mom in the problem, was another thing he couldn't very well do.

Only a week had passed since the time he got news of his big break and the time he left for shooting on the wide-open plains of Kansas. The story revolved around a group of young misfits and draft dodgers in the Midwest, living hand-to-mouth, stealing and robbing to get by. But the focus of the film was on the two main characters, Evan Easton—played by my brother—and Harold Bower, played by another up-and-coming young actor named Terry Hull, who has since gone on to become a full-fledged film star. Easton was naïve, honest, "idealistic and highly principled," as the production copy read—which Mike received a few weeks after the wrap—until he met up with Bower and his gang. They were petty thieves, rogues, all of them wanderers. I've since often wondered if my brother didn't base at least a little of his character and his relationship with Bower on my relationship with himself, except at this point in our lives he would've had to do a lot of guesswork. Because he hadn't yet found me out. Because, although he might've suspected me of being a thief and a bit of a rogue, he had no real proof of it. The only evidence might've been my short story, and in that he would've had to sort out the facts from the fiction.

When I rode past Mrs. Turner's house in the mornings I'd sometimes toss her paper in the bushes so that I had an excuse to stop and run get it. The idea was to familiarize myself with her place as much to save time in good planning as to overcome my nervousness. Once I nearly pulled a shoulder muscle throwing her paper clear over her Jaguar right up to the backyard fence at the end of the driveway. As I hopped off my bike, and hurried after it, I saw that the gate was made of wrought iron with ornamental spikes at the top. On the latch hung a heavy-duty Master padlock. It would need to be clipped if I wanted to bust in through the rear, which meant I'd have to bring bolt cutters. Another alternative was to break a window in the front, but that seemed too risky. A car might pass on the street at the wrong time. A neighbor might walk by. The chance wasn't worth taking. I decided to cut the lock on the backyard gate.

Now, instead of my brother waiting to hear about one of his big breaks, one of his opportunities, it was me doing the pacing and fretting. I had thought, although wrongly, that when Mrs. Turner asked about canceling her subscription for a week that she was about ready to take her trip. But the days kept passing, and neither my route manager nor Mrs. Turner had given me my cue. Again I collected her check. Again she gave me a fine tip. She said nothing about leaving, though, and I knew better than to bring it up myself, for fear of making her suspicious. I'd hoped to do the job before Mike got back from Kansas, just so I wouldn't have to worry about working my schedule around one of his nights out, but that's not the way it ended up happening.

I'd gone to my classes this particular morning, after my route, the same day I nearly pulled a shoulder muscle tossing Mrs. Turner's paper—and on my way home in the afternoon, as I rounded the corner onto our street, I spotted the mailman. He was crossing our lawn over to the next house. My heart sped up. As a general rule, whenever possible, I did my damnedest to get my hands on the mail before Mike or Mom. If my school sent a letter, it wouldn't be good news, and though they hadn't sent one yet, it didn't mean they wouldn't. So the second I saw the mailman I rose off the seat of my bike, pumped hard on the pedals and raced the last block home, straight up the lawn onto our porch. Parked it. Rushed to the box. Mom opened the front door just as I pulled out three letters.

"Anything important?" she said.

"Gas bill."

"Never late, are they?"

I shuffled to the second. "Water bill," I said.

"Of course."

"And one for Mike."

Mister Michael Casey. The return address was the William Morris Agency in Beverly Hills. Just seeing those names near my brother's gave an air of importance to that other side of his life—a side I envied, that seemed exotic, remote, and admirable.

Mom pulled the letters out of my hand and headed back into the house, staring down at Mike's letter as she walked. I followed her into the den. There she continued to stare at the envelope, holding it up to the window, turning it this way and that against the light. "It's about time," she said, smiling, though the smile didn't last. She looked down at me and frowned. "If you don't have anything better to do," she barked, "you can take out the garbage. And the cans need to be brought back in, too." Even though I knew there was a reason why she wanted me out then, one that had to do with more than just dumping the garbage, I did as I was told.

Normally Mom kept the bills on top of the desk in the den until she got around to paying them. And Mike's mail while he was gone—about a half-dozen fan letters forwarded from Aaron Spelling Productions, a whole lot of junk mail, and some correspondence with *Films in Review*—we kept for him in the top drawer. The bills were there, all right, because I checked soon after I'd hauled the cans into the backyard. The envelope from the William Morris Agency wasn't with them. I closed the drawer. Upstairs I heard water falling against the tile in the shower stall. I looked up at the ceiling and I thought to myself, Maybe you're wrong, maybe you're worrying about nothing. Maybe it's all in your mind.

About an hour later I helped her get the car out of the garage. She said she was going grocery shopping. The phone rang a few minutes after she'd left. I picked it up in the den.

"Hello?"

"This the writer Jay McKinney?"

"Hey."

"I'm headin' home." He spoke in a slow country drawl. "My work is done and finished."

"When you getting in?"

"Depends."

"On what?"

"When Evan and me get saddled up."

"You want us to meet you?"

"In Dodge City?"

"C'mon," I said. "Be serious."

Mike laughed. "I'll be flying in tonight," he said. "Is Mom there?"

"She's out shopping."

"Tell her not to worry. I have a ride home."

"I'll be waiting for you."

"It'll be late."

"That's okay," I said. "I wanna hear how it went."

"It went great."

"I knew it would."

"This is a major film, Jay. It's going to make my career."

"To the top."

"That's right."

"Mike?"

"Hmmm?"

I lowered my voice even though Mom was gone. "There's something I gotta tell you."

"What?"

"Something important."

"Are you okay?" he said. "Is Mom all right?"

"We're fine."

"Then what is it?"

"We'll talk when you get home."

"Sure it can wait?"

"I'm sure," I said.

"See you soon."

"Bye."

Leitha met him at the airport a few hours after he and I finished talking, the night of his big surprise. I can't think of anyone else he would've liked to have seen more first off the plane. The terminal had to be crowded, too, because it was a Friday and the businessmen were returning or leaving for home, families were starting vacations or coming back from one, while others sprawled in chairs, sleeping or reading the newspaper, waiting for a connecting flight. Mike came off the plane wearing the suit he had in the movie. A gift from the designer, it was, a kind of memento tailored just for him. As he headed up the ramp he felt inside his coat pocket, and it was there—the big surprise—safe inside its velvet-lined jeweler's box.

He grinned and began looking for Leitha in the crowd around the gate in the terminal. Already he'd had a couple of drinks back at the airport in Kansas City, and another couple on the plane to steady his nerves. Definitely he had to be nervous, thinking about what he was going to say, and how exactly to say it. His hands were likely sweating. Maybe his mouth was a little dry. But he must've also felt proud of himself, and it was that, I'd like to think—not the nervousness—that showed in his long broad steps, and in the way he held his chest up and out as he walked. And he was happy, too, maybe happier than he'd ever been before because today he'd accomplished what he'd dreamed of accomplishing since he was a boy. The film was done, he'd given his role all of what he'd learned over the years, what he knew of his character, and now he was home to wait for the reaction come opening night. From the critics. From the audience.

She saw him first. He was dressed in an old-fashioned black suit with a western-style bow tie around his neck. His hair was short, combed, his cheeks slightly flushed from the alcohol, and under his arm he carried a copy of *Variety* rolled into a tube. How handsome, she must've thought, even dressed as he was, like a small-town boy all gussied up for his first big trip to the city. That's really what he was, anyway—successful or not—still a small-town boy, still innocent with some rough edges left. And she admired that in him. He wasn't like the other boys she'd known. Spoiled. Too used to getting what they wanted. Leitha rose to the balls of her feet and waved to him from behind another woman. Only he didn't see her and the grin on his face began to fade. At the end of the ramp he stopped and scanned the crowd. Frowned. Other passengers stepped around him. Leitha ducked in front of the woman and waved again. In that moment, before he noticed her, she saw in his eyes a look of confusion and disappointment—almost a kind of resignation, as if he'd expected her not to show. The look made her smile, and that's how Mike first saw her, as he pictured seeing her when he came off his plane—smiling, waiting for him, just as he'd hoped.

They kissed there in the lobby of the terminal until Leitha broke it off. She caught her breath and leaned back to look at him.

"Didn't you have time to change?"

"Into what?"

"Your own clothes."

"These are my own clothes."

She rolled her eyes.

"Missed you," he said.

208

"Missed you, too."

Next they went for his luggage, talking and laughing all the way down the long white-tile hall to the baggage claim, holding hands while they watched for his suitcase on the conveyor belt that went round and round. Ahead Mike noticed a middle-aged man staring at his bow tie. He winked and the man looked down at a passing bag. A few minutes later he grabbed his suitcase off the belt and they headed out to Leitha's car in the parking lot.

They kissed some more before she started the engine because they at least had a little privacy now, and then Mike worked his hands up beneath her blouse for a second or two, enough to feel his hands against her skin and no more, tough as it was to stop. It had been so long. Each night in Kansas, when he'd finished working, he had lain in bed in his motel room thinking of her and wishing she was beside him. And now he had her, only the parking lot at LAX wasn't the best place for them, especially after they hadn't seen each other, especially in a sports car. So she straightened her blouse back down when he pulled away from her and sighed. Finally Leitha started the car and they drove to the Imperial Gardens in West Hollywood for a late-night dinner.

At the restaurant they had a couple of drinks. Mike loosened his tie, rolled his neck. Looked around. A Bengali in a turban sat in the booth across from them, talking to another man dressed in a white robe. They weren't listening, and the other customers were too far away to overhear him. He sat forward and rested his elbows on the table beside the menus. His face grew serious, stern for a moment, before it softened into a smile. Leitha raised her drink, sipped it, set it down. He looked her straight in the eyes.

"What do you think about us getting married?"

She blinked.

Just then the waiter appeared at their table. "Are you ready to order?" he said.

Mike leaned back in the booth.

"Not yet."

"I'll have another drink," Leitha said.

"Me too."

The waiter left.

Again Mike smiled and sat forward. He was just about to speak when Leitha glanced down at the table.

"Is there an ashtray around here?" she said.

"You don't smoke."

"I do sometimes."

"Since when?"

"When I drink."

She began rummaging through her purse on the seat. Found her cigarettes. Lit one. "I don't know what it is about alcohol but it makes me want to smoke." She shook out the match. "I need an ashtray."

He wagged his head and stood up and went and borrowed an ashtray from the Bengali in the other booth. Soon the waiter came back with their drinks. When he left, and they were alone again, Mike took a deep breath and exhaled hard. From inside his coat pocket he found the jeweler's box and held it out to her. Smiled.

"Go on, take it."

But she didn't move and after a while, when she lowered her eyes, he placed the box on the table in front of her.

"Try it on," he said.

"Not tonight."

"See if it fits."

Leitha picked up the menu and pretended to study it. "What are you going to get?" she said.

"Would you quit changing the subject?"

"Should I order for both of us?"

Mike sighed.

"At least open it and look."

She closed the menu. "I can't," she said.

"Why not?"

"Because I can't accept it, okay? You know how my dad is." Leitha stabbed her cigarette out in the ashtray. "I'm not sure I'm ready to get engaged, even if I wanted. To you or anyone. Okay? Just put it away." She glanced around the restaurant until she spotted the waiter and caught his attention. A few seconds later he was at their table again, opening his note pad, a pen in hand.

"The Peking duck," she said. "Does that come with egg roll? Can we order it for two?"

Mike reached for the box and put it back in his pocket.

The Mercedes idled with its headlights shining on the garage door at the end of the driveway. Mike yanked his suitcase out of the trunk and slammed it shut and started across the lawn to the front door. All the lights were out in the house. Leitha lowered her window and called to him.

"Aren't you forgetting something?"

He turned around.

"I don't think so."

"Your *Variety*." She held it out the window, waving it at him. He walked back to the car but stopped a step short of it. "Don't be mad, all right?" she said. "Just let me have a little time." Pause. "You caught me off guard and I need to think it over."

"For how long?"

"Don't stand so far away."

He bowed his head, nodded. Stepped closer.

"C'mere."

He put the suitcase down and rested his elbows on the window frame.

"Give me a couple of weeks."

"You going to tell your parents?"

"Probably."

"You already know what they'll say."

"I still have to tell them."

"Before or after you decide?"

"After."

"Good luck."

"I'm not a little girl anymore. I make my own decisions now." She handed him the *Variety* and then kissed him.

Mike looked down at the paper. "Ever hear of Henry Martin?" he said. *"The Swamp Monsters?"*

"What brought this up?"

"He played the lead doctor."

Leitha gave him a strange look.

"Do you remember him?"

"No."

"He died yesterday."

"You're morbid."

"Don't you want to know how?"

"I don't even know who he is," she said. "Bye."

"Two weeks?"

"About that."

"I love you."

Mike stepped back from the car and asked himself why, as he watched her drive off, did he have to mention Martin just then. What was the connection? Leitha would've been much too young.

Naw, he thought, picking up the suitcase. He wasn't morbid even if his timing was bad. The old guy had been a fine actor in his day, one her father certainly would've remembered. They mentioned his name in the obituary. Mike stuffed the *Variety* into his coat pocket, his fingers grazing the jeweler's box as he did so. Martin was the workshop's first successful disciple and the first, also, to go. A massive coronary. D.O.A. He headed for the front door. The porch light flashed on.

This part I'd watched from the living room, as I'd been waiting up for him, sitting in the dark with a cigarette, blowing my smoke out the window. Their voices carried well in the quiet of the night. I heard almost every word, and those that I couldn't make out I guessed at, given the nature of their conversation, the tone and its mood. All in all, it's a fairly accurate account of what they said, if not what my brother thought about the latest addition to his obituary collection, before he started back toward the house. Before I let him in. As for Mom, she'd returned from shopping earlier that evening, and for a few hours she'd waited up for him with me—because I'd told her about his call—but finally she went to bed. The clock on the mantle had read twelve-thirty. "Wake me when he gets home," she'd said, yawning, heading for the stairs. And I promised her I would, although I had no intention of following up on it. Now the clock read two. I flipped on the porch light and opened the door.

First thing he did was put down his suitcase and hug me. Then he sniffed at my collar and turned me loose.

"You've been smoking again."

"No way."

"Better knock it off, man," he said. "You're going to stunt your growth."

I'd smelled alcohol.

"What about your drinking?"

"What about it?"

"Better knock it off," I said. "You drink too much."

"Hey, is that any way to greet your brother? The movie star?" He punched me lightly in the arm. Chuckled. "Mom asleep?"

"Yeah."

"You got something to tell me?"

I dropped my voice to a whisper. "Let's go outside," I said. "I don't want to wake her."

So we went out back, after he'd gotten a couple of beers from the refrigerator, and sat under the stars on the lawn chairs in the middle of the yard. For a while we just stared up at the sky, listening to the crickets. The night was cool. He opened his beer and I did the same with mine. "Out with it," he said, finally. "What's so important you couldn't sleep without telling me?" I didn't know quite how to say it, because I wasn't completely sure it was true, and so that's how I told him. Carefully. The envelope. Mom's reaction. My suspicions. When I'd finished I felt as if I'd somehow betrayed our mother, yet I also felt I owed Mike my honesty when it came to his own welfare. It was for me to mention and for him to confirm. That was my duty as a brother. He was silent.

"What're you going to do?" I said.

"You think she cashed it?"

I shrugged. "She took it."

"Shit."

"Maybe I'm wrong, though."

"I doubt it," he said. "The check was supposed to come this week, and besides she shouldn't be touching any of my mail in the first place." He took a drink from his beer. "I actually used to think she'd change, that we could be a good family again even without Dad . . . that this stuff would stop, but it never will. She's a thief, man, it's in her character, it's in the blood." He reached over and put his hand on my shoulder and squeezed. "You're who I'm worried about now."

"I'm doing okay."

"That's not what I mean."

"What, then?"

"You ever think about moving back with Dad?"

"What're you talking about? I'm with you, man." Suddenly I felt my voice rising and weakening both at once. "Remember?" I crossed my middle finger over my index and held my hand up. "Where you go, I go. I made up my mind a long time ago and there's no changing it."

"Settle down, huh?"

"I ain't moving back."

"Dad loves you. He needs one of us."

"If he loved us," I said, "then tell me why the fuck, huh? Why the fuck did he let us go with Mom?" I stared at him hard for a while and he didn't say anything. Because he knew I had a damn good question for which he had no answer; a question, too, that he must've thought about himself more than once, coming up empty-handed every time.

"You're being unfair, Jay. You're being selfish," he said, raising his voice as I'd raised mine, except louder. He pointed a finger at me. "That's not why he let us go. It was me, man. *My* decision. Dad needs you as much as you need him and don't you ever think different, damn it." I looked down at the grass then. Neither one of us said a word for a couple of minutes. Finally he sighed and reached into his pocket and took out the jeweler's box and opened it and showed it to me. Inside was a diamond ring. "You listen now, you listen good . . . and don't tell Mom. Promise?" I promised. "I might get married, and if I do, Jay . . ." He snapped the box shut. Returned it to his pocket. "Don't you think I don't love you, ever, because I do and I always, always will. We're brothers, we've been through a lot of shit and it's brought us closer together, instead of apart—not like other families. Only there's one thing you got to understand." He fell silent for a moment. From him came another sigh but a deeper, heavier one than before. "I won't be living here too much longer."

I stood up.

"Her name's Leitha," he said. "And she's beautiful. You'd approve."

"Congratulations."

"You mean that?"

"Yeah, sure. I mean it."

He said something else after that but I'd quit listening, as the conversation, though the words may have been a little different, sounded awfully familiar. Already I was headed down the driveway with my beer, reaching into my back pocket for my Marlboros, lighting one up, taking the smoke in just as deep as I could get it.

I had half expected him to chase after me that night, only he didn't, and I can't say I was disappointed. What I needed then was to be alone. To think. Too much had happened too quickly. I walked around for maybe an hour, trying to figure out what I was

214

going to do next. There didn't seem to be any solutions, no good ones, anyway, or none that I liked. When I'd smoked my last cigarette, I wandered back home. The light in Mom's room was on by then, and so was the one in the living room. You could hear them shouting all the way down the block about his money. No way, no how, was I going back inside. I slept in the garage for what was left of the night and in the morning, and for the next month, things weren't quite the same between Mike and me. Not that I avoided him, or that he avoided me, we just didn't talk that much. No heart-to-heart conversations, anyway. Part of the problem was that he was just too busy now. He and Leitha saw each other almost every day after he got off the set, as Universal had put him straight back to work before *A Rough Kind* was even released. TV stuff, mostly. One prime-time show after another. "Junk," was what Mike called it, tossing the latest script on top of his file cabinet, on top of the others. "Rotten dialogue, rotten story. Why does every car have to end up exploding? I'm sick of this trash." Then he'd wag his head and slip downstairs to make himself another drink. Still, foolish as the scripts may have been, my brother never slacked off on a performance. Sober or not, he did the best he could.

Sometimes he and Leitha went to the house in Malibu when her folks stayed at the workshop. Now and then they met at our place when Mom was gone. Mike was right about her looks. She was a beautiful girl. I'm sure her parents must've known that they were seeing each other more than casually, but I don't think Marrin realized just how serious they'd gotten until the relationship was well under way. As for our own mother, I can't blame Mike for keeping his plans secret from her as long as he could and did. Breaking the news was bound to be disastrous. The night he showed me the ring, the night I took my walk, I thought hard about what I could say or do to change his mind. Nothing. But he didn't move out that month or the following one, though I knew it was inevitable.

I checked on the ring every day after he'd shown it to me. Mike had put it in his dresser drawer, and about two weeks later the damn thing was gone.

18

Saul Leiberman got off to a later start than my brother in that he didn't decide to become an actor until the night of his twenty-first birthday. He celebrated it alone in his studio apartment watching *The Treasure of the Sierra Madre* on an old Zenith perched on top of a chrome TV cart. On the window ledge rested a fan, its head turning back and forth, blowing hot air around the room. Outside ran the freeway, a steady stream of cars, soot, and horns. There had been a heat wave all week, temperatures reaching a hundred and five by noon, and at night it wasn't much better. Saul sat shirtless on the floor with a warm beer in one hand, a cigarette in the other, staring at the blue-gray screen. An unshaven Humphrey Bogart was cracking under the heat of the sun and the pressures of greed. He was alone, long without water, and nowhere could he find even a foot of shade. What Saul saw in Bogart that evening, as he watched him crawl hands and knees along the desert floor, led him to believe that he could do the same. Act. It didn't look too hard.

That was in the summer six years before, going on seven, since he'd enlisted in Theodore Marrin's workshop, and still he'd yet to land even a bit part. Seeing my brother's career take off so well, so quickly, while his own stagnated, had to make him a little desperate, a little on edge.

One afternoon he showed up at Leitha's place in Malibu. This was about a month after Mike had proposed and the summer was approaching. Her parents were gone for the weekend. She answered the door in her bikini.

"My mom's not here."

Saul cleared his throat. "I'm looking for Mike," he said. "He around?"

"What if he is?"

"Can I talk with him for a minute?"

"Some other time."

She started to close the door but Saul stopped it with his hand. "C'mon," he said. "I took the bus all the way to Santa Monica and

thumbed it from there." All I wanna do is ask him something."
He gave her a sad, sincere look. "It'll only take a second, I promise."

"Wait here."

She shut the door on him and got Mike from where they'd been
sunning themselves on the redwood deck overlooking the ocean.
He went out to the front porch in his swimming trunks, eyebrows
furrowed, curious.

"What's happening?"

"Sorry to bother you."

"No problem."

"I just wanted to know if you're going to class next week."

"Probably," he said. "You came all this way to ask me that?"

"I tried calling but you weren't home." He looked down at his
feet, kicked at the ground. "You being so busy and all lately, I just
wondered if you're trying out for *The Circle*."

"On Tuesday?"

"Regular class, man."

"I haven't even opened the script."

"So you're not auditioning?"

"Not this time."

"Thanks, buddy."

"For what?"

"Just thanks."

As he turned to go Mike called to him. "Hey, how'd you know
I was here?"

Saul glanced over his shoulder. "The Marrins are in Idyllwild,"
he said. "It wasn't hard to figure out."

Then he smiled and headed back down the mountain to the
Coast Highway.

Mike returned to the redwood deck. Leitha lay on a towel on
her stomach with the back strap undone. A bottle of Bain de Soleil rested on the guard railing.

"You scare him off?"

"He's gone."

"The guy's a loser."

"He'll do all right."

"As a janitor, maybe."

"Go easy on him," Mike said. "He's my friend."

"What'd he want?"

"Nothing."

"Friends like him always want something." Leitha raised herself up on her elbows, keeping her arms close together. "Did you know he's afraid to drive? Say boo and he jumps. My father only has him around to keep the theater clean. That, I guess, and because of my mother," she said. "Could you put some lotion on my back?"

A break was what the guy needed, he thought, reaching for the bottle. There were plenty of less talented actors in town who worked regularly. Some were stars. As Mike poured lotion into his palm, then onto her shoulders, and began working it in, he noticed the diamond on her finger.

"Have your parents seen the ring yet?"

"I take it off when they're around," she said.

"Leave it on."

"Uh-uh."

"Invite me over for dinner. We'll tell them together like we're supposed to."

"Wait until you move out."

"That won't be for a few more months."

"We'll survive."

"Quit stalling," he said. "Don't be scared."

Leitha rolled over onto her back without the top and grinned. "Boo," she said.

Every summer for the past six years Theodore Marrin had produced his own play, *The Circle*. It was a long one-act about a group of inmates in a private mental institution. The understanding among the students was that if you played one of the principals you were bound to get interviews for other parts, if not a job out of it. The play had an excellent reputation around Hollywood not only because it was a powerful piece but also because those in the industry knew Marrin cast only his two best students for the leads. And that's what a lot of the business folks wanted. His best, his brightest. Saul had tried out for the male lead for the last six years and not once had he made the cut. This time it was going to be different.

At the audition Tuesday Saul felt confident. He and Mike sat together as usual in the back row. A half-dozen others studied

their scripts in silence, and occasionally one glanced up and re-
cited a line aloud. Two more students came through the door.
Mike nodded.

"Who's the little guy?"

"The redhead?"

"Yeah."

"Some punk kid. He's new."

"Any good?"

"Do I look nervous?" Saul put his fingertips to his chest. "No
way." He nudged him in the arm. "You know Mick Toma?
Everybody thought the guy was nothing, like he wasn't going
anywhere. He played *The Circle* a couple of years ago and the next
thing you know he lands an equity tour with Heston. New York
and England, man. Can you believe it?" A big grin. "It's my turn
now. My fucking dues are paid."

A minute later the old man hobbled into the theater with Cindy
clutching his arm. She helped him up the stairs into his chair
upstage corner and then took a seat in the front row. Glanced
back at Mike. He smiled nervously and leaned closer to Saul.
"Where's Leitha tonight?" he whispered, but all he got was a
shrug. Auditions had begun.

For two long hours Marrin grilled and ridiculed his students.
Seven young actors had their shot and not one of them made it
through the entire scene before he pounded his cane and ordered
them offstage. The only one to get past the halfway mark was the
new kid with the red hair. He might've made it all the way, too, if
he hadn't stuttered and missed a line. The old man grunted, his
nostrils flared, he rose slowly from his chair. "One lousy page of
monologue and you fucked it up," he shouted. "Get off the stage."
Marrin sighed. "Take a ten-minute break." He looked around the
theater. "Mike?"

"Up here."

"You're on when we come back."

Students funneled out the door until Mike and Saul were the
only ones left.

"Mr. Marrin?"

"What now?"

The old man made his way down the stairs with Cindy at his
arm again. Mike approached him. "I haven't had a chance to look
at the play."

"Too busy for me?"

"It's not that."

"Too big for us now, eh?"

"I missed last week," he said. "I don't even have a copy of it."

"Borrow one." The old man started out of the theater. "You have ten minutes to study," he said. "Put in an appearance for the class."

At the door, as Cindy held it open for her husband, she looked back at Mike. "In case you're wondering, Leitha's been grounded for the summer," she said. "No calls, no dates." Marrin jerked his arm free from hers and wandered into the parking lot with Cindy right behind him.

The door closed.

They were alone now. Saul put his feet up on the seat ahead and threw him a copy of the play. It fell short into the aisle in a flutter of pages.

"Go on, man. Pick it up."

"Don't be mad."

"I don't give a shit."

So he reached for it, and when he looked up Saul was already headed for the door. Mike shook his head, asking himself as he settled into a seat why Leitha had been grounded and what it had to do with him. Everything. He opened the script then slapped it shut. For a moment he thought of confronting the old man, telling him off, only that's exactly what he wanted. A major scene. Fuck him. Fuck the workshop. Mike tossed the play onto the stage and walked outside into the parking lot and past the house in back of the theater. Cindy stood on the porch, smiling. He glared at her, then continued down Vine to the bar that served minors without any questions.

Mike called when he figured she was alone. Auditions had to be under way again.

"Hello?"

"Leitha?"

"Yeah."

"You break the news?"

"Not me."

The phone smelled of something foul, something sour, and Mike wrinkled his nose. Held the receiver a couple of inches from his mouth. "Your mom told me you're grounded," he said. "What happened?"

"We had a fight."

"Over what?"

"I don't want to say."

"Your old man find the ring?"

"Don't call him an old man."

"Sorry."

The jukebox blared. He turned his back to it and covered one ear with his hand. "Why don't you come by," he shouted. "Have a drink with me. I'm at the Rain Club on Santa Monica."

"Better ask your mommy first."

"Huh?"

"She called this morning."

"You kidding?"

"Uh-uh."

"Shit."

"I'm corrupting you, she said." Her voice was sarcastic. "Or that's what my mother told me, anyway. I didn't get a chance to talk with yours. Say hello to her for me, okay? And tell her thanks for the help."

She hung up.

Mike slammed the receiver down and stormed back to the bar and downed his drink. Ordered another. It was going to be awhile before he could think of heading home without wrapping his hands tight around Mom's neck.

Saul stopped at the liquor store before he caught the bus back home. At his apartment he opened the windows and turned on the fan. Although it wasn't a hot night, not the full-blown summer of six years before, the air was still muggy, still humid. Even the slightest rise in temperature made his place like an attic. Made him sweat. He opened a beer and flipped on the TV. Nothing but garbage. He turned it off and finished his beer and drank another. Then he had another and another until the six-pack was gone and he started on the vodka he'd bought. Finally he found the nerve to do what he thought he should've done a long time ago.

He set the phone on his coffee table and dialed the workshop number.

"Hello?"

"Mr. Marrin?" he said. "This is Saul."

"It's after eleven."

"I'm sorry, sir."

"Call back tomorrow."

"There's a purpose," he said. "I want to apologize for taking off like I did."

"Good night," he said.

"Apologies accepted?"

"Just don't let it happen again."

"But you forgive me?"

"Good night, Saul."

"Sir?" He swallowed, collected his courage. "I'm quitting the workshop."

"Fine," he said. "Good-bye."

"Don't you care?"

Marrin hung up.

Saul put the receiver in its cradle and rested his head in his hands and listened to the whir of the fan on the windowsill. The moment he'd said it he knew that he'd made a terrible mistake.

The door to Marrin's den was open about a foot. Leitha peered inside. She was wearing a flannel nightgown. Her father sat behind his desk.

"Who was that?"

"Saul," he said. "Why?"

"Just wondering."

"You expecting a call, honey?"

"No."

"Good," he said. "Because I don't want you using the phone."

"For how long?"

"For as long as it takes to straighten you out." He removed the receiver from the hook and set it on the desk. "Isn't it past your bedtime?"

Leitha pushed the door wide open. "I'm not a kid anymore," she said, her voice rising. "You can't keep me locked up. This is crazy. I haven't done anything wrong; I haven't hurt you or Mom." She stomped her foot. "All you're doing is make me hate you."

Marrin patted his thigh.

222

"C'mere, princess."

She didn't move.

He sighed. "I may be crippled but I'm not blind, baby. If there's anything I want it's to see you happy. Trust me, you'll meet another boy at college soon," he said, "and then you'll thank me. I don't enjoy being mean to you." He held his arms out to her and she bowed her head and went to him and sat carefully on his lap. "Actors are fine for amusement, and maybe that's okay for you now, but remember, they're professional liars, honey. Professional fools. You're never to take them seriously." Marrin looked her in the eyes. "Promise me you won't see him anymore."

She stared down at the floor.

"He's been with your own mother. We both understand that." Marrin stroked her hair, the back of her neck. "Now it's my daughter?"

But she was silent.

Busy signal.

Mike had had a few drinks and come home and now he sat in the den with the phone pressed to his ear. It was after the third try, the calls spaced about every twenty minutes, when he gave up for the night and slipped upstairs to Mom's room. Eased opened the door. In the light from the window he saw her curled up on the bed, her body hidden beneath the covers, only the back of her head visible from where he stood staring at her. For a while he thought of pulling the blankets off, cursing her, but he was too exhausted, too burned, and too drunk to fight tonight. What he needed was to be alone. As he watched Mom sleeping, her hair spread across the pillow, the anger and rage he felt passed into sadness. She looked harmless there in the bed under the moonlight that shone through the window. He thought of Dad and wondered if this was how he once saw her, gentle in sleep, warm beside him. They must've had some good years together. Sure, they must've. So he turned away then, he shut the door and avoided another confrontation as he had with Marrin hours earlier, and he wandered back down the hall to his room. Tomorrow there was work to be done.

As he sat on the edge of his bed, taking off one shoe, then the other, letting them drop to the floor, he thought of Saul. He thought of Leitha and his brother and he thought again of Mom and hung his head. He needed rest. Sleep. Tomorrow he began filming again for Universal, this time a *Cannon, M.D.* episode. In it he was to play Dr. Cannon's younger brother, a confused kid who believed—after studying the symptoms in a medical book— that he had Hodgkin's disease. The diagnosis he kept from his brother until his condition was almost beyond help. The character turned out to be sick, yes, but not with the fatal illness he thought. Mike lay back on the mattress, trying to remember his opening lines, but coming up blank.

A second later he passed out.

Every time Saul drank he said things he really didn't mean and always regretted it intensely when he awoke the next morning. Now his head throbbed. His throat was dry. He rolled out of bed and dragged himself into the shower and let the water pelt his back until it turned cold and stung. After he'd dressed he caught the bus into Hollywood and got off on Melrose a few blocks from the workshop. So far the sky was overcast, and cool, yet as he walked he began to sweat through his shirt. Saul drew the back of his arm across his forehead and looked at the hairs. Slick. Wet. It felt good, deserving, and somehow just that the toxins—all the poisons and garbage he'd put into himself the night before— should be seeping out of his system now, slowly, drop by drop. No more drinking. Ever. Because he'd made a hell of a mistake and if he could repair it, if he could set things right again, he promised himself never to look back—to just move forward and behave. He'd sign up at the YMCA, start working out, find himself a girlfriend, and get a steady job. "Sweat," he told himself, as he walked faster. "*Move.*" He made fists of his hands, squeezing hard, feeling the blood pressure rising. "Sweat the shit out of your body."

When he got to the theater he let himself inside with his key, took the broom from the broom closet, and swept the aisles and the stage. Mopped the floors. Pushed the seats back into place. Then he set about cleaning the bathroom in the dressing room, which was where Marrin found him, a minute later—leaning over the toilet, sprinkling Comet into the bowl.

The old man looked down at him.

"Shouldn't you have done that last night?"

Saul nodded.

"You have certain duties, certain responsibilities," Marrin said, "and you walked out on them. You walked out on me, Saul, and now this . . . this is how you show your respect, to come back the next day as if nothing happened?" He took in a deep breath and let it out slowly. "What am I to supposed to do?" Pause. "Forgive you? What am I supposed to think?" Pause. "Nothing?"

"I'm sorry, sir."

"Sorry?"

"Yes."

"How sorry, Saul?"

"Terribly sorry."

He reached behind the tank for the brush and dropped to one knee and began to scrub the porcelain, first the outside, then inside the bowl. Not a word was said for a long while. There was just the sloshing of the water as he worked the brush around. The old man put the tip of his cane to the back of Saul's neck and pushed a little. "You're a loser and a coward. You're a sick, pathetic boy." Pushed a little more. "You've never had any talent and you never will. I'm the best at what I do, Saul, and that's to train those who are worth training, who are worth my time, but even I can't shape something out of nothing and you're nothing, Saul. Nothing. You don't exist." Once more he jabbed the cane into his neck, hard this time—enough to knock the sweat off his brow onto the floor. "Get out," Marrin said, but in a calm voice, not a shout. "I never want to see your face again."

19

I robbed my last house the night before Mike's movie opened. Mrs. Turner gave her notice in the middle of June, I'd just gotten out of school for the summer, and my report card showed two F's, two C-minuses, and a D in English. A few months had passed since my brother quit the workshop, leaving as unspectacularly as the days that had slipped by, without incident or argument. He never did confront Mom about her phone call to the Marrins, or at least I never heard about it, and as far as I know Leitha cooled off soon enough. They still saw each other whenever possible, even though it had gotten harder to do than before, now that her father was on to them. The sonofabitch couldn't keep her locked up all summer.

The F's on my report card I was able to change to B's, but the D was a little tricky. Although I must've written fifty D's into B's on another sheet of paper, when I attempted it on the report card it came out looking like hell. I didn't know what to do, whether to say I'd lost it, or just hand it over to Mom and pray it would pass. In any case, as I said earlier, this was the day before *A Rough Kind* opened. I was alone. Mom had gone shopping for something special to wear the following evening, and where Mike was—if not with Leitha—I had no idea. Riding out the last hours in a bar?

When night fell, and the house was still empty, I wrote a note and left it on the kitchen table. The clock over the stove read a quarter to nine.

Dear Mom and Mike,
Went to get something to eat. I'll be back around 10:00. Don't worry, I know how to take care of myself.

Jay

In the garage I found my bolt cutters, duct tape, gloves, flashlight, and a screwdriver, and slipped them into the sack on the handlebars of my bike. I rode out onto the street, looking over my shoulder every now and then as I pedaled. The neighborhood was quiet, and the night was a perfect one—warm, dark, no moon in the sky. Be calm, I told myself. Calm but alert. Be fast and be quiet. In the middle of the block was her house, drapes shut, lights out inside. I coasted up the driveway to the gate at the end and got off and turned my bike so that it was facing the street and propped it against the cinder-block wall. Again I looked around. Nobody in sight. The sprinklers were on in the backyard next door.

From the gate hung the Master padlock. I put on my gloves and took the bolt cutters from the sack and slipped the jaws around the U-bolt. It was made of case-hardened steel but the cut still didn't add up to more than a few seconds' worth of work. The lock softened under the teeth without any real pressure, and soon I was making my way across the backyard to the patio and a set of French doors inlaid with small panes of glass. Ten minutes, I told

226

myself. Get in and get what's good and get the hell out. Quickly I taped one of the panes with the duct tape, then snapped it with the butt of the screwdriver, and froze, listened. Far in the distance I heard a dog bark. A moment later I slid the screwdriver into my pocket and peeled the tape back and reached inside and unlocked the door. Flipped on my flashlight. Entered.

My plan was to find the master bedroom and go through it first, as that's usually where folks kept the small things they liked most, and the small things were usually the most valuable. So I headed across the living room to the staircase, and on my way I passed the coffee table, where I spotted the two silver candlesticks I'd seen months before when I came collecting. I stuffed one in each of my back pockets and then started up the stairs a step at a time, pausing, listening, then continuing on. At the top I shined the flashlight down the hall and it faded against the door at the end. There were three other doors to the right, all closed. I opened the first one. Inside a nightstand separated two neatly made single beds. Opposite them was a dresser, but there was nothing on it. I checked the drawers and they were empty. There was nothing in the closet, either, except for a bunch of wire hangers.

The next door opened into a black tiled bathroom. A pair of panty hose, the legs hanging toward the floor, rested on the towel rack.

I moved on.

The third room was completely bare. Not even a carpet on the floor.

I moved on to the last door.

By this time I was getting a little irritated, a little too anxious, and much too careless. I pushed open the last door, which was already ajar, and found my flashlight aimed on the face of a man lying on a king-size bed in the middle of the room. He bolted upright. I spun around and dropped the flashlight and ran back down the hall, down the stairs, and through the living room, slammed into the coffee table, picked myself up, and shot out the doors, onto my bike, and pedaled like hell without once looking behind me until I was rounding the corner. The man stood in his bathrobe in the middle of the street, shaking his fist. And cursing, I imagined, though I couldn't hear the words.

Up the block I tossed the candlesticks into a patch of ivy growing in front of someone's house. The gloves I yanked off and threw into the gutter. As for the bolt cutters, and the duct tape, I'd left them on the patio, and there wasn't a damn thing I could do about it now. I'd never seen the man before, I didn't know what he was doing there, and I hoped—as I pedaled still faster— that I'd never see him again. A car passed by just then and my heart dropped. But it wasn't a cop. I popped the curb onto the sidewalk and lowered my head, and that's how I rode the rest of the way home, with my shoulders hunched, my face turned away from the street.

Mom was parking the Nova in the garage when I came up the driveway. She got out as I climbed off my bike.

"Where you been?" she said.

"McDonald's."

"There's plenty of food in the refrigerator."

"I just felt like a hamburger."

"If you want hamburgers, we'll have hamburgers," she said. "All you gotta do is ask, baby." She went around to the trunk and opened it. "Help me unload this stuff." One bag after another she piled into my arms, all from May Company, all large but light. She grabbed the last few and shut the trunk and we went inside to the dining room. I set the things on the table and flipped on the light. Mom hollered toward the stairs. "Mike . . . honey, you here?" But there was no answer. "Did he come home before you left?" she asked. I told her no and she sighed. "That boy better get some rest because he'll need it. I'm sure there's a big party after and we don't want to have to leave early." Mom dumped her bags onto a chair and smiled at me. "How's it feel to be out of school?"

I faked a smile. "Great," I said.

"You do good?"

"I did okay."

"How good's okay?"

I shrugged.

"Run get your report card," she said, handing me one of the bags. "Try these on while you're at it. See if they fit." She reached out and ran one finger above the top of my ear so that the hair fell behind it. "You could use a trim, you know."

I headed up to my room and put on the new clothes and dragged a comb across my head. From the dresser drawer I took out my report card, examined it again, and groaned. The D made

228

into a B looked as phony as I did. In the mirror was some nice kid in a stiff, fancy dress shirt with a clip-on tie and polyester slacks too big around the waist—not Jay McKinney. This guy was a fake. A cheater. I sighed and turned away from the mirror and went back downstairs with the damn report card. Mom was on the phone in the den now. She held a red satin dress against her chest with her free hand, checking its length. On the floor in an open shoe box was a pair of red pumps. "It starts at eight," she said. "At the Bruin in Westwood . . . it's right in the Village . . . uh-huh, we'll need it for the night." I stood there for maybe a minute before there was a pause in the conversation. Mom tucked the receiver against her shoulder for a few seconds and pursed her lips, eyeing me. "They fit fine," she said. "Lemme see your report card." I handed it to her and she looked it over. My heart went up to my throat as I studied her face, hoping it would pass. "Not bad," she said. "Actually it's pretty good except for the C-minus, but that's in P.E. I'm proud of you." Then whoever it was she was talking to came back on the line, she handed me the report card, and stared down at her feet. "Miller . . . Jenny Miller." As she spoke she lifted one of the shoes out of the box with her toe and slid it on. "We're in the Fairfax district . . . off Beverly." Something funny must've been said then, because she laughed, and I took the opportunity to slip back to my room and undress again.

Only I didn't come downstairs afterward. I hung my jeans over the chair and the screwdriver I'd used to bust the window fell out of my pocket. I put it in the desk drawer and then went to the bathroom and tore up the report card so that Mike wouldn't see it. The pieces I flushed down the toilet.

Later, while I was in bed, Mom checked on me.

"Honey, you asleep already?"

I lay silent, still.

"Good night," she said. "Love you."

When I heard her shut the door I pulled the sheet over my head and wished that I could shrink like the Shrinking Man, curl up, and dissolve into the mattress.

Five o'clock A.M. He stumbled into my room, pulled off his shoes, collapsed on the bed. At first I thought he was so out of it that he'd gotten our rooms mixed up. Gotten lost. His breath reeked, his voice was hoarse. The words came hard for him but he knew exactly where he was.

"You got something to say?"

I rolled onto my back.

"About what?"

"You tell me."

"Like old times, eh? Anything?"

"Anything," he mumbled. "But be honest, Jay. I want to help you."

"With what?"

"Don't lie to me."

I didn't know what he meant, if he was bluffing or what.

"I ain't lying."

"They're going to catch up with you," he mumbled. "The lies. You know what it's done to the family. Just level with me, okay, brother to brother? Old times, remember?"

I panicked.

"You're drunk, you ain't making any sense," I said, voice rising. "You're always drunk, man. Why don'tcha sober up for a couple of days?" And I climbed out of bed and hurried into my clothes. Mike propped himself up on his elbows for a second, then fell back onto the mattress. Outside, the sun was rising, and from the light coming through the window I could see him more clearly now—the jawbone, the sunken closed eyes. He'd lost too much weight for the *Cannon, M.D.*, role and he hadn't gained it back yet. "You better start eating, man, or you're gonna get sick." Whether or not he was listening, I couldn't tell. Mike didn't say anything, and for the time being I didn't care. I wanted away from him.

The first thing I did when I got outside was to pull out the ladder in the garage, climb it, and look up on the rafters. I took a deep breath and held it. It wasn't any bluff. My box of stuff was gone—the Rolex, the ring, the silverware, everything.

Including the gun.

Sonofabitch if I didn't know what to do but get on my bike, pick up my papers at the corner, and deliver them on schedule like it was just another day. The difference was that I had the good sense, or lack of courage, not to come home until it was almost time to leave for the opening.

A stretch limousine was parked at the curb. The chauffeur sat on the fender thumbing through a magazine. Our front door was open. Mom stood just behind the threshold in her new red pumps and satin dress. Her arms were crossed over her chest, and on her face was a scowl.

I rode my bike up the lawn. Hopped off.

"Where the hell have you been?" she shouted.

"Working."

"Get inside right now."

"The evening kid didn't show," I said. "I hadda do his route."

"You should've called."

"I forgot."

"Just put your bike in the house and get dressed," she hollered. "If we're late it's because of you." Mom stepped past me and hurried out to speak to the chauffeur. I rolled my bike into the foyer, where I spotted my brother staring at me from the living room, sitting on the edge of the couch, bent over the coffee table with a pair of scissors. He was cutting a page out of one of Mom's *Movielands*, maybe another obituary.

"I want to talk with you," he barked. I eased the kickstand down with my foot, parked it, started upstairs.

Halfway down the hall he caught up with me and grabbed my arm. Shoved me into my room. Slammed the door.

"You fucked up."

"I gotta get ready."

"Shut your mouth."

He pushed me onto the bed.

"Lemme alone."

"You idiot," he shouted. "You stupid fuck." He stormed over to the desk and picked up a book that rested there, turned around, and narrowed his eyes at me. "Found the typing manual for you, asshole." He shook it in front of my face. "Found some other shit, too, but I don't suppose you know anything about it." He raised the book over his head. "I ought to hit you, hit you hard." I flinched, leaned back. "Knock some goddamn sense into that head." But he didn't hit me—he threw the book down. He bit his lower lip. "Breaking and entering, man—taking what isn't yours like you don't know any better. What's happened to you? Huh? I don't understand." He spun around and went to the window, looked out, then turned and pointed a finger at me. "You're a fucking thief, Jay, and you didn't learn it from me. You didn't get it from Dad." He walked over to the bed and pushed me again. "The story's true . . . you're like Mom."

Silence.

"Please don't tell her."

"I might."

"Or Dad, you *can't* tell Dad."

She hollered up the staircase then.

"What the hell's taking so long? C'mon, c'mon. It's going on seven-thirty."

Mike grabbed my new pants off the chair beside the desk and tossed them at me. "Get dressed." He went to the door and yanked it open. "Get down to that thing outside. I'll deal with you tonight."

He slammed it behind him.

I stared at the wall, ashamed and sick to my stomach, wishing I hadn't come home. Wishing this day was over, gone, finished. My eyes stung. I hung my head and pinched the bridge of my nose until the stinging passed. At the foot of the bed was the typing manual, broken open at the spine, and after a while I picked it up, smoothed out the pages, and set it back on the desk. I wondered what he'd done with my stuff but I knew I couldn't ask, that it was gone for good. Again Mom hollered up to me. I dragged myself into the new clothes.

A couple of minutes later I scooted into the backseat of the limousine. The chauffeur shut the door for me, then ran around to his side and slipped behind the wheel. Soon we were moving. I sat across from Mom and Mike, but he wouldn't look at me. There were dark circles under his eyes, his complexion was pallid, his face gaunt, and the dress shirt that he wore fit him much too loosely. He stared out the window.

"What's the matter with you boys?" Mom said.

Silence.

She nudged Mike.

"Why so quiet?"

"We should've driven ourselves," he muttered. "This is overdoing it."

Mom laughed. "Better get used to it, honey, because we're gonna be riding in these a lot. You're a star now." Near her feet was a small compartment, which she reached down and opened. "It's your night and we're going in style, baby. *Style.* All the way." On the shelf were champagne glasses and a bottle of Dom Perignon in a silver bucket of ice. Mike uncorked it for us. I held the glasses as he poured and handed the first full one to Mom.

She raised it into the air. "A toast," she said. "To a new star."

We touched glasses.

"To your movie," I said.

"To the big time."

The limousine made a turn onto Sunset, and a little of my champagne spilled onto the carpet. We drank in silence for a while. At a red light I noticed a man in a station wagon, his arm hanging out the window, looking at us. A couple on the sidewalk stared, too, and I felt uncomfortable, as I imagine my brother did. "Think we'd ever be in a limo going to the opening of your movie?" Mom said. "Could you picture it? When we were back in San Jose?" Mike shook his head and poured himself another drink. She laughed her shrill laugh and poked him in the ribs. "Smile, baby. Why so quiet?"

"I'm just nervous."

"They're gonna love you."

We passed through Beverly Hills, past the mansions and into Westwood, where the streets were crowded with students from UCLA. Most were tanned and a lot were blond. They all looked healthy and strong, especially compared to my brother with his champagne, sitting slumped in the seat, silent, pale, and thin, sweating from the forehead. Mom gave me her glass, opened her purse, and took out a brush, a handkerchief. "Hold still," she said, leaning forward, patting the sweat from his face. The chauffeur pulled to the curb outside the Bruin as she was trying to brush his hair. Mike jerked away from her. "Wipe that frown off your face," she said. "Cheer up." She nudged him in the shoulder again. "Look happy for the photographers."

And he smiled.

The chauffeur left the engine idling as he got out and ran around and opened the door for us. Part of the sidewalk had been cut off with two red cordons, and there were maybe twenty or thirty people in line behind them, but there weren't any photographers, no snapping bright lights or screaming fans, just a red carpet that led from the curb past the box office into the lobby. Mom reached for his arm on the way in, and I saw the hurt in her eyes when he turned away, when he wouldn't let her take it. Instead, he jammed his hands into his pockets and walked a step ahead of us. The young man at the door asked for our names. "Michael Casey," my brother said proudly, "and two guests." He checked

233

us off on a sheet he had in front of him on a ticket stand and moved aside.

The lobby was packed, noisy. It was a beautiful old theater with high ceilings and murals on the walls, gold-leaf pillars, chandeliers, and baroque-style cornices. A group of men stood talking just inside the doors. One turned and clapped Mike on the shoulder and congratulated him. I suppose it could've been the director, maybe the writer, or one of the technical people or minor players. Mom and I stood near the buffet table, waiting for him to introduce us, but he never did. A waiter in a tuxedo gave her a glass of wine, which she sipped absently, scanning the lobby, trying to keep smiling. Mike disappeared into the crowd for a minute, and when he returned he had a handsome young woman clutching his arm. She wore a backless dress.

"Mom," he said, "this is Leitha Marrin."

"Nice to meet you."

"My pleasure."

"And my little brother Jay."

Leitha smiled.

"I've talked with you on the phone once," she said. "But we've never had a chance to meet. You have a beautiful family."

They reached out to shake hands, only Mike had already spoken, and Mom pulled hers back. She let it fall to her side.

"We're getting married."

The lobby lights blinked off, then on.

She flung her purse over her shoulder and started through the crowd, out of the theater, when Mike took hold of her arm. "Stay, okay," he said. "I want you to stay, Mom."

The audience was made up of agents and reviewers, actors and friends of actors, relatives of those in the industry, and maybe a few dozen others unconnected to the film who had actually paid to get in. The theater was almost full, and it must have held at least a thousand. Mike sat between Leitha and Mom. I took the seat at the end beside him. Before the lights went out everyone around us had been talking except us. The credits came after the title. On the huge silver screen, the soundtrack playing, appeared my brother's name in a single frame to himself.

STARRING

MICHAEL CASEY

I glanced at Mike and smiled as Leitha slipped her hand into his on the armrest. Mom stared straight ahead. The applause was good, as it was for Terry Hull—the other lead—when his name passed across the screen, as well as the ones that followed it. The movie opened with a young man being dragged out of an old house by two Union soldiers. He wore a dress with a bonnet on his head. On the porch was the mother, screaming, and in the background were more soldiers on horses. The scene cut then to the inside of another house not far from the first one, because you could hear the clop of horses approaching, and there was my brother. Michael David McKinney. The whole screen lit up, or at least that's how I saw it, saw him—in the same suit that he'd worn home the night he returned from Kansas. Before him stood a shrine table for his dead brother, and beside him were the actors who played his parents. They all looked scared, especially Mike, though he was trying hard to hide it.

For a moment I forgot that my brother was angry with me and elbowed him in the ribs, grinned. "You did it," I whispered. "You've made it, man." But he ignored me, and in that same moment I remembered what I'd done earlier and why there couldn't be any congratulations or teasing. Onscreen the mother shooed him under the black tablecloth of the shrine at the same time that a knock came on the door. The father opened it. Seconds later Union soldiers were searching the house.

They don't find him, though, and in the next scene he's headed out of town. That's when he meets the Bower character and his gang and from there on the movie moves as swiftly and powerfully as its opening. Only this was a realistic western, not stock-full of murderous Indians, black-and-white heroes, and bad guys. The gang was an awkward, bumbling bunch of young men and boys who couldn't hit a damn thing with a six-shooter unless the target was close and standing still. True to life, it was. No hundred-yard running kills with a .45. No smooth talkers and barroom brawls.

If my brother was tense about his work as he watched himself that night, or if he'd worried the months before about how he and the movie would be received, there was no need for it. He'd done a fine job, and it showed not just to me but most everyone else in the audience, objective or not as they may have been, considering their ties to the film. Still the applause came fast, loudly, sincerely. A reviewer from *Life* later wrote, ". . . *A Rough Kind* is a good kind . . . Go see it," and another from *Cosmopolitan* said, "It [*A Rough Kind*] has the ambiance of Mark Twain young male foolery overlaid by the stark realism of the Jack London genre." But I've gotten ahead of myself here, because the reviews weren't yet written, and for now the movie was just ending with a medium-close on my brother and Bower. A freeze frame. They were pointing Colts at a bank teller.

Mom rose suddenly from her seat. Her knees bumped against the back of the chairs, and in her haste she stepped on my foot. I rose, too. Leitha turned to my brother.

"You better go."

"I'm not chasing her anymore."

"She's your mother," Leitha said. "You can't let her leave like that."

"Hell if I can't."

"Go on."

He made a fist. Hit the armrest.

"Calm down."

"I'm calm."

She put her hand on his knee, patted it. "Hurry," she said. "Before you miss her." A man behind us leaned over his chair and congratulated Mike. Another in front did the same. People were rising all around us now, talking again, filling the aisle.

"C'mon," I said, nodding toward the doors. "Talk with her, huh?" He gave me a dirty look, and I think he would have cursed me if Leitha hadn't kissed him then, prodded him again.

"I'll meet you at Musso and Frank's later," she said. "Okay? All right? Just do what your brother says—talk to her, Mike. She needs you right now."

So he sighed, gave me another mean look, and we headed up the aisle into the lobby and outside. The limousine idled in the white zone behind a Buick with the door open. Mom sat in back, her face turned toward the window away from us. I climbed inside. Mike scooted over beside her and put a hand on her shoulder. "Don't touch me," she said quickly. "Get away . . . go back to that girl, you don't care about me."

"That's not true."

"You never did care."

"Would you just listen?"

The chauffeur was at the door now. Mike looked up at him and then to Mom again. "You want to go out to dinner?" he said. A long silence. "What about it? Someplace nice where we can talk?"

More silence.

"Just take me home," she said.

He nodded to the chauffeur, who shut the door.

On the ride back Mike kept sitting forward on the edge of his seat, trying to get her attention, to comfort her, but it was useless. She wouldn't even look at him. Once he gave up for a minute and crossed his arms over his chest and groaned in exasperation. "Fine night," he muttered. "Thanks, both of you for the fine night, for being so understanding, thanks." And in a way, though I knew it was wrong, it felt good to see him sweat as he'd made me sweat earlier, and because I thought he deserved it. Because he wanted to desert not just Mom but me for some girl neither of us knew or cared about. A traitor to the family, he was, and at the time I didn't question my own selfishness. Suffer, I thought. "Mom," he said, sitting forward again. "I'm going to be twenty years old. Don't you think it's about time I fell in love?" But she continued to stare out the window in silence. In the reflection I saw what my brother couldn't, due to where we were sitting—opposite each other—and what I saw was a faint smile on Mom's face. I'd seen it before and knew what it meant. The limousine stopped in front of our place.

Mom opened the door herself and got out calmly, paid the man with what must've been a hundred in cash, and headed into the house. I followed Mike up the path lined with birds-of-paradise to the porch, where I stepped in front of him. "Maybe you should take a walk," I said. "Give her time to cool off. Let her think about it. It's just gonna be bad if you go in now."

"I want to settle this."

"Do it tomorrow."

"Get out of my way."

"Mike," I said. "Don't go in."

"You don't want to hear it, fine. I don't want you to hear it either. Stay in your room until it's over." Pause. "We still have plenty to talk about."

"You ain't telling on me?"

He shook his head.

"Thanks, man."

"You don't have to thank me."

"I mean it."

"Don't think you're getting off."

"I know."

"You don't want to go to jail," he said. "You have to stop."

"I promise."

"And you have to return the stuff," he said. "We got to figure out a way to do it so you don't get caught."

He stepped around me and went inside. Mom was waiting for him in the living room on the couch that once belonged to Miss Swanson. She spoke in a noble, haughty voice. "This little girl, this little Leitha, do you honestly believe she loves you? Do you suppose, just for a minute, do you think, and I really, really want you to think hard now, that this little slut might ever look at you twice if you weren't up on the screen tonight?"

"Don't ever call her that."

"I know one when I see one, baby."

"Mom," I shouted.

"Go to your room."

"No."

"You're just like your father." She stood up from the couch. "Is that what you want, Michael? To be like him—dirty? Is that what you and I've worked for all these years?" Her voice was still haughty, yet calm, and that's what was scary. "Is that how I raised you? To sleep with some cheap slut?"

"Shut up," he hollered.

"Truth hurt?"

"She's a good woman."

Mom laughed.

"I came home to talk," he said, "not fight."

"So talk."

She went to the table lamp and adjusted the shade, which was tilted. Mike walked to the mantle and took a long, deep breath as if he were preparing to speak, but it was Mom who spoke first. "When's the big day?" She looked at him and smiled. "When do you tie the knot?"

"August."

"Tell me something?"

No answer.

"She your first slut?"

238

His face grew red. "Quit calling her that," he shouted.

"Is she?"

"It's none of your business."

"She is, isn't she?" Mom made a clucking noise with her tongue, as if she were disappointed. "Let me tell you, baby, there's gonna be a lot more wanting to get into your pants. You don't marry the first one that gives you a little."

"But she's not the first."

Mom glared at him and he glared back. Slowly she cocked her head, not taking her eyes off him, and came a little closer. They were within a couple of feet of each other now. "Is that how you spend your money?" she said, the calmness gone from her voice. "Dinners and movies on sluts and whores? But that's not enough, huh, baby? Huh? You gotta get married. How many," she said, "just how many have there been?"

"All kinds," he said.

"Stop it," I hollered.

Mike glanced at me. Shouted, "Get out of here."

"No."

"How *many*?"

"Dozens."

She slapped him.

"And Leitha's the best. Soooo good." He rolled his eyes. "All we do is fuck, all day long we fuck and fuck." She slapped him again. "You should hear when I make her come, Mom. She screams and it's a beautiful, glorious scream." Her hand flew up but he caught it at the wrist this time and squeezed until she was wincing. Up came the other hand and he grabbed it, too, as it landed on his chest once, twice. The blows made a hollow sound like a drum. "You bastard," she screamed. He pushed her and she stumbled back into the wall and hit her head hard against the plaster. For a moment her eyes grew dull, listless, and I thought it might've been over. Mike pointed a finger at her, his voice cracked. "No more," he said. "No more. I don't want to fight anymore."

Suddenly the dazed look passed from her eyes, she lowered her chin and cocked her head, smiled. Slowly she approached him now. "Big man, are you, baby? Hitting your own mother? That make you feel big, honey?"

"Don't touch me."

"But I'm not mad."

"*I said, 'Don't touch me.'*"

Mom held her arms out as if she had nothing to hide. "I won't hurt you," she said. "C'mere, baby. I don't want to fight any more than you do."

He backed up a step.

"Don't be scared."

"Get away."

"Hold me, honey. Please," she said. "Please, I need you to hold me."

Another step closer.

"Mike," I said. "Don't."

Her hand came up gently. At first he leaned away, avoiding it, and then in his eyes I saw him give in. Her eyes, too, had become fluid, tender. She stroked his cheek. He let her hand slide underneath his chin, down to his neck and around his throat then back up to his cheek and down again with the nails bared into his skin. A strange noise, as if he'd lost his breath—an animal noise—rose from his chest. And he slapped her, lunging forward with all of his weight, so that her hair swung one way and then again so it swung the other way. Again and again. "Stop it," I hollered. "That's enough." But he kept on until she fell to her knees. In that same moment her eyes flashed toward the coffee table, the scissors there on top of her movie magazine, and now she had them. Up Mom came, rising off the floor. Down went her hand, down with the scissors, down fast and hard.

Only she missed.

He grabbed the arm before she could raise it again and held it against his chest, both of them trembling, until her body went limp. Until, finally, she began to cry. The scissors fell to the carpet and I walked over and got them. My brother let her go then and left the house. I didn't know at the time, and I don't know now if he'd planned to return. Mom went and curled up on the couch against the plastic, knees pressing her stomach, keening. For a while I stood over her with the scissors tight in my fist, knowing I could do it, but letting my grip slacken. That was how I felt then and that was how I last saw her that night—crying.

I went upstairs to my room to wait for Mike, hoping he'd come back at least for our talk, and a few minutes later I heard Mom start the Nova in the garage. She was going out to look for him, I thought, as he was on foot and couldn't have gotten far. Could be she wanted to apologize or maybe try to kill him again. All I know for sure is that I heard the car leave the garage and roll down the driveway and soon afterward our doorbell rang. I'd intended to answer it, thinking it might've been my brother, that he'd forgotten his keys and needed in, that he wasn't meeting Leitha after all, as it was already past midnight. I looked out the window from Mom's room first, because of the hour, except it wasn't Mike on the porch but three men in blue. Another was walking up our driveway shining a flashlight. Two squad cars were at the curb. Before I turned away I saw the Nova cruise by, pause, then continue on. At first I thought they were after her and I imagine she figured the same. I wondered if maybe a neighbor had called them because of the fight and then I thought, No. The bell rang again, longer, insistent.

Downstairs, out the back door, I ran. Popped the fence into a neighbor's yard. "Over here," one of the cops shouted. "Over here." But I was moving, fast up another fence by then, from yard to yard, running so they'd never find me and knowing, too, that I could never come home again.

PART IV:

Raising the Roof

ON HIS FRONT DOOR in Echo Park was a warning from the Los Angeles city coroner: REMOVAL OF THIS SEAL IS A FELONY. No one, under penalty of the law, was to enter the house until investigations into his death had been completed. Only there was nothing for them to investigate, and if there was, the chore was mine, not some cop's. There were few clues and no clear motives that any homicide inspector could've understood. The details wouldn't fit in their note pads even if they belonged there, which they didn't. I shook my head. No seal would keep me out of the house my brother had lived in—not now or tomorrow, not until they said, Fine, ready, you can go in now.

Up the block neighborhood kids were playing flag football in the middle of the street, T-shirts tucked in hind pockets like tails. If they saw me, they didn't seem to care. I headed down the porch and up the driveway and stopped for a moment at his car. Looked through the window. In the backseat were empty cardboard boxes with the smaller ones sleeved into the bigger ones. The tape deck had been yanked out from the dash, stolen, and the wires hung free. Kids, the ones playing football, maybe? I wanted to go talk to them, not really talk but accuse the first one who gave me a wrong look, drag him back over here and *show* him, hard, his face against the window, my hand on his neck. But instead I went around to the gate and up a set of rickety stairs to a door with a plyboard panel that a cop had recently nailed over a rubber flap at the bottom. One kick, two kicks and the panel was down. In a few seconds I had the door open and had stepped into the upstairs bedroom, the one he never used, the one I once slept in. I held my breath. This was the day after the authorities had taken him away, all the windows had been shut and locked, it was July and hot, and the smell from downstairs was rotten, sour.

A few of his books were scattered across the floor, and there was a mattress in the corner, a rumpled blanket on top of it, and a brown paper bag with a pair of pants poking over the rim. I searched the rooms upstairs, then I went downstairs and looked through drawers cluttered with empty half-pints and blank sheets of paper, inside books and under chairs and even between the cushions of the couch, until evening fell.

By now I'd grown used to the stench; bad as it may have been, it was my brother's. My breathing came easily. I went finally to the bedroom where he had shot himself, though I did not want to go there again. The drapes were closed, and it was dark. The electricity hadn't been turned off yet and the light, when I moved the switch, shone across the bed. The pillowcase was damp, the color black except for around the far edges, where there was still some white left. Now I lost my breath. My stomach, too, felt buoyant inside as if it were going to rise into my heart. I searched the closet and the pockets of his clothes and rifled through his dresser drawers and the one in the nightstand before I gave up. You always expect a note, a letter, some explanation, poor as it may be. He'd left none.

In the corner stood his file cabinet. I opened the middle drawer. Under *C* I found the card and read it.

> Michael David McKinney (1953–19)
> Born Casey in San Jose, California. Died in ( ), Los Angeles, of self-inflicted wounds on ( ). Among his feature credits were *A Rough Kind*, and the made-for-TV movie *Where Are the Children?* He acted in more than 30 television shows, including episodes of *Cannon, M.D.; Down the Shore;* and *Vice Squad*, for which he was nominated for an Emmy as outstanding guest performer in a drama series.

But he hadn't updated the obituary with his last film, *Backstage Actresses*. It was from

New Land Productions, directed by a man who later went on to make better movies. I took a pen from the nightstand, filled in the blanks for him, added the last credit, put it back in its proper place in alphabetical order in the drawer as he would've done, and then turned off the light. Outside I could hear the kids still playing, shouting. I lay down on the bed and rested my head in the black impression that my brother had left in the pillow.

20

All night I sat awake watching farm communities and towns along the coast pass by the window in flashes of darkness and light. All night I thought of my brother, believing I'd deserted him, that I'd made a mistake. Come morning the driver turned off U.S. 101 and stopped at the Greyhound in downtown San Jose and I got off with the others. There I mustered the courage to phone Dad and tell him where I was. His voice sounded more nervous than I thought my own did. "Stay put now," he said. "I'm on my way, don't you go anywhere." When he hung up I went outside and sat at the curb. Across the street a half-dozen men stood at the corner in front of an old hotel, talking in Spanish, some sharing coffee from a thermos. I wondered if they were pickers who had missed the flatbed that would've taken them to the orchards on the east side. It was the season for cots again. Soon my father pulled to the curb in his truck and I climbed into the cab, more beat and exhausted than I'd ever been in my life, not knowing what to say or how to say it. We drove. The streets were empty compared to L.A. Only a few other cars were on the road. He spoke first.

"You wanna tell me what happened?"

"I just felt like visiting."

"Pretty short notice."

"Didn't think I had to give you any."

"You don't," he said.

"School let out. I thought maybe we could spend some time together." I shrugged. "You know, maybe go fishin' or something."

"I'm in the middle of a job, son."

"So we'll just hang out, okay?"

"Okay."

"Maybe I can help you."

"It's harder than pickin'."

"So whatta you sayin'?"

"Take it easy."

"You don't want any help? That what you mean?"

"Don't get upset." Dad looked away from the road for a moment and furrowed his eyebrows at me. "How'd you tear your shirt?"

"Caught it on the bus door," I mumbled.

"In a hell of hurry, huh?"

I kicked at the Skilsaw on the floorboard and didn't answer.

"Hell of a cut there, too. Driver drag you here?"

"Real funny."

"You ain't laughing."

The sleeve I'd torn on a nail hopping a fence ten hours earlier; the cut the same way—on the shoulder.

"No luggage, huh?"

"Why all the questions?"

"You tell me."

"No," I said. "No luggage."

"How long you plan on stayin'?"

"I can go back now if you want."

"That ain't what I meant, son."

"It's just for the weekend. That all right?"

"Fine."

Silence.

"How's your mother?" he said. "How's Mike?"

And I lost it then, too old to be crying, but crying anyhow. Dad pulled to the side of the road and set the shift in neutral and put his arms around me and hugged me, which only seemed to make it worse. "You stay here long as you want," he said, and his voice was cracking, too. "This is your home, son. Don't be so mean to your old man. I love you." Pause. "And I missed you, I missed you something bad." He held me as I held him in a way that I have never forgotten. I tried to tell him why I was there, what had happened and what I had done, but I couldn't get the words out for all the tears and anger and confusion. "Settle down now," he said. "Tell me what you want when you want. I won't ask you any more questions except one." He leaned away, ran a finger under my eye. "Answer true?"

I nodded.

"You eat breakfast yet?"

"No."

"Me either."

Dad grinned. As we drove on I saw clouds of steam rising from

248

the stacks of Del Monte in the distance. Fruit cocktail. The smell in the air was sugary sweet but bitter. I thought of Mom. I thought of my brother as we rode down the simple and familiar streets to the apartment Mike and I had left two years before. Not much seemed to have changed. Not the bright-yellow color of the buildings or the white trim around the windows. Not the driveway and the pothole in the middle of it. The difference was that the paint over the eaves had begun to chip and the open field behind the apartments, the uprooted orchard, was no more. A new stucco complex stood in its place. Dad parked in the carport, where against one wall, beneath the storage cabinet, leaned a stack of scrap rock and odd lengths of two-by-fours. Together we went upstairs.

Over minced ham and eggs, toast, and a tall glass of milk, I told him almost everything. Mom stealing Mike's first check. His plan to marry and his heavy drinking. How he'd lost too much weight. How I'd been cutting school again. The last big fight and opening night and the cops. Everything, that is, except the burglaries, which I was too ashamed to mention. Dad wagged his head through it all. "You think they got your mother?" he said solemnly when I'd finished. I told him no, that she'd kept driving and that I'd panicked, run. "Why didn't you tell me what was going on?" he said. "You could've called. If I'd known. . . ." His fist came down on the Formica table. I thought to myself, What if you'd known? What would you have done? And I said it, too.

"Come get you and Mike, that's what."

"She wouldn't let you."

"I don't believe I'd ask."

"Mike wouldn't go."

"He could do his acting here. Hollywood's no good for him, son. I don't care how well he's doing. You read all those bad things in the paper about the stars and they're true, aren't they? They're true." He looked at me as if I had the answer. "There's plenty of work for him in San Francisco." I stared down at my plate because he was wrong about San Francisco and there was no reason to argue over it. My brother wouldn't have listened. "Who's this girl, anyway?" he said. "How come he didn't tell me?"

I shrugged.

"An older woman?"

"About his age, I guess."

Pause.

"You don't think they caught your mother?"

"No."

"You sure?"

"All I know is she kept driving. How can I be sure?"

Again Dad pounded the table. "Damn the IRS," he shouted. "Damn Mrs. Glass." Then his voice grew calm, he sighed, and I suppose because I'd been fairly honest with him he now decided to be fairly honest with me. Without my having to ask, he told me about this phantom lady from the past who Mom called the "old bitch," one I'd never seen and never would, who had caused us much trouble for reasons I did not learn until this day. The property scam. The death of Mr. Glass. As he talked I saw not my father but an older beaten man with too many wrinkles around his eyes, sunburned cheeks, and arms so heavy with muscle that at times like these they seemed to weaken him with their weight. But all of what he said was washed in gray words, as if, maybe, Mom had never done the phantom lady any wrong—that she'd been unjustly persecuted, that there had been some mistake. I listened, believing the worst, leaving no room for innocence. As Dad ended the story he rose from his chair and went to the phone on the wall. Dialed. He let it ring and ring and when no one answered he hung up and turned to me and frowned. "Don't worry about nothing because I'm sure she's okay. Your mother's a smart one, or maybe she isn't so smart getting herself in all this trouble in the first place." Now he closed his eyes, opened them, smiled. "We're gonna do just fine, son, you and me—just fine." He started to put a hand on my shoulder then pulled it away, bent over, and squinted. "Let's clean your cut out so you can take a nap. How's that sound, huh? You look tuckered out."

A few minutes later he tried calling again, and I imagine he kept trying long after I'd eaten breakfast, long after he'd helped me wash the cut and swab it with iodine, all afternoon into the evening without an answer. That was how my first day in San Jose began and ended. I'd taken his advice and I slept well, not having had any on the bus the night before, until he woke me. "You want to help out?" he said. The room was still dark, and for a second I didn't know where I was or who was lying beside me. I sat up fast. My heart quickened, then I remembered and relaxed.

"Dad?"

"Yeah?"

"You get a hold of Mom?"

"Nope."

"Mike?"

"Nope."

"What time is it?"

He rolled out of bed. "Time for work," he said, "if you still plan on helping. We'll knock off early and call again. I don't know what else to do. C'mon, get dressed." Already he'd slipped into his Big Mac khaki pants and work shirt, laced his boots in the dark, and left the room. I fell back on the bed again, half asleep, thinking of Mike and Mom, when he switched on the light and yanked the covers off me. "If you don't want to go to school you're gonna have to learn how to work," he said. "You drink milk in your coffee? Sugar?"

The roof had already been stripped. Ninety-pound black felt had been laid out and nailed down neatly so that the heads made a straight line from one end of the house to the other. The remains of the old roofs, one of composition and one of tar and gravel, were scattered around the footing below.

"See those rolls?"

"Where?"

"Right there." He pointed to the backyard. "Run get me one."

I climbed down the ladder and wandered across the yard. Wrapped my arms around one of the rolls. Heaved. It didn't budge. I glanced up at Dad, but he was on his hands and knees in his carpenter's overalls, his back to me, stretching out his tape measure. So I wrapped my arms around the roll again, except I squatted this time, ducked my shoulder, and slipped under it. My back bowed. I staggered toward the ladder, the thing digging into my skin, and took hold of the first rung. The muscles in my thighs and the tendons at the back of my ankles ached. Each step came harder than the last but I was determined to make it. When I'd gotten about halfway Dad crouched at the edge of the roof and looked down at me. "That too heavy for you?" I shook my head. A drop of sweat fell from my brow to the ground. "C'mon then," he said. "We don't have all day. This stuff has gotta be nailed down before it gets too hot to work with. C'mon, c'mon."

At the top rung he took the roofing from my shoulder and set it down in the valley so it wouldn't roll off the roof. The rafters shook under the weight. I smiled in relief because I'd made it when he didn't think I could. "Whatta you grinning about?" he said. "Get back to work. You got fourteen more to go."

I went for another.

He used them as I brought them, rolling each out, cutting the ends with a drywall knife and tossing the scrap over the side, tarring the edges, nailing them down. The pounding of his hammer sounded through the streets. A neighborhood of tracts, it was, all built alike except for the design on the garage door. Tiny front lawns. Steel posts for porch beams instead of four-by-fours. Not once when Dad got to working, except to haul the rolls off my shoulder, did he even pause to catch his breath. I made it up with seven, three ahead of him. My thighs, arms, almost my whole body ached. I wiped sweat from my forehead. The sun was high now.

"Time for a break?"

"No breaks, son."

"What?"

"Don't tell the union," he said, winking.

"It's getting hot."

"And it's gonna get hotter the more we keep talking." He took a nail from the pouch as he spoke, set it, and with one clean blow drove it home. "Fetch the apron in the toolbox, right behind where I keep my wrenches," he said. "Get yourself a hammer and start pounding. The nails are in the bed. Use the half-inch galvanized, not the others sitting there."

I sighed and did as I was told.

Now every few minutes he stopped whatever he was doing to look over my shoulder. "Keep your nails straight," he said once. "Sight your line." Another time he wagged his head, as I'd driven the heads in too deeply and had damaged the composition. "Get the tar," he said. "Fill in the holes. Don't pull the nails, it'll only make it worse. Look at there." He pointed to an empty spot on the line. "Keep 'em spaced about three inches apart, son; we don't wanna have to come back here in the rain and try and find where you missed."

Four hours, maybe five, had passed since we'd started, though it seemed a hell of a lot longer. The skin between my thumb and index finger was raw from swinging the hammer. Sweat stung my eyes. And on my palm a blister black with tar had started to bubble, burn. A hundred times that afternoon I wanted to throw the hammer down and go wait in the truck—say fuck it, quit. Yet I kept pounding, one nail after the other, thinking if I could just get to the end of the row, begin another, and finish it, that this day, like the pain, would pass when it was over. We'd be that much closer to home.

"You want to fetch another roll?"

"Just one?"

"Keep 'em coming if you want."

I climbed up off my knees, using the hammer as a kind of crutch. Dad gave me a curious look. "Which hand you been nailing with?" he asked.

"My left."

"But you write with your right."

"Uh-huh."

"That how they taught you at school?"

I couldn't remember, but I imagined that that was the way, and I said yes. Dad smacked his lips. "You might wanna try writing with your left. It might come more natural to you." He wiped sweat from his brow. "Might also have something to do with how you see. Things still look backward to you sometimes?"

"Not too much."

"Don't you feel bad if they do."

"I won't."

"The world *is* ass-backward."

Dad smiled and returned to pounding nails. I started toward the ladder, stumbled, caught myself. He glanced over his shoulder with his hammer poised in midstroke. "Watch your step now, son," he said. "Forget the roll and start picking up down below. We'll knock off soon as I get this row nailed and see if we can't get a hold of them again."

And I was sorry he'd said it. Not that I wanted to keep working. Or that I didn't want to talk with Mom or Mike. I did. It was because, I thought, heading for the ladder more carefully this time—that there was bad news waiting for me on the other end of the line.

There was a telegram from Western Union under the door when we got back to the apartment later that afternoon. Dad picked it up and opened it.

CALL IMMEDIATELY 213-555-3265. MIKE.

I read from over his shoulder. The number wasn't ours. "Sonofabitch," he muttered. "I hope he's worried about you and nothing else." He went to the kitchen and dialed, his face stern, grave, while I went into the bedroom to lie down. Rest was the excuse. They must've talked for a half hour or so, but I couldn't hear much of what Dad said as he kept his voice low and I didn't get up to listen.

A while later the door opened and he peered into the room "Son," he said, "your brother's on the phone."

"Dad?"

"Yeah?"

"I don't feel like talking."

"Best you do, though."

"Can't you say I'm sleeping?"

"You better get up," he said, strict.

I swallowed and rose from the bed.

When I got to the phone I was feeling faint, a little light-headed.

"Jay?"

The line crackled.

"Hello?"

"I'm listening."

"You did the right thing," he said. "Leaving. I'm proud of you."

"Sure."

"I am."

Silence.

"We'll visit each other a lot, okay?" he said.

"Sure."

"You know I'll write."

Silence.

"The cops were at the house today," he said.

I wrapped the cord around my fist and squeezed it.

"You told Dad they came last night?" he went on.

"After you left."

"Where was Mom?"

"She took off."

"Where?"

254

"I don't know."

"Didn't she say anything to you?"

"No."

"They're looking for her again," he said. "She's gone, man. So are her clothes. No note, nothing, and I don't know where the hell she went." Pause. "That stuff of yours . . . I'm going to get rid of it at the Goodwill."

Felt to me at the time, as I gave the receiver back to Dad, that everything was going in circles. I reached for the edge of the stove, and in a rush of fear and relief I wondered where Mom could have run and if I would ever see her again. When my head cleared I found myself staring down at my hand. Beside it on the stove was a tray of Marissa's enchiladas loosely covered with aluminum foil.

21

What happened to my brother after I left L.A. is partly speculation, partly fact. Some things I know for certain. Other things I've had to piece together here and there over the years from old letters, photographs and memories, his personal papers and bank statements. As for Mom, she'd up and gone like Mike had said. From her there were no letters or postcards for a very long time. Dad, however, reassured us both that she'd be back. "Dragging her ass," he'd say. "You can damn well bet she'll come home." Sometimes, if he had had a couple of drinks, he'd even laugh. "And she'll be driving a Cadillac, probably, except it won't be her own." Still, the months kept passing, and the longer she stayed away, the more I worried about her, though there were also times when I didn't give a damn. Times, too, when I resented her for leaving. She had taken the Nova and closed out our bank account. It was mostly Mike's money.

After his death, when I was cleaning out his desk drawers, sorting what I wanted to keep from what I didn't, I came across his checkbook. The last deposit was nearly a year earlier. The balance had fallen from seven thousand dollars to eighty-two dollars and fourteen cents. Check number one-twenty-one was made out to the Arms Hotel in Hollywood for rent on a room that he never slept in. One-twenty-three, the last, went to a neighborhood liquor store in Echo Park. In the side compartment of the checkbook was an itemized receipt from a pawnshop on Melrose Avenue. My "stuff"—a Rolex watch, the set of sterling silverware, the class ring, and diamond earrings—never made it to the Goodwill.

I also found his address book, which led me to some people who knew him in a way that I could not, and I phoned them. Set up a time to meet and talk. What I got were stories and anecdotes from those who were his friends. The business people, except for his agent, were either too busy to be pestered or they just didn't want to talk. Up to a certain point, Leitha and her mother were fairly gracious about the whole thing in that they were willing to talk with me, but their stories conflicted a lot. I had to do some serious guesswork. Eventually, when I tried to get Cindy to confirm a couple of details over the phone, she cut me off. I tried calling again a few days later and this time she told me that she was having problems of her own and didn't need me bothering her anymore. The past was the past. Good-bye.

She hung up.

That same afternoon I came across a yellowed clipping from the Metro section of the *Los Angeles Times*. It was dated August of the same year that my brother and Leitha eloped. At the time he was on location in Reno, Nevada, filming an episode of *Down the Shore* for Universal. There was a scene in the program set in one of those roadside chapels, and I'd like to think that's where they were married, but it probably wasn't, though it must've been a similar kind of place. I do know for a fact that Leitha's father wouldn't talk to her after the marriage and that, if he'd ever intended to forgive her, he never had the chance. I also know that Mike drank a lot during the shoot, because it had begun to show now in his face—the bloat, a pastiness about the skin no makeup could hide—when the episode later aired. Part of the drinking was likely done in celebration of the wedding and the other part had to do with the failure of his movie. *A Rough Kind* closed two weeks after it had opened.

Mike took it hard, like it was his own fault. Like he'd done something wrong to make it sink. Dad and I never said anything to him about how it had disappeared so quickly, without a trace, as if it never existed. And how we, too, thought it a shame to see a good movie fade before it had a chance. We saw it at the Prune-yard theater in San Jose on a Tuesday night, and on our way out later, headed to the parking lot, we spotted a kid on top of a ladder perched against the marquee. He'd already removed the first word and was lifting the *K* out of the second when we passed. We looked the other way, as I imagine my brother tried to do in terms of his career, just to keep going, not to worry. The next one, he must've thought, would do better. Only no new film of-fers came along as he'd hoped and expected, considering the praise he'd won, and he began to blame it on the contract. "The ex-ecutives and producers have typecast me as a volatile, overly sen-sitive, almost psychotic character," he once wrote me. "All I'm given to play are junkies, hypochondriacs, love-stricken fools, and emotionally disturbed youths. But my range is greater than that, Jay—much, much greater. If they want a mannequin with a frozen talent they ought to hire one and get rid of me. I don't know how long I can keep doing this shit without losing what's left of my self-respect."

When Mike and Leitha returned from Nevada they bought a Datsun and rented a house at the top of Laurel Canyon. Life might've been good for them there, but it turned out not to be for reasons I'm only partly clear on. Which brings me back to the point where I left off—before Saul Leiberman's arrest, and long before I found the clipping. I'd often wondered what had hap-pened to him, as the news didn't make it to San Jose and my brother never saw fit to tell me the particulars on account of Leitha.

The topic was hushed up.

The picture showed a handsome man in a T-shirt. Sweat in the shape of a *V* outlined his chest. He was in midstride with his hands cuffed behind his back. A plainclothes cop gripped one arm. The night before a student had noticed an older Mustang parked in the theater parking lot and remembered it as being "un-usual for someone in our class, like a teenager's car . . . you know, flame painted on the hood?"

From what I've pieced together Saul finally found the courage to buy himself a new battery and hook it up, shoot some ether down the throat of the carburetor, get behind the wheel, fire the engine, and nurse the car to a Shell station. Fill the tank. Inflate the tires to maximum pressure. Next he cruised a few side streets so that the oil worked its way through the lifters and then he took it on the freeway to open it up and blow the carbon out. He ran it hard through the gears, his heart rising, zipping past the others, in and out through the traffic, fast then slow, until the engine breathed smoothly again. Come night he showed up for the workshop after having stayed away for a couple of months, hoping the old man might've forgiven him by now. Likely he'd gone in at the beginning of class, because I don't think he had it in him to plan it, and the old man kicked him out again. Belittled him in the process. In front of everyone.

So he would've had to sit outside in the parking lot on the hood of the Mustang and smoke a few cigarettes until the students left and then he followed Marrin into the dressing room or maybe he forced him there. There were signs of a struggle, though where and when that struggle began is debatable. Could be Saul only wanted to talk, except this time without the begging. Could be Marrin tried to soothe him, as he had before—because this came out in Saul's confession—by first asking him to sit as he had before and giving him a massage, maybe easing his way down the shoulders to the chest, working the muscles there, then placing his lips on his neck from behind. His hands moved farther down, maybe, unbuckled the pants, and maybe he reached inside and tried to pump some life into the young man.

Except the desperation and despair had crippled his love and it was bitterness now, not pleasure, that surfaced. That's when the resistance likely began, because the old man was persistent, and that persistence only made them both more frustrated than they already were. Then came that angry mouth of Marrin's and the slamming of his cane and to shut him up Saul took it away from him. The old man fell forward. From behind, it was used, the cane. Strong arms cinching up on both ends so fast that the quiet came a moment before the struggle could.

The Mechanical Man was like a bad dream come true. The script had arrived two weeks earlier but he couldn't bring himself to open it until tonight. Five past twelve, it was. Now he flipped through the pages, sipping Smirnoff over ice, counting the lines he was supposed to have memorized for tomorrow, when there came a tap on the door. He rose from the chair and turned on the porch light. Looked through the peephole. Saul Leiberman stood with his hands in his pockets, head bowed, staring at his feet. My brother undid the lock. Opened the door.

"Sorry to wake you."

"I was up."

"Leitha too?"

"Uh-uh."

"Asleep?"

"Right."

"Good," he said.

"C'mon in."

"Can't.. My date's in the car."

"Invite her in."

"We were just cruising by. Got better things to do, if you know what I mean. No offense."

Mike stepped out onto the porch and looked down at the Mustang parked at the curb. He couldn't see anyone inside but it was dark.

"That yours?"

"Yeah."

"Driving again?"

"Fuck the bus," he said. "You ask a lady out, whatta you say— we're taking the thirty-one? Listen, man. I don't wanna bother you but like I asked her where she wanted to go, right? Like a fool, right? She says The Islander and then what does she do? Orders this big meal and doesn't hardly eat it. Now she wants to go dancing. I had a hundred bucks when I started." He patted his pockets. "Can you pop for a loan?"

"How much you need?"

"Whatever you can spare."

He reached for his wallet and gave him what he had. Three twenties.

"Thanks, buddy."

"No problem."

"You understand, huh?"

"Don't worry about it."

"She's a looker, man."

"Good luck."

"I'm this close to making her," he said, holding up his hand, thumb and finger pressed together. "I'll pay you back soon as I can." As he hurried down the stairs to the car, Mike returned to the living room and picked up the script, started to open it, then sighed and slapped it shut. His role was an exchange student who comes to America, falls in love with his beautiful sponsor, and defects from East Berlin by jumping out of a helicopter amid KGB gunfire. The Mechanical Man catches him just before he hits the ground. Such bullshit. Such trash. He tossed the script on the coffee table and switched off the light and felt his way through the darkness into the bedroom.

Leitha rolled over onto her stomach and adjusted the pillow under her head.

"Who was that?"

"Nobody."

"I heard you talking."

"Go back to sleep."

"Who was it?"

"Saul," he said. "He needed a loan."

"You didn't give it to him?"

He unbuttoned his shirt. Dropped his pants. Boxers. Climbed under the sheets. He drew his fingers along the inside of her thigh, kissed her neck.

"Did you?"

"Just a few bucks."

His hand moved up to her belly and around her hip.

"You'll never see it again."

"I'm not thinking about that now."

"You memorize your lines already?"

"Almost."

She pushed his hand away.

He waited a moment then drew his fingers over her thigh again. Kissed her. Again she pushed his hand away. "You *reek*," she said. "The whole room reeks. It's repulsive and I'm sick of it." Leitha turned onto her side with her back to him. "Try fucking me sober for a change."

On the set he got the shakes something terrible. He botched his lines and missed half the others. The director was fed up. "Cut," he shouted. Sweat rolled down the side of Mike's face. His mouth was dry and his hands were trembling so he jammed them in his pockets. Tossed his head back. Closed his eyes. Beside him he heard the cameraman, the soft electric hiss of the dolly rolling forward, then backward, gauging distance, focusing. The director shouted again. "Ready?" Mike nodded. A loud buzzer sounded and he stiffened and opened his eyes. The spots shining down on him blurred together, then separated, doubled, then separated again. "Quiet on the set," the director hollered. "Let's get it right this time, damn it." Mike blinked.

The camera boy held the clapper boards in front of the lens. A slap of wood on wood followed the voice. "Scene three, take five."

The girl playing the sponsor ran her fingers through her hair once and, flinging open a false door, entered center stage. There was a nervous, apprehensive look in her eyes. She delivered her line. A moment passed, then two. Mike stepped toward her. More silence. Finally the director sliced his hands through the air clean and fast like an umpire. "Cut." He glared at Mike. "And it looks like what? *Like I'm going to have to return to my country*. What's the big problem here? *It looks like I'm going to have to return to my country*."

"Excuse me."

He walked off the set.

"We're not finished."

"I need a drink of water," he said, pinching the bridge of his nose. "I'm not feeling too good."

"Water won't help."

"What was that?"

"Take a break."

"Give me a minute," he said. "I'll get it the next time."

Mike headed to the water cooler at the back of the set, paused to glance over his shoulder, then wandered into his dressing room.

The director turned to the A.D. when Mike had shut the door. "Who's that other kid under contract?"

"Jason?"

"Is he any good?"

"He's okay."

"Call him in."

"What if he's busy?"

"Just tell Mike he can go home and then get me someone responsible. I don't care who," the director said. "Call his agent, too. She has to know."

*   *   *

Cindy had gone to breakfast at Du Par's in Studio City with the new working scholar. On their way out she bought two jelly rolls to go. Later she dropped the young man off at his apartment in Hollywood, kissed him, then drove to the house behind the theater and went inside. The door to the den was closed, as Marrin usually kept it when he was at work, which was fine with her—he could hide there all day for all she cared. With Leitha gone, so was the pretense. Cindy stayed at the place in Malibu now. Marrin lived at the workshop. This time she hadn't bothered to shower and wash away the smell of the young man and his cologne. Nor did she make a point of buying and using the same soap she used at home anymore, if she happened to sleep out. Or to change her clothes as soon as she came in. Or to make a point of looking cheerful when she climbed out of the car, prepared to stare him in the eyes when he asked where she'd been, or to act hurt that he suspected her.

She took a saucer from the kitchen cabinet and opened the bag with the jelly rolls, placed them side by side on the plate, and set it in the middle of the table. Today she had planned to wash, as she still did his laundry, still cleaned the place, and kept enough groceries stocked to carry him through the week. But when she went into their old room to strip the bed she saw that it was made. She hurried to the den and opened the door. Empty. So she went outside and let herself into the theater, thinking that was the only other place he could be—that at worst he'd fallen down, maybe, and he couldn't get to his feet and had had to lie there for the night. And that's where she found him, sprawled on the dressing-room floor with the lights still on. His neck was twisted to one side and his shirt collar was turned up at the throat. The cane rested on the floor near his chest.

All the air suddenly rushed out of her lungs.

When he returned from his dressing room, face washed, smiling, and rolling a Certs under his tongue, the director had already begun to shoot around him. He stood on the sidelines and waited, thinking he'd be up again shortly, only after the take the director told the electricians to shut down the lights and set up for the next scene. It wasn't on the shooting schedule for the day. The A.D.

took him aside and put an arm around his shoulders and told him he could change and go home.

Later he walked him out to the Datsun.

"I'll be better prepared tomorrow."

"Just get some rest."

"I'm beat is all."

"Of course."

"You understand."

"Don't worry about tomorrow," he said. "Sleep in. Am I clear?"

For a second Mike stared at him, not stunned or surprised, but wondering if he'd heard right, knowing he had. Quickly he slipped behind the wheel and closed the door. As he drove his heart sped and he felt his face flush hot. *The Mechanical Man* was garbage anyway, he thought, rolling down his window, passing the guard's station in a daze. At Ventura Boulevard he made a right and continued up to Laurel Canyon, dropped it into third, and climbed the grade into the mountain. His throat felt tight, dry. The engine was lugging. He downshifted to second, then drew his hand across the back of his forehead and swallowed.

At the house, as he unlocked the door and stepped inside, he heard water running in the bathroom down the hall. All Leitha needed to know was that the shoot had been canceled. He had the day off and they could take in a movie. Go for a drive or something, anything just to get the hell out of here for a few hours. Maybe he'd tell her different later, maybe not. Right now he needed a drink. He went to the kitchen to make it when the phone rang. He reached for the receiver.

"Hello?"

"Let me talk to Leitha."

"She's in the shower," he said. "Want me to have her call you?"

Cindy began to cry.

"What happened?"

More sobbing.

"Tell me."

More sobbing.

"Hang on."

"No."

"I'll get Leitha."

Cindy cleared her throat. "Tell her to come to the theater," she said, and he heard in her voice the strain of control. "Her father's dead."

After they hung up he opened the cupboard and reached for the bottle of Smirnoff and uncapped it and took a good drink. Shuddered. He waited for Leitha to finish showering and then, when he heard the water stop running, he brought her a fresh towel. "What're you doing home?" she said. Steam fogged the mirror and the window overlooking the backyard. He put his arms around her. All wet, she was. Leitha laughed. "How am I supposed to dry myself?"

The cops had roped off the theater and the house. Small red seals were posted on the doors. Black-and-whites blocked the driveways. Passersby stopped on the sidewalks and stared and talked in hushed voices. Traffic on the street moved slowly. By two o'clock in the afternoon the body had been loaded into the back of an ambulance and driven to the city morgue. Now the homicide inspector stepped past a young officer standing guard at the front door, sighed, and took a seat beside Cindy and Leitha on the living-room couch. She held her mother's hand. They'd both been crying off and on for the last three hours.

"Can I ask you some questions?"

Cindy sniffed, nodded.

"And you?"

Leitha nodded, too.

The inspector frowned. "Do you know anyone," he said, pausing, as if to consider the words. "Anyone who you think might've wanted to see Mr. Marrin dead?"

"No."

"No one at all?"

"No."

"You do want to get the sonofabitch?"

Both of them nodded again.

"Think, then."

A dozen seconds passed.

"Mrs. Marrin?"

"A lot of students didn't like him."

"Someone in particular?"

She shook her head.

264

"Did he have a run-in with a student?"

"Not lately."

"When was the last time?"

"A few months back."

"Who was it with?"

"A young man."

"What's his name?"

"Saul," she said. "Saul Leiberman."

"And what was the fight about?"

"He quite the class and then wanted back in," she said. "But my husband wouldn't let him. I don't know if they fought or what. My husband wouldn't say. He had a bad temper."

"This Saul?"

"Both of them."

Leitha wiped her eyes and looked at Mike, who had been leaning against the wall all this time, listening. "Tell the man," she said.

"There's nothing to it."

"Tell me what?"

"He came by late last night—Saul Leiberman," Leitha said. "For money."

The inspector exhaled. Mike glanced at him, then Cindy, then Leitha. He shook his head at her. "The guy loved your father," he said. "Why involve him in this? He's got enough problems already."

But the inspector persisted. So he took a seat on the couch and told the story, even described the car, though he felt it was a waste of time. Anybody could've killed the old man. And with good reason, he thought. There were lots of times when Mike had wanted to grab the cane and hit him with it—hit him hard, too, only he didn't mention any of that. Leitha and her mother were torn up enough. When he'd finished the inspector called to the cop standing on the porch and ordered an APB. Mike winced. Leitha turned to him then, her eyes so swollen that when he looked into them his own began to sting. "I'm staying with my mother tonight. We need to be alone with each other," she said, her voice faltering toward the end. He didn't know what to say, if there was anything he could say to ease the pain, that ought to be said, and decided there wasn't. Instead he kissed her on the forehead and felt for her hand and pressed it into his own. Outside, through the open door, he noticed the cop getting into the black-and-white, shutting the door.

Earlier that morning Saul had blown a head gasket on Highway 10 between Indio and Blythe in the middle of the Chuckwalla Valley. Desert land. He got out of the Mustang and threw open the hood. A cloudburst of steam dissipated into the dry air and he cursed and kicked the front grill and looked down the road. Nothing in sight. He began to walk. By noon heat waves rose from the asphalt, shimmering in the near distance, vacillating like clear liquid. Saul yanked off his T-shirt, mopped sweat from his face with it, and continued walking.

Occasionally a car went by and he'd stick out his thumb, but no one would stop. Once a truck swerved too close and ran him off the road. He spit into the wake of dust left behind and gave the finger to the driver. A mile up the way he spotted what looked like an overpass and he walked a little faster, hoping it led to a town, maybe one where he could catch a bus. Only when he got there it turned out to be an old bridge built over a shallow gully of tumbleweed and rock. Again he cursed, settling into the shade and resting until the hottest part of the day had passed. Must've reached a hundred and ten. A few hours later, when he climbed out of the ditch into the setting sun, he heard the distant whine of an approaching car. Saul shielded his eyes with a hand and stared in the direction of the noise. The hum of the engine grew closer, he stepped into the middle of the road and waved his T-shirt over his head, first wildly then hesitating, waving it only a little, then finally not at all. The colors undulated in the heat waves. Black and white and glint of chrome. CHP. Its tires made a crackling sound, slowing, pulling off to the shoulder.

22

The Vietnam War was nearing its end by the summer of '72. Although it wouldn't be over for another year yet, I'd never have to worry about the draft as my brother had. "I wouldn't have voted for Nixon if he was the last sonofabitch on earth," Dad had said one morning, the paper spread before him on the kitchen table. "It's taking the weakling long enough, and we're losing thousands of boys in the waiting, but we finally got him up against the wall. He's bringing some of our boys home, and look at here." He pointed to the headlines of a small article and smiled. "By God if there's not talk about ending the draft." He nodded firmly. "Looks like you might be free to do what you want." Except that freedom, at least for now, didn't include work. Like it or not, every morning I rose from bed, we had breakfast, and then it was off to the job.

That summer my father taught me how to hang doors, to find leaks in a roof from inside the attic, how to tear out a window and frame in a wall and vice versa, and how to cut a straight line with his Skilsaw, the model before they started mass-producing them. "Hold it tight," he'd say. "Don't let her bind and kick on you. Always keep the guard on, son, and be afraid of this thing 'cause it'll take your hand off if you blink." Then he'd hold out his thick fingers and say, "All ten still here." Flex them. "A lot of carpenters can't make the claim. Thirty years in the business, and still every time I squeeze the trigger I say this could be it if I ain't careful. You tell yourself the same."

And I learned to keep it from kicking. To follow the pencil mark he'd made on the wood without flinching. To give the saw a quick last push toward the end of the cut so that the board wouldn't splinter. I also learned how to drive the truck that summer, as I'd turned sixteen, and Dad needed me to sometimes run and pick up supplies—stucco mix or lumber, maybe just a fender washer. He paid me eight dollars an hour for my labor, which was better money than I ever made delivering papers, though the job itself wasn't nearly as exciting as robbing houses or busting into machines. There were times when I considered taking advantage of the situation. A lot of the homes we worked on were empty during the day.

There were also times, usually in the morning, when I felt proud to be a carpenter. Strapping on my leather tool pouch, breathing the smell of freshly cut lumber, seemed somehow romantic. And knowing I could pull a ten-foot four-by-four off the lumber rack on Dad's truck onto my shoulder without straining much gave me a certain satisfaction. Doing it, however, was another matter altogether. By the end of the day my body was sore and the pride was long gone. I was beat, as my father was beat, too tired to do much else when we got back to the apartment but eat and turn on the TV. I'd like to think he worked harder than usual that summer to show me what it was like, only I don't believe it to be the case. The prospect of my starting school soon seemed like a vacation.

Occasionally when we came home there would be a casserole in the oven waiting for us. On the table would be a note from Marissa with directions on what temperature to heat it and for how long. Dad had made her a key to our place. She had moved across town after the divorce and taken a job cashiering for Penney's. "She wants to help us out a little, son," he'd said, the day I found the enchiladas on the stove. "Nothing more to it than that." Which I knew was a lie, though I thought better than to say it.

Another, quieter couple now rented the apartment below ours. The unit down the way where Eddie García once lived had been vacant since my return. In any case, it was toward the end of summer before I saw Marissa again, the first time she came to make us dinner. She wore a loose cotton dress with a sash tied around her waist, and her hair was still damp from a shower. Dad was in the bathroom when she arrived. In her arms was a bag of groceries, and I took them from her—not just to help, but to have something to do, as I didn't know what to say, or how I felt about her yet, or how she felt about me. Marissa stared at me for a few seconds. I lowered my eyes.

"Good to have you back."

I nodded.

"Where's your father?"

"Taking a bath."

"I heard you're working with him."

"Just for the summer."

"He says you're good at it." She made a clucking noise with her tongue. "Sure have grown. I remember when I first started taking care of you and your brother and you were just this high." She held a hand out a couple of feet from the floor. "Now look at you."

"Where do you want the groceries?"

"The counter's fine."

I turned my back to her, went to the kitchen, and set the bag down. Slid my hands into my hind pockets. Dad came into the living room then, smiling, freshly shaven and smelling of Old

Spice, wearing his favorite Hawaiian shirt. He patted her on the arm. "Excuse me," I said. I slipped by them into the bedroom, where I stayed until he called me out for dinner about an hour later.

Partway through the meal, as I was passing him the salt, there was a knock on our door. He wiped his mouth with his napkin and rose from the table to answer it. A man in a suit stood in the hallway.

"Mr. McKinney?"

"I have company right now."

"I'm from the Internal Revenue Service," he said.

"I know where you're from."

"We're looking for your wife, sir."

Dad glanced over his shoulder at us, then stepped outside. Marissa looked at me and shook her head. "They just won't let up," she said. A minute passed and when he hadn't returned she threw her fork down, pushed her plate away. "Do you know how many times they've dragged your father into court? How many times he's gone to Sacramento and tried to bargain with them? They've even camped outside the apartment all night to spy on him. Damn," she said, "he wants to settle up for your mother but they won't accept the offers. Can't they see he doesn't have anything anymore? Is he supposed to be hiding money somewhere?" She stormed out of the kitchen into the hallway with her napkin in her hand. "Leave him alone," I heard her holler. "Even if he knew, what kind of man would inform on his wife?" she said. "C'mon and finish your dinner, David. Your son is waiting."

She stormed back into the apartment. I didn't say a word to her but I was smiling inside, for I believed she'd done him right. Dad returned after a few minutes and sat down at the table again, but that's all he did, just sat there, staring at his plate.

I passed him the salt.

"What's this for?"

"You wanted it."

"Before we were interrupted," Marissa said.

"Your steak's getting cold," I said. "Better start eating."

Dad absently picked up his fork and turned it between his fingers. "I gotta see if I can't try to make another offer," he muttered. "See if I can't make some kind of headway with these people." He stabbed the fork into a chunk of meat. "This shit has got to stop."

After dinner I did the dishes while he walked Marissa out to her car. When I figured enough time had passed I went to the window and looked down at the carport and watched them kissing as I had once before. It struck me as a little ridiculous, considering how the circumstances had changed, and I told him so when he came back upstairs.

"You don't have to kiss her outside," I said.

He looked more stunned than surprised.

"What're you talking about?"

"I mean you don't have to hide."

"We're just friends," he said.

"Go out," I said, waving a hand. "Do something together. You don't gotta hang out with me all the time."

The following night he showered and got dressed up and took her "out on the town," as he called it. I made myself a pot of coffee, got out my cigarettes and notebook, and spent the evening at the kitchen table working on what I thought was going to be a short story, except it kept growing. This one was about a family similar to my own, one that moves from San Jose to Los Angeles as we had—without the father, too, only he's dead from the beginning. A construction accident. Not as a carpenter but as an ironworker. There were three brothers instead of two and the youngest, like myself, found himself in trouble on a routine basis. The oldest brother, I decided, would be an actor. Of course I didn't figure all this out that evening. What I started with was one thing and what it became later was another. All I had when Dad came home were two paragraphs on a kid my age arriving at LAX as a ward of the court, a plainclothesman at his side. He'd gotten caught running away and was being returned.

On the table beside me were another dozen or so pages crumpled into balls. The kitchen was full of smoke. Dad swung the door back and forth, trying to clear the air.

"Building a fire, are you?"

"Sorry."

"Smoking like that," he said, wagging his head. "You're gonna get emphysema before you're twenty. If you don't want to quit you better cut way down. I can't hardly see in here."

"It ain't that bad."

"Bad enough."

"You have a good time?"

He closed the door and began loosening the top button on his shirt. "Always do with her. Marissa's a fine one." He nodded at the table scattered with the balled-up papers. "What you up to?"

"Writing."

"Can I read it?"

"It's personal," I said.

"A letter?"

"Yeah."

"Looks like you're having a go of it," he said. "Don't get frustrated if the words won't come out right. Just keep at it and it'll get easier."

"I hope."

"Writing Mike?"

"Uh-huh."

"Tell him to come visit."

"I already did three times."

"Can't hurt to remind him again. I'm sure he's just been busy," Dad said. "Finish up and let's get to bed or we'll be dragging ass tomorrow."

I don't know if it was the coffee I drank or what but I couldn't sleep worth hell that night. Or the next, for that matter, and many of the ones that followed it. All I could think about was the characters I was working on, visualizing how they looked and dressed and walked, listening to how they talked, trying to imagine what they would do in the course of a day, where they would go and what would eventually happen to them all in the end. I also thought about Mom and where she was and wondered if she was okay. I thought about my brother and what life in L.A. with him would have been like if I hadn't run. He'd written me one letter to my four in the months since I'd left. We had talked on the phone, yes—which was how Dad and I learned about Theodore Marrin's death—but it wasn't as personal as getting a letter. And half the time Dad and I called he wasn't even home. I wrote him a fifth letter, a couple of months after I started school at James Lick High. In this one I was curt.

Mike:

What's going on there? We called yesterday and three times last week but you weren't home or you just don't want to answer.

Too busy for us? Why won't you write back? I don't even
know if you're getting my letters. Why don't you come visit?

Love,
Jay

A strange reply arrived a month later. The handwriting was so
small and sloppy that I had to guess at a few of the words.

Dear Jay:

Your letters arrive at a time when I'm in no position to return
them. I'm busy interviewing new agents as I've had to get rid
of Betsy (she continued to fuck with my personal life despite
repeated warnings not to) until I had no choice but to hire an
attorney to do what she should've done long ago. In the
meantime I'm getting new pictures taken and just in general
trying to keep a low profile, which is why I'm not answering
the phone. Apologies to you and Dad. I love and miss you
both. Any word from Mom yet?

Your brother,
Mike

P.S.—Keep writing even if I don't answer promptly. Leitha's
still in mourning over her father and the stress on our
relationship has been tough as a result, understandably so.

I continued to write my brother, though not as often as I would
have if he'd written back more than occasionally. His last letter
had frightened me, and I tried not to think about the implications
of it. I tried not to worry, and instead concentrated on my story,
in part because I wanted to show it to him when I'd finished—to
show him I'd been doing something he could be proud of me for;
and in part because the characters seemed to have taken their own
course once I set them on it. In class I dreamed of the family I was
creating, preferring now to call them people instead of characters,
as they told me about themselves and their lives in such detail that
they became, if not my real friends, at least good imaginary ones
who usually behaved the way I wanted them to. I took notes on
what they said and did, some of which I later used, some of which
I did not. The point was that while I was listening to my thoughts
the teacher would also be talking and I had to shut out one or the
other. So I did poorly in school again, only for different reasons
now, not that I cared much one way or the other. I attended all of

my classes. The alternative, my father had warned me, was to drop out and go to work. "Learn yourself a trade," he said. "Nobody's gonna pay you to sit on your ass and look pretty, son."

In the afternoon, if Dad needed help, and the job happened to be nearby, I'd find him parked at the curb in front of the school gates when I came out. If he wasn't there, I'd either wander home and write or go to the gym and lift weights for a while with some of the wrestling team. In a few months my maximum bench press went from a hundred and ten pounds to a hundred and fifty-five, and I added a couple of inches to my chest. What I liked about the weights was that I could actually feel myself growing stronger. Maybe my muscles would be sore after the workout, but the next day, stiff or not, and if time allowed, I'd lift again. Soon it took considerably more than a half hour in the weight room to wear me down. Yet there was also a practical purpose in it aside from the exercise, which had to do with looks—not looks for the sake of looks themselves, but as a kind of protection. *Mallates* stuck with *mallates*. *Cholos* hung with *cholos*. White boys like myself, what few there were at Lick, either took a hell of a beating on a regular basis because they were outnumbered, made buddies fast with someone big, as I did—in fact the biggest in terms of muscle—or learned not just to be tough but to talk it and walk it and look it. A combination of all three was the ideal. Like it or not, and I didn't, that's the way it was. I learned more in the schoolyard about getting by than I ever did in the classroom. The teachers didn't have a chance to do much other than baby-sit and scream for quiet.

But I was growing disgusted always having to act bad, always having to be on guard for some punk. The whole routine had begun to bore me. It seemed that there were better, more important things to do with myself than fight. Although I still put on the badass act, I did my best to stay in the background, to sit quietly in my chair in class, and not to lock eyes with the jackasses who wanted to hassle me because of my color. My third month at Lick, my teacher Mr. Allen, the woodshop instructor, was hospitalized when the punk I shared lockers with split his head open with a billy club he'd made for his semester project. The class cheered him. The kid was suspended for a month. That stuff wasn't uncommon.

I got into my share of trouble, though I also avoided a lot of it on account of an acquaintance I'd made the first month. Once after school I went to the gym to lift weights, and as I was crossing the basketball court a *cholo* smaller than me hollered over.

"Paddy," he said. "Even the sides, *ese*." He tossed the ball to me and I caught it. There were three of them, the two others *mallates*, playing half-court, and they wanted another.

I threw the ball back.

"No, thanks."

"Chicken shit."

I ignored it.

"We need you, *gabacho*."

As I was walking away he threw the ball and hit me in the side of the head.

They laughed.

The ball bounced against the wall and I picked it up and carried it into the weight room with me and waited. My buddy Danny Lopez—or rather this was how we became buddies—was pressing the limit on the squatting machine—six hundred pounds—without grunting. He was our one-ninety-one wrestling champion, who took state in his junior year and who a few years later became a defensive lineman for the Miami Dolphins. "Big Jay," he said, as that's what he called me, and always in the best of humor. "What's happening, man?"

I didn't have time to answer him.

The small one came through the door first. I slammed the ball into his stomach and hit him roundhouse-style in the temple. He went down and then the others were on top of me, but not for long, as Danny was there for me in the next couple of seconds. He didn't even have to touch them.

"Get off him," he hollered.

They climbed off me.

Danny poked the biggest one in the chest. "You got a problem with him," he said, "it's with me now, *machucón*. You come to me from now on."

Word like that got around and I didn't have to worry too much. Danny and I never really became close friends because he was awfully popular and he didn't have a lot of time to waste outside the weight room, but he did watch over me while I was at Lick, and he did help me train. At the end of the school year I'd probably spent more hours working out than I should have, as my grades weren't the best, and I hadn't written much on my story beyond the opening two paragraphs. I did, however, have a notebook full of ideas and bits of dialogue.

My report card, which I brought home and showed to Dad, averaged out to a D-plus with a C in English. I had passed my sophomore year. Although I had to make up one of the two courses I'd failed as a freshman, I'd gone on to the next grade and struggled through it. Getting that year behind me was a major achievement. A D-plus average seemed pretty good as far as I was concerned, considering the circumstances, for it was a passing grade, yet Dad thought I could do better.

"You gotta think ahead."

"I will."

"You're going on seventeen, son," he said, in his most earnest voice as if, at that age, the world would suddenly shift beneath me.

The next time I saw my brother came unexpectedly, eight months after I'd left L.A. Something strange had happened to him. The changes scared me, as there was no clear explanation for them. To blame it all on his drinking would be too easy. He called late one Friday while Dad was out with Marissa. I remember the cheerfulness in his voice and how it had sounded faked. He was in a bad way. I held the receiver to my ear.

"Can you pick me up?"

"Where you at?"

"The airport, man."

"In town?"

"Surprise," he said.

"Great."

"I been thinking about you."

"Same here."

"Thought I ought to visit," he said. "It's long overdue. Let me talk to Dad."

"He ain't here."

"Where he'd go?"

I paused for a moment. In the background I heard the blare of a flight announcement. "He's out with Marissa," I said. "They've been seeing a lot of each other."

"Good for him."

"That's how I think."

"I'll take a cab."

"I can drive now," I said. "Meet me in front of the baggage claim."

When we hung up I wrote a note for Dad in case he came home before we did and then hurried out to the truck and drove to the San Jose airport. At first glance I didn't recognize him, as he had on dark glasses and a heavy coat with the collar turned up. On his head was a cowboy hat. His pants looked like part of some uniform with blue piping down the legs. As I pulled to the curb he threw a big cardboard box into the bed of the truck and opened my door. Gave me a big hug, he did, which I returned. "Putting on some muscle," he said, leaning back to size me up. "Your shoulders feel solid, man." I smiled, proud he'd noticed, for I had gained a good ten pounds, none of it fat, and almost an inch in height. "Mind if I drive? Always did want to see how this thing handled." So I scooted over and he climbed behind the wheel and tossed his head back and laughed. "Local Boy Makes Good." He spread his arms, framing it, grinning. "Headlines, huh? Capital *m* . . . small *c* . . . only where's the fucking parade?" Glanced left, then right. "We have to call the *Mercury* and let this little town know that Michael McKinney is *back*." I laughed along with him, but it was a nervous one. He clapped me on the shoulder, then put the truck into gear and drove. When we turned onto a dark road, just outside the airport, he reached into his coat and removed a pint of whiskey, had a drink, and offered it to me. "Warm you up," he said. "Lot colder here than L.A."

I took a drink. "Why don'tcha take off your glasses?" I said.

"Can't."

"It's night."

"Somebody might recognize me."

"Come off it."

"People stop me all the time. They know who I am," he said, very seriously. "You just don't star in a major movie and go unnoticed. It's one of the reasons I had to get away, Jay. A little relief, you know. I didn't come up here to be harassed."

For a while I didn't say anything.

"Mike?"

"Yeah?"

"You're kidding, right?"

276

"Don't you believe me?"

"No."

"You're talking like the others," he said, disgusted.

"What others?"

He glanced away from the road to look at me. Raised his voice. "Others, man, others. Where's the reason for me to lie? You're my brother. Trust what I tell you." Pause. "Pass the whiskey."

At the end of the road he turned onto what during the day was a busy street but now was deserted. The gas station on the corner was closed. Our headlights glanced across the windshield of an older car parked at the curb. The glass was white with frost. We passed over a set of railroad tracks. "Make a left at the next light," I said, except he didn't turn when we reached it.

"Where we going?"

"Home."

"You just missed the turn."

"We're taking the long way," he said, the faked cheerfulness back again. "Have yourself another shot and relax." He looked down at the dashboard. "We got plenty of gas and plenty of time and if we run out of whiskey I got another bottle right here." He patted his coat pocket. "Cheer up. Don't look so somber."

Soon we were driving along First Street through downtown San Jose. The old Fox Theater had gone out of business and the marquee lights were either busted in the sockets or missing. The box office had boards over the window. I remembered the night with Eddie García and winced, wondering as I had then what had happened to him, where he had gone. Other stores were dark and abandoned. We finished the first bottle of whiskey and opened the next, but I didn't feel drunk. Once, as we passed the bottle, I asked Mike to turn around. Dad was probably home by now. What was the point of this, anyway?

"Why does there have to be one?" he said. "I can circle back and drop you off if you're scared."

"Scared's not the word."

"What, then?"

"Take off the glasses," I said. "It irritates me not to see your eyes."

He grinned again.

By now we had come to our old house, the street quiet and dark, the walnut orchard still in the night, the many branches swaying slightly, skeletal against the light of the moon. My brother parked the truck in the driveway and shut off the headlights. The house appeared smaller than I remembered, though it was still large, and for a long while we stared at it in silence. The front lawn was neatly cut and there was an upturned tricycle on the porch and a potted fern hanging from the eaves. All the windows were dark and the top of the hedge along the side of the front porch, the one our father had let grow, had been manicured into a perfectly shaped tube. Ahead in the driveway was a new Country Squire station wagon.

"Dad built this place," he mumbled.

"He built a lot of places."

"Not like this."

"Let's go," I said.

Mike opened the door. "They don't belong here," he said, climbing out. "Strangers are sleeping in our room right this minute."

"Get back in the truck."

"This is our home."

"It was."

"Still is, man."

"You're drunk," I said. "I'll drive back."

"A little kid named Jay is in your bed and the other one's empty. The mattress is bare. No sheets, nothing. You know why?"

"Why?"

"Because I'm here," he said, looking at me through his dark glasses as if I were stupid, as if what he'd said made all the sense in the world. "Isn't that right?"

"Right," I said. "C'mon."

"But where should he be?"

I slid behind the wheel. "I'll leave you," I said. "I swear it, Mike."

He just smiled and stripped off the coat. Beneath it he had on a shirt the same color as his pants with patches on both arms. On the breast pocket was a badge of some kind. He adjusted the cowboy hat. "Cover the front door," he said. "I'll take the back."

"Get in the truck."

"Keep your voice down."

"I'm gonna make you if you don't."

278

"Threatening an officer?"

"You're fucking crazy."

"Don't say that."

"Get in."

Mike placed a finger to his lips. "Shhh. They're going to hear you," he whispered. "They're going to hide and make the job harder. That what you want?"

As he started up the driveway I jumped out of the truck and ran and grabbed his arm.

"Quit playing games."

"No game, Jay."

"It's sick," I said.

He jerked his arm free and hurried up the driveway. I caught him again at the backyard gate while he was reaching over the top to unlatch it. "You sonofabitch, you," I whispered, and this time I wrapped my arms around his waist, lifted him off the ground and started carrying him to the truck. He began to laugh.

"Bet you could get in and out quicker than I could," he said. "Thief."

"Shut up."

"Jay the thief."

I pushed him into the truck.

"Lots to steal here."

He tried to get out and I pushed him back in again. The dark glasses fell off his face. I slammed the door while he was feeling around for them on the floorboard.

In a second I was behind the wheel, throwing it into reverse, backing out.

Mike rolled down his window.

"You're forgetting our brother. Hey," he hollered at the house. "Wake up, Jay, we're leaving without you."

A light in the living room came on.

On the way back he finished what was left of the whiskey. I didn't say anything to him for a long time and he didn't say much to me. Because he knew I was angry. Because he knew I was confused. "I didn't mean to scare you," he said, as I parked the truck in the carport. "I was just having a little fun. You mad? Don't be mad." But I didn't answer him. I was disgusted and felt, at the time, that he deserved silence for having behaved like a child. I unlocked the door and we slipped inside quietly. It was past one, the kitchen light was on, and Dad was asleep. He had scribbled a note on the one I'd left on the table, asking us to wake him when we came in, only I thought it better to let him rest. My brother agreed. The truth was that I didn't want them to see each other until Mike had sobered up.

I shut off the light and we pulled out the sofa bed together, then undressed in silence. He took one side of the mattress and I took the other with my back to him. "Talk to me," he said. "Don't cut me off, man. I love you and I'm proud of you, Jay, for stopping me tonight." Pause. "What happened is between you and me, not Dad, and I don't want you opening your mouth about it, okay? He's got enough worries as it is, and besides," he said, "you owe me one. I never told on you. Respect my privacy—I respect yours."

His words only made me angrier.

"I think Leitha is planning to leave me."

A minute of silence passed.

"I don't know what to do," he mumbled.

Still I said nothing.

"Please talk to me."

I opened my eyes but I didn't move. Another minute passed. I had intended to make him suffer by my silence, if I could, but with the news of Leitha I decided he'd had enough. After a while I rolled over, propped myself up on an elbow, sighed. Mike lay on his back with his head on the pillow and his arms straight at his sides. The dark glasses had slipped down the bridge of his nose. "Since when did we start owing each other things? That's not the way it works, man," I said. "Take those stupid glasses off and let's talk." Except I'd waited too long, for he had already begun to snore.

Dad shook me awake.

"Where's Mike?"

"Huh?"

"Mike. Where's Mike?"

I bolted upright, looked beside me. The spot was empty.

"Didn't you pick him up?"

"Yeh."

"Well?"

"He was here last night."

"He ain't now."

I jumped out of bed.

"Mike?" I called.

"I told you he's not here."

"He was when we went to sleep."

"Why would he leave?"

"No reason," I said.

"You boys didn't fight last night?"

"No."

"Then he probably just went for a walk," Dad said. "C'mon and get dressed. I need you to help me this morning."

"It's Saturday."

"Name of the day don't make a difference."

"I oughta stick around for Mike."

"We'll leave the door unlocked."

"Can't we do it tomorrow?"

"Line's backed up over at old Mrs. O'Brien's place," Dad said. "We'll be home to get breakfast on the table before he comes back."

So I slipped into my clothes and went out on the job with him that morning. He was right about it not taking long. Old Mrs. O'Brien's bathtub wouldn't drain, which wasn't any big emergency that couldn't have waited a day, but she was a good customer. Dad had remodeled her kitchen a few years before, two other rentals she owned, and when she called he made a point of taking care of her fast—small job or big one. I removed the plunger with a screwdriver and Dad ran the snake down the line, busted through the blockage, filled the tub and tested it, then told me to pack up the tools.

We were home again in an hour.

In the bed of the truck was the cardboard box my brother had brought with him, forgotten there last night, and I grabbed it on my way up. It was strapped with filament tape and twine and it was heavy. Dad and I made and ate breakfast but Mike didn't come back.

He phoned from the airport at ten that morning before his plane left.

"Had to get going," he said.

"You just got here."

"I'm sorry."

"So am I."

"You forgot your stuff."

"It's yours."

"Mike," I said. "Come on back."

"I called my new agent this morning." A faked cheerfulness entered his voice. "I'm up for another movie, man, and I have to get home. The script's at my house."

"Bullshit."

No answer.

"Don't leave yet."

"Business is business."

"I'll come get you."

"Can't do it," he said. "Remember what I told you about Dad now; you owe me. Don't go worrying him."

"Cut the *owe* stuff."

I gave the receiver to our father. He'd been standing beside me with a solemn look on his face. They talked while I went and got a knife from the silverware drawer and cut the tape on the cardboard box. When they hung up Dad was smiling and I knew that my brother had convinced him that all was fine. "Short visit," he said. "Too bad he couldn't stay longer but this movie sounds like a winner, don't you think?" Pause. "Was your brother drinking last night?" It was as if I could affirm some hope for him with my smile, a simple No, and erase the doubts he had about his other son. I settled up the debt by doing both. Dad wagged his head, chuckled. "Sometimes I worry about nothing," he said. "Damn how I wish you would've woke me, though, like I asked. You know I wanted to see him." I nodded and looked away from him to the box at my feet and peeled back the flaps. Inside was my typewriter.

23

I'm tired of fumbling for the answers. There comes a time, and it is now, when I have to stop imagining how things could have been, or how they might've happened, and instead let the truth take its own awkward course in the way I observed it. I could say that Hollywood blackballed my brother, but for this I have no proof. I could say it was the alcohol that ruined him and that he was just self-indulgent and naturally self-destructive and let it go at that. I could say a lot of hasty things. The fact is he never worked for Universal again. I doubt if it had to do only with *The Mechanical Man*, getting fired and all, but combined with maybe a couple of other similar incidents, along with the breaking of his contract, I can understand how he got a bad reputation. Mike was soon known around town as a drinker with a volatile temper. I once spoke with Betsy Grotz about him and she said certain people in the business felt that my brother "wasn't all there half the time." He dressed in character on the few auditions he went out for during the last two years of his life, becoming incensed when the casting directors were taken aback by the costume or his refusal to drop the voice he had assumed for the role, even in casual conversation. Later, when he heard that the part was given to another actor, he'd call the casting director or the producer and reprimand them for failing to recognize his talent, for their cowardice and narrow-mindedness. Betsy had her own reputation to protect and quit sending him out after a while.

I suspect that's when he began looking for another agent, although not for the same reasons that he mentioned in the letter. The few I received after that were increasingly disjointed and angry. He kept talking about moving to New York for the theater "to do what the real actors do," he wrote. "Stage work. Fuck small-town Hollywood and the TV shit." Yet I knew he'd never just pick up and go. Film was what Mike knew best and what he most wanted to succeed at. As for this new agent he said he had when he phoned from the airport, and about the movie—having to get back to study the script—it sounded much too convenient to be true. If he wasn't lying, he didn't get the role, or at least I never heard anything more about it. I don't know if he had another agent at that time, either, though he did eventually find one at a smaller agency that handled a lot of commercial work.

Through Mike's address book I found and phoned the actor who'd played the Bower character in *A Rough Kind*. I asked him about my brother, what he knew of him, where he thought he might've gone off the track, and he said that Mike had a pattern of bouncing back and forth between sobriety and drunkenness. There were whole weeks when he cleaned himself up, quit drinking, and showed up on the set knowing his lines, ready to work again. This was still during his contract period. "Then something would set him off," the guy said, "some little thing and he'd go on another binge. You should talk with Darlene Cassidy. They worked on a couple of shows together. She liked your brother," he said. "She could probably help you more than me."

So I thanked him and called this woman. They'd done a *Davis County* episode a couple of years earlier, which was her first role, and my brother's fifteenth or twentieth—I don't know for sure. Universal had jobbed him out on this one. "Anyone who saw your brother on *Vice Squad* had to be convinced they were watching a real retarded boy and not Mike," she said. "That's the first time I ever watched someone who was so good and then got to work with him. I was pretty proud about it." Here she paused, and I knew she was trying to find the right words to say something I might not want to hear, for I had asked her how he behaved on the set and she'd avoided the question. I reminded her of it. "A little strange," she said, finally. "He was playing a psychopath and Lawrence Marlin, you know him, he kept stopping the shoot and calling the makeup girl over for 'Man-tan.' That's what your brother called it. This guy was a real star asshole," she said. "All the close-ups had to be on him and they all had to be perfect. Mike was very irritated. They had this scene together where he had to slap Marlin, and let me tell you—they kept doing it over and over because 'Man-tan' didn't really want to be hit, so it never looked quite real. Finally your brother did the slap right so we could all finish up and go home. But it wasn't acting. 'Man-tan' was so pissed he walked off the set. I can't blame him for being angry but he deserved it." Pause. "The director had a big talk with your brother after that and made him apologize to the asshole. The next day when he did his lines they came off kind of mechanical. It was like he just wanted to get it over with. I took him to lunch that afternoon," she said, "and he drank two double margaritas. Is any of this helpful?"

I told her it was.

Afterward I tried calling his last agent but I couldn't get through. I believe Mike made the switch from Betsy to this other agency around the same time that Leitha left him, as he'd predicted she would, only I don't know this for sure.

I learned of the breakup quite a while before his death, when I phoned one night and the voice of another woman answered. A Bob Dylan song played in the background.

"Leitha?"

"She's not here."

"Who's this?"

"Who are you?"

"Mike's brother."

"He went to the store," she said, "but he'll be back in a few minutes. Want me to have him call you?"

"Soon as he gets in."

"Will do."

"Tell him it's important."

"Bye."

I waited an hour but the phone didn't ring. So I called back. Busy signal. I tried once more before I went to bed and it was still busy. In the morning it was the same thing, and I thought to myself that either one of them was having a hell of a long conversation or else the phone had been taken off the hook. I told Dad about it, the woman, about what I suspected regarding Leitha. He sighed, as he often did, as if this were just another complication with a simple answer that precluded panic. "I'm sure he would've let us know if it soured," Dad said in his slow, methodical drawl. "Don't jump to conclusions, son. Could be the other girl was just visiting, could be a friend of Leitha's. No matter the case," he said, "you best keep quiet till you know different." Yet I could tell he was worried, as I was, for we both knew that a marriage gone bad meant more drinking for Mike.

A couple of days later I tried again and got a recording. The line had been disconnected.

It was five weeks before he phoned with the new number. Mike had moved now into the house in Echo Park. The rent, he said, was cheaper, and he apologized for not calling sooner. Leitha he refused to discuss except to say that yes, she was gone, but that they were going to get back together. "In time," he said. "It was all a horrible mistake. As soon as this shit blows over . . ." And I changed the subject then, because I knew what he was doing, and it scared me to hear it. Instead I asked him about the new place and told him I wanted to visit. He said fine. That night I wondered if, like at a lot of other bad times in his life, he hadn't brought the marriage down intentionally, knowing its outcome from the very start. First he predicted it and then he made it come true to fit the plan.

I did a similar thing with my story.

As the months had continued to pass I developed a certain momentum with it. Scenes became chapters, one leading into another, and I soon found myself writing regularly after school. I'd set up my typewriter on the nightstand in the bedroom and stay there for hours. As usual Dad would bitch about my smoking when he came home, for cigarettes and writing had become one and the same thing to me. With each completed page I rewarded myself with a Marlboro. Of course he wondered what I was writing, so finally I told him. This was the week I turned seventeen. He'd just gotten off from work.

"It's a story," I said.

"What about?"

"A family."

"Am I in it?"

"No."

He peered over my shoulder. Whistled. "Lots of cuss words," he said. "You don't show this to your teachers, I hope."

I covered the page with my hand.

"Nobody sees it."

"Not even me?"

I shook my head.

"You stick to it, son. Bad words and all, I like knowing you're busy." He clapped me on the arm, handed me an envelope. "A card come for you today."

I leaned back in my chair.

"Open it."

The address was written in an elegant hand.

Suddenly my ears felt hot. For a moment I wondered if I should crumple the envelope into a ball and toss it into the wastebasket with the other garbage. The postmark read Orlando, Florida, and there was no return address. "Go on," Dad said. "See what she has to say." I split the seal. Inside was a Hallmark with a picture of a cute squirrel eating an acorn. I opened the card and read:

286

Thinking of you on your birthday
with a warm wish for all that makes
you happiest

Love,
Mom

I gave it to Dad.

"What'd she write?"

"Nothing."

He turned the card over a couple of times, then shook his head. "She wrote she loved you. And she didn't forget your birthday," he said. "That counts for something." He clapped me on the shoulder again. "She'll be back."

"I don't care."

"Don't be talking like that."

"I mean it."

"No you don't."

"Forget it. I don't wanna argue."

Dad placed the card on the nightstand and began pacing the room. "I don't know about your mother and me anymore, son. I love her but it don't seem like we're ever gonna get together. Does it to you?" I shook my head. "You know I'm fifty-nine years old now and that ain't no young man. I'm tired of sleeping alone." He stopped pacing. "Marissa's got her eye on an old house. . . . It's in poor shape, needs lots of work, but we been thinking if she can swing the down payment I could maybe remodel it." Pause. "Could be we sell it when we finish and make ourselves a profit." He threw a hand in the air. "She goes one way, we go the other. We're all richer for it." A shrug. "Maybe," he said, raising his voice, "maybe we just fix it up and stay there. Permanent. Think about it. We'd have to move in together while we're working on it 'cause we can't both be paying rent on two places," he said. "I want your honest opinion. Do you like Marissa?"

I looked down at the card.

Then I looked up at him.

"She's okay," I said.

"What about moving in together?"

It didn't seem as if I had a whole lot of choice. "That's okay, too," I said.

And he looked hard at me.

"It's gotta be more than okay, son. On both accounts."

I turned back to the typewriter and pretended to concentrate.

The Strangler murdered another young woman about a week before I boarded flight 302 on PSA bound for Los Angeles. The body was found in Elysian Park, a couple of miles from my brother's house. My plane arrived at nine o'clock in the evening. Dad had bought me the round-trip ticket for the weekend of my seventeenth birthday.

For over an hour I sat on top of my suitcase at the curb outside of the terminal, watching the cars pass on the street ahead, looking for the red Datsun Mike said he would be driving. I wavered between exasperation and worry—my mood one of anger, as the memory of our last meeting still weighed on my conscience. I was determined, if not to do battle, to be the brother he had once been for me. My approach was probably the wrong one but I was young, and, as I said before, determined and angry. Three times while I waited I stepped into a nearby phone booth and dialed his number. Three times there was no answer.

Finally the Datsun swerved to the curb and Mike unlocked the door and pushed it open. Again he wore sunglasses, though a different pair than the last time I saw him. His hair had grown to his shoulders, it was stringy and needed washing, and he hadn't shaved in a few days.

"Hurry," he said. "Get in."

"What's the rush?"

"*C'mon, get in.*"

No greetings, nothing.

I threw my suitcase into the backseat and hopped inside and slammed the door. In the next second we were moving fast; I grabbed the dash. "Slow down," I shouted.

He glanced at me, grinned, and I knew then he was drunk. "I'm on business, man, business. There's work to be done—no time to play; I'm running late. You picked the wrong week to visit." Mike stepped on the gas and we shot past a taxi into the other lane without signaling. Soon we were speeding down the ramp onto the San Diego Freeway.

288

"I want to tell you something," he said, turning to look at me. "But it can't go any further than this car. You have to promise me that."

"Watch the road," I said.

"I'm watching."

We were coming up fast behind a truck.

"Look where you're going."

He switched lanes at the last moment.

"You promise?"

"I promise," I said. "Just be careful."

Now we were boxed in by cars on both sides and he put on his signal, tried to edge his way into the other lane, had to back off, speed up, then slow down. The driver behind us flipped on his brights. Mike ignored it. The turn signal on the dash continued to blink. "You understand about the Strangler?" he said. I told him I'd read about it. "Then you realize he's out there right now, man, you understand that? I can use your help. Together," he said gravely, "we can take him or . . . if need be, put him out of his misery. You want in on it?"

"Quit joking around."

"I asked you a question."

"How much you been drinking?"

The blinker continued to flash.

Mike took a deep breath, exhaled. "Listen now," he said. "Listen closely. I'm working with the police on the case and that's no bullshit. They needed a real undercover man, a professional, Jay, a real actor for the job."

"I don't wanna hear it."

"Are you with me?"

"No."

Mike grinned. "You're missing out on some good writing material."

"The blinker's on," I said.

He turned it off and glanced into the mirror. The car to our left had fallen behind. He swerved into the next lane and switched from the San Diego to the Santa Monica Freeway; then to the Harbor and finally to the Hollywood. From there we took the Alvarado Street exit and cruised for a few blocks. I let go of the dash and stared down at my feet. On the floorboard was a

crumpled McDonald's bag. I kicked at it. "Mom sent me a card,"
I said. "For my birthday."

"Must've been someone else."

"I just told you it was her."

"Impossible."

"She's in Florida."

"Mom's dead."

"You're talking crazy."

"She's dead." His voice rose in anger. "We had a mother once
but she's dead." Down the block, across from the Burrito King at
the corner, he pulled to the curb and shut off the engine. "Be back
in a minute," he mumbled. "Keep your eyes straight ahead and
don't blow my cover." He jumped out of the car. I sighed. Overhead a silver neon sign shaped like a martini glass blinked off and
on as if it were tipping back and forth. A red olive rolled at the
bottom. There were curtains over the doorway, which my brother
parted as he entered. I put my hands on my temples and
massaged them. Part of me thought he was faking it all, playing a
childish game, but the other part said he believed it. That's the
part that frightened me.

I waited and waited.

The minute passed into ten, maybe fifteen minutes. I was about
to go in and get him when he came out with another man. They
stopped on the sidewalk near the doorway of the bar. The man
swayed on his feet, nodding as he spoke, once pointing down the
block. He, too, wore sunglasses, and there was a hole in the knee
of his slacks—plaid slacks that looked too loose for his skinny
frame. After a while my brother glanced one way, then the other,
and reached out to shake his hand. He pressed something into it.
The man smiled and headed back into the bar. Mike returned to
the car smelling of whiskey.

I asked him about the man as he started the engine. "A little
cash, a little information," he said. "I got us an address." We
pulled away from the curb. I fell back in my seat and tried to keep
my temper.

Up the block I lost it.

"You gave money to that guy?"

"A few bucks is all."

"He's a drunk."

"That's only his cover."

290

"Why you hanging out with bums," I shouted. "He's ripping you off."

"I got plenty of money."

"That ain't no way to think."

"And there's more coming," he said. "Lots more."

"From what?"

"Acting."

"In what?"

"All kinds of things."

"What?"

But he wouldn't tell me, because there was nothing to tell. Instead he swore me to secrecy again.

Supposedly, according to his "informant," the address belonged to one Walter Johnson, who had seen the killer but who was afraid to describe him to the police. "The job," my brother said, as we rode across town, "is to guarantee him protection and get him to talk." I didn't believe it, nobody else in their right mind would've, and I don't know how or if Mike really did himself. Another game, maybe, another fake?

"This is stupid," I said. "Let's just go back to your place. I came down here to visit with you, man, not this shit." But he wouldn't listen, and after a few more protests he completely ignored me, and I quit trying. We ended up driving to this address in West Hollywood and parking at the curb outside of a nice old Spanish-style house. The blue glow of a television shone against the drapes in the front window.

Mike got out of the car. "Remember," he said, in a deep voice, "I'm only here to ask a couple of questions. Sit tight and relax. I'll be right back." I went with him, though, because I felt that I had to. Because he might've needed my help if he irritated the wrong person. I was ready to apologize for him.

As he knocked on the door I stepped to one side, a little behind him. "You're making an ass of yourself," I whispered. A few seconds later the porch light came on and a small iron grill in the middle of the door creaked open. The face of an old woman peered out. For the first time that night my brother removed his sunglasses, and for the first time in months I saw his eyes—red around the rims in the light, the whites bloodshot. He cleared his throat and reached into his coat pocket, flipped open his wallet, and showed the old lady a badge. "LAPD," he said. "We'd like to talk with Mr. Johnson, ma'am."

"I'm Mrs. Beal."

"It's Mr. Johnson that we want."

"No," she said, her voice in panic. "No . . . I don't know a Mr. Johnson."

"Ma'am, we know he's in there."

"Excuse me," I said.

I grabbed his arm and pulled him back down the walkway toward the car. "Gimme the badge, man." The wallet was in his hand and I reached for it but he held it away. "You're scaring the hell out of the woman," I said, louder. "You got no right. Gimme the goddamn badge."

Mike shrugged me off, half smiled.

"I can still kick your ass, little brother."

Which only made me angrier.

I thought of tackling him, wrestling the damn wallet away, and I might've done it if I hadn't glanced back to the house at that moment. The old lady was staring at us from the little iron door. Suddenly it slammed shut. "She's calling the cops," I said. "Get in the car." And this time Mike listened, we hopped in the Datsun, he put on his sunglasses, and we drove. I was steaming. "What's happened to you?" I hollered.

No reply.

I jabbed him in the arm. "You ain't my brother, man, you're a fake." Again I jabbed him. "Know what I think? I think you're losing your mind. I think you're a drunk." I hit the dash with my fist. "Look at me." But he just kept driving and I got still angrier and reached out and yanked off his sunglasses.

"Give 'em back."

"No way."

I rolled down my window.

"Don't do it," he said.

Out they went.

Mike turned to me, winked. "No fake, Jay," he said. Then his eyes grew wide, he clenched his teeth. "Gonna kill us all."

He began to swerve back and forth across the road.

The headlights glanced across an old dilapidated house at the top of a hill as we turned into the driveway. Two stories tall. The attic window at the pitch was busted. A plank fence that separated the yard from the one next door was covered with *placa*. My legs felt weak, rubbery. I had a bad headache. Mike killed the engine. Twenty minutes earlier I didn't think we'd make it. He had jerked the wheel left and right until I took hold of it and screamed for him to stop.

We hadn't talked since then.

I got my suitcase out from the backseat and followed him in silence. Inside the house he switched on the light and wandered into the kitchen and returned with two glasses and a bottle of Ancient Age. One glass he set on the coffee table. The other he held in his hand as he sat down on an old couch, resting his elbows on his knees, hanging his head. The bottle of whiskey was clamped between his thighs with the neck pressed against his stomach. I stood with my suitcase in the middle of the living room. All the drapes were drawn, and on the wall behind my brother I noticed a crack in the plaster that someone had once tried to patch. Down the hall was a wicker basket overflowing with dirty laundry.

For a long time he kept the position, motionless, as if exhausted or ashamed. When he finally raised his head to pour himself a drink I started for the staircase at the back of the room. At the top I found a bedroom with a mattress on the floor, some blankets, and began to undress.

The same pattern.

A similar story.

He came to me later that night as I was falling asleep, at the point of a dream, lucid now he was, penitent, moonlight filtering through the window onto a bluish pale face that only resembled that of the brother I'd known years before. The skin shone of oil, the eyes appeared heavy, and his cheeks were bloated as if that portion of him had been submerged under water too long. Still, the sadness I felt in seeing him like this was mixed with disgust, anger. He sat on the edge of the mattress with his whiskey bottle. "I hit her—Leitha," he said. "Like I hit Mom, I hit her. But not as hard and I didn't mean it. I honestly didn't mean it. She wouldn't shut up about her old man." He bowed his head and ran his hand through his hair. "They weren't talking because of me and that hurt her. She wants a divorce, Jay, but I love her and I need to get her back. I need to start over. Fresh, from the beginning, I gotta get to a place where there are no memories, man. Do you understand me? I don't want to be like I am anymore. I'm repulsed by what I see." And now I sat up, pulling the blankets warm around my neck, shivering beneath them, though not from the cold.

"You have to stop drinking."

"I will."

"You mean it?"

"Yes."

"And you need to see a psychiatrist."

That wasn't what he wanted to hear, but he smiled anyway and held out his hand. "Yours," he said. In it was the badge, which I took from him, not even metal—plastic painted silver, almost weightless. I patted the mattress beside me and in doing so I like to think I sent the years running backward then, if only for the moment. "Sleep here tonight," I said. "Please, sleep here."

But he only shook his head.

I returned to San Jose a day earlier than planned. What happened was that I woke up the next morning to the sound of a door closing, got dressed, and wandered downstairs. The clock on the living-room wall read seven o'clock. Mike stood before the coffee table with a brown bag in one arm and a newspaper tucked under the other. He put the paper on the table. I stopped at the end of the staircase and watched him, unnoticed, as he reached into the bag and pulled out a fifth of Ancient Age, fumbled with the seal, twisted the cap off. His hands were shaking so bad he couldn't raise the bottle to his lips and drink without it spilling down the corners of his mouth. I winced. I think he saw me then, though I'm not sure, for I had started back upstairs.

A minute later I came down with my suitcase. At the door I paused to see if he'd say anything, if he'd try to stop me, because I really didn't want to leave. He sat now on the couch reading the newspaper. "The Strangler murdered another girl last night," he said.

"I'm going," I said.

He didn't say anything.

"I'm going."

He reached for the bottle. Without looking at me, he held it up, as if to toast, and took a good long drink.

That's when I left.

I caught the bus into Hollywood and from there I transferred to one that dropped me off at the airport. The woman at the PSA counter exchanged my ticket for another flight that left in an hour. While I waited to board I stepped into a phone booth and called Mike. I didn't know what I was going to say, didn't know if there was anything to say. The line rang and rang and finally I hung up.

My plane left soon afterward.

By noon I was back in San Jose. I phoned Dad and he and Marissa picked me up outside the baggage claim. They both had sullen, worried looks on their faces. Marissa was silent, and I thought to myself that they must've spent the night together. Why else would she be here now? I threw my suitcase in the bed of the truck and squeezed into the front with them. Dad grazed her leg as he shifted the stick into first. She scooted a little closer to me. When he'd gotten it up to third he leaned across the seat and patted my knee. "You wanna tell us what happened?"

"Nothing happened."

"You just come back early for the hell of it?"

I stared out the window.

"Maybe I got homesick."

"I don't believe it."

"Believe what you want."

Up came his voice, and for good reason, though I didn't think so at the time. "Damn it, son. I'm worried about your brother," he said. "Tell me what the hell happened."

"Go find out for yourself."

"Don't you be so nasty."

"I'm not your spy."

"You want to walk home?"

Marissa put her hand on top of his on the wheel. "Come on now," she said. "It's not going to do any good to fight. He'll tell you in his own time." She looked at me and smiled. "You want to see the house your dad and I are trying to buy?" I stayed silent. "He said you liked the idea." She nudged me with her leg, still smiling. "Quit frowning," she said. "Don't be such a little shit."

All the way there Dad had a grimace on his face, and his lips were pursed tight, but as soon as we got to the place his mood changed. It looked like a real dump. An ivy plant had wrapped itself around the post of the FOR SALE sign in the front yard. The lawn was overgrown with weeds, the house was painted an ugly turquoise, and whoever had built it had designed it somewhat like a boat, with small porthole-shaped windows and black pipe for porch railings. The roof was tar and gravel while the other homes up and down the block were older, well-kept custom-built houses with thick shake roofs. "First thing we gotta do," Dad said in his serious, businesslike voice as he climbed out of the truck, "*if* the loan comes through, is to tear out those windows and put in some big ones. Let the light in." He walked through the weeds, rubbing his chin between two fingers, eyeing the house. Marissa and I trailed behind him. "Next we put on new siding. Mind you, this is just the outside I'm talking about. We also gotta tear off the roof and maybe put on shake, maybe terra-cotta. . . ." A pause. "Son," he said, "run get me the tape." I went to the truck, opened the glove compartment, and came back with the fifty-foot reel. "Hold it at the edge of the house there," he said, which I did. Dad stretched the tape out to a spot on the lawn he'd marked with his boot heel. "Picture the bedroom here," he said. "If we bring it out flush with the rest of the place, it'd give us . . ." A glance at the measurement. ". . . another hundred and fifty square feet." He reeled in the tape and slipped it into his pocket and then leaned back to look at the house. "It could be beautiful, best on the block," he said. "Just gotta use your imagination a little." At that he wandered off through the weeds, through the gate, and into the backyard. I watched him pick up a short rickety old ladder from the ground and set it against the side of the house.

Marissa walked over to me and crossed her arms over her chest.

"Happy, isn't he?"

"I guess."

She stepped away then to cup her hands and peer through a crack in the drapes over the front window. "What a mess," she said, more to herself than me. "I wonder if your father knows what he's getting into."

"Course he does," I said.

"It might be more work than it's worth."

"He knows what he's doing. You ain't got any idea how good he is," I said, "or you wouldn't be saying that. I've seen him tear out rooms and when he puts 'em back together you'd never think it was the same place."

Marissa turned away from the window.

"Mind if I tell you something?" she said.

296

"Depends on what it is."

"It's personal."

I reached down and grabbed hold of a weed and pulled it up and twisted the root end between my fingers. Watched the dirt come loose.

"I never meant to hurt you," she went on.

"Let's change the subject."

"No," she said. "If I've hurt you, or your brother, I never meant to. I love your father and I would never do anything to come between you and him. Your mother," and here she paused to pick a weed as I'd done. "I'm sorry."

Just then we heard the crack of wood on concrete followed by a chuckle. We looked up. Dad sat at the edge of the roof with his feet dangling over the side. "Bumped the damn ladder." A few seconds passed. "Jay?"

"Yeah?"

"You wanna set it back up?"

"Set what back up?"

"The ladder."

"Ladder?" I turned to Marissa. "You see any ladder?"

"What ladder?"

After we dropped her off at her apartment, and had gotten back to ours, I told Dad why I'd left Mike a day early.

"He's drinking way too much."

"How much is that?"

"He was drunk when I got there," I said. "He drank a fifth that night."

"I'll talk with him."

"Gonna take more than talk. The shit's making him crazy," I said. "You know he hit Leitha?"

"*My* boy?"

"He told me he did."

"Jesus Christ."

"And he thinks he's a cop."

"What?"

It sounded ridiculous when I said it but it was true.

"We went looking for the Strangler."

"Now you're making this up."

My voice rose suddenly. "I got no reason to make nothing up.

297

We gotta do something." I made a fist and shook it. "He bought another bottle in the morning, no breakfast or anything. I just couldn't take seeing him that way anymore."

Dad wagged his head and went to the phone and called Mike. His voice was gruff at first, full of anger, then slowly it grew softer until he was speaking calmly. I began to worry. "Could be, could be," he said, glancing at me. "Yes, but . . . Yes . . . Yes, I don't think he'd do that. . . . No . . . I suppose it is possible. Let me talk to him and call you back." When they hung up Dad sighed and came over to where I was sitting on the couch. "Your brother says you're not telling the truth. He says you boys got in a fight about your mother, you blamed him, and now you're trying to get even. That so?"

I stood up.

"It's a lie."

"Who am I supposed to believe?"

"Me."

"He sounded sober."

"He wasn't."

"How do you know?" he said. "Did you talk to your brother just now?"

The tone of his voice, the disbelief in it, was enough to set me off again. "Go see him for yourself," I hollered. "See who's lying."

"Maybe I will."

"Do it."

"I just might."

"Sure," I said. "Sure, you will."

But I knew he wouldn't go, because he hadn't the many times before when there was trouble, and I was right. I suppose he called Mike back that afternoon and listened to more of what he wanted to believe, as parents will often do. My brother could be very persuasive and our dad easily convinced. Neither one of us ever discussed it again. On that particular day I had hurried into the bedroom and slammed the door behind me. My typewriter stood on the nightstand and I went to it, pulled up a chair, and returned to that place in my story where I had left off. A quiet place without dialogue. A place where things usually happened the way I designed them to happen, the way I wished them to happen, not this other way around.

24

Dad made another offer to settle up with the IRS but they rejected it again. The refusal arrived by letter around the same time that we got some good news. The loan for the house came through. Now my father went to work on his regular jobs in the morning, came back to the apartment for dinner in the evening, then went off again to the house, and didn't return until late at night. He wanted to remodel the three bedrooms and tear out a wall in the kitchen to put in a service porch before we moved in. Working around furniture would've been too much trouble. A lot of the time I went with him and helped, while other times I stayed behind and did my homework. "More important you do your studies," he'd say, "than flunk out on account of me. You don't got much longer to go." And I did study, though I spent at least equal time, if not more, on my writing, as I was nearing the end of my story as well as my junior year at James Lick High.

On weekends Marissa met us at the house dressed in blue jeans and tennis shoes, with a red bandana covering her head, tied at the back of her neck. She picked and hoed weeds, trimmed the bushes and trees, sawed big limbs from on top of a ladder and piled them into the bed of the truck. Later she'd haul the load to the city dump. Sometimes Marissa and I switched off so that she could help Dad while I worked the yard, gathered scrap wood, or swept. Together we poured the foundation on the addition to the bedroom where she and my father would eventually sleep, then framed it up and walled it in. We hung drywall and taped and textured it all by hand. We tore out the bathroom floor because of dry rot, installed a new toilet and an almost-new vanity Dad had left over from another job, and paneled the walls in dark oak.

At noon we'd set up a box in the living room, sit Indian-style on the floor around it, and eat the lunch Marissa had made for us. "Babe," he'd say, as that's what he called her, though until recently he'd never said it around me, "it don't seem like much now but you just wait." He'd grin and she'd roll her eyes. They'd both look around the room and sigh or maybe laugh. The floor was cluttered with tools, the walls had Dad's pencil marks on them where he planned to put in more outlets, there were water stains on the ceiling. It was a great mess, and hard to imagine any other way. Then came his stern voice. "Your money ain't going to waste, babe. This is gonna be a beautiful home you'll be proud of."

Often, while we worked or ate lunch, I thought of Mike and wished that he could be here with us. I thought of Mom, too, and wondered how she was getting along. I had received another card from her with the postmark of Houston, Texas, saying only that she was well, hoping the same for me. At this point in time Dad and I rarely talked about them. The house and how it was to be remodeled filled most of our conversations, few as they were. With the long hours of work came fatigue, and at night, when his day was finally over, I didn't have the heart to remind him about Mike, that we should be worried, that we hadn't heard from him in several months. I'd phoned him a dozen times in as many weeks. He had an answering service now and I left messages for him, but either he couldn't get ahold of us, because we weren't home much anymore, or else he just didn't try. After a while I stopped trying, too. As for letters, between helping Dad, working on my story, school and working out in the gym, and the chores around the apartment, I didn't have much energy to write them. That was my excuse, anyhow, though I learned much later that during this time he was still playing cop.

Another person I found in his address book after his death was Terrance O'Dell, who had acted with Mike in *Edelman: Attorney at Law*, and I phoned and asked him what I had the others. "I was high when I met your brother," he said. "He was playing a crank, making all kinds of calls, you know, just to scare people? He got along fine with everybody except this little starlet who was banging the producer. She couldn't act worth shit, man. She kept blowing her lines. So she had the director throw all the extras off the set so she could, like, concentrate. Mike didn't have much patience for that kind of crap and he let her know it. The producer nailed him. I'm sorry about what happened, really. Your brother was cool." He laughed. "We got drunk one time, and we were driving in his car and this jerk cuts us off, right? What's Mike do? He pulls up next to him right on the freeway and flashes a badge. Then he waves the guy down. Man," he said. "He was going to give him a ticket. I laughed so goddamn hard I . . ."

"Thanks," I said, and hung up.

Terrance O'Dell had played a public defender on *Edelman: Attorney at Law*. I know this because I scanned the *TV Guide* every week for Mike's name and saved the clippings whenever he was listed. O'Dell's name was alongside his on that episode. Mike also did a *Jill & Mrs. Hamilton* that year. I watched both programs but missed the rerun of *Edelman*, as the show aired early on Saturday night and I wasn't home for it. Every weekend, aside from Dad and I working on the house, there was also the laundry and grocery shopping to be done. It was on a Saturday evening at the P&W market, the night of the *Edelman* rerun, and where we did our "trading," as my father called it, that I happened to see Eddie García again.

The Shrinking Man.

Except he'd grown, not in height, but outward. I spotted him a couple of carts ahead of us at the check-out counter with his foster mother. His shirt was stretched over his stomach, pulling at the buttons, and although his hair was still short it wasn't cut to the scalp. The box of Marlboros was missing from his shirt pocket. But what had changed most, I thought, were the eyes—the way they used to shift back and forth, wince or blink every few seconds. Now he stared intently ahead as the food passed on the conveyor belt into the checker's hand. Meat and ice cream. Potato chips. Pop-Tarts. I thought of ducking under the chain across the other register, approaching him to see if he remembered me, and I would've if not for my lack of confidence, if not for his foster mother being there. Dad nudged me in the shoulder just then and whispered, "Look at that sonofabitch." A muscle-bound man in a tank top passed us with a packet of food stamps in his hand. The cart was loaded to the brim. "A strong man like him can't dig ditch?" Dad glanced down at our own cart, which was never more than half full, and then only with the basics. When I looked back to Eddie he was pushing the cart out the door into the parking lot. His foster mother led the way.

"Got himself a bad back, you suppose?"

"Shhh," I said.

"Lifting all those weights?"

On our way out a few minutes later Dad stopped at the news-paper machine and bought the Sunday *Mercury*. I looked for Eddie in the car that was pulling out of the parking lot but he wasn't in it. The clang of the lid closing, of metal on metal, startled me. Dad was already headed for the truck, a bag of groceries in one arm, holding the paper in the other and reading it as he walked. I caught up with him. In the light of the parking-lot lamp I saw him smile. "Tired?" he said. I told him that I was. He set the bag of groceries in the bed of the truck and then took the bag I was carrying and did the same with it.

"Know what I was doing at your age?"

"Working."

"You bet."

"For the Southern Pacific."

"With a crew of men," he said, as we got into the truck. The paper he rested on the seat beside us. Soon we were riding toward home. "When I quit twenty years later I was a supervisor and most of the others were still working the tracks. And they hated it, son. They bitched constantly. All the job meant was a check enough to fill their wallets so they could go out and get drunk and have a little fun come Friday night. I'd hate to see you wind up doing something you didn't want to do." He glanced across the cab at me. "You know," he said, "there ain't been a McKinney on our side ever made it to college. I hoped your brother to be the first."

"He did fine without it."

"That's not what I'm saying."

"I know what you're getting at."

A grin. "You do, do you?"

"We ain't got that kind of money."

"I been reading up on it," he said. "There's loans, there's grants, and you gotta take a test called the S.A.T. You could study your writing." He placed his hand on top of the Sunday paper between us. "Do this kind of work, huh? Maybe you can even get a scholarship if you set your mind to it."

I half laughed, half coughed.

"Nothing funny about that."

"I don't have the grades."

"You could if you tried."

"I ain't smart enough for college," I said, loud. "And you know it."

At that he fell silent.

We turned down the block and passed the corner where Eddie and I had sometimes hung out. I wondered if he was living close by and thought to myself, Yes, he had to be, and that we'd meet again. Next time I wouldn't be so shy, I told myself, though I knew it was a lie. Dad pulled into the driveway. In the carport he turned off the engine and climbed out. I met him on his side of the truck. "I want to do what you do," I said. "I want to learn the trade. What's wrong with that?"

He handed me a bag of groceries but he didn't look me in the eye. "I'll teach you," he mumbled, finally. "If that's what you really think you want, I'll put you on my license after you graduate. You do have to graduate from high school, son, and I want you to take that test. It's not open for debate."

Upstairs, while he was frying us hamburgers and potatoes, I went into the bedroom and took out my story. I kept it in a box that once held five hundred blank pieces of white paper. It was almost half full now, about as full as it was going to get, and the pages were just that—pages—no longer blank. There were a hundred and seventy-five of them, or three hundred and fifty counting the carbons, which I kept in a manila envelope. I removed them from the box and held them in my hands, feeling their weight, feeling proud. Good story or not, I'd gone the distance. Another couple of chapters would tie it up. In my mind I pictured the last scene with the youngest brother, the runaway, about to take off again, this time for good, only he wouldn't steal a car to do it as he had before. Instead he'd buy himself a ticket at the Greyhound on Vine Street in Hollywood. As the kid was boarding the bus his older brother would catch up with him, because he knew he was planning to leave, and he'd talk him out of going. In the end they would live together in their own apartment without the mother or the other brother, maybe happily ever after, maybe not. The story ended there on a hopeful note.

I took a pen from on top of Dad's dresser and addressed an envelope to Mike, though it would be another few months before I actually sent it. And a few more would pass before I would hear back from him. By then another summer would come and go, I'd

303

complete my junior year with a C-minus average and begin my senior year, except it would be at a different school, for by this time Dad and Marissa and I had moved into the house on the better side of town in Willow Glen. The kids at my new school were almost all from upper-middle-class families—soft kids, they were, compared to the ones at Lick. Almost all of them dressed well; almost all of them had parents who bought them nice cars for their sixteenth birthday. At first I was a bit resentful, not so much because of how they seemed to have it so good, so easy, but because some were smug about it. That's what bothered me most. It was as if they knew no different and that they never would, and as a result I felt a little wiser, a little tougher and less vulnerable than them. The main thing, though, was that I didn't have to worry about looking over my shoulder anymore. The teachers could teach without hollering. Fights were rare.

I received another postcard from Mom about a week after we'd settled into the house. This one came from Carson City, Nevada. Dad had also written Mike and told him about the move. About Marissa. About the postcards. I wrote my own letter and told him that we had become a family. With it I enclosed the carbon copy of my story. He wrote me back at the new address in April without a word about the manuscript. All he said was that he was coming to visit and for Dad and me to be prepared to take the week off. "I have a surprise for you all. Plan on some fishin' on the Chetco," he wrote. "Plan on having a hell of a time."

We set the date by phone.

He called the day before he left to confirm it. Dad said fine, that we'd be ready, and I thought to myself that now he would finally see the changes in Mike that I had. That night Marissa helped us pack our clothes and air out three sleeping bags Dad had bought long ago when he lived in Eureka. I'd never slept in one before. Marissa was quiet, sad, as she arranged canned goods into a cardboard box on the kitchen counter, because she wasn't going with us. Because she had to work. It turned out to be for the better. Somehow I felt, the day I sent the manuscript off with the letter, before we took this trip, that if my brother read the story closely he'd know what was in my heart, what had been lost, and some way, however naïvely, I hoped that it could return to us what time and distance had stolen.

304

25

One of the last times that I saw my brother alive he was driving a thirty-foot Winnebago. Dad and I had just loaded the truck with the camping gear when the thing pulled up across the driveway on the morning of our trip. The horn sounded. We turned to look but there was glare on the windshield from the sun and we couldn't see inside of it. We figured he'd be driving up in his Datsun and from here we'd take the truck, either camp out or stay in a motel if it got too cold. The month was May. There might still be snow on the ground. Nothing had been said about a big Winnebago.

"Who's that?"

Dad shrugged.

"The thing's blocking our driveway," I said.

An aluminum door in the middle of the body opened and out stepped Mike. His hair had grown to his shoulders. A scraggly beard, thick at the chin but too thin on the sides, grew on his face. On his head rested the Stetson that he'd worn in *A Rough Kind*. He tipped it back and winked. The voice was a good imitation of our father's drawl. "You all packed and ready?" He slapped the side of the Winnebago. Grinned. "Ain't this the way to go, boys?" And then he spread his arms, laughing, and Dad and he hugged. A couple of seconds later they parted.

Dad leaned back and looked him up and down, then nodded at the Winnebago. "You'd do better to spend your money on a hair cut," he said, "than this monster here. How much it costin' you?"

"Plenty."

"That's what I thought."

"We're going in style."

"Roughin' it woulda been okay."

"Dad," he said. "Okay ain't good enough for you and Marissa." He put his arm around him. "I didn't come all the way here to be scolded about my hair or about what I should or shouldn't do with my money. We're out to have ourselves a time." He winked at me. "Ain't that right?"

I didn't say anything.

"Son?"

"What?"

"Marissa can't come with us."

"Just the boys again, eh?" He slapped him on the back. "Except this time around we got you."

Dad and I exchanged looks.

"Mind if your brother drives?"

"It's up to him."

"Jay?"

"Fine by me," I said.

Mike grinned. "Think you can handle it?"

I nodded and began to unload the truck.

Two narrow twisting lanes bordered a cliff that dropped hundreds of feet to the waves below. Highway 1. A strong wind rocked the Winnebago. Behind me I heard a plastic cup fall from a shelf and hit the floor.

"Can't you keep this thing steady?" Mike shouted.

"Leave him be," Dad said. "He's doing fine."

"There's a parent who sticks up for his kid."

"I'd do the same for you."

"Would you?" he said. "Mom wouldn't."

"Don't be bitter."

"Who's bitter?"

They were in the living-room area. I couldn't turn to look at them but I heard Dad sigh.

"She tried her best, son."

"How do you know?"

"I trust she did."

"You trusted wrong."

"Quit it," I shouted.

Dad was silent.

I glanced into the rearview mirror and saw a dozen cars trailing the bumper. Our top speed was twenty-five miles an hour, ten around the sharper curves. And there was no place to pull out. I stepped on the gas. Cursed. The idea was Mike's, taking Highway 1, as he'd wanted to see the ocean. Dad wanted to take the inland route because it was faster and safer. That was our first disagreement, shortly after we'd crossed over the Golden Gate.

Now we were passing through Bodega Bay.

"Hey, Jay."

"Yeah?"

"This is where Hitchcock set *The Birds*."

"How about that?" Dad said.

"How about a drink?" Mike said. "Assumin' little brother don't mind."

I didn't say anything.

"He thinks I'm overdoing it."

"Are you?" Dad said.

Mike came up toward the front of the cab so that I could see him now. He put his fingertips to his chest. "Do I look like a drunk? Do you see me stumbling? Look at the feet. Firm on the ground even in this thing." He winked at me. "Jay here's a little old prohibitionist, you know? Ought to revive the temperance league."

Dad laughed uneasily.

"But I won't drink without his permission."

I glanced away from the road to give him a dirty look.

"Can I?"

Silence.

"You mind?" he said. "Mind if I have just a short one? Promise you won't tell?"

Another gust of wind hit us. I jerked the wheel straight. "Hold her steady," he said, "like you hold a grudge." He patted me on the shoulder and returned to the back of the cabin. "You know that kid of yours has almost written a pretty good book," he said. "I say *almost* because of your ending, Jay. Pure sugar and sap. It's sweet enough to gag a person. You read it, Dad?"

"He wouldn't show it to me."

"For good reason, too."

"Shut up," I said.

"Something to hide?" Mike said. "It's all fiction, man. All make-believe. All in the mind. Ain't that right, Jay?"

I ignored him.

"Let your brother concentrate on the road."

"Tell me, Dad," he said, "what's that they say about folks who won't look you in the eye? I wouldn't trust what he told you about me any farther than I can spit." Over the hum of the engine I heard the refrigerator door open, close, the clatter of ice in plas-

307

tic cups. "All these years," he said, "all this talk 'bout huntin' and fishin', but us never getting no chance to do it. It's gonna be nice. To you, Dad." The cups joining made a clashing noise. "To the Chetco. Tell you what I'm gonna do." Pause. "Sittin' tight?"

"Son?"

"Let me finish."

"Why you talking like you do?"

"Huh?"

"Like an uneducated man," Dad said.

"I'm talkin' like you."

"Worse."

"Just listen, listen," he said. "I'm buyin' us the piece of land."

"Say that again."

"You heard right."

"Now . . ."

"Don't you *now* me."

"You save your money."

"To hell with that. Right on the river, I'm buying it, while the money's here," he said. "I got another role."

"Good for you."

I called back to him. "In what?"

"A movie."

"Congratulations."

"About this land," Dad said. "You mean it?"

"Damn right."

"Because if you do I'll build you a place."

"Ain't only for me."

Dad grew excited. "Jay," he said. "You hear your brother? You hear what he wants to do for us?"

I was skeptical.

"You sure you got it to spare?" I said.

"Do you?" Dad said.

"Would I mention it if I didn't?"

"Of course not."

"It sounds like Jay don't believe me."

"Maybe I don't," I said.

"I believe you," Dad said.

"Little brother thinks I'm making it all up like he does with his stories," he said, raising his voice. "But I'm a star, man, you hear me, Jay? The only real one in the cast. They're paying me plenty, and you can bet your ass there'll be plenty more where that came from. My career's looking up. I hit a slump but I'm on my way back to the top." Pause. "Let's have us another drink."

I heard them clap each other on the back. A gust of wind hit the Winnebago just then and an oncoming car swerved over the line a little too closely. I gripped the wheel tight. "Son," Dad said, "your brother and I don't doubt you. You're in a tough business. There's bound to be ups and downs but you got the talent, and you're a McKinney, and you're gonna keep doing well like you say." Another clap on the shoulder. "You make me proud. Not many boys would do this for their father, especially after what happened. I want to make it up to you in the best way I know how." And as I drove they continued to drink, and as they drank Dad's voice became more animated. And more cars, each time I glanced into the side mirror, continued to pile up behind us. Still there was no spot to pull over. "First off we get the land," Dad said, excited, "then soon as we get a little money ahead we start saving for material. Lumber's cheap compared to labor and that's where we got the edge. We'll build it to last, son. Build it good and strong, we will. Your brother and I know our stuff. It'll be a beautiful summer home for you to get away from that Hollywood and get your bearings when you need to. And it'll be a good investment, too," he said, "because it'll go up in value come the day you boys wanna sell, if you wanna sell. Maybe you'll have your own kids by then and wanna share it with them." Dad chuckled. "We'll build the fireplace outta natural stone, make us a sunken living room, a den for you and Jay to study in. Believe me," he said, "it'd be my pleasure to build you a good home."

Finally we reached an open stretch of road. I stepped on the accelerator. About a hundred yards ahead I spotted a shoulder large enough for the Winnebago. Beyond it was another road. "Like you told us," I heard Mike say, "I got this." And I don't know it for a fact, because I couldn't turn around to see him, but he must've patted his own chest like Dad would've done and had many times before. "Heart . . . and this." He must've nodded. "Brains . . . and this." Now he likely made the fist. "To fight with, huh? A McKinney. Can't keep us down, Dad. Gotta work harder than the next guy. No room for the half-assed. Gotta make something of yourself. Gotta grab the opportunity when it presents itself. Am I right? If Marissa were here she'd agree, considering the initiative taken. You're not even divorced. How is it shacking up," he said, laughing, "as your generation calls it. Mine just say living together. Pretty progressive for your age," he said. "Jay wrote me that you're all a regular family now."

Dad didn't say anything.

"Be quiet," I hollered.

"Don't be so touchy, little brother."

"Cut the *little* brother crap."

More silence.

Mike laughed again. "Guess who called from the dead?" he said.

"No more drinkin' for you."

"I'm just gettin' started."

"You've had enough, son."

"The bitch is back," he said. "She phoned."

"Don't call her that."

"It's true," he said.

"Change the subject," I hollered.

"Why?"

"You know why."

"She's back in L.A.," he said.

Solemn. "How is she?"

The turnout was getting closer. I flipped on the blinker and began to slow down.

"She's found a live one."

Dad was silent.

"Guess what else?"

"Shut up," I hollered. "Shut up."

"He's an electrical contractor," he said, "and he has loads of money."

More silence.

"But not for long." Mike laughed. "The poor dumb bastard. I told her about you and Marissa, Dad. She wants a divorce. She told me to tell you she's sending the papers." And I heard my brother clap him on the shoulder again. "Hell, don't be so glum about it. I signed mine a few months back." More laughter. "Like father," he said, "like son. I say fuck 'em both. Let's have us another drink."

The second I pulled over the other cars sped by us. I put the monster into park and yanked on the emergency brake, for I was sick of it. Sick of listening to my brother's shit. "Dad," I said, turning in the seat, "you okay?" But he had his head down and I'm not sure if he heard me, because he didn't say anything for a long time. Mike sat beside him with an arm around his waist. A fifth of bourbon rested on the refrigerator nearby. "You wanna go back?" I said. "You don't gotta take this."

No answer.

"It's no problem to turn around here."

"That's just like you," Mike said. "Always wantin' to run home."

"Fuck you."

"Up yours, man."

I rose from my seat, as did Mike, when Dad finally lifted his head. His eyes had a weary, sad look about them. "Settle down, boys. Keep drivin', Jay," he mumbled. "I'm fine. We made it this far, we might as well keep going."

Highway 1 became U.S. 101 and turned inland at Rockport in Mendocino. We rode past Garberville, then Rio Dell, back to the coast, and past the town of Eureka, where our father was born, past the great redwoods and pine and the green fern of Humboldt County toward the Oregon border. I saw snow on the mountains in the distance before the sky grew dark. Another hundred miles or so and we'd reach the Chetco.

By the time we got to Crescent City they had finished the bottle of bourbon and I turned off the road into a gas station. Mike put on his coat and stepped outside. "Last chance for supplies," he said. "Any store worth doing business with is closed across the border."

I followed him up the street toward a liquor store while Dad was filling the tanks. "Why you trying to hurt him?" I said when I caught up to him. As we walked he pulled his hat down low, turned the collar of his coat up, and bowed his head. We could see our breath in the light from the streetlamp. "Answer me, Mike. You telling the truth about that land? Because if you're not, man, if you're bullshitting . . ."

"The name is Greg Ribbs."

"Be serious."

"In case anyone asks," he added, winking at me. "You know how it is in small towns. All they do is watch TV."

I drew my hand down my face.

"Stop it," I shouted. "You're pissing me off."

"These people live for actors," he said. "They know them all. Put yourself in my place for a change. Why do you think I've grown a beard?" He grinned, pushed open the door to the liquor store, and whispered, "Greg Ribbs. Got it?" I paused and let him go a few steps ahead so people wouldn't think we were together.

Mike browsed the aisles for a minute until he found the Jack Daniel's. I stood beside him as he brought a fifth of it up to a pretty girl working the register and put it on the counter. He smiled at her, glanced at me, then looked at the girl again.

"You know, don't you?"

"What?"

"Who I am."

She squinted her eyes at him. "Should I?"

"*A Rough Kind?*"

"Rough what?"

"The movie," he said. "That's how you know me."

"Are you an actor?"

Mike smacked his lips. Nodded at me.

"What I tell you?"

She cocked her head to one side and stared harder at him. "I didn't see the movie but I can tell you're from California. What's your name?"

"Michael Casey."

"It sounds familiar." She paused to rub her chin with her thumb and forefinger. Again she squinted. "What else have you done?"

"Lots of TV."

"*Ironside?*" she said.

"Must've been somebody else."

"*Dragnet?*"

"C'mon, do I look that old?"

"Let's go," I said.

Suddenly her eyes lit up. "Yeah," she said, "yeah, I've seen you before. But without the beard." She snapped her fingers. "Weren't you on *Cannon, M.D.*?"

Mike smiled proudly.

"Wrong again," I said.

His smile disappeared.

"I was too," he said.

"Quit lying."

"You know damn well I was."

I shook my head. "He does this all the time. They look like the same guy but they aren't," I said. "Pay her, Greg, and let's go."

"You sonofabitch."

I left the store.

When I got back to the Winnebago it was parked in the lot away from the pumps. Inside I found Dad curled up on the bed in the back room with his face toward the wall. The plaid quilt was pulled up around his neck. The sour smell of whiskey hung in the air. "I'm tired," he said. "Wake me when we get to Brookings and I'll take it from there."

Around nine o'clock that night I made the wrong turn. I didn't do it on purpose. The right headlight burned out after we crossed the state border and I couldn't see the signs along the highway very well. One read CHETCO NORTH FORK, which is where I thought I turned, but the road began to grow more narrow, the brush and the trees more dense, and I wasn't so sure anymore. My plan had been to surprise them to the sound of the river rolling when they both woke, for Mike, too, had fallen asleep soon after we left the gas station. The fifth of Jack Daniel's was clamped between his thighs on the couch. Before he passed out he called me a sonofabitch again. I ignored him. That had been two hours earlier.

I continued up the mountain, leaning over the wheel, the engine lugging it in low up the steep grade. There was snow now along the sides of the road. The radio, which I'd been playing to help keep awake, turned to static. I switched it off and rolled down my window and the cab filled with cold air. I tried to listen for the sound of the river but all I could hear was the grind of the engine. The road grew more and more narrow until branches began to scrape the side of the Winnebago as I passed them. Suddenly, what up until now had been a paved road became a dirt one, or rather a muddy one, because of the snow, and I put on the brakes. Killed the engine. Rose from my seat. Found the flashlight. I was slipping into my jacket when my brother sat up and uncapped the bottle and had a drink.

"Where are we?"

313

"On the Chetco, I think."

"Whatta you mean you think?"

"Shhh."

"Dad still sleeping?"

I nodded and opened the door. Mike grabbed his coat and followed me outside into the cold and down the road with the Jack Daniel's. The sky was so dark you couldn't hardly see your hand unless you held it to your face. For a while we walked in silence. "If we're not on the Chetco," he said, "then where the hell are we?"

"I'm not sure."

"Oh great."

"Keep your voice down," I said, because we weren't far enough away from the Winnebago yet. Because I didn't want to wake Dad. "See if you can't hear the river."

We stopped and listened. Nothing. "Leave it to you, man," he said. "Lost in the middle of nowhere." I shone the flashlight around the trees but that's all I saw—branches, bark, a few patches of snow on the ground. "The great outdoors, eh?" His voice became soft, lucid. He slipped his hands around my neck from behind. "The Strangler's alive and well. He's hiding in the hills and he's gonna getcha." I reached up and pried his hands off me and told him to quit fooling around. We walked on in silence for a while. "I got another story for you," he said, "one that you might want to use someday." I said I didn't want to hear it, but he carried on with it anyway. "I went to see Leitha after you left, the time you visited. I needed to talk," he said. "I wanted to make up but she wouldn't even come to the fucking door, man, and her mother said she was going to call the cops. It's over. There's nothing I can do about it anymore, nothing, so I get myself a bottle like this one." He held it up and had another drink. "And I go down to the beach and sit there and talk to the ocean instead." Pause. "It's rough and it's dark, like tonight—no moon out—and the waves keep breaking closer and closer and pretty soon one gets me. I'm soaked. So you know what I do, because it won't listen?" Mike punched me lightly in the arm. "I holler at it, man. *Back off*, you arrogant sonofabitch. Back off and be quiet. *Listen*." Mike jumped in front of me and I stopped again. "Suddenly the whole ocean is calm. Me," he said, jabbing a thumb into his chest. "*I* did it."

314

I stepped by him and continued along the road. "Next thing you know," he said, "I hear this voice calling out, 'Bobby . . . Bobby, is that you?' and there's this beautiful girl, but when she sees I'm not the guy she turns away. I follow her up the hill to this big house and she lets me come in, because I'm wet, right? I need a towel. All these people are sitting in a circle on the floor in a big living room listening to this little guy play a guitar. He's drinking Jack Daniel's straight out of the bottle. I sit down, right, but he's not offering me any and I'm thirsty. My whiskey's long gone. Finally," he said, "and here's the clincher." Mike paused for another drink. "The guy stops singing and I look at the different faces and then at his and I say, 'You know you sound a hell of a lot like Dylan. Pass the bottle.' Then all the people laugh and I know it's *him*, man. He doesn't smile, either. He just hands over the bottle and breaks into another song—this one for me except I was too drunk to remember the words." Again he punched me in the arm. "How's that for a story, huh? I'm telling the truth. I wouldn't lie. I'm going to tell the truth to Dad, too," he said. "The old man's a failure."

I walked faster.

"You hear me?"

"No," I shouted.

"Listen to me."

"I'm tired of listening."

"Don't think he's so great," he said. "Either he couldn't keep the family together because he was incompetent or else he just didn't give a shit enough about us to try." I put my head down and walked still faster and he hurried and caught up. "He was fucking Marissa long before you and Mom found out. You were too young to realize it but I did. Acting," he said, "it wasn't the only reason I went with her and it wasn't the only reason he let us go. You got out in time, because I helped you, I made the way for you to run and don't ever forget it." He paused to have another drink. Be calm, I told myself. Calm. "You're my Frankenstein. I created you, understand, but not to write sickly sweet endings because that isn't the way it works. I'm the material. I'm the one you've written about, the actor, and it never was happy." He slapped me on the back. "You had me on your side. I tutored you, I was there when you got in trouble, I'm your fucking father, not the old fool you call Dad. Understand? I watched out for you the best way I knew. Now you tell me," he said, "tell me who the liar is and where the man was for me?"

"Be quiet," I said. "Please?"

"Can't take the truth?"

Silence.

"Would he have come for you if you hadn't gone to him? No," he said. "I'm not going to be quiet anymore."

"Shut up."

"Does it hurt?"

He stopped then, and I think he pointed up to the Winnebago, though it was too dark for me to tell for sure. "Where was he ever? With his goddamn back to us like it is now," he said. "Sleeping or working or fucking Marissa. That's our father. A gullible old country fool. Remember, man, remember, I'm the only one who ever really cared about you." He put his arm around me but I pulled away from him and turned off the road into the snow. He followed me close behind, through the brush and the trees until we were far enough away from the motor home so that I didn't have to worry about Dad.

There, in what I thought was a clearing, I stopped and aimed the flashlight on his chest.

Now I hollered.

"You're not buying any land."

He didn't answer.

"You're bullshittin' us, man, like always."

In the light I saw him smile. Because he knew I was right. Mike turned his back to me and walked a little farther toward where the mountain had begun to slope downward. He dropped to one knee, uncapped the bottle, had another drink, and shivered. "I hear the water," he said. "C'mere . . . c'mere and listen to the water." I went to him and we were quiet for a few seconds, for we both knew now what was coming, and what had been coming for a long time. The silence rang in my ears.

"Ain't any river down there," I said. "Ain't any water, ain't nothing down there." And up he came then with the first one, round through the darkness against the side of my head, so that my ears rang now not with silence but from the blow. I hit him low on the side of the neck. He threw another, which missed, and I hit him again on top of the head as he ducked and wrapped his arms around my waist and slammed me up against a tree. The flashlight fell. A great rush of air lifted from my lungs and for a moment I couldn't breathe.

"C'mon, little brother," he hollered. "You self-righteous little sonofabitch. C'mon . . ." I couldn't see him but I heard a branch snap, felt the breeze from his fist pass my ear, and I leaned into him hard with my shoulder. He groaned. Down we went to the snow, rolling, slipping down the slope, throwing one punch after another, connecting with the ground about as often as we connected on each other. His breath was hot on my face. "I can still kick your ass," he shouted. "Don't think I can't. Don't think I won't." When we stopped rolling he was on top and he hit me in the forehead, the eye, and I grabbed him by the lapels and pulled him down and then over, and again we were rolling until we bumped up against what had to be an old log. Now I was straddling him. Another fist caught me in the jaw near my ear. The cold made it so that all I felt was a brief stinging and numbness and then, when I finally reared back and let it go hard, very hard, there came a splash of warmth across my cheek. He groaned and cupped his nose with his hands. My heart skipped a beat. I rolled off him. He groaned again.

A few seconds later he raised himself up on one elbow. The other hand still covered his face.

"Where's the whiskey?"

"Fuck the whiskey."

"I think you broke my nose."

"That's what you get."

"Just find me the bottle."

"Find it yourself."

The flashlight was shining in the snow up the slope about fifty feet away. I ran and got it, found the whiskey and his hat next to a tree, and brought them to him. He was lightly touching the bridge of his nose with two fingers when I knelt beside him with the light. There was blood on his hands and all down the front of his coat. He winced. We were both wet and shivering. Mike had a long drink, then capped it. "Dad doesn't need you hurting him," I said, angry. "I oughta hit you again, hit you harder. Knock some goddamn sense into that head. I swear I will if you hurt him anymore." Pause. "You gotta forget all the shit in the past, put it behind you, man. You need to come live with us for a few months and get sober for a change. See how it feels. You're fucking up." I

317

nudged him with my knee. "What happened, huh? I don't understand. You listening?" I tapped him hard on the head. "We got an extra bedroom. It's yours if you want," I said. "You can't do shit in L.A. like you are."

And in the dim light, because the batteries were already getting weak, I saw him wipe the blood from his nose on his coat sleeve and give me a smile. "This isn't your story, Jay. No pretty endings," he mumbled. "Go on back. I'll be up in a bit. I need a little time to think." I turned the flashlight toward the road to set my direction straight, then switched it off and dropped it in his lap.

Halfway to the road I stopped and glanced over my shoulder for him but I couldn't see a damn thing. "You're gonna freeze your ass off out here," I shouted. When he didn't answer I walked on, feeling my way through the darkness and the trees back to the Winnebago. The lights were on inside. I took a deep breath and opened the door. Dad was sitting on the couch, elbows resting on his knees, hands folded between them. He looked at me and wagged his head. "Damn it," he muttered. "Damn it if I didn't know you boys were gonna get in a fight. Where's your brother?"

"He's okay," I said. "He'll be coming along soon."

"Get in here."

Dad took me by the arm and steered me to the bathroom and flipped on the light. In the mirror I saw that my eye had already begun to swell and close and that there was a long purple break down the middle of my forehead. "Look at your face," he said. "That what you come here for? To fight? Get yourself washed up and out of those clothes." By the time I'd finished, and had changed into a dry shirt and pants, Dad had the first-aid kit opened. "Hold still now," he said, as he dabbed the cut on my forehead with iodine. "You want to tell me what you boys were fighting about this time?"

"He'll tell you."

"Where is he?"

"He should've been back by now."

Dad put the cap on the iodine bottle and sighed. "I don't know what to do. He was always such a good, strong boy." A moment of silence passed. "I been thinking about maybe having your brother come stay with us for a while, if you two can get along without killing each other." He turned away from me and stared out the window. "Where are we?" he asked. I told him where I thought I'd turned, my plan, and he sighed again. Ten minutes or so had passed and he began to pace the floor. Finally, when Mike still hadn't returned, he cursed and threw on his coat, grabbed another flashlight, and we went looking for him. I led him back to the spot where we had the fight and we shone the light all around the area, but he wasn't there. We walked up and down the road calling his name. If he heard us he didn't answer. We returned to the motor home and checked to see if he'd returned. He hadn't. We waited another half hour.

Again we went out to look for him.

We retraced our steps.

It was long past midnight. Our fear and worry had grown so great by then that when we finally heard him the tension we felt suddenly became anger.

Mike laughed.

Dad shone the light on him. He was kneeling behind the rear wheel of the Winnebago, traces of blood caked around his mouth and nose, nursing the last of the whiskey. "Looking for me? I've been here all along," he said. "Waiting for you." And watching, I thought. Watching us walk up and down the road, through the brush and the snow and the trees, calling for him, but never answering us.

26

We never made it to the river. It was somewhere behind us. Another fight broke out that night and come dawn we'd had enough of each other and headed back to San Jose. There we parted on the note that all was well, in the way families will sometimes do when they know different but have nothing more to say to each other. The offer to live with us was turned down. He hugged Dad at the curb outside the house and as he did so I heard him whisper that he was sorry. Dad told him that there was no need for it. I hugged him, too, and then we waved good-bye and watched him drive away. From here on out, there's not much more to tell.

The divorce papers arrived as Mike said they would and Dad

signed them and sent them back to a post office box in Reseda. This happened about a week after we returned. Marissa made us a special dinner in celebration and they told me of their plans to marry when the divorce became final. "We're gonna have the preacher come here and tie the knot," he said, "if we can get the place fixed up in time. I think we can." The wedding was set for the last week in August, which would've given us another three months or so to get the house in shape if things hadn't turned out like they did. Dad also met with the IRS again, or rather they came to our house again, only this time he gave the news of his divorce. He hoped it might change their outlook on the matter. The agent said that he'd "report it" to his supervising officer and get back to us.

About the new film Mike said he'd landed, it wasn't a complete lie, though he wouldn't live long enough to see it open. He phoned late one night in mid-June. "That movie I told you about, it's called *Backstage Actresses*," he said. "It's a terror film, and not exactly what I made it out to be. I just thought I should set things straight with you. No more lies, eh? I did it as a favor for the director. He's a friend. You won't find my name on the credits because I worked below scale. The union, you know? They wouldn't appreciate it." The line crackled. "Hope I didn't wake you. Is Dad up? I need his turkey recipe." Pause. "I'm moving again," he said, "and I want to throw a party before I go." By that time our father had rolled out of bed and was standing barefoot beside me in the hallway, a worried look on his face, tying the sash on his bathrobe. Marissa stood behind him in her nightgown. The clock on the wall read just after twelve.

I cupped the receiver to my chest.

"It's Mike," I said.

"He okay?"

"He wants your turkey recipe."

"At this hour?"

"I think he's drunk," I said.

He took the receiver from me.

As I returned to my room Marissa looked at me and shook her head. I couldn't go back to sleep that night for wondering what to do, how to feel or think besides scared. I remembered how Mike used to look after me, and I wondered how much of what he was going through now had to do with the loss of that responsibility. I didn't know then, and I can't rightly say I know it any better today. But I do know one thing for sure about that night and that is that he lied again about the movie. A few months later I talked to the director. The part was given to him, not because the friend needed him, but because he knew my brother needed the money.

The next day we put up drywall on the living-room ceiling. The week after that we had new carpets laid, clean white drapes hung, and the fireplace fronted with brick instead of the smoked glass there originally. Next we paneled the outside of the house in pine to cover up the old chipped boards, painted, and built a flower box under the kitchen window and installed shutters on the others. At the end of the third week of June, when there was no longer any threat of rain, Dad arranged for an industrial Dumpster to be placed in our driveway the following Friday. Soon we would begin tearing off the roof and throwing the scraps into it. There were four roofs already on the house, one laid over the other, and three of them had to come off before we could nail down the new one. I also graduated that same month with a C average. The ceremonies I won't discuss except to say that Dad and Marissa insisted I attend them and that they were extremely proud of me and afterward we went out to a fancy Chinese restaurant in Saratoga.

My S.A.T. scores, because Dad had wanted me to take the damn test, were 400 in the verbal part and 500 in math. How I came out higher in math than English, I don't know. The former was my worst subject. The results arrived late, which was fine by me, as I didn't care one way or the other about them anyhow. I showed Dad the letter when he got home from work and had begun making dinner. He wiped his hands on a dish towel that was stuck into his pants waist for an apron and then took the letter from me. He furrowed his eyebrows. Studied it.

"The numbers," he said. "Whatta they mean?"

I shrugged.

"Are they good enough for college?"

"Who cares?"

"I do."

"It doesn't matter," I said. "I'm not going to college."

Marissa came home then and set her purse on the kitchen counter and gave Dad and me a quick kiss. Nearby on the stove a frying pan crackled. She reached for the lid. Removed it and wrinkled her nose. Peered inside. "Smells great," she said. "What is it?"

"Salisbury steak."

He handed her the letter.

"Can you make heads or tails outta this?"

She stared at it for a few seconds with the same puzzled look Dad had had. "It's just his scores," she said. "I don't know how good they are but I'm sure we could find out if you want."

"Skip it."

"Skip nothing," Dad said.

"What's the point?" I said, raising my voice. "I already told you I wanted to learn the trade."

That's when I went to my room, for I had my own now, and I spent a lot of time there before and after dinner in the evenings. While Dad and Marissa relaxed in front of the TV, over the sound of game shows and movies filtering through the living-room wall into my room, I read the novels of Hemingway, Sinclair Lewis, Jack London, some Faulkner short stories, and more of Nelson Algren. I'd begun a new story of my own, too, or at least I had started taking notes on one, which was what I was doing late that night after the Salisbury steak dinner, long after the television was turned off and Dad and Marissa had gone to bed, one week before the fatal week when my brother called for the last time.

I answered it on the second ring.

"Jay?"

"Yeah?"

"Did I wake you?"

"No."

"I changed my mind." Pause. "About coming to live with you guys. Is the offer still open?"

"Of course."

"You better ask Dad first."

"He's sleeping right now," I said. "But don't worry. He wants you here."

"You sure?"

"I'm sure."

"What about Marissa?"

"We'll ask her tomorrow," I said. "I know she'll understand."

"I need a change."

"I know."

"But I can't stay away too long or I'll have to start over when I get back. This town's got a short memory, man. Maybe that's for the better, considering my reputation." He laughed. "It's not too great anymore." Pause. "You think it'll be okay?"

"It'll be fine."

"I just put a deposit down on another place."

"Get a refund."

"A really fucking sleazy room."

Silence.

"I hate the thought of moving again," he said. "I hate the thought of living there."

"So don't."

"That's why I called."

"You're welcome here."

"It's just for the summer, all right?"

"All right."

"Some of my stuff's already boxed."

"Good."

"When can you come?"

"This Saturday."

Silence.

"I can help you guys fix up the house."

"We can use you."

"Thanks, Jay," he said. "I'm sorry for all the shit I pulled."

"Forget it."

"Bye."

"See you Saturday."

"Call me when you talk with Marissa, okay?"

"Okay."

"Bye."

"Love you."

"Love you, too, man."

I hung up.

The day was Tuesday. In a few more minutes it was Wednesday. I went to my room and set my alarm clock so that I was up before Dad and Marissa. He wandered into the kitchen at five-thirty that morning, still groggy and sleepy-eyed. I offered him a cup of coffee and waited until he'd had a couple of sips. "Dad," I

323

said. "If you and Marissa don't mind, I need to borrow the truck to pick up Mike's stuff this weekend. He wants to come stay with us for a while." Dad set his cup down on the table and blinked as if he hadn't heard right. But Marissa had. She stood in the doorway. "The truck's all yours," she said. "I think it's a great idea."

The next evening, when Marissa returned home from Penney's, she had two shopping bags with her. In one was a new bedspread and in the other were new curtains. That same night we picked up a double mattress and box spring that she'd ordered and we put it in the spare bedroom. We mounted brass rods and strung the curtains through them. She made the bed. We aired the room out and we drove a couple of nails into the walls and hung a painting of a lion from one and a seascape from the other. Dad moved a bookcase from the hallway into the room and a dresser in from the garage. Marissa lined drawers with flower-print paper and polished the mirror. It was a nice room when we were finished. We stood back toward the doorway to look at our work. I thought Mike would be pleased, except for the seascape painting, but at least it broke up the monotony of the blank wall.

Dad put his arm around Marissa just before we shut off the light.

"No second thoughts?"

"Absolutely none."

"Because this is your house," he said.

"It's ours."

"You'll be good for him," I said.

"I sure as hell hope so," Dad said. "He's got a lot of anger in him, babe. He might be tough to get along with for a while."

Marissa elbowed him lightly in the ribs. "Don't forget I helped raise your boys and I love them," she said, reaching out to rough up my hair. "Even this stubborn little shit here." A firm nod. "This is their home if they want it. Mike's always welcome."

At that Dad shut off the light and we went down the hall to phone him. I dialed the number and let it ring a dozen times. He wasn't there and his answering service, I guess, had been disconnected. Because nobody picked it up. An hour later Dad tried calling him. "Must be out saying his good-byes," he said as he hung up. Once more, before we went to sleep, I tried calling but without any luck. And first thing in the morning I phoned again.

Still there was no answer. I slammed the receiver back in its cradle and started for the kitchen to have breakfast when suddenly it rang. I grabbed it on the first ring.

"Mike?"

"Who's this?"

"Jay McKinney," I said.

The voice was frantic. "This is Mrs. O'Brien," she said. "Put your father on. Quick. It's an emergency."

The last time Mrs. O'Brien called in a panic was when her bathrub wouldn't drain. That was no emergency. It was just an old lady, I thought, exaggerating her problems so we'd hurry out there and take care of it. That's exactly what I thought again when we pulled up in front of her house that morning—another needless rush—but this time around I was wrong. This time it was for real. Not only would her bathtub not drain but her toilet was also backing up. The same for the sink. Dad wagged his head as we stood in the bathroom, myself slightly on tiptoe, for I had tennis shoes on and the floor was sopping wet with rancid water.

"No use even running our snake here," he said. "We gotta find the clean-out valve outside and try that first. I hope it isn't what I think it is."

So first we found the clean-out valve on the side of the house and tried clearing it there. It didn't work. We tried flushing it with the garden hose. It didn't work. "Well, son," he said, wiping his brow of sweat with the back of his hand, "we'll try the line in front of the house." Which is what we did. Dad sent me into the house then to try the toilet and I did and it overflowed. I stepped into the bathtub to avoid getting wet and hollered the results out the window to him. He pointed to a tree in the yard. "Here's our problem," he shouted back. "Gotta be roots getting into the main line somewhere. Pack up the tools. We'll rent a snake with a motor and teeth and see if that don't cut her."

An hour later we returned with a hundred-foot steel snake with teeth at the end, the kind the Roto-Rooter people use, and ran it through the line. Fifty feet up the blades jammed. By now our arms were weak from shoving and pushing and hanging tight to it, because the thing whips around as it works, and still we'd had no success. We'd also worn out two pairs of old leather gloves holding it steady. Our hands were beet-red and sore.

325

Dad let out a big sigh.

"I was afraid of this."

"Can't we get sharper blades or something?"

He chuckled.

"Fetch the shovels out of the truck and start digging."

"What about lunch?"

"What about it?"

"We haven't had any."

"You'll lose your appetite soon enough, son," he said. "You might even lose what little breakfast you got left in your belly."

We measured off to the spot in the front yard where our snake had jammed and began to dig. And dig. When I paused once to catch my breath he looked at me and grinned. "Better work a little faster," he said. "We gotta knock this job out so you can leave to pick up your brother in the morning. Sooner we get through here, and the sooner you get back, the sooner we can get to work on our own place."

I stabbed my shovel into the ground.

We continued to dig.

Late that afternoon we had a big mound of dirt piled off to one side of the lawn. The hole was about four feet deep and just large enough for the both of us to stand in and work. A terra-cotta sewer line lay at the bottom of it. At the flange where the pipes joined was a tree root about the size of my finger and a mess of smaller ones that had squeezed their way into the flared end of the line in search of water. I threw down my shovel and put my hands on the small of my back and groaned. "Just as I figured," Dad said. He squatted down in the hole and scraped the dirt off around the roots and dug out beneath the line with his hands. "I been thinking, if it's okay with you and you don't feel jealous about it, if you can understand my reasonin', I'd like Mike to be my best man." He glanced up at me. "I think he could use it more than you—the reassurance, I mean. No hard feelings?"

"No."

"You won't take it personal now?"

"He needs that," I said. "To know."

Dad stood up straight, smiled.

"Run get the hatchet, a ball peen hammer, my concrete chisel, and the drywall knife," he said. "I'll teach you how to clear the line." As I climbed out of the hole, and half limped to the truck, he called out to me. "And bring the bucket—it's under the tool-box."

When I came back he pulled himself out of the hole and told me to hop in it, which I did, and then he began to instruct me. I cut the roots going into the joint. I dug out a little deeper around the pipe and marked it with the knife and carefully chipped away at it with the chisel.

Finally, as the sun was setting, a beautiful orange ball in the sky, I broke through it—a round hole the size of my fist. Fifty feet of pipe full of Mrs. O'Brien's waste and rancid water that had been backed up in the line for days filled the ditch in a second. I was knee high in it. The stench was thick, vaporous, overpowering. I held my nose and tried my best not to gag. Dad handed me the bucket. He kept a straight face. "Start bailing it out," he said in a drawl, "or if you prefer you can just reach on down there and see if you can't cut the roots now."

I swallowed.

"Let's get a move on," he said.

Again I swallowed, feeling sick to my stomach. I looked down at the putrid water and felt even sicker. Somewhere beneath it was the pipe. Suddenly I felt dizzy. "Whatta you waitin' for?" Dad said. I set the bucket on the side of the ditch and took hold of the other side of it for balance. He lowered himself into the hole beside me. "Son," he said, "maybe you oughta seriously consider another line of work." And at that, both knee high in shit now, the sun setting in the distance, holding our breath and watching it go down, we began to laugh.

I left San Jose for Los Angeles at five o'clock on Saturday morning. Dad and I had tuned up the truck and changed the oil and checked the radiator and replaced the fan belt later that night after we repaired the sewer line. It was his way—to always make sure the engine was running well and ready for a long drive, to warm it up five minutes before you left, not to rev it. "You keep her down to fifty-five or sixty and you won't have any problems," he said as he walked me out to the truck in the darkness that morning, the sun not yet up. "Tell your brother I send my love. Tell him I'm looking forward to this." And I nodded and then I got into the truck and started the engine and let it warm up. Dad stood in his bathrobe in the glare of the headlights and waved to me as I backed out of the driveway onto the road. Marissa was sleeping in.

We had phoned Mike the night before and there was no answer. I phoned him again when I woke up and there was no answer. Dad thought I might want to wait until we got ahold of him to confirm it, but I said, "No, he'll be there. He knows I'm coming." And I said it with such certainty, almost a shout, that my father became silent. I drove well beyond fifty-five that morning on Highway 101, again headed south, no radio, just my thoughts. And the thoughts weren't very profound. A young man's musings. Foolish thoughts, they were. Thoughts that all would be well and that this was what my brother needed and that we would get along and that he would learn what I had learned, what he had first taught me and what I believed he had since forgotten.

By noon I was in L.A.

I thought of riding past Debra Swanson's last home for the hell of it, or our old home, although I never did feel that way about it. I could have but I did not. Instead I followed the Hollywood Freeway straight to the Alvarado exit and got off and drove a few more blocks. I parked behind his Datsun in the driveway of his house that was all run down and in need of repair. The day was hot, very hot and very smoggy, and I had my shirt off and I was sweating. And I remember thinking to myself, Good. He's home. At least I don't have to worry about waiting and wondering where he is. I went up the set of rickety stairs and knocked on the door but there was no answer. Again I knocked. Again no answer. I tried the door. Locked. I tried to look through the window but the drapes were drawn. I tapped on the glass. "Mike . . . hey, you here, man?" I shouted. After a while I went around back and tried the door there. It was locked, too. By this point my heart was pounding.

Above me I noticed another door, up another rickety set of stairs, one with a rubber panel that a dog once used to come in and out of the house. I hurried up to the landing and reached through the panel and felt for the knob, turned it, let myself inside. Immediately a sordid stench far more powerful than that of the sewer line struck me. For a moment I didn't move. The house was quiet except for the hum of the refrigerator below. "Mike," I shouted. "Hey, you home? Time to get a move on. Got the truck out there ready to load." But I knew it then, I already knew from the stench and the quiet, from his car still being in the driveway, yet I kept talking. I went downstairs. "Old man's a-waiting on us. Your room's all ready. Work to do, Mike." My voice faltered. "Plenty of work to do still. Why?" The door to his bedroom was closed and I put my hand against it and pushed. "I was coming for you, man," I said. "I'm *here*."

27

The wedding was held in our living room. Dad and I hadn't yet finished remodeling the house, so there were a few odds and ends that our guests had to overlook, mainly the roof, as they arrived outside in their cars. We'd torn off the tar-and-gravel and two layers of old composition but we hadn't time to take up the last and put on the new. It was a small wedding, with a dozen of Marissa's relatives present, one of Dad's brothers from Oregon, a photographer, and myself. I gave the ring. The Lutheran minister, or the preacher, as Dad called him, was a sober sort who skipped the long sermon and got quickly to the point. After all, it was my father's third time around and Marissa's second. They didn't need the advice.

She looked beautiful in a lavender dress and matching pumps. Dad wore a brown suit and wing tip shoes and he had doused himself for the occasion with a little too much cologne. Although he smiled, there was a sadness about him, in the quiet way he held his head, in the folds beneath his eyes and the deep lines around them that hadn't been there the month before. When the preacher proclaimed them man and wife, my father kissed Marissa sweet and long, and the photographer snapped their picture. Up came the cheers. Out came the champagne.

I watched them from across the room.

"Jay?" Dad called.

"Over here," I said.

"Get in between us."

The photographer had them posed in front of the fireplace and I went and joined my parents for the shot and a couple of others. A minute later Marissa's relatives had surrounded her and Dad and I headed off to the kitchen to help serve the champagne.

Later my father broke away and took me by the arm. We slipped outside onto the porch, where it was more quiet. He loosened his tie.

"It went good," I said.

"She looks great, don't she?"

"Beautiful."

Behind us I heard the people laughing and talking in the house.

"I'm gonna miss you."

"Gonna miss you, too."

"The first ever of the McKinneys," he said. "I'm proud of you." He patted me on the back. "You're going to do okay. You're going to do just fine, just fine. Try to smile," he said, slowly now, "like I'm trying." He put his arm around me. "We better go inside."

We went back into the house.

The party carried on until night fell, when Dad and Marissa went out to the car, got in, and left for Lake Tahoe. They were gone for three days. Alone, though I tried not to, I thought constantly of my brother. How I had found him. The funeral. He was buried in an expensive casket at Forest Lawn on a hill overlooking Warner Brothers, surrounded by the "other stars," for our mother had insisted he deserved the "finest" as a fitting final gesture. Money was no longer a problem for her on account of her fiancé.

The day of the burial she pulled into the mortuary parking lot in a new El Dorado with her new beau. Dad, Marissa, and I stood on the steps of the chapel, waiting to go inside, watching them. Mom wore a knee-length black dress, black pumps, and dark stockings, as she had the day of her arrest years before, and her black hair was piled in a bun on top of her head. As she came up the steps, one hand locked in the fiancé's, I saw that her eyes were red and that she'd been crying, only what sympathy I might've had for her was no longer there. She wrapped her arms around me. "Honey," she said, "I'm sorry, I love you." And now it was my face, not my brother's, that went stone blank and pale against her shoulder in the same kind of scene, replaying itself once too fucking often. "Why?" she said. "Why did he do it?" My body stiffened. Mom leaned back to look at me. "Don't be like this to me, baby, not now. How could we know?" I pushed myself free. She frowned as if she were confused and reached for me again and

I turned away, this time for good. "David?" she said, as if she expected him to step forward, to step in on her behalf. But he turned his back to her, too. That's when I put my arm around Marissa and we went inside and took our seats in the chapel.

I haven't seen her since.

After the funeral, after the wedding, when Dad and Marissa came back from their honeymoon, we put on the new roof and then he helped me move into a studio apartment in the Mission district of San Francisco. I had applied and been accepted to the state university there. My grades were poor, but combined with my test scores, which Marissa had checked up on and found out to be fairly decent, I made it in. They had a program where I could do the kind of writing I liked and get credit for it. As for the novel I wrote, small though it was, I looked up Betsy Grotz's address in my brother's book and shipped it off to her. I had talked with her once before about Mike and thought that because she had liked him that she might like me enough to at least read it. I was right. In her reply she wrote that she enjoyed the book and that she was giving it to another agent in the New York office for a second opinion. "But don't get your hopes up," she wrote. "Just keep at it."

As for the IRS, they did finally settle up with Dad. And the old bitch Mrs. Glass, as our mother called her, was put in a rest home. The case against Mom was dropped. As for my brother's last movie, it opened four months after his death, toward the end of my first semester at college. I had to take off for Los Angeles again the following week. The police department had sent a final notice: either retrieve his personal effects or they would be destroyed. My father didn't want to go all that distance for a few last things that would only bring back sad memories, and I didn't want to go either, but I'd made the trip before and felt certain now I could make it once more and that I should.

I borrowed the truck.

With the notice had come a form of authorization for Dad, which he had signed, and which I gave to a tight-lipped clerk in the property division the afternoon I arrived. I put my signature on a line in a ledger on the counter and the clerk handed me two manila envelopes and I left.

In the parking lot, in the truck, I opened them. Inside the first was a roll of Certs. His wallet. Car keys. Five quarters. Inside the other was the .38. The grip, I noticed, the moment before I slipped it back into the envelope, was crystalline, the color amber. I remember thinking to myself that they ought to have cleaned it up.

I WAS AT the Gordon in Hollywood,
watching *Backstage Actresses*, when he
appeared in the seat beside mine. The movie
had just begun.

"Where'd you come from?"

"Take a guess."

I turned away. "Just leave me alone," I
said.

"Is that any way to treat your brother?"

"Go sit somewhere else."

"I like it here," he said.

Onscreen the New Land logo faded into a

medium close shot on a young woman
undressing in a bedroom. Mike jabbed me in
the arm as the camera pulled back to reveal
the shoes of a man creeping up behind her. "I
told you it was one of those horrible terror
movies," he said matter-of-factly. "You're
wasting your time." The tempo of the music
increased. "Did you get all my stuff?"

"Out of the house?"

"From the cops," he said.

"Yeah."

"What about the gun?"

"You'll never lay your hands on it again."

At that he laughed. I looked around to see
if anyone had noticed us. A couple of
teenagers in the row across from ours were
staring straight ahead. "Relax, little brother,"
he said. "They can't hear us. And anyway I
don't need the gun anymore." He patted my
hand on the armrest. "I just thought since it
was stolen they might hassle you when you
came to get it." I shook my head. "Never
used any of the stuff you ripped off, did you?
Didn't get the chance," he said. "Maybe you
can make good use of it now. How's the
writing coming?"

"Go away," I said.

"How's Dad?"

"Can I watch the damn movie?"

"Don't get angry."

I nudged his elbow off the armrest. "You
knew I was coming for you, man," I said,
raising my voice. "How come you couldn't
wait?"

"Figure it out for yourself."

"I'm tired of trying."

"But it's good material," he said.

I gripped the armrest.

"*Go* away."

"If that's what you want." Mike nodded up

334

at the screen as he rose from his seat. "Don't blink, little brother," he said, "don't flinch or you'll miss me."

Then he was gone.

I settled back into my seat and sighed. Ahead onscreen I saw him dressed in a security guard's uniform, escorting a man and a woman into a holding cell. They'd been caught trespassing on corporate property. My brother had four lines. That was all. That was it. I kept expecting him to appear again, only he never did.

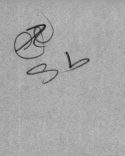